A SHATTERED LENS

Praise for *Written in Blood*

"5/5 . . . This smart mystery by Layton Green [is] a real page turner."
—*San Francisco Book Review*

"[A] fascinating new protagonist who's both tough and sensitive."
— *Kirkus Reviews*

"A satisfying page-turner for readers who appreciate literary references and existential questions with their corpses."
—*Publishers Weekly*

"Dostoevsky and Poe would be proud."
—*Knoxville News Sentinel*

"*Written in Blood* provides the delights of a whodunit, esoteric clues that refer cleverly to classic literary works, and, at the same time, offers the gritty sense of place and the kind of psychologically complex characters ordinarily associated with noir. These elements combine to make a smart page-turner as dark and deep as the Carolina woods."
—Gordon McAlpine, author of *Hammett Unwritten* and the Edgar-nominated *Woman with a Blue Pencil*

"*Written in Blood* combines bookishness and murder in brain-teasing ways, doubling the pleasure of a more conventional procedural. Fast paced and braided with twists, it's terrific entertainment."
—Andrew Pyper, author of *The Only Child* and *The Demonologist*

"[W]ritten with profound elegance and clever misdirection that brings the book to a surprising climax."
—*Ellery Queen Mystery Magazine*

"*Written in Blood* is a relentlessly paced mystery that's part old-school whodunit, part modern police procedural and part psychological thriller, with a knockout ending that the reader will never guess... and never forget. Highly recommended!"
—The Internet Review of Books

"[A]ny fans of the dark crime genre will be sure to enjoy this. I'm definitely going to look out for Layton Green's books in the future."
—The Eccentric Trilogy

A SHATTERED LENS

A DETECTIVE PREACH EVERSON NOVEL

LAYTON GREEN

SEVENTH STREET BOOKS®

Published 2019 by Seventh Street Books®

Inquiries should be addressed to
Start Publishing LLC
101 Hudson Street, 37th Floor, Suite 3705
Jersey City, New Jersey 07302
PHONE: 212-431-5455
WWW.SEVENTHSTREETBOOKS.COM

10 9 8 7 6 5 4 3 2 1

Library of Congress Cataloging-in-Publication Data

Names: Green, Layton, author.
Title: A shattered lens : a Detective Preach Everson novel / by Layton Green.
Description: Amherst, NY : Seventh Street Books, an imprint of Prometheus Books, 2019. | Series: A Detective Preach Everson novel ; 2
Identifiers: LCCN 2018042003 (print) | LCCN 2018043594 (ebook) | ISBN 9781633885394 (ebook) | ISBN 9781633885387 (paperback)
Subjects: | BISAC: FICTION / Mystery & Detective / Police Procedural.|FICTION / Mystery & Detective / General. | FICTION / Suspense. | GSAFD: Suspense fiction. | Mystery fiction. g
Classification: LCC PS3607.R43327 (ebook) | LCC PS3607.R43327 S54 2019 (print) | DDC 813/.6--dc23
LC record available at https://lccn.loc.gov/2018042003

Printed in the United States of America

To Bonnie Jean Perdue, hometown girl

All changes, even the most longed for, have their melancholy, for what we leave behind us is a part of ourselves; we must die to one life before we can enter into another.

—Anatole France

1

The camera felt so right in her hands. So natural. The sheer heft of it made her feel important, as if she were already more visible to the world. Everybody everywhere needed something to help them belong, Annie knew. For some it was obvious: money, drugs, guns, sex, power. For others, it could be something as simple as a pet, or a child, or a single friend.

Something no one else could claim.

Something to make you feel alive and special.

What Annalise Stephens Blue wanted, what she had craved since she had first seen *ET* and *The Goonies* and *The Princess Bride* and countless other movies sitting on her daddy's lap before he left home, was a camera. Not just any old transmitter of encoded images, but a *real* camera. A vehicle for Blue to realize her dream of becoming a filmmaker. A caster of magic spells, a chronicler of her generation, an artist who would throw a light in dark corners and speak for voices unheard.

Guided by the pewter light of a full moon, she trod down the forested path behind her trailer park, pine needles swishing under her feet once she got past the soda cans and beer bottles and fast food wrappers clotted with dried ketchup. The stench of garbage bins faded, replaced by earth and pine and an explosion of insect chatter.

A few hundred feet in, she stopped to peer through the night lens. What she saw gave her chills. Not just the clarity of the images, but the way the experience made her feel. Though Blue had lived in the trailer park for fourteen of her sixteen years and knew these woods like she knew her own face in the mirror, seeing the forest through the high-powered lens made her feel like someone new and beguiling, a stranger in a strange land, a pioneering explorer in the wilderness of life.

She was no longer Blue from the trailer park, Blue with the Goodwill clothes and the mother who cleaned roach motels, Blue the shoplifter, Blue the alley cat, Blue the anorexic who loved to eat but couldn't gain weight and had no curves, Blue the high school junior who was held back a year because of behavioral issues.

All that was behind her now. She had taken the first step on her journey. Now she was someone full of curiosity and discernment, a budding filmmaker, a sculptor of popular culture. Someone clever and funny, wise in the ways of the world, destined for great things.

Someone who mattered.

Despite her giddy thoughts, her new acquisition made her nervous. Resembling some kind of advanced alien weaponry, the Canon EOS C100 was a prince among cameras, a piece of equipment so beautiful it had taken her two days to work up the nerve to touch it. What if she pressed the wrong button and broke it?

In her head she knew her fears were unfounded, because she had read everything she could find on the camera. She knew it was made for a European market and was hard to get in the United States, that it had a Digi DV 4 processor, an EF-L series lens, and weighed only 2.2 pounds without accessories. She knew the extended ISO range allowed filmmakers to shoot under low light conditions, essential for low-budget filmmakers like herself.

She knew all this, yet holding the Canon in her hands, using it, was a different story.

Her destination was just a few hundred yards into the tract of forest that separated her trailer park from the Wild Oaks subdivision. She was going to set up inside the tree line on the far side of the common space, close enough to observe the nighttime activity of the Creekville upper crust. Wild Oaks was new money, not old money. A blend of professors, young professionals, and Creekville's typical array of progressive oddballs. *Modern Family* in semirural North Carolina.

Sure, old money had scandals and depraved patriarchs, but Blue didn't care about the dirty secrets of the smattering of business tycoons and trust fund babies in town. Everyone in Creekville hated them and wished they would move to Chapel Hill. New money was where the action took place. With the movers and shakers, the strivers, the upwardly mobile who professed their allegiance for a litany of trendy causes, but who would rather die than give up a single morning latte.

Night Lives.

That would be the name of her first film, an exposé on the nocturnal activities of the people who lived just across the forest from her but who thought they were so much better. Not just the parents, but the kids. The popular ones those Wild Oaks parents bred like minks. She imagined they came out of a celestial assembly line, little blond babies wearing Ralph Lauren onesies in the car seats of their BMWs and Mercedes. The Morning Star himself lived there, David Stratton, the high school quarterback and resident golden boy. Despite herself, she fantasized about dating him, though not for his popularity or good looks. No, she recognized something inside him. A darkness like her own, born not of evil but of sadness, a searing aloneness that scraped at the edges of the soul.

How could someone that beloved ever be lonely? Did no one really know him? Was he lost and didn't know how to escape the trunks of the longleaf pines hemming in his neighborhood like the bars of a giant prison?

When they were kids, she and David used to play in one of the tree houses the Wild Oaks fathers hired someone else to build, until David's parents found out and banned him from associating with the trailer park kids. In the years that followed, the forest between them became an ocean to cross, a Maginot line, a barrier more mental than physical.

What had happened to that little boy?

The true story of the Morning Star, both devil and angel, was one of the many mysteries she aimed to expose in *Night Lives*.

David Cronenburg, she thought, *watch the hell out*.

Halfway through the woods, she heard the murmur of angry whispers, too low to make out the age or gender. Blue froze. She couldn't be seen with the stolen camera. At first she debated turning back, but teenage trysts took place in these woods—repurposing the tree houses. This could be her first big scene. Why else would anyone from Wild Oaks be out in the woods after dark?

The thought excited her. She scurried off the path and looked for a place to hide, breathing in the damp forest air. She spotted a fallen trunk covered in fungi and tried to step over it, but her foot plunged through the rotten wood and an image of a writhing mass of insects filled her mind, a sinkhole full of centipedes and slugs and fire ants. She resisted the urge to jerk away. An artist had to suffer for her art! Instead she sucked in a breath and plowed forward, not wanting to alert her subjects, stepping over the trunk and then squatting on a rock behind it. She knew the clearing up ahead, where the voices were headed. It was a common meeting spot. After hurrying to focus the camera, she hunkered down, breathless with anticipation. She was Citizen Kane, Lois Lane. The Girl with the Dragon Tattoo.

Just before the voices entered the moonlit clearing, a noise in the bushes startled Blue. She jerked her head to the left but saw nothing. After a few tense moments, she realized it had probably been a squirrel. People always thought a noise in the woods must be a snake, but that was because they didn't know any better. Snakes didn't make noise unless they wanted to.

Though she had lurched away, the camera remained pointed at the clearing: a subconscious reaction that pleased her. An instinct to always maintain focus on her subject. She bent to peer through the lens when a muted gunshot echoed through the forest, followed by the dull thud of something collapsing to the ground.

Not something, she thought.

A body.

At first she thought it might have been a hunter, but she realized at once how ridiculous that was. No one hunted at night inside the town limits.

After whipping the camera back and laying flat behind the log, she became a deer, a hibernating bear, as silent as anything that had ever walked the forest. Though she had never fired a gun, they were all over the trailer park. She had recognized the muffled *thwap* of a silencer too.

A low, prolonged moan of pain came from the clearing. Though human, the desperation in the sound reminded her of a dog on the verge of death, whimpering with sudden knowledge, right before its owner put it out of its misery. A series of harsh whispers accompanied the moan, followed by a second gunshot.

The moaning stopped.

Blue's pulse hammered against her chest. Had someone just been murdered right in front of her? Not daring to breathe, she knew she had to hide there in the mud and leaves and insects, under the cloak of darkness, for as long as it took.

The whispering had also ceased. Now there was grunting, followed by a prolonged swish, as if something were being dragged down the path. An insect crept onto Blue's ankle and felt its way underneath her jeans. She swallowed her revulsion and let it crawl.

As the sound drew further and further away, a riff from her favorite indie rock band sounded loudly from her pocket, shattering the quiet like an errant baseball crashing through a window during church.

The ringtone on her cell phone.

No no no.

The dragging sound paused.

Blue jumped to her feet. A quick glance told her no one was within sight range in the darkness. She couldn't risk staying put and catching the beam of a flashlight. As she turned and fled, the canvas shoulder satchel in which she kept her schoolbooks and personal belongings, a worn old thing she had found at Goodwill, snagged on a branch. After fumbling to grab her bag, spilling the contents in the process, she vaulted over the log and sprinted down the path.

Moments later, footsteps pounded the earth behind her. Blue ran as fast as she ever had, fear pumping through her, adrenaline giving her wings. The trail split before it spilled into the trailer park, and she took the left fork, stuffing the camera into her backpack as she ran. The new path would put her out much further from home, but it would keep her in the forest longer, as well as stop the nosy neighbors and alcoholics in the trailer park from pointing her out to whoever emerged behind her waving a gun.

The trail split again and again. The footsteps behind her faded.

After jumping a creek that led to a new series of trails, Blue scrambled up a steep embankment and emerged in a weed-filled playground behind an apartment complex where she used to sift through the dumpster for discarded treasures. She slunk into the parking lot and, when no one was watching, emerged onto the road a half-mile from home. Shaking, she decided to hole up in a late-night diner a few blocks away on the edge of downtown. After slumping low in the booth and ordering a coffee, she tried to process what had happened, keeping her camera tucked safely in her bag.

It wasn't until an hour and a half had passed, after the waitress with sunken cheeks and tobacco-stained nails had told her she had to leave, that Blue risked the lonely walk home, flinching every time a new set of headlights swung into view.

2

Detective Joe "Preach" Everson set down the hatchet and wiped a line of sweat from his brow. A gust of wind caused a flurry of pine needles to drift down, adding to the layer covering the yard of his bungalow in the woods outside Creekville, North Carolina. Though the early October air remained mild, he had decided to get a head start on splitting wood for the season, knowing the weather could turn at any time.

After spending a decade as a homicide detective with the Atlanta PD, he had moved back to his hometown over a year ago, searching for a measure of peace and solitude after a case that had broken his spirit and changed the course of his career.

Eyeing the stack of logs with satisfaction, he took off his boots and stepped inside, where Ari was still working on the sofa in one of his sweatshirts, legs curled under her, poring over a legal file. After graduating from UNC law and passing the bar, she was barely a month into her job as a Durham County prosecutor.

"Even Jesus took a break on Saturday night, counselor."

"You're finished already?" she asked, without glancing his way.

"It's dark."

"Oh." She looked up with a sheepish smile, dark hair scattered, eyes straining from the text. "In case you think I'm having fun, this expert report makes IKEA instructions seem exciting."

"The accountant who ripped off his clients to buy his twenty-year-old girlfriend a Porsche?"

"That's the one. The guy can launder money like a Sicilian but doesn't think anyone will question a waitress with a new 911."

Greed and sex accounted for a vast portion of crimes in America, Preach knew. Where they were both involved, rational behavior had a way of taking a vacation to a distant tropical island. "How's a cold beer and Chinese food sound? The good stuff, not takeout."

She sighed. "Lovely. Just give me a few."

"Sure," he said, though her attention had already returned to the folder.

For the most part, Preach's year with Ariana Hale had been a thrilling one, filled with long passionate nights, bleary-eyed coffee in the morning, and intense debates on his screened porch in between, sipping bourbon as they waded through the murky lagoons of life, literature, and the meaning of it all. She challenged him, he challenged her, and they loved each other—what more could one ask?

Still, dating a woman studying for the bar and beginning life as an attorney had its challenges. In the last few months, Preach could count on one hand the number of times Ari had stayed the entire weekend. While she was in law school, their odd schedules had seemed to mesh, but now she worked nine-to-five, or more like nine-to-nine. With his irregular hours, they struggled to find time to connect.

After he washed and toweled off, Preach ran his fingers through his short blond hair and threw on jeans, a black sweater, and a pair of slip-on shoes. After tucking his badge and wallet into a pocket, he sipped on a tumbler of whiskey while waiting for Ari to wrap up. Unlike Atlanta, where he had carried a loaded Glock 22 everywhere he went, in Creekville he relied on the nine millimeter locked in the dash of his car for most off-duty outings.

And he was the cautious one.

"I'm sorry," she said, once they had settled into a faux red leather booth at the Happy Buddha, a Chinese restaurant just off Main Street. She was wearing a long black skirt, matching boots, and a forest green sweater with lacy sleeves.

"For what?" After all these months, he couldn't stop looking at her face. Like her smoky dark eyes and expressive mouth, both of which hinted at layers unpeeled, Ari possessed a combination of innocence and world-weary insouciance that drew him in like an explorer discovering a lost city.

"For working all the time," she said.

His eyes lingered on the silver bangles sitting loosely on her left wrist. Thin by nature, Ari looked almost gaunt these days from her late nights and stressful career.

"Do you like it?" he asked her. "The job?"

She started to open the menu, then paused. "I feel like it's where I need to be. At least for now."

"It can take time to be sure."

"It's hard," she said, with a rueful, self-effacing chuckle. "Harder than I thought it would be."

"Really? I think most people understand that being a trial attorney is a difficult job."

"I thought law school was hard. This," she waved a hand through the air, "is hard in a different way. C'mon, let's order."

After a moment, as she perused the menu, he said, "There are lives at stake now."

Her eyes lifted to meet his gaze.

"What you do matters," he continued in a quiet voice. "The pressure makes it hard to sleep at night, and your decisions can haunt you. It's real now."

She pursed her lips, digesting his words, and nodded.

He reached over the table and squeezed her hand as the waiter approached.

Two hours later, deliriously full of dumplings and Dan Dan noodles and Tsingtao beer, Preach took Ari in his arms once they returned to his house. "What are you reading these days?" he asked, kissing her neck as he removed her cropped denim jacket.

"Legal briefs."

"Besides that," he said, lifting off her sweater and then his own.

She pressed against him, running her nails down his broad back, her flesh like warm caramel on his skin. "The *Triangle Business Journal.* Law blogs. Police reports. Sexy stuff, huh?"

He scooped her in his arms and laid her down on the couch, as easy for him as lifting a jug of milk. "I know you've got a book hiding somewhere at work. In your purse or your briefcase or a desk drawer. No way you get through the day without one."

"You know me that well, do you?" she purred, as he wedged in beside her and unhooked her bra. "I'm a career woman now. Those carefree days of meeting you on your breaks at the nearest coffee shop are gone forever."

He leaned on an elbow. "Forever's a long time for a wandering soul like you. So which one is it?" he asked, cupping a hand over her breast.

She gasped, arching in pleasure at the gentle massage. "What?"

"Which book is it?"

She gripped his hair as he eased his weight down on her. They kissed and intertwined their legs, hips grinding on the couch like teenagers.

"*Ghana Must Go,*" she whispered in his ear. "I listen to the audiobook when I walk to work."

"Oh yeah? What else?"

As he pushed her skirt up, she unhooked his belt, and the two of them giggled as they worked to remove his jeans without losing contact. "The latest Murakami is on my nightstand."

His fingers curled into the edges of her silk panties. "And? Confession is good for the soul."

"A little Jane Austen when I cook. Her letters. That's it, I swear. Joe?" she said, breathless, as his hands slid into the divots below her pelvis, gently probing.

"Yeah?" he said, his voice husky.

"Why don't we do this more often? Like, five times a day?"

"Good question." As her legs locked around his hips, a vibration from the coffee table broke the spell. Both their gazes slid to the table, coming to rest on his work phone. "One sec," he muttered. "I have to check."

She lifted her hands over her head, stretching in pleasure as he bent over the phone. "Should we move to the loft?" she murmured. "Bring some wine?"

He knew the optimism in her voice, despite the call from work, was reflective of the fact that Creekville rarely had the sort of situation that would result in Preach having to report in while off duty. Violent crimes were rare, and there hadn't been a homicide since the terrible events of the year before.

"I'd love to," he said slowly, staring at the message and then easing off her, sitting up on the edge of the couch. He turned to meet her gaze. "But there's a body in the woods."

Preach veered off the old country road and into a gravel parking lot, the lights of his cruiser strobing the side of the abandoned mill. The old brick wall seemed to swallow the flashing light. Despite the weeds and broken windows, the mill had stood for a century and would stand for countless more, a remnant of a time when everything manufactured did not seem fleeting and ephemeral.

No reporters yet. Just a few police cars parked at odd angles and a cluster of officers standing beside the mill. The forest loomed a few yards away.

The mill was just inside the Creekville city limits, less than a mile from the county line. As Preach walked over, he saw the postures of the other officers straighten, hands fidget, conversations cease. They still didn't know what to do with him. Though born and raised in Creekville, he had left town far too long ago—right after high school—to still be considered a local. He worked the same beat as the rest of them, but he had years of hard-nosed, white-knuckled homicide experience in Atlanta under his belt.

It wasn't just the job. Over the water cooler, he discussed novels with the administrative staff instead of telling jokes or swapping hunting stories. While most of the officers kept sports memorabilia and family photos on their desks, Preach had a Purple Heart from the Atlanta PD and a framed quote from Kierkegaard.

Which was okay. When a bad one hit, the Creekville police department didn't need a drinking buddy. They needed a leader.

"Where's the body?" he asked.

Officer Terry Haskins stepped forward, pointing out a footpath behind where they were standing. "At the edge of a sump, a hundred feet inside the woods. I'll take you in."

Among the gathered officers, Preach considered Terry the most promising, though Bill Wright had the most experience. Bill was nearing retirement and had long since lost that drive that caused officers to go the extra mile for a case, if he ever had it to begin with. Terry was young, had mouths to feed, and possessed a moral code that ensured he always gave his best effort. He was untested in battle, though. Preach didn't think he had ever fired his gun in the line of duty.

"Forensics is en route," Terry said.

After pulling on a pair of blue surgical gloves, Preach flicked on his flashlight and aimed it at the dirt path snaking through the trees. "Who called it in?"

"Animal control, believe it or not."

"What?"

Terry turned to point at a house across the road. It was an old, rundown country manor with a wraparound porch and a pair of pickups parked in the grass. "Around dusk, the neighbors heard a god-awful racket in the woods. It got so bad they called it in, thinking it was a pack of pit bulls on the loose. Animal control showed up and heard it too. Said it was coyotes. They fired off a few times, went to investigate, and saw a body chewed up on the side of the water. Animal control said they've gotten bad in recent years. Global warming, humans encroaching on their territory and all that."

"Wait—the coyotes killed someone in the woods?" Preach asked in disbelief.

"Oh. No. Sorry, I didn't say that right. The vic has two gunshot wounds. The water must have lowered to expose the body, and the coyotes dragged it out."

To ward off the chill, Preach buttoned his double-breasted, forest green overcoat, the same one he had worn his entire career. Ari teased him about it, but the musty smell kept him grounded. Connected to all the cases that had shaped him as an officer, for better and for worse.

"Lead the way," he said, as the forensics van pulled into the parking lot.

Looking unsure for a moment, Officer Wright fell in behind them. The others stayed behind to help the forensics team, manage the reporters once they arrived, and preserve the integrity of the crime scene.

Preach walked slowly down the path, waving his flashlight around, absorbing the crime scene on a visceral level. Tall pines creaked in the wind. The insects sang a primeval chorus, and every few feet something unseen rustled in the underbrush. A few times he almost tripped on a root or a large rock jutting out of the ground.

Less than a hundred yards in, the smell of death hit him, rancid and familiar. Terry put a cloth to his mouth, but Preach breathed it in slowly, adjusting, overcompensating with his other senses. The earth had turned spongy, and his light revealed a sunken area off to the left of the path, at the bottom of a slope. A small pool of water glistened in the moonlight like oil on asphalt. They shooed away the rodents, and Preach grimaced as he viewed the waterlogged corpse. Two bullet holes, one in the stomach and one in the head, left no question as to the cause of death.

His boots sank in the muck as he stepped off the path. The stench of fetid water commingled with the decomposing corpse made his stomach tighten. He focused on breathing through his mouth and, as was his custom, squatted on the ground beside the body to stare into the victim's eyes. Though the coyotes had taken chunks of flesh from the legs and the torso was a mess, the face was bloated but intact.

The victim was a teenage boy with a strong jaw and good cheekbones. Sandy blond hair cut close to the scalp, wide shoulders, long limbs, dressed in jeans and a form-fitting gray sweater. Shoes too muddy to identify. No apparent rings or jewelry. Calloused palms that Preach recognized as the product of gripping a barbell.

An athlete, then.

After a time, he pushed to his feet. "I know it looks bad, but that body's a few days old at most. Swamp water takes a rapid toll."

"It's two days old," Bill said, in a matter-of-fact tone.

When Preach glanced back, surprised at the certainty in the older officer's voice, Terry said, "You don't recognize him? Oh—you've been off the last few shifts, haven't you? We passed his photo around the morning briefing yesterday. Kid's name is David Stratton."

"I heard about a missing kid," Preach said, though Terry was looking at him like he should know the name. Preach held up a palm. "Is he famous or something?"

"Around here he is. He's Creekville High's star quarterback."

"Is that right?" The detective's gaze slipped back to the body. It was not often, even in the big city, that popular kids with preppy clothes showed up dead in the woods.

"His parents split a while back, but he lives with his mom. You might even know her. I think she was around in your day."

"Yeah?" Preach said in a distracted voice.

"Claire Lourdis, class of '99. That's around your time, isn't it?"

The name caused Preach to suck in a breath and give the junior officer a sharp glance.

"Tall and thin, good tan?" Terry added. "Still a real looker, judging by the photos. Like a model or something. You know her?"

The question recalled a vivid memory of long brown hair and designer sunglasses, toned calves and crossed thighs that seemed to go on forever, a coy smile tossed his way at the after-game parties. For a moment, he went back in time to one of those humid summer nights with Wade Fee, top down and a case of beer in the trunk, trolling the town's hangouts for a glimpse of feminine perfection.

In Preach's day, Claire Lourdis was the girl in school everyone wanted but no one could ever have. Despite having flirted with him a few times, she only went for college guys and was the one girl who had rebuffed his advances. She was smart and beautiful and cool, talented and ambitious. A year older than him, her plan was to head to Hollywood after graduation, until an unexpected pregnancy changed all of that. After she married the father, Preach lost track of her, though he still remembered how besotted he was with her as a junior.

To young Joe Everson, the Creekville High bad boy and heartbreaker of his day, Claire Lourdis had been the one who got away.

"Yeah," he said, staring down at the corpse and feeling unbalanced, flooded by memories as well as empathy for a mother whose world was about to implode. "I know her."

3

Preach forced away thoughts of Claire Lourdis and concentrated on the crime scene. With the steady hand of a surgeon, he moved the flashlight slowly over the body and across the top of the water. The sump was about twenty feet wide and smelled like a sewer. He walked the perimeter, stopping to examine the impressions in the mud, poking the light into the trees and clumps of undergrowth.

No sign of a weapon. No evidence of a struggle.

Just the looming presence of the forest, thick and dark, secrets lurking like ghosts.

Bill started walking toward him. Preach held out a hand. "One of us is enough. I want forensics to check for shoe prints."

"All I see is animal tracks."

"Me too," Preach said. "Which is why I want forensics. The kid didn't fly in here, and neither did the perp."

"The path we came in on looked clean," Terry said. "Think someone swept it?"

"That, or they came in another way. I don't see another path. But we'll have to check where these woods lead in the daylight."

"Any first impressions?"

As he thought, Preach blew into his hands to warm them. "Two shots, close in, small caliber weapon. One in the gut, the second in the right temple. A kill shot."

"You mean, like a professional?"

Preach shook his head. "Too messy for a pro. If you're in that close, why not just go for the head? No scratches or bruises on the face, either." He looked down at the body. "If I had to guess, I'd say it was someone he knew. Or at least knew well enough to get in close."

"Drug deal gone bad?" Terry asked.

"As good a guess as any, at this stage."

Bill crossed his fleshy arms and peered into the water. "What were they doing out here, anyway?" he muttered. "It smells like shit."

"I don't think anyone was doing anything," Preach said, "besides dumping a body. There's no sign of blood on the trail or anywhere else. I suppose the kid could've been standing in the water when he was shot, but that doesn't ring true. As you said, there's nothing here. That kid was tossed."

"Makes more sense," Terry agreed, but Preach had already moved on. He could hear forensics lugging their equipment down the trail, and he wanted another moment alone with the body. A barred owl hooted in the distance as the detective knelt again beside Claire Lourdis's son, studying his face, trying to read his story before the floodlights came on and forensics treated the body as the lifeless husk it was.

David Stratton, star quarterback. Town golden boy. A demigod in his insular little world.

What had brought him to this foul, rotten, mud-soaked conclusion to a promising young life?

Who had looked into his eyes and pulled the trigger? What had happened between them?

What dreams and thoughts and regrets had passed through David's mind between the first shot and the second, knowing he was about to die?

When Preach turned back, vaguely aware of the commotion behind him but lost in his reverie, he saw a handful of new faces in the clearing, dressed in blue nylon jackets and hovering over a pile of equipment.

Lela Jimenez, the new deputy chief of forensics, met Preach's gaze. "Okay to proceed, detective?"

"Yeah," he said, with a final glance at the body. "Do your thing. Make sure to drag the water for a phone."

Lela flicked a switch and a flare of white light lit the clearing.

Later that night, when he had finished with the crime scene, Preach left the woods and returned to his car. So far, forensics had uncovered nothing new. He hoped the full report would add some color.

He started the engine and sat with the heater blowing, knowing what he had to do. More than anything, he wanted to go back home, climb in bed with Ari, and dream away the memory of the boy's sightless eyes. The last thing he wanted to do was face the mother's grief. It was the worst part of the job, or one of the worst, but Preach wasn't about to hand it off to anyone else. Not when he was the only officer with any real homicide experience. Not when he knew the mother personally.

Nor was he willing to wait until the morning. It wasn't his place to judge whether Claire's suffering for her missing son was worse before she knew the truth, or after.

At 4:00 a.m., the town of Creekville was as quiet as an ocean bottom, the night a burden of dark water pressing down on the detective as the empty streets whisked by, bringing him closer and closer to Claire Lourdis's house.

He drove down the oak-lined sidewalks and expansive lawns of Hillsdale Street, then through the tiny resting heart of downtown, a few blocks of shops and restaurants centered around the repurposed cotton mill. The closer he drew, the more it felt as if he were journeying back in time, pushing through some kind of reverse womb where death awaited on the other side, instead of life.

The worst death of all.

The death of a child.

Soon after passing the Wandering Muse bookstore, Ari's former employer, he turned left onto Highline Street, a busy two-lane road that linked up with an old state highway. A mile down Highline was the first of three entrances to Wild Oaks, one of Creekville's more desirable neighborhoods. After glancing at the GPS, he turned into the second entrance, past a series of houses with front-yard gardens enclosed with chicken wire to keep out the deer. Most of the residents had accented the pine needles covering the ground with boulders and locally sourced wood chips. This neighborhood was built when he was a kid, and he remembered how his mother had once scoffed at the new construction and labeled the new owners as hopelessly bourgeois. Now, the quaint bungalows and wooded tracts of common space were the very definition of Creekville, and flat grassy lawns that reeked of normalcy were frowned upon.

Still, it was hardly bohemian. Most of the houses had undergone extensive renovations and cost far more than most working-class people, including Preach, could afford. The housing prices in Creekville were pushing out all of the artists and students and starry-eyed dreamers who had given the town its character in the first place.

On his left, 122 Howard Street appeared, the address Terry had given him. Preach parked on the road and sat with his hands gripping the wheel, eyes shut for a long moment before he stepped out of the car.

The walkway to Claire's front door stretched before him like the plank of a pirate's ship dropping into the icy dark. He took a deep breath and started walking, gravel crunching underfoot. Halfway to the two-story house, twin lights kicked on beside the front door.

Preach knocked and shifted on the balls of his feet as he waited, his badge held high.

The door cracked open, stopped by a chain. A moment later it widened, and Claire stood in the doorway wrapped in a silk bathrobe, hair mussed and falling past her shoulders in gentle waves, her long face smooth and beautiful even without makeup. Though she looked more mature and dark circles floated beneath her eyes, no doubt due to worry and lack of sleep, Claire Lourdis was still the same bombshell she had been in high school.

Preach saw the recognition in her eyes at once. Normally when someone answered the door at night, they did so with sleep-filled eyes, blinking, addled from the sudden interruption.

Claire looked very much awake. She peered right through him, as if trying to see into the back of the car parked by the curb.

"Claire, do you remember me?"

She swallowed before she spoke. "Of course, Joe. Everyone knows you're back. I'm sorry about last year."

He gave a curt nod. "Me too."

Her eyes flashed, and he knew the niceties were over. "Do you have him?" she said quietly. "Tell me you have him."

He stepped forward and lightly touched her arm, trying to project as much strength as he could in the hope that some of it would flow into her. "Claire," he said as gently as he could. "I'm sorry. We—"

She smacked his arm away, hard. "What do you mean you're sorry? Where is he? Where the hell is he?"

Preach gripped her by the arms, just hard enough to stop another blow. "We found him in the woods, Claire. He's gone. I'm so very sorry."

In the split-second it took her to register his words, her head cocked to the side in a confused manner, as if disoriented. Then her eyes rolled back and she ceased to have weight. He caught her as she fell, eased her to the ground, and held her as she screamed, a knife of grief slicing into the calm center of the night.

When she finished screaming, her nails dug into him as she clawed her way to her feet, using him as leverage. She looked as if she might bolt, but he applied an ounce of pressure on her arms, suggesting, and she convulsed with sobs as she fell into him. It took all of his willpower to maintain his own composure.

"Joe," she moaned. "Joe, my baby boy."

He hugged her tight, trying to absorb her pain. "I'm so sorry," he whispered.

"Tell me it's not true. Tell me it might not be him." She gripped the hair on the back of his head so hard it made him wince. "Tell me, Joe!"

It was the one thing he couldn't do.

When Claire was coherent again, Preach told her how her son had died and where they had found the body, though he wasn't sure she was listening. Worried she might be a suicide risk, he flipped through her cell phone and called her mother, a local retired nurse. After her own breakdown on the phone, she rushed over to console her daughter. He left them huddled together on the sofa, weeping, calling out the name of their lost one.

Unable to imagine their grief but feeling it twisting inside him, he drove home and drank bourbon on the screened porch until he was numb enough to sleep.

A piercing siren sounded over and over in Preach's dreams, a foghorn on a boat adrift in a wine-dark sea. The boat started rocking as the waves crashed in, and an image of Claire's face was superimposed in the moonlit sky like an ancient goddess gazing down on her creation with infinite sadness. Then it was Ari's face and she was leaning over him, shaking him awake.

"Joe! It's almost eight. You slept through the alarm."

He blinked and sat up. "I did?"

"When did you get home?"

The events of the night flowed back into him like a returning tide of polluted water. "I don't know. Late. Then I stayed up a while."

"Why?"

With a sigh, he dressed for work and gave her a recap.

Ari pressed a hand to her mouth. "God, how terrible. I can't imagine."

"I know the mother," he said. "Or I used to. We went to high school together."

She approached and cupped his cheek in her hand. "I'm sorry. You're handling the case?"

"Yeah. Though . . ."

"What?"

"I'm afraid it might get worse when I dig. Worse for Claire, I mean."

She took his hand. "Does it have to be you? Maybe it's time for Terry to step up?"

"He's got a full plate right now, and he's not ready for this. Besides, I think I . . . I should be the one. It's why I'm here, you know?"

Preach had over a decade of homicide experience in the war zone of the Atlanta PD. Besides Chief Higgins, who had cut her teeth in Charlotte, no other officer in Creekville had worked lead on a homicide.

She reached up to kiss him. "I understand. Come to breakfast, okay? I made French toast."

"You did?" he said, surprised.

He followed her to the table and saw the first volume of Proust's *In Search of Lost Time* sitting beside a plate of buttered toast, along with a cup of coffee and a bowl of scrambled eggs.

He gave her a rueful grin. "Cute."

Ari never had time to cook, but even when she did, culinary innovation was not one of her talents. He always appreciated the effort, but decided to reach for the Cackalacky sauce. The eggs would need it.

She sat across from him, dressed in gray sweats and one of Preach's old T-shirts. It was nice to see her relaxed. These days he usually saw her in business attire, and he knew she resented the conformity of it all. But she had kept the same hairstyle, a disheveled look that he loved, and that resembled a pile of straw assembled by a diligent family of squirrels. She also still wore her silver thumb rings, and instead of covering up the twin Jane Austen tattoos on the undersides of her wrists, half hope and half agony, she had added another: the scales of justice, just above her left ankle.

As they ate, she pored over a legal brief while he made the daily news rounds on his cell phone. On the local scene, it was all about an issue that had inflamed Creekville in recent months: the push from developers to buy up real estate downtown, change the zoning laws, and shove in big-box stores and high-rise apartments. The locals were fiercely opposed to change, and everyone Preach talked to was convinced the developers would lose. But he knew money talked, and walked, and sifted through nimble fingers beneath tables.

Nationally, the news had grown so absurd he had stopped paying attention. The unending litany of agenda-driven vitriol did nothing but divide a nation that needed desperately to be working together.

Still, his eyes flicked over the headlines. Children buried alive after an earthquake in Mexico, displaced families wading through a filthy river in Bangladesh, another Hollywood mogul crashing through life with the mindless depravity of a Greek god.

He slowly closed the phone. "Remember when we used to sit side by side and talk over breakfast?"

She glanced up. "Mmm?"

"Do you really have to read that right this very moment?"

She frowned. "Yeah. I kinda do."

"It's Sunday."

"You know I have an important witness interview tomorrow."

"Life's short, Ari. The whole world is buried in their cell phones or in their work."

He glanced away, knowing his outburst was unwarranted, and she laid a hand over his. "I know you're processing last night."

"Yeah."

"Listen, I understand you're busy all day, and I've got to run, but maybe we can meet for lunch tomorrow, if I get done in time?"

From her tone and the way her gaze slipped away, he could tell that the very thought of meeting him during the work day stressed her out. "It's okay," he said quietly.

"You're sure?"

He downed his coffee, stood, and carried his dishes to the sink. "Knock 'em dead tomorrow."

The Creekville police station was located on the second floor of a brick building with white awnings, situated above a gluten-free bakery and an ice cream parlor that specialized in frozen custard.

Even though it was Sunday morning, the station was buzzing with the nervous energy of a murder. As soon as Preach passed through reception, Chief Higgins called him into her office and slapped a piece of paper on her desk.

"What's this?" he asked. "Preliminary autopsy?"

"An autopsy already?" the chief said. "What are we, McDonald's for the dead?"

"It's the second murder in a decade."

"Check back tomorrow."

"They find a phone?" he asked.

"Nope."

The chief was a top-heavy redhead with oily skin, a thin determined mouth, and arms as thick as barrels. Her personality, like her voice, was an odd combination of Southern matriarch, hardened police officer, and Zen Buddhist.

"Tell me about the kid," he said.

"What do you mean?"

"Does he have a record?"

"You spent too much time in Atlanta," she said. "This is Creekville High we're talking about. He was a model student, no discipline problems we know of." She held up a palm. "Though views can get distorted when the star quarterback is involved."

"Who was looking into his disappearance?"

"Bill."

"Great."

She wagged a finger. "Be nice."

"Nice doesn't solve murders."

She picked up a stress ball marked with a yin-yang symbol, leaned back, and started gently kneading it. "You're right. Talk to Bill, but you should probably start from scratch."

"I was going to anyway."

She nodded, and her mouth tightened as she gripped the ball harder. "Dig, Preach. Coaches, friends, neighbors, Sunday School teachers. Short-term pain can be forgotten. But the longer this thing goes unsolved . . . this is one of those crimes that can tear a town apart."

"Thanks for the added pressure. What I can promise is that I'll do my job, the best I know how."

"I want a list of suspects by Friday."

Before he left, he picked up the piece of paper the chief had set in front of him. "What's this?"

"Bill's report on the missing person case. Look at the second paragraph. The night David disappeared, one of the neighbors heard a disturbance at the Lourdis house. A screaming match."

He finished reading Officer Wright's notes from Friday, October 3. In response to Bill's inquiry, Claire had blown off the incident, saying her son was a typical angst-ridden teen upset with his mother's boyfriend. "So Claire and David were fighting about her new fling. That's not uncommon after a divorce."

"The divorce was years ago."

"It's hard to see your mom date around." A long breath seeped out of him. "God, she'll never forgive herself if she drove him away that night."

"Probably not. But you need to ask her a few questions."

"That's the plan."

"You need to ask her if she owns a gun."

He started. "With an execution-style shot to the head? A mother? I don't think now's the time—"

"We're not positive about the time of death, but it looks like it's going to be soon after he left the house. How many people could he have run into?"

"It just takes one. He was distraught and could have gone anywhere. Who the hell knows what happened?"

"That's right," she said softly, pointing a finger at him. "It just takes one. So ask."

4

After Preach left the station, he wanted to order his thoughts before he talked to Claire, and he felt the need for more coffee. Good coffee, that was.

Minutes later, he pulled into the gravel lot of Jimmy's Corner Store, a café and local market that served as Preach's second office. He entered the packed cafe and sat on a barstool at the counter, facing the chalkboard menu and an old tin Sunbeam Bread sign that had probably been there for fifty years.

Over the years, the aroma of roasting coffee had permeated the tables, overstuffed chairs, and blue clapboard walls. Preach hunched over his mug and thought about how best to approach Claire. He hated to impose on her grief so soon, but a timely investigation was essential. Evidence degraded over time.

Officer Wright's case file was painfully thin. It was obvious he hadn't thought David was in imminent danger. Bill had made a few calls but, except for David's argument with his mother, uncovered no evidence of enemies or disturbing behavior.

Which Preach wasn't buying. That kind of crime, the murder of a healthy male from close range and a careful dump of the body, didn't scream spur-of-the-moment decision to Preach. What he thought was that past events had initiated a chain reaction that for some reason had come to a head after David left his house. Whether the argument with his mother had anything to do with that, well, he would just have to see.

On Monday, he planned to visit the school. Talk to the teachers and coaches and David's friends. Where else did teenage boys hang out these days? Preach thought about his own youth and the hell he had raised, but things were different now. He and Wade and the crew had drunk themselves silly and smoked a little pot, but they hadn't had drugs that could ruin your life with one puff or pharmaceutical concoctions mixed in bathtubs that could make you claw your own face off.

Had David been into drugs? Gotten involved with the wrong crowd?

There were other possibilities, ones Preach had seen with homeless teens time and time again. Ones that made him shudder. He still didn't like to look at a missing persons report for children, or even the back of a milk carton. A crime against a child was a stain on the human race.

Still, none of that rang true here. He needed to know more, peel back the layers.

It just pained him to do it with Claire's child.

The town was buzzing as Preach drove through the leaf-strewn streets to the Lourdis house. The activity still surprised him. In his day, Sunday was for church and nothing else. Fancy clothes and fried chicken on the table, shuttered shops throughout the town. His own parents would rather have slept in the snow than pass through the doors of a church, but the Creekville of his youth was still steeped in Southern tradition.

Over the years he had done some reading on how secularization and religion waxed and waned in various cultures over time. He had some thoughts on the matter, most of them involving societal norms instead of any sea change in spirituality. But now, as far as he could tell, cafés and brunch spots were the preferred form of worship in Creekville on a chilly Sunday morning.

He swung into Wild Oaks, and driving through the neighborhood in the daylight, with its abundance of wood chips and wire fencing in the front yards, made Preach feel as if he were inside a giant chicken coop. Yippies, he liked to call the residents of Wild Oaks. Half yuppie, half hippie.

Claire's handsome, traditional two-story home was much more all-American than the others. Featuring white siding with brick trim, along with dogwoods, accenting an ivy-covered arbor, the home was one of the few with a manicured lawn. About the only solidarity with the Creekville vibe was a patch of solar panels on the roof.

After parking, Preach shrugged on his overcoat, stuck his notebook in an inside pocket, and walked to the front door. A burly man in his forties answered the knock. He looked Preach up and down. "Can I help you?"

"Is Claire home?"

"Who are you?"

He had the quick speech of a businessman, along with a hint of Carolina twang. Preach took a moment to answer, noting the man's tanned skin, cunning eyes, and clipped dark hair. His two front teeth were a touch too long, and the one on the left was shinier than the other. Probably reconstructed. With his loafers, slacks, and Ralph Lauren sweater, he looked as out of place in Creekville as a farmer in Manhattan.

"A friend." Preach took out his badge. "And a detective."

"She can't talk right now. Jesus," he said, his eyes darting to the side, "have some respect."

"What's your name?"

"Brett. Brett Moreland."

"And you are?"

"Her boyfriend."

"I understand your concern, but I promise to be gentle. Given the circumstances, I think she'll want to talk to me. Timing is crucial to a murder investigation."

Brett steepled his fingers on his forehead. "Murder. God, how did this happen? What was that kid into?"

"Why do you think he was into something?"

"Oh, I didn't mean—hey, aren't they all? I just don't know what to do. Claire isn't doing so well."

"I'd expect not."

Brett didn't seem to notice the remark. "You said you're a friend?"

"I knew her in high school."

He looked the detective over again, with new eyes, and then

grunted. Before he could respond, Claire shuffled into view behind him, wearing lavender sweats and a Creekville Football hoodie. The cuffs were rolled so the sleeves would fit her.

Brett turned, laying his hands on her shoulders as she approached. "You don't have to talk to him right now, baby. You have rights."

She stepped away from him and hugged her arms across her chest. "You think I care about *rights*?" She started to break down but composed herself with a shudder. Come in, Joe. I'll do everything I can to help."

"I guess I'll go to the store," her boyfriend called out, as Preach stepped past him. "Unless you need me?"

She waved him off.

"You still need almond milk?"

Her face twisted, furious at the innocent tone, the intrusion of daily routine on her grief. "Just go."

Preach watched him walk toward a Mercedes S-Class and beep the lock. After Claire closed the front door, Preach asked, "What's he do?"

"He has an Internet marketing company. Vertical Integration or something." A hiccup of a laugh slipped through the sadness. "To be honest, I don't really know. Every time he tries to tell me, my eyes glaze over."

"So he's probably got a *lot* of money."

She gave a sad smile and looked away. Preach heard the unspoken story, saw the quick clench of her jaw.

The interior was a modern open floor plan that comprised most of the first floor. Moving as if dazed, she led him to a sectional sofa across from a stacked stone fireplace. Preach shrugged out of his coat and sat a few feet away. Before he started the interview, he leaned in and took her hand. "I can only imagine how hard this is. If you need to stop, let me know."

"I want to help."

He gave a slow nod. "Okay."

"Thank you for coming. I know it didn't have to be you."

"It kind of did. But you're welcome."

She gave a little shiver, still huddled within the protective embrace of her own arms. "What do you need?"

"I'll need to see David's room, but why don't you take me through the day he disappeared?"

Her arms uncrossed and moved to her lap, her thumbs rubbing against each other as if she couldn't sit still. "It was a day like any other. A school day. I made him eggs and toast and bacon . . . I still make him breakfast . . . and he left for school."

"Is the old Wrangler outside his?"

"It breaks down all the time, but he loves it." Her face crumpled as she looked down. "Loved."

"Who brought it back?"

Her eyes lifted. "Sorry?"

"I assumed . . . go ahead and finish, please."

"After he left, I went to work, as I always do. I've been at the boutique for a few years now. I get home at five and make dinner. He got home from practice late, around six-thirty. He seemed a little preoccupied and wouldn't talk about his day."

"Was that strange? Was he open with you?"

"He used to be, until he started high school. Except for my mom, we're all the family each other has. My dad is dead, and David's father's parents are in a nursing home in Pennsylvania."

"Have you contacted his father?"

"Brett sent him a text this morning."

Preach's eyebrows lifted.

"We don't talk," she said.

"What about him and David?"

"Barely. I don't really know anymore."

She didn't explain further, and Preach made a mental note. "Does he live close?"

"Richmond."

The absence of emotion on her face, as if all feeling had long ago been stripped away, spoke louder than words.

"Do you think something happened at school? Maybe at practice?"

"I don't know. He'd been acting weird all week."

"In what way?"

"Just . . . preoccupied. But he was a teenager, you know? That's more usual than not."

"Was he a well-adjusted kid in general?"

"As well adjusted as a kid can be whose father abandoned him."

She said it deadpan, with as little emotion as her earlier mention of her son's father.

"No recent fights at school?" he asked.

Her hands moved to cup the back of her neck, gently massaging. "He was such a good boy, Joe. Never in trouble. Good grades. Lots of friends." Her voice lowered to a whisper. "He had his whole life ahead of him. He was so young. My baby . . ."

She began to cry, shielding her brow with her hand. When she didn't stop, he reached for her hand and gently squeezed it. In return, she dug her nails into his palm with the strength of the bereaved.

After letting her hand slide away, she blew her nose and composed herself.

"I can come back later," he said.

"No. We do this now."

His eyes flicked to the fireplace, taking in the photos strung along the mantle. David throwing a football, David at the prom with a tall blond girl, David and Claire posing on a mountaintop, David in the back of a boat with some friends. He was a strikingly handsome kid, with a fine-boned face and large expressive eyes. Gentler, more refined than Preach at that age. There was also a depth in David's eyes, a brooding self-awareness that Preach knew had never been present in his own. At least not until his senior year when he had watched his cousin Ricky suffer a horrible death, and Preach's self-awareness had come swooping in like a vicious homing pigeon.

But enough of all that. "So he came home, was acting a little off, and you sat down to dinner?"

"Fried chicken and waffles with chocolate sauce." She flashed a wan smile. "His favorite."

"Homework after dinner?"

"We didn't finish until eight or so. He disappeared to his room for a while, maybe for homework, probably for Snapchat, and by the time I washed up and saw him again it was after nine. We—" She paused and looked out the window to her left, at the pine cone–strewn yard behind the house that sloped down to a tract of woods. "We had an argument."

"About school?"

"About Brett."

She stood and walked to a cabinet in the kitchen. After sloshing Jack Daniels into a rocks glass, she took a long drink, her face wrinkling in displeasure. "I assume you don't want one?"

"No."

She returned to the sofa and stared into the glass. As the silence lengthened, despite the professional nature of his visit and the terrible circumstances behind it, he caught himself looking at the curve of her neck, and a jolt of attraction coursed through him. As beautiful as Claire still was, it was not so much a physical longing for the grieving, disheveled woman on the sofa, but rather a ghost of unrequited lust rattling its chains, the return of a supernatural force that had once consumed him.

He forced the intrusion away, thinking of Ari, berating himself for the weak moment.

"David didn't approve of Brett," she said finally. "He didn't think he was good for me."

He left the unspoken question hanging in the air. "How bad was their relationship?"

"It wasn't physical, if that's what you mean. I doubt Brett could have laid a hand on David even if he'd wanted to. David was a strong kid."

Preach wasn't so sure about that. David may have been an athlete in the prime of his life, but he was still a kid. Adults had a different kind of strength, and a different outlook on violence. Grown men fought for keeps.

But he could talk about that with Brett.

"Let's keep going. You argued. What happened next?"

She resumed staring into the glass, her head sinking lower, as if she hadn't the strength to hold it up. "He ran out of the house and got in his Jeep. I heard him leave, and then—" she sobbed once, "that was the last time I saw my son alive."

After giving her another moment, he said, "How did the Jeep get back here?" When she looked at him in confusion, he continued, "Did you find it somewhere? Or did someone report it?"

"Oh. No. It was here when I woke up the next morning."

"You didn't hear him come in the night before?"

"I was really upset about the argument. I . . . took some pills."

"What kind?"

She waved a hand. "Just something to help me sleep. Does it matter?"

"It might," he said, then caught himself when she flinched. He wondered if he was overcompensating for his earlier moment of weakness. "If you were too far gone to hear a struggle."

"You mean you think someone might have come to the house?"

"I don't know what I think."

Her face fell. "It was just an Ambien. God, Joe, if I missed something that night—"

"Don't think like that. You didn't know." She put her head in her hands and began to softly weep again. He yearned to leave this woman to her grief, but there was one more question he had to ask. He knew how the question would affect her, and it seemed as if he had to rip it out of his own gut. This wasn't a hardened criminal in Atlanta or Charlotte, this was Claire Lourdis, grieving mother, lifelong citizen of Creekville, and denizen of his own past.

"Claire, do you own a gun?"

Her head slowly rose, and he winced at both the accusation and the suffering in her eyes. "I have a Ruger. It has a pink handle."

"It's called a grip," he said, with a faint smile. "What's the caliber?"

"I have no idea."

He could tell by the curtness of her answers what she thought of his line of questioning. He didn't want to upset her by pressing further, and it would be easy for forensics to verify the type of gun that was used.

"Joe," she said, shaking her head. "Don't waste your time."

"It's a standard question. I'm sorry I had to ask. Do you have David's phone?"

"No. It wasn't . . ." She couldn't finish.

"We didn't find it either. Can you give me his number? I'll request the phone records."

After she wrote the number down, he pushed to his feet. "Could I see his room, please?"

She pointed. "Up the stairs and to the left. I can't . . . I'll just stay here."

"Of course."

As he made his way upstairs, he noticed expensive furniture and elegant touches throughout, signs of careful selection at high-end department stores. Shiny pottery displayed on a mantle, a trio of diamond-shaped mirrors in the hallway. There was also a series of framed watercolors, impressionistic stick figures dancing in the moonlight that Preach suspected might be Claire's. In high school she had been very artsy, a talented painter and singer as well as an aspiring actress. Her taste for clothes and jewelry was always impeccable, though she never had any money. Like most everyone else in the Creekville public school system, Claire's family had gotten by just fine, but they were solidly middle class. Her mother had worked as a bank teller, and he couldn't recall what her father had done. But Claire had never needed money to stand out. A born fashionista, she had bargain hunted and shopped at thrift stores and, if he remembered correctly from their few conversations, designed some of her own clothes.

In David's room, a queen bed faced a television mounted on the wall. There was a set of dumbbells and dirty football pads in the corner, and a desk scattered with schoolbooks, notepads, pens, a photo of Claire, and one of David with his father. Stacked on the desk chair were a few college information packets: Davidson, Emory, Furman, and NYU. Atop a nightstand, he saw a leather cross necklace, three books, a football-shaped alarm clock, a recent copy of *Men's Health*, and an iPhone stand with speakers.

Preach read the book titles. *A Tale of Two Cities* he guessed was a school read. The other two were *American Gods* by Neil Gaiman and a nonfiction book titled *Why Does the World Exist?*

When he returned to the living room, he asked, "David didn't have a laptop?"

"We shared one, but he rarely used it. Kids are always on their phones these days."

"Was he religious?"

"You saw the necklace?"

"And the books."

"He picked the necklace up on a spring break trip to Charleston. He didn't go to church or anything, though since he was young"—she gave a smile so wistful Preach felt a lurch in his stomach—"he always wanted to know where we came from and what happened after death. And now . . ."

As her eyes teared up again, he gave her his card. He had intruded enough for the day. "If you think of anything else," he said quietly, "anything at all, let me know. The smallest detail might matter."

She stood to see him out. When they reached the door, she teetered on her feet, as if she had lost her balance. He put a hand on her shoulder to steady her, and she gripped it. "It doesn't feel real, Joe," she whispered. "I don't know what I could have done—"

"Claire!" he said sharply. "You can't let yourself go there."

"Go where? Where is there left to go?" She snarled and stepped closer. "Somebody murdered my baby boy. Shot him and left him lying in the bottom of a goddamned swamp." She jabbed him hard in the chest. "You find out who did this, you understand? Find him and hide him somewhere, then take me to him. I'll do the rest of your job for you."

As he backed through the door, the intensity of her stare burned into him as if cauterizing a wound. "I'll do everything I can," he said. "You have my word."

"You find him," she said, right before he turned and walked away. "*You find him.*"

On his way out, Preach searched David's Jeep and found nothing of interest. A few smelly clothes on the back seat, empty Gatorade bottles, candy wrappers, a pair of movie ticket stubs, and an iPhone charger. He called a tow to impound the vehicle so forensics could search for hair and other fibers.

As Preach was pulling away from Claire's house, he saw Brett's black Mercedes with custom rims turn onto her street. Preach reversed, lowered the window, and pulled alongside the sedan. "Can I talk to you at home later?"

Brett frowned. "I guess. Why?"

"Just a chat."

"About what?"

Preach didn't bother with a reply. "What's your address?"

He hesitated. "212 Baddington Street. Chapel Hill."

"Six o'clock sound okay?"

"If we need to talk," Brett said, "why don't we do it here? I'm free for a few minutes."

"I think Claire could use a break."

"We can go in the garage, light a stogie—"

"Brett." Preach stared at him until the other man glanced away.

When Brett turned back, his eyes were more wary. "Sure. I get it. I eat early, so maybe we could push—"

"I'll see you at six."

5

Ever since the night in the woods, Blue had known someone would come.

The reality was even worse than she had imagined. The gangbanger going door to door in the trailer park was a certified killer, a twenty-something Latino who everyone called Cobra. His quick knife strikes had earned him the nickname, along with the hooded black jacket he favored. Blue had never crossed paths with him, but she knew him on sight. His gang, Los Viburos, controlled the drugs that ran like diarrhea through the trailer park, and Cobra was their top enforcer. Whenever he rumbled in on his Honda CBR Interceptor, kicking up clouds of dust, the busy trailer park suddenly resembled a desert in the heat of the afternoon.

She peered through the plastic blinds in her bedroom. Sunlight glinted off the discarded toys and bicycles in the weed-filled yard of the trailer across the gravel drive. To her left, three doors down, Cobra was holding something in his open palm and asking questions about it. No doubt about it: the murderer who had chased her through the woods had found the items from the bag she had dropped. Maybe Cobra himself had been in the woods, maybe not. Didn't matter. He was here now, and he was looking for the owner.

Looking for her.

When she had watched the film footage she had shot a few nights ago, all she had seen was the flash of a gunshot and then a swish of brown, which she assumed was a burlap sack used to drag the body away. She hadn't seen the murderer or the victim, though whoever had committed the crime didn't know that and would never believe her.

Over the last few days, she had run through the missing contents of her bag a million times in her head. Food stamps. Lipstick she never used. A stolen cigarette lighter. Her father's *Ghostbusters* keychain. A flyer for the end-of-semester variety show at the high school.

No doubt the food stamps, recovered so close to the trailer park, had led Cobra here. The fancy silver cigarette lighter might have thrown him off for a day or two, or maybe he had assumed it was stolen. She didn't know why he had waited so long to come.

The crazy part was the victim.

David Stratton, the Morning Star, shot dead in the swamp behind Barker's Mill.

No way there were two murders in Creekville that close in time. David was the victim, and someone had dumped his body in the swamp.

And she had heard the whole thing.

It didn't seem real. Popular kids didn't get killed in the woods, and contract killers didn't hunt down witnesses in Creekville. Had David been mixed up in the drug scene? It seemed to be the only explanation. She had heard nothing like that at school, though she was hardly part of his circle. Still, gossip from the popular kids usually trickled down. She knew Elliot Jacobson and Fisher Star, two of his closest friends, used pot and coke and pharmies.

Or maybe David was a dealer. Maybe that was how his mom afforded that house between boyfriends. Maybe the Morning Star had slung some rock on the side and skimmed off the top, and Javier Ramirez, the head of Los Viburos, had signed his death warrant.

She watched Cobra finish another home visit and walk through the yard to the house next door to Blue's, his boots squashing the tiny pyramids the fire ants made in the dirt.

As she let the shutters close, her hands trembled like an alcoholic's. If she didn't calm down, Cobra would know she was hiding something. For once, she wished her mother was at home and didn't work two jobs and sleep at her boyfriend's house most nights.

Whenever she needed to leave without leaving, whether to flee the soul-numbing reality of the trailer park or a humiliating situation at school or to escape an abusive stepfather, all three of which had come and gone like bad weekends, Blue went to the safe space in her head.

She went to the movies.

Was this an *Indiana Jones* problem? *Crocodile Dundee*, *Lethal*

Weapon, *Beverly Hills Cop*? Just thinking about those films brought a smile to her lips, calmed her down a fraction.

But no. This was not a time for larger-than-life, sugar-coated eighties films. The danger outside was all too real. She had to channel true emotion. *Raging Bull* territory. *The Color Purple*. *The Killing Fields*.

Grit, realism, survival.

Blood and fury.

With a deep breath and a snarl, Blue strode to the cabinet above the sink and grabbed the bottle of Southern Comfort. The whiskey burned as it went down, so bad it made her choke. But she kept it down and felt better. Calmer, more in control.

Okay, Blue. Think.

Cobra didn't know who had been in the woods that night, or he wouldn't be going door to door. Should she hide? Run away? Give him the camera and come clean?

All of those options were risky. Hide, and she looked guilty. Give him the camera, and he would probably decide to tie up loose ends. She could run if she had to, but she didn't have the money to get very far, and she feared he would find her. Contrary to what regular people thought, people on the street all knew each other. Unless she took to the woods—and she didn't have the skills to survive long term—Cobra would catch wind of her before long. Someone would narc.

She couldn't go to the police, either. Cops didn't protect people like her.

Pushing out a breath, she decided she had to face him and throw him off the scent. The variety show flyer suggested a high school student, or maybe the parent of one. But there were a dozen teens living in the trailer park. Blue kept her dark hair short, as short as a boy's. She had worn a denim jacket the night of the murder. With any luck, whoever had glimpsed her in the woods would assume he had seen a young man.

The only other identifying object was the *Ghostbusters* key ring. No one had seen her with it, she was sure of that. She never took it out. It was one of the few things she owned that belonged to her father, a private thing she kept from the world.

A knock at the door. Soft but insistent.

This was it, then. More deep breaths. She bit down hard on her lip to calm her nerves. Right before she opened the door, Blue took another swig and let the whiskey fire spread through her belly. She channeled the working class sneer of DeNiro, the helpless rage of a young black woman in rural Georgia in the 1930s.

In the open doorway, so close she could smell the musk of his cologne, a clean-shaven face peered at her from deep inside the hood. His stare was like an ice pick, cold and bladed, unfeeling.

"Yeah?" she said, somehow managing not to croak the word.

He thrust his hand forward, causing her to flinch, but instead of striking her, Cobra opened his palm to reveal the food stamps, key ring, and flyer she had dropped. "These belong to you? I found them in the woods."

It was the first time she had ever heard him speak. His voice was soft and calm, with the faintest trace of an accent. Though she yearned to grab her father's key ring and slam the door in his face, she flicked her eyes down at his palm, noticing the underside of a black ring, then gave a nonchalant shrug. "Nope."

His stare lingered so long she felt tendrils of fear creeping up her legs and down her arms, slow and malevolent. "What about a friend?"

"I don't have any friends."

"That's too bad."

Blue put a hand on the door frame. "That's life."

His eyes roamed past her, studying the interior. The intelligence in his eyes unnerved her. She had imagined him as an empty vessel, a dumb thug with a gun.

Then again, that was probably the assumption people made about her. Ignorant white trash from the trailer park.

"You smoke?" he asked.

"Sometimes."

He was still holding his left palm out. With his other hand, he reached into a coat pocket, withdrew a packet of Marlboro Lights, and offered her one. She accepted. With a deft series of movements, he shook the cigarettes out, returned the pack to his coat, then took a lighter out of his back pocket. At first, she thought it was the silver lighter she had lost, and her knees felt watery. Watching her the entire time, Cobra lit her cigarette, and then his own.

It was a stainless steel lighter, but not the silver one. He closed his palm over the lost items. "Ask around for me. Find out who these belong to."

Was he toying with her, she wondered? Did he know?

"Okay," she said, forcing indifference into her voice.

"There's something in it for you if you do."

"How do I find you?"

"I'll be back. Soon." He blew smoke, backed away slowly, then turned and started walking down the gravel drive pockmarked with potholes that snaked around the trailer park.

"Hey," she called out.

Cobra stopped, did a half-turn.

"Thanks for the smoke."

He took another drag, raised the cigarette in acknowledgment, then continued on to the next trailer.

With a shudder, Blue shut the door and sank to the floor, shivering as if she had the flu.

6

After leaving Claire's house, Preach returned to the office to start on some paperwork. Top of the list was getting a court order for David's cell phone records. That shouldn't be a problem. In general, privacy concerns ceased at death in the eyes of the law.

His eyes lingered, as they often did, on the cubicle that had belonged to one of his old partners. Preach visited him every now and then in prison, wincing at the gradual dimming of light in his eyes. From Preach's time as a prison chaplain, before he joined the Atlanta PD, he knew the true horror of incarceration was not the loss of freedom, but the daily choices one was forced to make to survive. Navigating the jungle without becoming one of the animals.

Most people who landed behind bars—not all, but most—had disadvantaged upbringings and poor choices to blame.

It was prison that turned them into criminals.

After finishing the paperwork he tapped his pen on his desk, thought about what to do, checked in with forensics, and headed back to his cruiser.

The crime scene in the woods behind the mill was almost more eerie in daylight, a square of yellow tape screaming for attention in the ancient silence of the woods. An aberration of nature among the foraging squirrels and the bucolic chirps and whistles of the birds.

The pines swayed and creaked in the wind as Preach took a knee and stared at the muddy remains of the sunken pool where David's body had lain. An old, shredded bird's nest hung like a shroud from one of the branches extending over the drained sump. No new insight came to him, and he slowly circled the crime scene.

Nothing stood out among the carpet of wet leaves except for discarded beer cans and a few plastic bottles. So far, forensics had uncovered a few heel prints on the dirt path. Most likely a set of work boots, most likely male.

That meant little. Even if someone had swept the ground, a few old prints might have been missed. It would be impossible to ascertain whether they were related to the murder.

Again, the fact that called out most to the detective was one of detraction. The lack of evidence of broken branches or other signs of a struggle.

Where, he wondered, was the real crime scene?

Preach gathered his thoughts while grabbing an early dinner at his favorite 'cue shack. The special of the day was burnt tips, the caviar of the barbecue world. Though considered a delicacy of Kansas City style, the true provenance of burnt tips was shrouded in culinary lore. All Preach knew was that he was biting into a succulent, fire-crisped, wood-smoked, fat-caramelized, swoon-worthy piece of cubed pork so good he had almost forgotten, for a brief moment, about David and Claire.

Almost.

Preach had never been good at leaving the job behind. There was a fine line between lazy detective work and healthy detachment from a case. Another razor-thin margin separated diligent investigative work from dangerous obsession.

The pressure of a murder, the heightened emotions and public scrutiny, blurred the lines even further.

He took a few bites of fried okra and sipped on his sweet tea as the other patrons gave him sidelong glances and tried not to sit too close. They either recognized him from the news last year or sensed from his demeanor and overcoat draped across the chair that he was not a regular civilian. When he had first started on the job, the isolation had bothered him, but over the years he began to wear it like a second skin.

After he finished eating, he steepled his fingers and continued to think. The most common motives for a murder were, by far, money and love. A slew of related motivations fell under the umbrella of these two broad categories, such as jealousy, lust, greed, or revenge.

Of course, there were always outliers. Motives and murderers that defied easy categorization, or even reason. Psychopaths, sufferers of weird fetishes, political or religious fanatics.

But in terms of domestic homicides, money and love accounted for so many murders that it was foolish to look elsewhere unless presented with compelling evidence.

On paper, David's case should be less challenging than most. A high school student narrowed the playing field. Unless the kid had a secret life, his world should be limited to family, friends, and school. A small town like Creekville shrunk the possibilities even further.

Yes, David might have had a secret life, or his murder might involve some bizarre motive. Those were always possibilities.

But if Preach had to bet?

He was placing his chips on money or love. A drug deal gone bad, a jilted rival. He hated to think about it, but someone even closer to David might be involved.

With this case, he worried less about failure and more about what skeletons he would dig up in the process.

Brett Moreland lived in a sprawling granite house in a Chapel Hill subdivision full of similar McMansions. In contrast to the leafy, graceful environs that defined most of the beautiful college town, Brett's treeless neighborhood stood out like a hippo in a trout pond.

An old town filled with old money, home to the oldest public university in the country, Chapel Hill had long been the state's genteel uncle. Raleigh was the heart of government and Charlotte was the business hub, but if one wanted to rub shoulders with the North Carolina elite and make a deal with the true power brokers over a fine scotch in the back of a country club steak house, then one delved into the oak-lined heart of Chapel Hill.

In the dying light Preach glimpsed a lake between the houses. He parked on the curb and walked to Brett's front door. Above him loomed a twenty-foot portico supported by white pillars, and he estimated the house was six or seven thousand square feet. In Chapel Hill this type of place would run a few million. At least.

Brett answered the doorbell after the second ring, dressed in a tracksuit and huffing from exertion. "Sorry, just finishing up a workout." As Preach took off his coat, Brett noticed the officer's thick chest and arms. "You lift?"

"I do."

"Nautilus, free weights, isometrics?"

Preach shrugged. "Sometimes I pick up heavy things to try to clear my head."

Brett gave him a quizzical look and dabbed his forehead with his towel. "Come on in. Glass of water? Tea? Something stronger?"

Why did people always feel the need to offer an on-duty policeman a drink, Preach wondered? "I'm fine."

Brett waved at the living room. "Make yourself at home. Let me grab a beer and I'll be right with you."

After an annoyed glance at his watch, Preach absorbed the cream-colored walls, a chandelier dangling from a high ceiling, and bands of wrought iron wrapping the balcony on the second floor. Almost no knickknacks, very little art or furniture, and a giant television above the gas fireplace. A bachelor's pad.

As always, the detective chose his seat carefully, selecting a high-backed armchair with his back to the wall. The chair faced a windowed nook that afforded a view of an expansive green lawn ambling down to the lake. An electric blue speedboat was tied off to a wooden dock.

Brett returned with a mug of foam-topped beer. He held it up. "You sure?"

"I'm sure."

The host sat on the edge of a suede sofa. "So, what's up?"

Preach waited before he spoke, hoping Brett would absorb some of the gravity of the situation. As successful as the man obviously was, Preach got the sense he didn't absorb very much.

"*What's up*?" Preach repeated.

"I mean, I know what's up. I can't believe the kid's dead." Brett looked down at his beer and let out a long breath. "But what's up with me? What do you want to know?"

"What do you do for a living, Brett? Claire mentioned marketing."

He brightened and began speaking very fast. "Strategic management consulting for online companies. Mostly vertical integration marketing. You familiar with that?"

"Nope."

"The product, the industry: doesn't matter. I can leverage it all. There's unlimited growth potential. I teach companies how to find their own customers online, keep them invested, and sell to them throughout the year. Inbound, automation, outbound distribution. Cutting out the middleman. Sound good? You want to see it in action?"

He reached for a laptop on the coffee table, and Preach held out a hand. "Some other time. It looks like you're doing all right for yourself."

A cunning light entered Brett's eyes, revealing, Preach thought, a bit more of his true self.

Brett talked fast and hard and might like to play the fool, but he was not stupid.

"It's almost too easy," Brett said. "The vast majority of business owners, they're in love with their product, so they can't see the big picture. You know how they say you should never represent yourself in court? My motto is no one should be in charge of their own sales and marketing." He draped an arm across the sofa and took a satisfied swig of beer.

If I had to have dinner with this guy, Preach thought, *I might have to poison my own drink*. "I guess we have a similar job."

Brett's eyes narrowed. "How's that?"

"We both clean up after other people's mistakes."

Brett looked unsure whether he should laugh or not. "I prefer to think of it as strategic management consulting."

"So do I. For the police chief of Creekville. I need to know where David went the night of the murder, Brett. Do you have any insight on that?"

"Claire said they had an argument—" he paused for a beat, as if wondering if he should have disclosed that detail—"and David drove off. She said that's the last time she saw him. I have no idea where he went."

Preach thought Brett's hesitation was a little too obvious. Was he making sure the detective knew about the argument with Claire? "When was the last time you saw him?"

"They came over for dinner the night before. Rib eyes on the grill. Pittsburgh rare, melted blue cheese, the works."

"Do you know what they argued about that night?"

Brett's eyes slipped away. "Dunno. Grades, girls. Maybe me, I guess."

"You?"

"Hey man, it's no secret the kid and I didn't get along. What can I say? I wasn't daddy."

"You mentioned his grades," Preach said, keeping him off balance. "They weren't good?"

"Oh, they were great. Claire was always pushing harder."

"And David resented that?"

"Wouldn't you?"

Preach let that go. "Did David have a girlfriend?"

"Claire didn't talk about that?"

"I'd like to hear it from you."

Brett spread a hand. "Okay, okay. Not a regular one, but the kid did alright, you know? Football star, got his mother's looks. He was chasing after this one girl who wouldn't give him the time of day, but isn't that how it always is with chicks?"

"Which girl was that?"

"Mackenzie Rathbun. She was older, a college girl."

Preach took out his pen and pad and made a note. "How did he know her?"

"Over the summer, David bussed tables for a few bucks at The Courtyard. It's a high-end restaurant near—"

"I know it. Did they ever go out?"

"According to David, she barely knew he existed."

Could be an angle, Preach thought. Maybe David got himself in trouble trying to impress her. "Tell me more about the tension between you two. He worried you were trying to replace his father?"

Brett took a drink of beer, sniffed, and crossed his legs. "I'd marry Claire today if I could. I mean, have you seen her? Hey, she said you knew each other in high school."

"Small world."

"Yeah. Anyway, she wanted to wait until David graduated."

"That's almost a year away."

"Tell me about it. I tried to move them in here, but she wasn't having it. Because *he* wasn't having it."

"Why not?"

Brett gave him a sharp look. "I already told you. I'm not his father."

"That was the extent of it?" Preach said calmly. "He resented another man in the house?"

"To be honest, I think the kid just didn't like me."

I can't imagine why not. "Did your arguments ever get violent?"

"What? No. Hey man, are we just talking here, or are you accusing me of something? Because I can call my lawyer."

"Do you need a lawyer, Brett?"

"No," he muttered, and took a swig of beer.

"Then we're just talking."

"Okay, then. It was nothing serious. We just didn't get along."

"Did you worry that would impact your future with Claire?"

"I mean . . . not long term. Once the kid was gone, we'd have been fine. Claire and I are pretty tight, man. We get along great. Never argued, except about the kid."

"What did you think of David? Apart from the tension between you two?"

"He was a little moody, but a good kid. Stayed out of trouble. A little cocky too, but who isn't at that age?"

"Did you two ever hang out without Claire? Go to dinner, catch a flick?"

Brett shook his head. "I asked. He wasn't interested."

"Do you have any idea whether he was in some kind of trouble?"

"Nothing that would lead to . . . not that kind of trouble. God, no." Brett slapped a knee and stared at the floor for a long time, as if the emotions had just hit him. "I can't believe we're having this conversation."

"What do you mean, *not that kind* of trouble?"

"Huh?" He took another long swallow of beer. "Hey man, whatever we say here, it's between us, right?"

"I can't promise that."

"Oh."

"There's no such thing as client confidentiality with the police, if that's what you mean. Why don't you tell me what's on your mind?"

Brett considered the question, then said, "About a week ago, David came home from football practice with a black eye. He told his mom he got it in practice."

"Hard to get a black eye beneath a helmet."

"That's what I thought, and I told him so. He insisted it happened when the pads were off. I said, who lets their star quarterback get hit in the eye during the season, without pads?"

"What did he say?"

"He admitted he got in a fight with one of the players after practice. He wouldn't go into detail and made me swear not to tell his mom. So if you tell her, I'd appreciate it if it didn't come from me."

"Why didn't you tell me earlier?"

He shrugged. "It's just kid stuff, right? Claire flips about little things."

"It may be kid stuff, but a kid's dead." He made a note about the fight. "Do you know the other kid's name?"

"No."

"Maybe I'll take that glass of water."

"Oh—sure."

Once Brett returned, Preach took a swallow and said, "You don't have any guns, do you?"

His eyes became guarded again. "A few, yeah. I collect them."

"Is that right? Do you mind if I take a look at the collection?"

Brett hesitated. "Sure. I suppose cops and guns go together, don't they?"

"We respect them."

He sniffed. "They're in the basement," he said, then led Preach down a staircase to a furnished lower level as big as the first floor. The wood-paneled main room housed a pool table with a novelty glass playing surface. On the way through, Preach glimpsed a guest bedroom, a wine cellar, and a room with stadium seating and a projector screen.

"What's in there?" he asked, as they passed a doorway cracked just enough for Preach to notice the finished concrete walls.

Brett pushed the door open. The room was empty except for a bed bolted to the wall, a monitor beside the door, and a kitchenette recessed into a side wall. "My safe room."

"Your *safe room*?"

Brett grinned like a schoolboy. "Two-foot concrete walls, blast-proof door, control panel, separate internet. Pretty cool, huh?"

"Why do you need a safe room?"

"Hey, man, crime is rampant in this country. I shouldn't need to tell you that."

"In suburban Chapel Hill?"

"I've got money. You can't be too careful."

Preach was unable to stop picturing someone held against their will inside the concrete bunker. He let his gaze linger on the room and said, "Let's see the guns."

Just past the wine cellar, Brett entered a room with mahogany cabinets filled with a dizzying array of firearms. Stuffed deer and boar heads filled the space on the wall between the cabinets. Preach guessed the room held a few hundred guns, and he supposed the two plush armchairs in the middle allowed guests to observe the magnificence of the collection.

"This is *a few*?" Preach said.

"I know people with a helluva lot more."

"Fantastic. You've got a permit for all these?"

"Every single one." Brett gave a conspiratorial roll of his eyes. "Not that it's hard. Hey, man, I love my guns, but we've got to tighten up those regulations. No one wants deadly weapons in the hands of the wrong people."

Preach didn't bother answering. By this time he knew Brett mostly talked to himself.

After Preach took a walk around the room, they returned upstairs, and he picked up his overcoat. On the way out, he said, "Do you mind if I take a look at your phone?"

Brett stilled. "Why?"

"We haven't found David's yet, and I'd like to read any texts he sent you. See if I can get some context on what was going on in his life."

"We almost never texted."

"Then it shouldn't take too long."

A vein in Brett's neck started to pulse. "You know, I do mind. I'd tell you if there was anything on there."

"I'm a detective. It's my job to see things other people don't."

"I just don't think you need to see my phone."

Preach shrugged into his coat, eying Brett the entire time. "Maybe you do need that lawyer."

Brett mumbled something and looked off to the side.

"Sorry?" Preach said.

"I said, maybe I do."

"Why don't you stick around town for a while?" Preach said, knowing he could get the texts from the phone records even if Brett deleted them. "We might need to talk again."

The host's face darkened. "And if I don't?"

"You should probably ask your lawyer the answer to that question."

7

Not one for bubbly displays of emotion, Ari corralled her excitement as she stepped up to the counter at Choco-latte, a coffee shop in the heart of downtown Durham. It wasn't just the smell of fresh grounds and steaming milk foam that had brightened her Monday morning. An hour from now, after less than three months on the job, she would be interviewing her first witness in a murder case.

We like you, her supervising attorney, Fenton Underwood, had told her. *We think you're smart and we think you're ready*.

Ari thought she was ready too. Then again, she was smart enough to know she didn't know very much. Murder cases were the big leagues. High profile. Fenton was the lead attorney on the case, but if it went to trial, Ari might get to handle a minor witness in court. This was one of the many reasons she had chosen the path she did. In a large law firm, she might not see the inside of a courtroom for years. In the overburdened DA's office, trial by fire was a necessity.

Would the case go to trial? Not many did. Most defendants were guilty, and they pled out rather than risk a maximum sentence.

The defendant in the case at hand, Ronald Jackson, was a known drug dealer. One of the more vicious in town. Local police, when responding to a 911 call, had found him in a stash house with two dead bodies, warm blood still pumping from the gunshot wounds. The vitims were a fourteen-year-old girl and an eighteen-year-old male.

The police believed the young couple had tried to rob the stash house, and Ronald had gotten wind of it and taken care of the matter himself. The couple had known the location of the stash house because the fourteen-year-old was Ronald's niece.

Classy.

The case had a wrinkle. Bentley Montgomery, the person who had made the 911 call and the witness Ari was about to interview, also dealt drugs—at least by reputation. He had a clean sheet, and they didn't know much about him, except the cops said he was an up-and-comer out of East Durham, the city's most dangerous neighborhood.

While the facts of the case could lead to an interesting interview, they made for a terrible trial witness. Ari knew they couldn't put Bentley in front of a jury. She also knew this was the reason she was being given the nod.

After browsing the pastries, she ordered a latte from the pierced and tattooed counter clerk. A refurbished mechanic's shop that threw open its tall garage doors in nice weather, Choco-latte was the hub of the city's counterculture. Ari loved to walk down from her apartment and absorb the stained-brick, alt-music, sustainable-living, starving-artist, mismatched-sofa,coffee-straight-from-the-dirt-encrusted-hands-of-Peruvian-farmers vibe.

Despite the recent prosperity, Durham was still a grungy town. "Keep Durham Dirty" was the town motto. Like Creekville, most of its residents wanted nothing to do with suburban America and the status quo. Durham, however, was an older and much larger city, complicated, reflective of the New South.

Once a prosperous tobacco and textile town, Durham had also been an early hub of African American business. Black Wall Street, it had been dubbed before the fortunes of the tobacco companies had waned, the manufacturing slump hit, and the city built a freeway through the historic black neighborhoods, gutting them. The warehouses downtown emptied. Businesses fled. Grandiose Southern homes had devolved into crack houses, and weeds strangled the neglected streets. For the last few decades, Durham was the town in the Piedmont that no one visited after dark.

The Renaissance began when the Research Triangle took off, fueled by cheap land and smart tech investments. In a startling turnaround that Ari herself had witnessed over the last few years, downtown Durham had transformed almost magically into a hipster haven full of repurposed brick warehouses, Duke graduates who decided to stay instead of fleeing to Manhattan, new residents who poured in daily, and a legion of small businesses so local and specialized it made her laugh. What does a city that small do with eight bakeries? A Basque-themed cider bar? So many wood-fired, locally sourced pizzerias she had lost count?

She hoped the trend continued, but she also wondered if the optimism of the long-suffering residents had not outstripped the limits of the economy.

Not only that, but a legacy of violence and poverty still loomed beneath the surface. As a district attorney, she knew all too well about the gangs and housing projects and quiet desperation that existed in more neighborhoods in Durham than anyone wanted to admit.

Still, the city was making leaps and bounds, struggling to succeed. Before she left the café, Ari's thoughts turned elsewhere: to the whirlwind of graduation, taking the bar, and starting a new job. She gave the other patrons in the café a lingering look. Not long ago, she had been one of them. Hovered over a laptop, slumming in ripped jeans and an oversize sweater, earbuds in place. Now, dressed in a sleek gray suit and high-heeled black boots, her hair pinned above her head, clutching a case file and hurrying to work, she was firmly entrenched on the other side.

One of *them*.

As a professional, she thought she was ready to meet with this witness. It was the transition to responsible adulthood she wasn't so sure about.

"Ready?" Fenton Underwood asked, with a grandiose wave toward the conference room door.

The corners of Ari's lips upturned. "As I'll ever be."

Fenton was as old school Southern as they came. Colored pocket squares that matched his ties, seersucker suits, gray fedora with a black ribbon, courteous and polite at all times. Nearing retirement age, he was something of a local legend, one of the best attorneys in the city yet never desirous of a political run. Ari liked him but knew very little about him. No one did. He protected his private life like the child he'd never had.

"Good luck in there," he said, shuffling toward his office. Unlike lawyers in large firms, district attorneys were too busy and pressed for resources to double up in depositions and client meetings.

"Thanks."

"Let's chat when it's over. Ari?" he called back.

"Mm?"

"Remember you're in charge. Every witness, favorable or not, has their own agenda. You stick to yours."

"Thanks, Fenton."

His craggy face, always ready with a grin, turned serious. "Some prosecutors lose sight of the goal. Somewhere along the way, or maybe before they started, they decide that making their numbers is more important than putting the right people away. Don't be one of them."

There were other attorneys within earshot, and he hadn't bothered to lower his voice. With a tip of his fedora, he turned and disappeared down the hallway.

Cup of coffee in hand, Ari opened the door and saw a black male in his late thirties waiting on the other side of the conference table. A tall and bulky man, his arms were crossed over a conservative brown suit, and his hair was cut an inch from the scalp. He watched her enter with shrewd, close-set eyes that shone with an unnerving vibrancy that made them seem much larger in size. It felt as if he was absorbing everything about her and stashing it away for later use.

Not wanting to seem weak from the start, Ari stared right back at him. "Mr. Montgomery," she said evenly, "thank you for coming. I'm Ari Hale."

He offered his hand. "Just doing my civic duty," he said, with a crooked smile that highlighted the asymmetry of his features. Bentley was not a handsome man.

Ari accepted the gesture, though she found handshakes a pointless, sanitized, outdated ritual that emphasized physical strength. Bentley's grip was powerful, and she quickly disengaged.

Transitioning from law school study groups to dealing with hardened criminals was not an easy thing to get used to. She thought she was beginning to understand what Preach must go through on a daily basis, and she had quickly learned to keep a shield over her emotions while at work. That level of exposure to the depravity of mankind had to take a toll.

She offered Bentley water and coffee, which he declined. After sitting, she took a moment to compose herself. Northern lawyers, Fenton had told her, tried to steamroll their opponents with their intelligence. Southern lawyers preferred to be underestimated, right until they won in court. Neither Northern nor Southern, nor from anywhere in particular, Ari was still feeling out her own style.

She had her suspicions as to Bentley's motivation, but decided to treat him the same as any other witness. Focus on the truth. "Let's start with some background information."

He spread his hands. "All right. Awful young to fly solo, aren't you?"

Taken aback, she said, "I'm assisting Mr. Underwood. This is a meeting to gather information, not a formal deposition, so you're not under oath. But please stick to the facts."

"Or you'll subpoena the hell out of me?"

"Or we'll get nowhere. If this goes to trial, you'll be under oath there."

"So you want the truth, huh?"

"Of course."

"Not what you want me to say, counselor?"

Ari leveled her gaze at him. "That's right."

He chuckled, his eyes boring into her. "Not many people want the truth, Ms. Hale. Not in this country."

She glanced down at her outline for the interview. "Let's start with some background information. Where were you born?"

"In the back seat of a Chevy Nova."

Ari blinked.

"Momma was homeless at the time, and the battery died on the way to the hospital." He flashed another uneven smile. "Some people like to talk about getting a jump-start on life. I had a real one."

Ari could tell from the frankness of his tone that he wasn't joking—nor would he tolerate any pity. "You're from Durham?"

"If your records search hasn't turned up anything, that's because my real name isn't Bentley Montgomery. It's Javontis Washington."

She made a note. "When did you change it?"

"As soon as I realized I wanted to make as much money as possible. It's a white world, counselor, and I knew I had to work extra hard to fit in." He plucked his bottom lip, then reached up and held a stiff piece of hair between his fingers. "It doesn't get much blacker than this, and I'm not pretty like Denzel. Add a ghetto first name and a slave-owning surname, and my story was told before it began."

She sensed he had an agenda for giving out this information. In fact, judging by the controlled manner of his speech and the deliberate nature of every facial expression or hand movement, she sensed he had an agenda for everything he did. His eyes flicked to her hands, which she had just folded on the table, and he continued, "There's no need to squirm. I'm the furthest thing from an activist. I'm a realist. A *business*man. Someone trying to do the best I can in the world as it stands. But to answer your question, I changed my name when I was twelve. I took it off the shelter wall, from two different donors, once I decided to make a go at it."

"A go at what?"

"Life. Bentley's a pretty white name, don't you think? As white as fresh cream on a frat boy."

"You changed it legally?"

"Once I found out how."

"What's your level of education?"

"You mean my IQ?"

"I mean your schooling," she said.

"Ah." He gave an amused smile, as if he'd uncovered a secret part of her personality. "I almost finished the fifth grade."

"Are you married?"

"Nope."

"Any children?"

"Not that I know of."

"What's your profession?"

"Like I said. I'm a businessman."

Ari tapped her pen against the table. She knew better than to probe his alleged drug dealing, but she also had to ask some basic questions. While she was forming her next question, he said, "What have you heard about me, Ms. Hale? Maybe I can clear up some misconceptions."

"I'd prefer if you just tell me anything you find relevant."

He tipped back in his chair. "I'm an entrepreneur. I sold my software company a while back, and now I'm an angel investor, mostly for local start-ups. I also develop apps, and I've got a patent portfolio."

At first, she thought he was joking. But his expression never changed until he chuckled at her confusion.

"Not what you thought you'd hear?" he asked.

"I didn't say that. What's the name of your company?"

"I have a few. The parent is New Hawk Holdings. The software company focused on business analytics for real estate companies. Mostly geared toward property developers, foreclosure sharks, and the like."

"Where did you learn those skills?"

"I'm a self-taught man. Self-made and self-paid."

She took a sip of coffee. "That's very impressive."

"Never mistake education for intelligence, and especially not for drive. I think too much education hampers a man, personally. Gives him something to fall back on. Especially with the knowledge at our fingertips in today's world. You know what you can learn from books, from the Internet?" His gaze pulled her in like a car crash in slow motion. "*Everything*."

She made another note, mostly to break away from his stare. His story could be double-checked later. After asking a few more background questions, she pressed forward. "Let's talk about the 911 call."

"That's why we're here," he said.

"Can you take me through the day of September 21?"

"The whole day? Grits and bacon on up?"

"Just describe for me where you were that night and what you were doing."

"Taking my evening walk."

Ari looked down at the address he had provided, on Angier Street.

"My house is about a mile away," he continued.

"A mile from the location you called in? 1620 Prosperity?"

"That's right."

"Were you alone?"

"I was."

She doubted anyone would walk a mile on the streets of East Durham alone at night, especially if he was a drug dealer. Maybe he hadn't witnessed anything at all and had made the call from his house. According to the police report, he had used his cell phone.

"East Durham isn't Iraq," he said, as if reading her thoughts. "Despite what y'all might think."

"Do you take a walk every night?"

"Almost." He patted his ample belly. "Doc says it's a must. Especially since I believe gluten free is the greatest heresy since socialism."

"Did anyone see you out? Opposing counsel will want verification."

He gave a thin smile that sent a chill inching through her. "A few people can be rounded up, I'm sure."

"Okay." She studied her notes again. "Why don't you take me through the rest of the night?"

"There's not much to it. Prosperity Street is near the middle of my walk. Right when I passed the house—"

"1620?"

"That's right. I heard the gunshots right there."

"The police report said a silencer was used."

He cocked his head. "You're new to this, aren't you? Suppressor is the correct term, and they ain't silent. Still easy to hear from nearby. I was close enough there was no debate. Right across the street, in fact."

"What happened next?"

"I took out my phone and called 911. What any concerned citizen would do, I hope."

"In the middle of the street? After hearing gunfire?"

"You're right," he said, with a tip of his head and a flicker of approval in his eyes. "I was armed—like I said, East Durham isn't a war zone, but it isn't Chapel Hill, either—but I hustled off behind a tree as I made the call. Once the cops came, I walked home and saw what happened on the news."

"Did you see anyone leave or enter the house before the cops arrived?"

"Not a soul. I saw his car in the driveway too."

This was the crux of his testimony, she knew. If Bentley was telling the truth, then that was strong evidence that Ronald had murdered two people inside the stash house. Or at least watched it happen.

"You know his car?"

"It says *Ronald* on the plate. With dollar signs on either side."

"Oh." Ari pursed her lips and considered his story. "Why do you think he didn't run away after he shot them?"

He shrugged. "Cleaning up the mess, I guess. Why expose yourself? No one in that hood's coming inside."

"Except the cops, when they're called."

He smirked. "That's right."

"Do you know Ronald Jackson?"

"I know *of* him. Everybody does." He leaned forward. "Do *you* know him, Ms. Hale?"

"What do you mean?"

"What kind of a man he is? Or maybe a better question: Do you know who that girl he killed was?"

"According to the police report, it was his niece."

He chuckled. "His niece. Yeah, he called her that 'round the way. That girl was eleven when her momma loaned her out to Ronald to pay for her junk habit."

Ari's fingers tightened around her coffee cup.

"Why do you think she was dumb enough to hit the stash house?

She wasn't dumb; she was desperate. She knew the consequences but didn't care anymore."

"How did she know about the stash house?" Ari said quietly. "Or do drug dealers make a habit of telling their prostitutes where their money is?"

His chuckle turned low and dangerous. "Well I wouldn't know much about that, Ms. Hale. I suppose you'll have to get Gallup to take a poll."

After Bentley left, Fenton signaled for Ari on his way out of the door. "Walk with me."

"Where are we going?"

"Just around the block. My mid-morning constitutional."

The older attorney grabbed his walking cane, along with an expensive wool peacoat with extensions on either side that looked like wings. Ari thought the custom-made, billowy coat made him look like a wraith, a revenant of justice, drifting down the streets of Durham.

Once outside, they turned right on Mangum, a busy street sandwiched between the county jail and a gleaming performing arts center. A microcosm of Durham.

"We can't use him," she said, still unnerved by the interview. "I don't trust anything he said, and I think he might have set the whole thing up."

"What do you mean?"

"The raid on the stash house, the murder, the call."

"That bad?"

She gave a little shudder. "He's highly intelligent. And I think he might be evil."

"You think he's trying to take out a rival?"

"Probably."

Fenton walked in silence for a moment. "So far, Ronald's defense is that he was nearby and heard shots, then drove over to the house. He had two bodyguards with him, and they're spinning the same story. There's nothing tying Ronald to the stash house, no eyewitnesses, and no murder weapon so far. We won't be able to hold him for long."

"So what do we do?

He glanced over at her. "Unless we think of a novel legal theory or the police do a better job with the evidence, we watch him walk. Maybe your tech mogul isn't as smart as he thinks he is."

Ari couldn't stop thinking about an eleven-year-old girl pimped out by her own mother to a monster. "Ronald can't walk. That's an abomination."

"We win some, we lose some," Fenton said calmly. "Hopefully the ratio is favorable. The real question you'll ask yourself in this career is how many abominations you can handle."

"Maybe I don't want to handle any of them."

A soft smile creased the wrinkles around his mouth. "I was young once too."

"Why don't we get both of them?" she said. "Ronald for murder, and Bentley for lying to the police?"

When they stopped at an intersection, he turned to face her. "Dig a little bit. Just remember you're an attorney and not the police." He tilted his head down, peering at her beneath his bushy eyebrows. "And never make a case personal."

An eleven-year-old girl, sold like chattel to a drug dealer and then murdered by his own hand.

Ari shuddered again.

It was already personal.

8

After spending the morning handing off most of his caseload to junior officers, Preach walked a few blocks to a Korean food truck for lunch. Over the years he had found that he never really got to know a town until he walked the streets. There was something primal about having to go from one place to another on foot, watching life unfold at a slower pace, truly observing instead of relying on fleeting glimpses from a car.

It was also a window into another world. In modern America, those with means bought the most expensive vehicles they could afford and zoomed down wide, paved streets, pulling into office parks with landscaped grounds and gurgling fountains.

The other half went unnoticed. Not those stretching their legs like Preach, out for a stroll, but people who had no choice but to use the streets. The brown-skinned woman hugging her infant to her chest as she waited for the bus, the homeless man with the vacant smile pushing a shopping cart, the white teen in Goodwill clothes and a Hornets cap walking hunched under a canvas backpack, alone during school hours, forced to write his own story.

Preach observed it all.

The food truck was parked across the street from a converted brick cotton mill that housed the local co-op as well as a slew of restaurants and specialty shops. The spacious grounds in front of the co-op served as the beating heart of downtown, where people from all walks of life ordered takeout from the organic grocery, relaxing on picnic tables on the wood-chip covered lawn as they enjoyed the dappled sunlight streaming through the bower of oak trees.

A portion of spicy beef bulkogi set Preach's mouth on fire. Soy and garlic and sesame oil dripped from his fingers and lingered in his nose. After washing it down with a ginger beer, he walked a bit further to the high school on the south side of town. The journey made him ache with memories, drawing closer to the lost horizon of his youth.

A few students on lunch break watched him climb the steps of the mammoth brick building and push through the double doors of the main entrance. The linoleum hallway and the scuffed glass cabinets filled with trophies, some of which he helped win, sent him careening back in time.

Leaning against a locker on his forearm, cocky grin in place.

Girl after girl brushing against his letterman jacket, their hair perfumed with beauty and vitality.

Everything easy, everything right, everything his.

Until his cousin Ricky had died, and then it wasn't. Young Joe Everson's worldview, his entire gilded childhood, had been exposed for the sham it was. Life was no longer his personal playground, this endlessly optimistic, carefree voyage that was supposed to end in some distant but equally perfect future.

Life was suffering and senseless death and a mockery of his juvenile confidence.

It had taken Preach a long time to learn that life, real life, was all of those things and infinitely more. The hardest lesson of all, the lesson of adulthood, was that he might never come to grips with what it all meant.

"Sir, can I help you?"

A red-haired older woman had opened the door to the administrative office, eying his musty overcoat with unease.

"Sorry, ma'am." He flashed his badge. "I'm Detective Everson with the Creekville Police. I was wondering if Principal Marcy might be able to spare a few moments?"

Her eyes lowered. "This is about David?"

"Yes, ma'am."

"Come with me."

The staff in the white-walled front office was somber, hushed. The red-haired woman knocked on the principal's door and slipped inside. She returned in a moment and waved Preach in.

"Thank you," he said, then walked into the office and found himself standing in front of a Creekville High principal for the first time in nearly twenty years.

Principal Marcy was a stern, birdlike woman with clipped gray hair and hazel eyes that burned with authority. "Good afternoon, Detective. I understand you're an alum."

After the publicity associated with the literary murders, Preach had grown accustomed to the recognition. He tipped his head. "I survived my four years, yes."

"We made a formal announcement this morning. I'm sure the students saw the news on television, but we wanted to soften the blow."

"Not much to soften about murder."

"An unspeakable tragedy," she agreed, then paused for a moment, somber. "But we must do our best to appreciate David for the time in which we had him."

With a glance, Preach took in the office: a mélange of warm paneling, framed certificates on the walls, and forest-green carpet. He put a hand on the back of a chair. "Do you mind?"

"Of course. How can I be of help?"

He took off his coat and sat. "I'd like to speak with David's teachers and coaches."

"Which ones?"

"All of them."

She folded her hands on the desk. "I believe they're in today. If you want to talk to his friends, that would be better with the parents present."

"I agree."

"I'll set you up in a conference room, if that's okay."

"Sure. Thank you." As she ran her finger down a calendar, he asked, "How well did you know David?"

"As well as I knew most of the students, except for the disciplinary cases. Which David wasn't. If I recall correctly, I've only seen him in relation to one incident."

"What was that?"

Her lips compressed. "About a month ago, he wrote the word *slut* in capital letters on the Facebook page of Lisa Waverly, his AP English teacher."

Preach's eyebrows rose.

"We talked to them both at length," she said, "and found no evidence of an inappropriate relationship."

"What did you find?"

"Ms. Waverly claimed she had no idea what it was about. David took the post down and apologized to her in person, in this office. He swore it had nothing to do with the two of them but wouldn't discuss it further, even under threat of suspension. In the end, we talked to his mother and decided not to take that step. He served detention for a week."

Detention? If he hadn't been the star quarterback, he might have been suspended or expelled. "Was there further trouble between the two?"

"None. He stayed in her class, and she reported that he was well behaved."

After a moment, he said, "What do you think that was about?"

"Ms. Waverly is . . . an attractive young woman. I'm not privy to her personal life, but it wouldn't surprise me if she had plenty of suitors. I believe David might have been expressing," she lifted a palm, "teen frustration? Trying to impress his peers?"

Simple teen frustration, Preach thought, doesn't cause a kid to publicly shame a teacher. Maybe another student, but not a teacher. The whole incident lowered his opinion of the principal. "You're sure that was the only violation?"

"I'll check, but I believe so. David was an excellent student. Popular and conscientiousness. I just can't believe . . . do you have any suspects? A possible motive?"

"I'd prefer not to discuss the investigation."

"Of course."

"Unless there's something on your mind?"

She drew back in her seat. "No, no. To be honest, I'm just overwhelmed by all this."

"It's a hard thing to wrap your mind around."

After a hard swallow she said, “How would you like to proceed?”

“Why don’t you call in Lisa Waverly? I’d like to talk to her first.”

Five minutes later, a young woman in high heels and a baby blue blouse, her auburn hair piled high into a bun, swayed into the conference room in which Preach was waiting. Lithe and of medium height, her gray pants hugged her hips when she walked, and a pair of designer glasses with red temples rested primly atop a thin nose. Her blouse sat low enough to straddle the line between suggestive and professional.

Consider that line crossed, Preach thought, as she leaned in to shake his hand, exposing a glimpse of a lacy black bra.

“Thank you for coming,” he said.

“Of course,” she murmured.

After the pleasantries, she looked him up and down as if he were a window full of designer shoes on sale and then settled into the chair across from him. A tear formed as she pressed a hand to her temple. “God. Poor David.”

Her voice was throaty, almost raspy. The detective noted a pair of tiny wings tattooed on her left ankle, as well as a silver bracelet with two pendants: a butterfly and a rainbow-colored peace symbol.

A free spirit, then.

Though attractive at first glance, Lisa was not beautiful. Her jawline was slightly askew, her eyes set too close together. He found the confident sexuality she exuded, while not affected, to be a small portion of the truth. Despite her flirtatious entrance, he found her sadness genuine, and she struck him in those first few moments as someone who felt very deeply, very quickly.

Most people, he guessed, probably mistook her chimeric emotions for insincerity.

“Thank you for coming,” he said. “I’m talking to his teachers to get a better picture of who he was.”

She gave a small, miserable nod. "He was a wonderful person. Smart, thoughtful, aware."

"Aware?"

She waved a hand, causing the pendants to tinkle. "He felt the things he read, noticed who was around him. Not just what they looked like or their outward emotions, but what they were thinking and feeling on the inside. I can see you looking at me, asking how does she know all of this? I'm sure Principal Marcy told you about the Facebook post."

"She did."

He waited for her to elaborate or become flustered, but the air of detached melancholy never wavered.

"I'm an English teacher," she said. "I observed him in class, read his essays and journal entries. It was quite obvious he was special, though he suffered from the effects of his appearance."

"What do you mean?"

"People, even teachers, often assume that bookish and unpopular kids are deep—and their counterparts shallow. But no one chooses their looks or their level of popularity, do they? Does it really say anything about a person?"

"I suppose not."

"David was popular and very good-looking, but for whatever reason, he chose to conceal himself from the other students. At least from what I could observe." A hint of challenge entered her eyes. "I know what people thought about the Facebook post. I'm sure I was deemed guilty of some fantasized inappropriate behavior, and it's a disgusting assumption. It was very hurtful."

"Tell me more about him. From what you observed."

She gave him a frank look, acknowledging that he had switched the subject. "He didn't have to try too hard at anything. Girls, sports, class. That's one reason I appreciated his effort. He wrote thoughtful, philosophical essays. He loved Faulkner, Toni Morrison, and plays of all sorts, especially Wilder. Anything to do with the dissection of a small town." A bitter smile tugged at the corners of her lips. "I could tell David was aware of the absurdities of his surroundings."

"Such as?"

She crossed her legs and flashed a magnetic smile that made him reassess her attractiveness. "Don't tell me you don't see it. You're a detective, after all. This town is so buried under its own pretension it can barely breathe. Do you know what true progressiveness is? It's not judging others for not being progressive—or for not being like you at all."

He wondered what she had been judged for. "Do you think David had a crush on you?"

She was quiet for a moment. "Yes."

"Are you involved with anyone?"

"A number of people," she said evenly. "I don't try to hide it."

"Do you think that's why he wrote what he did on your Facebook page? Out of jealousy?"

She crossed her legs. "I think it's because he saw his mother in me."

"What do you mean?"

"I'm not sure if I should be telling you this—"

"There's nothing you shouldn't be telling me about David right now."

She bobbed her head. "He wrote a piece about his mother. A very private journal entry. He wrote about how they were very different people and how he blamed her for the divorce. He even claimed she . . . had an affair. I'm not sure if this is public knowledge, or even if it's true."

"Do you still have the journal entry?"

"I can give you a copy before you leave."

"Please. Did you talk about it with him?"

"The students know I read them, and I give them feedback on their writing, but I never ask them to explain or discuss the substance in class. I find this leads to more honest writing."

He interlaced his fingers atop the table. "What about the Facebook post? Did you talk about that?"

"I tried. He apologized and said it would never happen again, but he never told me why he wrote it. He wasn't the same after, either. He was sullen in class and wouldn't open up in his work."

"Do you think there might have been other factors involved? Something else going on in his life?"

She gave him a level stare. "I would say that's rather obvious now."

He slowly nodded. "Any idea what those were?"

"None at all."

"Maybe you should give me all of his journal entries."

"I'd be happy to."

He sat quietly for another minute, waiting to see if she would volunteer more information. When she didn't, he said, "Did you ever see David outside of school?"

Her eyes flashed. "Never."

"Did the two of you have any contact on social media that was unrelated to class?"

"No."

"Where were you on the night of October 2?"

"You mean the night David was murdered?" She stared back at him. "It was a school night. I was home alone, planning lessons and watching television."

"Which show?"

She thought for a moment. "I was streaming *The Deuce*, I think. The new show by the guys from *The Wire*."

He made a note and stood. "Thank you for your candor, Ms. Waverly. That's all for now."

She smoothed her pants and rose. "I understand you had to ask the questions. It's just painful to hear them. I'll get those journal entries for you."

After she left the room, Preach got a cup of coffee and considered the conversation. The information about Claire was troubling, especially combined with the argument on the night David disappeared. Had something set him off in recent weeks? Was the English teacher telling the truth about their relationship?

He needed to know more about David's life. Earlier, he had taken a look at his Facebook page and found nothing of interest to the case, but he decided to pore over it again.

He needed those phone records. He needed to talk to his friends.

Except for the last interview of the day, the rest of the teachers proved unhelpful. Everyone reiterated the common theme: great kid, easy to teach, smart, didn't open up in class. Eyebrows rose when he mentioned Lisa Waverly and the Facebook post, though no one could point to any inappropriate contact between the two. As the day went on, he compiled a list of David's best friends and planned to compare it to Claire's list.

The last interview was with Bill Simpson, the Driver's Ed teacher and head football coach. Though he had never met the man before, as soon as Coach Simpson swept imperiously into the room, Preach felt as if he already knew him: the polyester slacks and crinkled green windbreaker; the thick fingers and heavy brow and thinning hair; the slabs of muscle hidden beneath a layer of middle-aged fat; the cocksure swagger of someone who believes he has the most important job in town.

"Joe Everson, huh?" Coach Simpson said, after a pissing contest disguised as a handshake. Preach found a perverse, juvenile pleasure in having a firmer grip than the coach. "You wrestled back in the day, didn't you? When Ray Logan was coaching?"

"I did."

"Helluva coach."

"The best."

"Took state your junior year, didn't you?"

"Second place."

"What happened the next year? You get injured?"

"Something like that."

Coach Simpson grunted, and his expression soured. "It's terrible what happened, just terrible. Y'all got any idea who did this?"

"We're working on it. What can you tell me about David?"

"What do you mean?"

"What kind of kid was he?"

"On the field, tough as nails. He wasn't the best athlete I've ever had, to be honest. Good enough to start, maybe all-district this year, but he wasn't going D-1 or anything." He shook his head. "But that boy could take a hit. You can't teach that. He didn't back down from anyone. Had a decent arm, too, but his leadership got him the job. The other kids followed him without question."

"Why do you think that was?"

He spread his hands. "Who's to say why some men are born to lead and others are born to follow?"

"Some were born not to do either," Preach said.

Coach Simpson didn't respond. Preach could tell he didn't think much of the comment.

"What about off the field?" Preach continued.

The coach shrugged as if the question was meaningless. "Good grades. Stayed out of trouble."

"Someone told me about the fight at practice."

"What?" the coach said.

"I heard David came home with a black eye after practice one day."

The coach sniffed and swiped his hand across his nose. "There might have been a fight. But it didn't happen at practice. I would have known."

"What can you tell me about it?"

The coach frowned into his chest. "Been a few weeks, at least. Maybe a month. Best I can remember, David came to practice one day with a black eye, and one of my assistants pointed it out. I asked David what happened, and he told me he got it playing basketball in his neighborhood."

"Did you believe him?"

Another shrug. "Why not? It happens."

"Was there anyone on the team he didn't get along with? Any rumors of trouble?"

"As I said, he was well liked. Anyone had a beef with David on or off the field, the whole team would be behind him." He wagged a finger. "I'll tell you, though, there's one bad apple that lurks around school after hours. Nathan Wilkinson. Word among the kids is he runs a pissant little gang. Come to think of it, I did see him having words with David after practice once. He'd never try anything around all the guys, which is why I never gave it a second thought. But yeah, he might have had it out for him."

"Any idea why?"

"Probably a girl, right? That's what kids fight about. Or maybe he was just bitter he didn't play ball. Who isn't jealous of the QB?"

"Nathan is a student?"

"Yeah, but he got suspended a few days ago. Too many skips, I think."

Preach made a note of the kid's name and stood. "I appreciate your help."

"Anytime, champ. See you at a game sometime? We could use the support."

"You never know."

9

"Update me," Chief Higgins said later that day, after Preach walked into her office and collapsed into a chair.

As the chief sipped her herbal tea and murmured little *mm-hmms* of acknowledgment, watching him with that tough-love gaze of hers, peach cobbler with a cast-iron crust, he told her what he had learned over the last two days.

"You don't have enough to subpoena Brett's phone," Chief Higgins said. "You know that."

Preach fiddled with an hourglass paperweight on her desk. If this were Atlanta, they would *find* enough. But this wasn't the big city. Paperwork wasn't as easy to push through the system.

"One tiny link," she said, "and the judge will play ball. But we need something. A person's got a right not to turn over their phone."

"Tell me something I don't know."

"How about what was on David's phone?"

Preach sat up. "The records are here?"

"They will be day after tomorrow. We just got word."

He resumed fiddling with the paperweight, watching the inexorable passage of the sand, wondering what stage of life the constricted portion of the hourglass represented.

"Do you believe her?" the chief asked quietly. "Claire?"

"Why wouldn't I? I've read the journal entry his teacher mentioned, and there's nothing in there beyond what she said. The kid harbored some resentment toward his mom, and yeah, maybe she slept around some back in the day. We haven't heard her side of it, and nothing I've heard makes me think she's lying."

"She's still the last one to see him alive. After an argument."

He shook his head. "Not the last."

The chief held his gaze for a moment, calmly took another sip of tea, and said, "Does he remind you of you?"

He looked up. "Who?"

"The boy. David."

"Oh."

"You seem awful thoughtful on this case."

"Ari calls it brooding."

The chief snorted.

"I didn't play football, you know. Everyone seems to think I did."

"It's a funny thing, to look back at ourselves," the chief said. "Wondering what we could have done different, who we might have been."

"I prefer not to ponder that particular version of myself."

She cupped her ceramic mug in her hands. "Maybe it would help the case if you did."

"Why? From everything I'm hearing, David and I were nothing alike. He seemed like a great kid. Good student, kind, thoughtful. I was . . . none of those things."

"Suit yourself," she said with an enigmatic smile.

He glanced to the side, annoyed. "Listen, what do you know about Nathan Wilkinson?"

"He's been in and out of juvie a few times. His daddy used to work at the county prison, before he ended up on the other side of the bars."

"What for?"

"Taking bribes."

"The football coach said Nate might be involved with a local gang. There's no one on my radar locally, except for Los Viburos. And they don't take white kids. Anything else you know of?"

"Nope, but you should ask the troops."

"What about the kid's mom? Any idea what she does?"

"Waits on food stamps and welfare checks, most likely. She depended on her husband, from what I remember, and they lived in the Carroll Street trailer park even then. Dunno if the kid and his mom still do."

"I'll check it out later. That's the park by the water tower?"

"Yep."

He whistled. "Tough place to grow up."

"Yep."

Later that day, Preach stepped out of his car under a bottomless blue sky, greeted by the rustle of dry leaves as an army of Latino gardeners raked the yard across the street from Claire's house. He breathed fall in through his nose and tasted it in his mouth, the dying of the land and the coming of the frost, sage and pumpkin and chili, damp and decay and wood smoke.

Brett's car was nowhere in sight. Claire met him at the door wrapped in a gray shawl, hair loose and framing her face. She had applied a touch of eye shadow and lavender lipstick.

"Hi," she said, with a melancholy smile.

"Is it a bad time?"

She moved aside. "Come on in. Are you just checking on me, or do you need something?"

"Mostly the former," he said, taking off his coat. "But I was wondering if I might take a look at David's emails?"

"Of course." Her eyes widened. "Something I should know about?"

"Just covering all the bases."

She led Preach to a spare bedroom with flowery wallpaper. A bay window overlooked a leafy side yard. After booting up the family computer, a MacBook Pro, she pulled up David's Gmail.

"Would you like some tea?" she asked. "Water?"

"I'm fine."

"Just let me know. I'll be on the couch when you're done."

"Okay."

Her fragrance lingered after she left, a floral and vanilla scent that brought back a sharp sensual memory. Had she worn the same perfume since high school, he wondered?

Annoyed by the distraction, he pored through the last few months of David's emails, accepting Claire's offer of coffee as the hours ticked by. He quickly learned that David's generation, or at least David, was not big on email. His Instagram and Snapchat pages had far more activity. Most of the emails pertained to college football recruitment, online shopping, and every so often, an exchange with his father that was notable for how impersonal it was.

After checking the Deleted and Sent folders, satisfied he had seen all there was to see, Preach closed the laptop and sat for a minute, thoughtful. He looked around the room and noticed the built-in bookshelves, brown suede loveseat, desk made of reclaimed wood, and a Persian rug that looked expensive.

Even without the pricey furnishings, how much did a house like this cost in Wild Oaks? Five hundred Gs? Six?

He couldn't help wondering how Claire could afford it.

When he returned to the living room, he found her on the couch in front of the gas fire. Beneath the shawl, she wore a pair of black leggings that accentuated her long legs. She set a glass of wine on the coffee table and patted the sofa. "Sit."

He obliged. "I've just got a few minutes."

"I'll take what I can get." A wan smile made a brief appearance and then vanished. "Sometimes I can't stand the thought of being alone. Other times I just want to curl up by myself and die."

"Maybe I should stay and make sure that doesn't happen," he said, as a joke.

"Maybe you should."

After a moment, he said, "Is Brett coming over tonight?"

"I'm sure he will," she said without emotion.

"Claire, I don't mean to pry, but were you and David okay? Were there any major arguments recently, besides the night he disappeared? I'm just trying to get a handle on his emotional state."

She reached for her wine and seemed to sink deeper into the sofa. "I take it you've never raised a child?"

"No."

"Parenting is the hardest thing in the world. At least, trying to do it right is. We mothers always receive the brunt of our child's emotions—the ups and downs, the joys and fears and frustration—but when you're a single parent, you get it *all.* All those normal roller coaster teenage emotions, all the daily stress. Add to that the pain of a child whose father doesn't love him, and . . . it can be overwhelming."

"You don't think his father loved him?"

She sighed. "When his father left, David spiraled. It grew even worse when he remarried, moved to Richmond, and wanted nothing to do with us. Do you see him here? In response to Brett's text, he asked when the funeral would be."

"And when is it?" he asked gently.

"Wednesday." She dabbed at her eyes. "Will you stop by? I could use the support."

"Sure."

"You were always such a good listener."

"Was I? I don't think of myself as doing much listening in those days."

"Look at us now. Are you involved with anyone?"

"I am. She's great. An attorney in Durham."

"An attorney." Claire studied her wine, then slowly looked up at him. "Did you ever wonder what might have been? If we had actually gone out?"

"You mean if you'd given me the time of day?"

She opened her mouth in mock surprise. "Is that how you saw it?"

"That's how it was."

A long strand of hair had fallen into her face, and she eased it away. "You know what they say about missing what's right in front of your face." She took a long drink of wine, and he started to feel uncomfortable with the turn the conversation had taken. He realized he had been subconsciously leaning closer to her, and he straightened against the back of the couch.

"Claire, I need to ask you something. It's about Lisa Waverly."

She waved a hand in dismissal. "What about her?"

"Were you troubled by what David wrote on her Facebook page?"

"Troubled? Of course I was troubled. Angry with him? Disappointed? Yes. Shocked? Not really."

Her answer surprised him. "Why do you think he wrote that?"

"Have you met her? She's about as subtle as an alley cat in heat. She flirts with her students, for god's sake."

"You don't think there was something—"

"Of course not. I would have known."

"Did he tell you why he did it?"

"He said she gave out grades based on looks and by how much attention the male students paid her. He got fed up with it and decided to do something about it. According to David, she calmed down after his post."

Preach wondered how much of this was a mother's rationale. "I didn't hear anything like that from the principal. She said David never disclosed his reasons."

Claire gave a thin smile. "He didn't have any direct proof, so he made me promise not to say anything. He was afraid he'd get into even more trouble." She seemed to sense he wasn't convinced. "David had a temper, but it was always connected to his hero complex. He was always sticking up for kids who were bullied."

The explanation for the Facebook post didn't ring true to Preach, but he could tell Claire had chosen to believe the story David had fed her. Now that he was dead, he didn't have the heart to press her. Not unless he had to.

But he was damn sure going to double-check Lisa Waverly's alibi.

"One last thing," he said. "I'm sorry if this is insensitive, but when I asked Brett for his cell phone, he refused to give it to me."

She grew very still. "What? Why?"

"I don't know. It's probably nothing. He has a right to privacy. But have you ever had any reason to . . . suspect him of being dishonest?"

It took her a moment to find her voice. "Brett has his faults, but as far as I know, he's been up front with me."

She looked as if she wanted to say more, then didn't.

"Claire? If there's anything I need to know, please tell me."

"It's nothing concerning David. I just . . ." She reached over and laid her palm atop his hand. "You don't need to know about my relationship issues. You have a job to do."

She let her hand linger long enough for a tingle of warmth to spread through him, then withdrew it before it veered into inappropriate territory.

The room, the gas fire flickering a few feet away, the heat from Claire's touch: it all felt far too warm. Thoughts of Ari flooded his mind, and he pushed to his feet, feeling guilty. "I'll be in touch," he said, a little too sharply.

She didn't seem to notice the change in tone. "Please do." Her voice turned cold, and a flash of fury consumed her eyes. "And you can expect Brett to turn over his phone today."

After leaving Claire's house, Preach sat in his car with his hands on the wheel, still unsure about what had transpired between them at the end of the conversation, but not liking it one bit. Her scent lingered in his mind, and he worked furiously to displace it, summoning a memory of Ari and drinking deeply.

It was natural to look at another woman and feel attraction, even arousal. That was biology. He understood that.

It was how one acted in response that mattered.

Feeling the need to hear Ari's voice, he tried her phone but got her voice mail. He decided to send her a text instead. She would see it long before she listened to her messages.

<*Thinking about you*>

After pushing out a long breath, he stepped out of his car to talk to a few of the neighbors. He scanned the houses within view and saw no sign of a security camera. No easy insight into the night David disappeared.

He left his car in front of Claire's house and walked next door to a mid-century modern with tall windows. No one answered his ring. He tried the next one over and got a similar response. Moving to the other side of Claire's house, he knocked on the door of a blue Cape Cod with a tidy front garden. A gaunt black woman in her sixties answered the door, wearing house slippers and a beige cotton wrap.

He introduced himself, flashed his badge, and explained why he was there. The woman, who introduced herself as Sharon Tisdale, retired professor of sociology at UNC, was the same person Bill had interviewed.

"We're all in shock," she said. "He was so nice, so . . ."

Alive, Preach wanted to finish for her. *He was so alive.*

Though a homicide was always difficult to process, he knew it was the abruptness of death, the sudden cessation of a living thing, that caused the dazed look of incomprehension in witnesses and surviving family members. The brute shock of mortality.

How could someone whom you talked to every day, broke bread and shared life with, simply cease to exist?

"I've only lived here a year," she continued, "but he mowed my lawn a few times during the summer and always stopped to chat. God, how do these things happen? It's so unfair." She pressed a hand to her forehead and squeezed her eyes shut.

After a moment he said quietly, "Let's talk about the night David was last seen alive. October 2. I understand you were home."

"Yes. I was. I already talked to another officer."

"That's okay. I'm the detective in charge, and I'm just revisiting a few things. What do you remember about that night?"

Her angular face turned solemn, which lengthened it even more. "I'm retired, my husband passed, and my daughter just moved to Raleigh. I spend a lot of time in my living room, and I have a good view of Claire's house."

She seemed to be apologizing in advance, and he let her continue.

"I remember them arguing outside that night—"

He cut her off. "Wait—did you say outside?"

"In the front garden."

It was probably just a slip, but Claire had told him they argued inside. He said, "Would you characterize it as a typical argument?"

Her head wove back and forth, waffling. "It was loud. Claire must feel so awful about that."

"There was shouting?"

"Yes," she said quietly. "Screaming."

"Could you hear anything that was said?"

She mumbled something, and he asked her to repeat it.

"I hate you," she said. "David told her he hated her."

"And what did she say in response?"

"It got quiet after that."

"Was there any physical violence?"

"I don't think so."

"But you weren't watching and can't be sure."

She gave a miserable nod. "What is this about, Detective?"

"I'm just gathering information."

He could tell she wanted to ask if Claire was a suspect. As her eyes slid away, he said, "Did you hear anything else strange that night?"

She gathered the fabric of her wrap tighter at the throat. "Not that I can think of. David left and came back later that night—"

"Wait—you saw him come back home? What time?"

"I heard him. The Jeep has a distinctive engine." She thought again. "I finished Jimmy Fallon and read for a while, so maybe midnight? Twelve-thirty?"

"Ma'am, I need you to think carefully. This could be very important. Did David come home alone that night?"

"I don't know. As I said, I just heard the Jeep."

"You're sure you didn't hear another voice? Two sets of footsteps?"

"Can one make out footsteps from inside a house?" she asked mildly.

"You're right. Okay. What else do you remember?"

"Nothing. I caught a glimpse of Claire and David in the house just before I turned out the light, and that's it."

He felt a prickle of gooseflesh creep along his arms. Claire had told him that David had driven off in a rage after their argument, and that she had taken an Ambien, fallen asleep, and never seen him alive again.

"Caught a glimpse?" he said. "What do you mean? Were you outside?"

"No, no. It's—I can show you, if you want."

"Please."

She led him down a hallway to the master bedroom at the rear of the ground floor. "Excuse the mess," she said, picking up a few clothes and then pointing at a set of sliding glass doors that opened onto the back garden. The bedroom wall angled slightly to the left, enough to afford a view of one of Claire's windows. A set of gauzy curtains covering the window did little to conceal the interior from view.

"Do you know what room that is?" he asked.

"Claire's study, last time I was inside. At night, if there's a light on, you can see right through the window. Not perfectly, but enough to see an outline. I can't say for sure who was there that night, but David had just come home, so I assumed . . ."

She trailed off, and he felt his hand tightening at his side. "You assumed what? Were you able to get a look at the other person?"

"I tried not to look, to be honest. I wish they would change those curtains." Her eyes slid over to the glass doors, and she sounded as if she didn't want to answer. "But I saw two people for sure, in the center of the room. A larger figure who looked like David, and someone thinner I assumed was Claire."

10

"I need you to think very hard," Preach said, watching the retired professor carefully. "Do you remember anything at all about this woman you saw through the window? Hair length, clothes, shoes, hat, glasses?"

Sharon was staring intently out of the sliding glass doors, as if trying to recreate the image. "From the position of the window, I could only see her from the waist up. I don't remember any distinguishing clothing, and I can't even remember if I saw long hair or not."

"What made you think it was a woman? Besides the slim build?"

"That's it, I guess," she said after a moment. "I hadn't thought about it before you asked. The memory just sort of . . . slips away."

"Recall is hard," he said, distracted as he considered the implications. The fact that someone was with David later that night, in his house, was monumental.

The person Sharon had seen could have been any woman or, for that matter, one of David's smaller male friends. A prosecutor would have a hard time, maybe an impossible one, using the testimony in court. But in terms of the investigation, it meant that someone David knew—and knew well—was with him that night.

And that person could have been Claire.

His throat felt dry as he pressed Sharon for more information. After failing to learn anything else of use, he told her to expect a sketch artist, thanked her for her time, and stepped outside. He ran a hand through his hair as he walked back to his car, his gaze slipping back to Claire's house.

Anything could have happened that night. The murderer and an accomplice could have confronted David in the house while Claire was asleep. Or David might have brought a friend or a girl back to the house, then gone off with someone else.

If I think long enough, I can come up with anything.

Yet Claire had lied about where the argument had taken place. Why? Was it a lapse of memory, or was she covering something up?

Should he confront her now or wait for more evidence? Was he allowing their personal connection to impact his judgment?

Or, God forbid, his *feelings*?

He snarled and walked faster to his car. He wasn't that kind of police officer. He wasn't that kind of man.

There was zero evidence of motive. He couldn't even imagine what it would take for a mother to kill her own son, even in a fit of rage. He had never heard of such a thing, outside of severe mental illness.

Check your facts, buddy. Just the other day, a stepfather in North Carolina took his three-year-old daughter out to the woods and shot her. It was all over the papers.

That was a stepfather, he chided himself. *A male. A soulless bastard.*

No sane mother would ever harm her own child.

But there are cases like that every year, all over the world.

There's always an exception. Always a case for evil.

Yet the night he had told Claire about David's death, every instinct Preach possessed screamed that her response to the news was genuine.

Claire is very intelligent and has been an actress since high school. She even got a few professional gigs. Or maybe her guilt is genuine because she killed him in a fit of rage, and now she's aghast at what she's done.

With one hand on the car door, he took a moment to steady himself. *Just investigate*, he told himself. *Do your job*. Still debating as to whether to confront Claire, his gaze slipped to the tract of woods behind the houses.

He still believed the swamp behind Barker's Mill was a dump site. He needed to conduct a full forensics search of the house, and he wasn't sure why David might have gone or been lured outside. But if nothing else, it would give him something to do while he considered his options.

As he left the car and strode through the space between Claire's house and Sharon's, out of the corner of his eye he thought he saw Claire watching him from a window. He turned and saw a flutter of curtains.

Jaw firm, he thrust his hands into the pockets of his overcoat, reached the tree line, and stopped to peer at the back of Claire's house. The kitchen was at the rear of the first floor. Between the kitchen and her office was a mudroom with a door that opened onto the back yard. The same door he was looking at right now.

His eyes ran along the wall of hardwoods lining the edge of the forest. Pine and hickory and sweet gum. The woods bookended the entire subdivision, and he wasn't sure how far they ran, or to where. He made a mental note to have Terry check.

A footpath cut into the woods about twenty feet past Claire's house. After toeing through the leaves piled alongside the path, he stopped to listen. Songbirds chirped, a hawk shrieked in the distance, and squirrels clambered over tree limbs. His own pulsebeat pounded in his head.

Walking as slow as poured syrup, he proceeded down the path, canvassing the terrain for anything out of the ordinary. Thirty feet in it linked up with a wider trail, and plenty of footprints made it obvious the path was in use. Most of Creekville's neighborhoods were connected to a greenway or a wilderness trail of some sort.

A few hundred yards in, something caught his eye. A fallen tree trunk beside the path, covered in moss and fungus. The woods were covered with them, but this one had a jagged impression a few feet from the end of the log nearest the path. He bent to inspect it. The width of the impression was about the size of a shoe.

The position of the hole raised Preach's hackles. As if someone had stepped off the path in the dark for some unknown reason, and their shoe had plunged right through the rotten wood. It could have been an animal or kids playing chase, or a split in the wood when it fell. But something felt off.

He bent to inspect the log and took a picture of it. After that, he rose and slowly circled it, toeing through the leaves and brush. He turned over the top layer, displacing moldy pine straw and a host of insects. After widening his search, he caught a glimpse of sunlight glinting on metal. Expecting a coin, he leaned down, brushed aside the leaves, and found a silver cigarette lighter. It had a protruding lip to aid the thumb swipe and an elegant floral pattern etched in gray lines on both sides. A vintage piece. He carefully dropped it into an evidence bag.

Another hour of searching turned up nothing else in proximity to the log. He could have spent all week digging through the woods. Still, his interest piqued, he kept an eye out on the way back, letting his gaze roam higher, not focused on the path alone. A hundred yards or so away, he spotted a pile of leaves that gave him pause.

Hundreds of leaf piles dotted this stretch of woods alone. Leaves sitting atop fallen logs and brush piles, leaves bunched in mounds over time by the wind. This one looked different for two reasons. First, the pile was structured in a way that looked abnormal to his eye. Too circular, and not contoured enough on the top. Second—and he wasn't positive about this—the area between the mound of leaves and the path, about ten feet of woods, looked as if it contained fewer leaves than the area around it.

Almost, he thought, *as if it had been raked.*

A layer of leaves still covered the ground, but leaves were dropping every day. If someone had wanted to cover something up, they would have tried to deflect suspicion by leaving some of the leaves in place.

When he probed the pile using a long stick, it went all the way through to the ground. He poked a few more places to be sure. After that, he used the stick to sweep off the top layers. The leaves in the middle of the pile weren't as damp as he had expected. In fact, they weren't very damp at all. He was no forest ranger, and was probably making something out of nothing. Still, stubborn as a rusty lock, he kept going, unable to let go of the thread once he had started to pull.

Moments later, his breath stuck in his throat, and he stood staring down at the pile. Suddenly feeling as if someone were watching, he glanced around the woods, then bent to sort through more of the leaves. After uncovering a few more handfuls, he was sure of what he was seeing.

Starting about halfway down the pile, some or all of the leaves had dark spots on them, ranging from dabs of discoloration to large splotches. They were all the same color, as if saturated in the same ink or painted with the same brush.

The splotches were not the sort that appear from water permeation, because these leaves were not even wet. These leaves—the entire middle of the pile—had been stained by a different substance.

And that substance, he was guessing, was blood.

11

Night Lives.

The Creekville tell-all would be Blue's ticket to stardom. It was going to be a hit, she knew it in her bones. How did she know this? Because America, above all else, liked to be shocked. This great big, lumbering, confused, color-streaked colossus of a country had conquered the world, put a television in every house, and provided access to the information highway on every laptop. Like all great empires from history, it had nowhere left to go but down.

Blue, of course, knew all too well how flawed the popular narrative was. She knew firsthand how the other half lived. But the other half weren't the ones who bought shit.

And the half who did?

They liked to be titillated. Force-fed. Abused.

She planned to release her masterpiece straight onto the Internet, because she knew no one was ever going to give her a chance. She had to go and rip her opportunity right out of its smug fortress. She would release her film, and then she would do whatever it took, *whatever it took*, to help it go viral.

Naked videos of her neighbors. Cheating spouses revealed. Domestic violence caught on camera. Every single piece of latte-encrusted dirt on the holier-than-thou residents of Wild Oaks brought into the light. Every lurid detail of the lives of Blue's trailer park neighbors exposed. *Honey Boo Boo*? *Duck Dynasty*? Hollywood producers clearly had yet to discover the Carolina sticks. She had stories to tell that would make Jerry Springer's toes curl.

She didn't care if she went to jail for invasion of privacy. The notoriety would be a blessing, because she would be famous. And in today's world, in the Roman Empire of the digital age, that was all that fucking mattered.

Only one problem stood between Blue and her destiny. A terrifying, implacable, knife-wielding problem named Cobra.

People in the trailer park were scared. Desperate. Alibis were being revealed or invented, laid at Cobra's feet like an offering to appease some brutal young god.

Thinking about what to do occupied her every waking moment. She had gone so far as to consider investigating David's death herself, so she could give the police the evidence needed to find the killer and get Cobra off her back. The desperation of that thought made her laugh out loud. What did she know about investigating a homicide? She would only get herself picked up by the police or killed by the murderer.

But she couldn't sit around and do nothing. The noose was tightening. She estimated she had a week, at best, before Cobra eliminated all the possibilities and zeroed in on her. He, and whoever he worked for, knew there was a witness out there. The *only* witness. They would do whatever it took to find her.

Someone knocked at her door, and a chill swept through her. Her hands shook as she went to the bedroom and pulled back the blinds, just an inch, enough to see that it was one of her neighbors. Old Billy Flynn, a retired plumber who eked out an existence on Social Security and Medicare, a useless drunk if ever there was one. A pedophile too. He had given Blue the eye ever since she turned ten.

What the hell did he want?

She opened the door, flinching at the stench of alcohol and cigarettes and unwashed flesh leaking from his pores. His long gray hair, stiff and shiny with grease, fell like oily strands of rope atop his bony shoulders.

"My mom will be home soon," she said, her first line of defense against the predators in the trailer park. *Mention an adult. Get them thinking.*

"It ain't your mom I'm after."

She started to close the door, but he stuck a wiry hand out, holding it half-open. "Just wait."

She tried to force the door closed, but he was stronger than he looked. After casting a furtive glance to either side, he hopped inside her trailer and shut the door behind him. Blue screamed and backed away, looking for a weapon. Trailer walls were thin. Someone could hear her, she was sure.

But would they care?

"Shush, girl. I ain't gonna hurt you." He put his hands up and stayed by the door. "See? I won't come no closer."

She fled into her bedroom, yanking her phone out of her pocket as she ran. She managed to unlock it just as Billy stepped inside the room, his eyes whisking greedily over the unmade bed and pile of undergarments on the floor.

"Put it down," he said, stepping closer. "If you do, like I said, I won't hurt you."

She started to dial 911, and he smacked the phone out of her hand. When she started to scream again, he said, "Shut *up*. Shut up or I'll call Cobra right now."

Blue slowly closed her mouth.

"That's right," he said, a nasty grin spreading across nicotine-stained teeth. "I know it's you he's looking for."

"What are you talking about?"

"I seen that keychain before. That Ghostbusters one. Yeah, I seen you with it."

Her first thought was that he was lying. She almost never took the keychain out, unless she was in her bedroom. Then she looked out of the window and saw his trailer parked a hundred feet away. She almost always closed her blinds, but maybe she had left them open once or twice, when she was depressed or really tired.

She saw the knowledge in his eyes.

"I seen that and more," he said.

The leer on his face made her wish she had a gun. "Get the hell out of here. I'm not kidding, my mom's on her way."

"You think I ain't lived here for twenty years? Your momma gets home after eight, when she gets home at all."

Again Blue looked around the room, her eyes resting on an old baton in the corner. Not the best weapon, but if she could poke him in the eye . . .

"Even if it was mine," she said, "which it's not, you can't prove it to Cobra."

"It ain't a court of law. And I got nothing to gain from lyin'. I seen you leave the night that boy disappeared. I seen you go in the woods with that camera. What do you think Cobra will do when he hears about that?"

"If you don't get out of my house right this goddamn second, I'm going to scream until my throat gives out."

He put his hands up. "I ain't gonna force myself on you, if that's your worry. But you listen up and listen good. Next time that wetback killer comes around, and I'm guessing it'll be soon, I'm telling him what I know. That is," the sly grin returned, "unless you and I can work out some kind of arrangement." He backed toward the bedroom door, slowly, his eyes roving up and down her body. "I'll stop by real soon, and you can tell me what you decide. Ain't no one gotta know but us."

After he left her trailer, Blue choked back her vomit and walked straight to the kitchen. She reached for the whiskey again and took two quick shots, welcoming the burn. Anything to help wash away the stench of that foul man.

She curled up on the stained cloth sofa, hugging her knees and staring at the brown paneling on the wall. Knowing what she had to do, a cherished remembrance sprang into her mind, a memory of sitting beside her father on Christmas Eve and watching *The Christmas Story*. She hadn't laughed so hard since. If only life were that corny, and a little mishap with a BB gun was the worst thing that could happen. That same night, her mother, in a rare moment of domestic inspiration, had made reindeer sugar cookies and hot chocolate while snowflakes as big as silver dollars had drifted down from outside, mesmerizing Blue, transforming her little world into a winter wonderland.

On that night she had been sitting on this very same couch, in the same mobile home, in the same grimy trailer park. Yet back then, when her daddy was still around and magic was real and the rusted swing set by the creek was all she ever needed, life couldn't have seemed any better.

Blue knew it wasn't the food stamps, or the sagging couch, or even the trailer park that was the source of her unhappiness. The immediate problems, yes. But not the *foundation*. She imagined people in North Korea or Guatemala would kill to have what she had.

Her problem, the problem with all of America as she saw it, was one of expectation. She saw the wealth that existed all around her and knew how low on the ladder she was.

Even worse: She had known a father's true love, and because she once had, she felt her loneliness all the more keenly.

Expectation.

She was ready to start her masterpiece, aching for it, but it would have to wait a while longer. She wasn't about to make a deal with disgusting Billy Flynn, and she had no doubt he would make good on his promise. And once that dirty old man told Cobra about her, the gang assassin would never leave her alone. Not until she, too, was rotting in a swamp.

Her decision was simple now. She had to lower herself even further, into the streets. As much as she despised the trailer park, it was all she had ever known, all the memories she had. She had no idea where to go next or what to do.

But if she wanted to live another week, she knew she had to leave Creekville.

12

As the tech vans and patrol cars arrived, blue lights strafing the sides of the houses, sirens slicing through the cold air, Preach stood on the street in front of Claire's house like the calm center of the storm, his chin level, hands tucked in the pockets of his overcoat.

Yet he felt anything but calm as Claire stepped out of her house with a bewildered look on her face, cringing as if she had not seen daylight in months. She had added a sleek calfskin jacket atop her shawl, as well as a pair of pink and purple sneakers. Her expression turned incredulous as Preach led an evidence team into the woods without speaking to her. After he pointed out the pile of bloodstained leaves and ordered a thorough search of the area, he left the woods and walked toward the circle of officers clustered around his car.

Claire cut across her lawn and stepped in his path. "What's going on?"

He stopped walking and eyed her for a long moment. "I found something in the woods. A pile of leaves covered in blood." He decided not to tell her about the silver lighter. "It might be the crime scene, Claire. The real one."

She put a hand to her mouth and stepped back, knees buckling. At first he thought she was going to fall, and he took a step forward to catch her, but she found her balance and straightened. "I don't understand. Here? Behind the house?"

"Are you sure you didn't see David again that night? After he left?"

She drew back. "Of course I'm sure. Do you think I wouldn't remember the last time I'd seen my son?"

"What about any noises in the house? Footsteps, voices, anything at all?"

"Have you ever taken an Ambien? I took two that night."

He pressed his lips together and glanced at the officers by his car.

"I have reason to believe David returned home that night, and that someone was inside with him."

"*What*? Who told you that?"

"Doesn't matter right now. Are there any of his friends who come around more often than most? Especially women, or males smaller than David?"

Claire put her fingers to her forehead. "I can't believe this. Someone he *knew*?"

"It's almost always someone familiar," he said quietly.

With a disbelieving shake of her head, she said, "He doesn't really bring girls around. There's one, Victoria Summit, who he studies with sometimes. Most of his friends were big guys. Football and all, you know? The only smaller one I can think of is Wes Hood. He lives down the street. They've been friends since childhood."

"He comes over often?"

"Once a month or so. He's a good kid. Smart. I think they play video games together. They went their separate ways a bit in high school but stayed friends."

Preach wrote down the information. "Brett mentioned a girl he really likes. The one who works at the Courtyard."

"Mackenzie Rathbun."

"Has she ever been to the house?"

"Not to my knowledge. And I think I would have known."

"Why?" he asked.

"Because I'm his mother," she snapped.

He paused a beat, keeping his tone neutral. "How often do you take Ambien at night, Claire?"

Her eyes flashed, and she jabbed a finger at his chest. "How dare you?"

"It wasn't a barb. I need to know how often David was alone, or virtually so. How many times a week does Brett sleep over, and how often do you take Ambien?"

With an effort of will, she composed herself. "I only let Brett stay on the weekends. The Ambien," her eyes slid away, "maybe two or three times."

"Per week?"

With a sob, she clutched his arm. "This is all my fault. I should have known what was going on. I'm a horrible mother, Joe. And now he's *gone*."

He wanted to pull her close and comfort her, as he would any grieving parent. Yet as much as she appeared to be telling the truth, he had to do his job. "Claire, I'd like permission to search your house."

Her eyes flew upward.

"It's standard procedure. I wanted to give you time to grieve—but I didn't realize the murderer might have been inside the house."

She touched her temple again. "God."

"Claire?"

She slowly looked up. "Of course. Yes, you can search."

"I'd also like to take the computer to the station."

After a few blinks, she swallowed and said, "Okay."

No one liked their house searched, especially their private communications. Yet he knew his next request would hit home.

"Can I have your permission to search everything on there? Not just David's documents and communications?"

Claire's gaze slipped away. She looked from the woods to the house and then back at the detective. "Am I a suspect?" she whispered.

"I just want to see everything on the home computer. Did Brett have access to your password?"

"You didn't answer my question."

"Did he?"

"Yes." She took a step forward, her voice hardening. "I told you not to waste your time. I didn't kill my son, Joe. Are you going to arrest me?"

"I'm not anywhere close to making an arrest."

"So I'm a suspect."

"I'm simply looking into all the angles. Why did you tell me you argued inside with David that night, Claire?"

She looked perplexed. "Because we did."

"I heard otherwise."

Her eyes went distant, and she shivered into her jacket. "The whole night is fuzzy. And the Ambien . . . sometimes it distorts my memory. Maybe I stepped on the porch as he was trying to leave, and we exchanged words. To be honest, I don't really remember." She held his gaze, chin uplifted. "Do what you need to, but if the other person inside was a woman, make sure you look into Lisa Waverly. Something about her . . ."

"I'll look into everything, Claire."

She took another step forward, close enough to grab his hand. The challenge in her eyes turned to grief. "I mean it. Anything that helps. Take my house down brick by brick if you need."

Her hand was soft and warm, and he felt uncomfortable, as well as self-conscious in front of the other officers. He stepped back, told her she was welcome to stay inside during the search, and strode away to give orders.

That evening, after Preach was the last to leave the office, he wolfed down a yellow curry at his favorite Thai restaurant, pondering the case.

The evidence team in the woods had matched the blood on the leaves to David's. For some reason, Claire's son had gone into the woods behind his house, and he hadn't come back out.

On further reflection it might make sense, if the murder had occurred in the home or in the backyard, to move the body to the woods. Maybe the pile of leaves was the initial dump site, but someone had gotten nervous and moved the body again, to the sump behind the mill.

A thorough search of Claire's house had revealed nothing suspicious. This made him doubt the murder had occurred in a fit of rage inside the house. Forensics would have uncovered a spot of blood somewhere. Still, that did not preclude a cold-blooded kill when David was sleeping and a quick removal of the bed sheets.

The very thought of that made his head throb. That scenario meant Claire had murdered her child while he slept, or someone had known she was out cold and decided to take advantage.

There was also a third choice: Claire hadn't committed the murder herself, but ordered it done.

But still—*why*?

Nothing else had turned up in the woods, though the search would continue the next day. Before Preach left the office, the forensic report for David's body had come in. Besides the bullet wounds, there were no other injuries except the type of minor bruising typical of football players during the season. No skin under the nails, drugs in the system, or signs of sexual intercourse. No identifying fingerprints, shoe prints, blood, hair, or slivers of unknown material. No residue of lipstick or makeup or cologne that had survived the water saturation. On David's clothing, they did find soaked fibers from the sisal plant—used to produce hemp—which reinforced Preach's theory that someone had used a burlap sack to drag or carry the body into the woods behind the mill and dump it. The same fibers had turned up near the leaf pile behind Claire's house.

The two bullets, one lodged in David's spine behind his stomach cavity and the other in the parietal bone, near the back of the skull, had come from the same gun. A garden variety nine millimeter. At least it wasn't Claire's Ruger, but only a true fool would shoot someone with a home weapon, deny it, and leave the weapon in place.

Though impossible to pinpoint after a few days of water immersion, the coroner had estimated that David had been killed soon after midnight on the night he had argued with his mother.

Exactly when Sharon Tisdale said she had seen him.

After dinner, Preach headed to Jimmy's Corner Store. He needed to get a grip on the case in his head. Different detectives did this in different ways. Some preferred the familiar buzz of the station, some preferred a home office, some the shooting range or a running trail or the gym.

When Preach thought through a case, he liked to be out in the world, in the community where the crime had occurred. Watching. Absorbing.

In his experience, the best detectives were regular people. Not ex-Special Forces or braniacs or charismatic types, though all of those skills were useful, but real people who wanted to make things right and who could relate well to other human beings. Someone who used their instincts and experience to draw information out of witnesses from a wide range of backgrounds.

Tenacity, drive, and cunning helped shape a good detective as well, but like the best poker players, the most successful sleuths of all were masters of observation.

He parked in the gravel lot beside Jimmy's Corner Store. On his way inside, a violent wind whipped a flurry of leaves into the air. Two obese men were sitting on the lawn in Adirondack chairs, one in a suit, the other with greasy hair and a beard and overalls. They were drinking root beer and smoking cigars, hands waving as they engaged in a vigorous debate.

When he had first moved back home, Preach had experienced mixed emotions. Despite the depression from his failure in Atlanta, the nostalgia of his childhood home had almost overwhelmed him, fluttering like a rare tropical bird in his chest, hard to pin down but shimmering with vitality. It was so beautiful here, so warm and lush, so peaceful at night. There was a sweet melancholy woven into the fabric of the place, an intimacy with nature and the community, tempered by the daily struggle to survive and the troubled history of the South.

He felt a duty to protect his hometown, preserve its innocence and its people, yet he knew he no longer quite belonged. Like all those characters in his favorite novels, he struggled with his choices, his sense of belonging, his definition of self, and the feeling of being lost in time.

Welcome to the human race, he thought.

Inside the café, he purchased a bottle of brown ale from the refrigerated goods section, had the counter clerk pop the cap, and found a seat by the window. Scuffed wood floors, clapboard walls, cheap aluminum tables that hadn't changed in fifty years. Jars of elderberry preserves and barbecue sauce on the shelves. He noticed a woman in camel print leggings and colored jewelry breastfeeding her child, a table of college boys with T-shirts and ball caps pulled low and faux worn jeans, a man dressed all in black with a scraggly beard and large hoop earrings, and a pair of old ladies conversing with graceful hand movements and careful nods.

His father used to bring him to Jimmy's for quarter ice cream cones while he strummed on his guitar in the corner and young Joey played with the wooden toys and board games. A few hours later, they would go home with local meat and milk and cage-free eggs, not because they were trendy or sustainable, but because they were cheap and delicious.

What could Preach's collective observations about Jimmy's and his hometown tell him about the case?

Maybe nothing. Maybe everything. That was how it went.

What did he know for sure? Claire and David had argued that night, loud enough for a neighbor to notice. David had left in a huff. He had gone somewhere unknown and returned sometime after midnight. He had talked to someone in Claire's study and turned up dead soon after. He likely had been killed in the woods, stuffed in a canvas sack, and dragged off, probably to the trunk of a car. Preach wondered if Claire was strong enough to drag someone of David's size that far. Probably not. In the morning, the evidence team was going to search for a trail of hemp fibers in the woods behind the mill. He made a mental note to add the car trunks of all the suspects to the list.

During his search of the house, Preach had stood in the study, a small room with leopard-print carpet and a custom-made liquor cabinet. For some reason, Claire had moved the family computer, a MacBook Pro, from the spare bedroom to the built-in mahogany desk in the study. Still an aspiring fashion designer, she used the Mac for her clothing blueprints and kept her works in progress on display in the sewing room.

Maybe Claire and David had argued again that night, about something on the computer. Maybe David had gone inside to get booze. Half of all homicides involved alcohol. The initial toxicology had revealed a limited blood alcohol content, but that was a nonstarter. Alcohol production in the body after death, due to microbial contamination and fermentation, was chemically analogous to a BAC resulting from drinking. Corpses recovered from water were especially problematic, due to decomposition and dilution of bodily fluids.

In the house he had kept an eye out for signs of a missing lighter, though he didn't know what that might be. A matching purse or cigarette holder? He could see Claire using a lighter like that, and after he had found a pack of Benson & Hedges in a bedside drawer, she had admitted she still smoked on occasion.

Nothing else in the house raised an eyebrow. An initial search of the computer uncovered nothing new. Claire rarely used email.

He sorted through the other suspects in his mind. Brett he simply disliked. Was the man capable of murder? He exhibited signs of a violent temper, had easy access to firearms, and was one of two people with a motive. On the other hand, he was larger than David, and Sharon had seen a smaller person in the house that night.

A sudden thought struck him. What if Sharon had mistaken Brett for David? Meaning David was the smaller person she had seen?

It was possible, but unlikely. It would be hard to mistake either of them for a slender woman. On the other hand, and he was starting to hate the sound of his own logic, anything could have happened. Sharon could have seen David with a woman, and then someone else could have stopped by later and murdered him. Or Brett could have been in the house at the same time, but in a different room. A collaboration?

Yet the elephant still remained, the key to the entire puzzle.

Why?

So far, the other person with a motive was Lisa Waverly. Preach didn't know what was behind that Facebook post, and the English teacher didn't scream *murderess* to him, but she was about Claire's size. The Facebook post itself was sinister, and he didn't believe *anyone's* story about the origin.

He took a long swig of beer, glanced around the café again, and tapped his fingers on the table. More nervous energy. More avoidance.

Another angle: After hearing someone else had been in the house with David that night, Preach had started to look at Claire with new eyes.

He estimated she pulled in fifty or sixty thousand a year, at best, from the boutique. She belonged to a country club, had a wardrobe full of designer shoes and clothing, took trips to Hawaii, and leased a BMW X-5. How could she afford all of that?

Did Brett foot the bill?

If so, that changed the dynamic.

For a moment, he wondered if he wasn't overreacting to his own flaws, his unwanted attraction to her. Pushing too hard to be evenhanded.

Stop thinking so much about it. About her. *Observe, follow the evidence, and don't assume. Treat it like every other case.*

He finished his beer and sat twirling the bottle between his palms.

The problem was, as much as the evidentiary process was the same, it was nothing like his other cases. There was an inherent bias he couldn't avoid.

It was his own past he was dissecting.

Ari came over at 10 p.m. that night. Preach was surprised she didn't just stay at her apartment in Durham. After Preach heated up some leftover pasta for her, she sat on the couch with a glass of wine, looking preoccupied.

Preach joined her. "I can make a fire on the porch. It's a nice night."

She flashed a tired smile. "Thanks, but I need to read through a few files."

"Want to take me there?"

"What? Where?"

"Wherever it is your mind is."

He thought he might get a chuckle, but instead she took her

bottom lip between her teeth, held it for a moment, and said, "Not tonight, okay? It's just this case I've got."

"Okay," he said, after gazing at her long enough to know that, while it might be work that was bothering her, it certainly wasn't just another case.

The next day brought no new developments. Just before noon on Wednesday, Preach and Ari stepped into a church on Highline Avenue, less than a mile from Wild Oaks. The carpeted foyer of Arrowhead United Methodist spilled into a modest chapel divided into three sections of pews, each twenty rows long.

"I've never been to a funeral in a church," Ari whispered, as they slid into the last row. "Is it a Southern thing?"

"Not that I know of," he said, bemused. "Lots of people choose to have funeral services in a church rather than a mortuary. Especially with cremations."

"Poor Claire," she whispered.

Not many seats remained. He noticed Brett up front next to Claire, and an older woman covered in gold jewelry who shared her high cheekbones and creamy skin tone. Her mother. The jewelry seemed odd, as Claire's family had grown up with very modest means.

Brett turned and caught Preach's eye, frowned, and looked away. People murmured throughout the chapel, a few women wept in the front row, and a harpist strummed soft notes by the pulpit.

"If it were my son," Ari said quietly, as she looked straight ahead, "I'd want the funeral in a church too."

"You would?"

Ari, he knew, had not been to church since she was a child. Her parents had never attended, but her grandfather took her whenever she stayed with him on the weekends.

"If I have a child who dies before I do, I'll believe in heaven."

Preach kept canvassing the crowd, searching for familiar faces. Not just for their reactions to the service, but to his presence. Statistics showed that a shocking number of murderers attended the funerals of their victims. With a case like David's, in a town as small as Creekville, there was a good possibility the killer was in the room with them.

The high school principal was there, along with a slew of students and most of the teachers Preach had met. No sign of Ms. Waverly.

"Is it strange that you're here?" Ari whispered. "Even though you know the family?"

"I don't know. It's never happened to me before."

"Better question: Do you *feel* strange?"

"Why would I?"

"I don't know, because you're investigating?"

After a moment, he said, "A little." He hadn't even admitted it to himself, and more than ever, the case brought home the fact that he was probing the lives of his friends and neighbors. In a city like Atlanta, a metropolitan area pushing seven million, that had never been an issue.

"How well do you know Claire?" she asked.

"Now? Not at all."

"Did you . . . date her?"

As he mouthed "No," an organ started to play, and a white-haired preacher stepped through the choir entrance and strode to the pulpit. While everyone settled into their seats, Claire turned to arrange her shawl on the back of the pew.

"Is that her?" Ari asked.

"Hmm?"

"The woman in the front who just turned. Long brown hair and black dress. Is that Claire?"

"Yeah. That's her."

Ari looked at him askance. "She's gorgeous." When Preach didn't respond, Ari held his gaze for a moment, then hid her iPhone in her lap and checked her texts.

During the service, it was obvious that the pastor, who kept referring back to his notes and never once used a personal pronoun when speaking about David, had not spent much time with the deceased. After the service ended, Preach debated leaving but thought that would look rude, as if he had attended just to scope out suspects. He told Ari he wanted to quickly pay his respects before he left.

"I don't mind if you skip," he said. "I know you have work."

Maybe he imagined it, but he thought her smile was a bit forced. "I'll stay with you," she said.

"Okay. Thanks."

They milled about in a large common room in the basement, drinking fruit punch and nibbling on sugar cookies. As soon as Claire entered, flanked by Brett and her mother, Preach and Ari joined the receiving line. Before they reached Claire, they shook hands with a few more relatives, including a tall and handsome man Preach recognized as Claire's ex-husband, Dylan Freeman. Though a few years older, Dylan had starred on the high school basketball team, and Preach remembered seeing him at games and around town. He was now an attorney in Virginia, with a successful employment law practice.

"Joe Everson," Preach said, introducing himself.

Dylan gripped his hand. "Ah, Joe. That's right. I heard you were working the case."

Still lean and youthful, Dylan had the easy charm, as well as the deep and earnest voice, of a trial attorney. If Preach remembered correctly, he had been a junior at Duke when Claire had gotten pregnant her senior year.

"Nice to meet you," Preach said. "I'm sorry about the circumstances."

Dylan looked down for a moment, and Preach saw a spasm of regret contort his face, a man who knew he had not done right by his boy.

And now he could never change it.

When he looked back up, the expression had morphed into a charismatic smile. "Thanks for coming."

"Sure."

With his grin fixed in place, still gripping Preach's hand, Dylan leaned in close and whispered, "You get the motherfucker who did this."

Preach locked eyes with him, gave a curt nod, and moved on. Dylan turned to Ari and smiled.

After a wordless handshake with Brett, Preach was standing in front of Claire, worried she would reject his presence. Instead she pulled him into a hug. "Thank you for coming," she said, leaning back but still holding onto his arms. Dark circles tugged at her eyes, and her face was drawn and pale.

"Of course." He introduced Ari, and the two women shook hands.

"It was a nice service," Preach said.

Claire nodded absently at the comment. Preach and Ari moved on. He knew it had been a trite thing to say, but all of a sudden he had felt—just as Ari had intimated—self-conscious of his own presence, of standing before Claire in her time of grief while knowing she was a person of interest in the case.

Outside the church, Preach walked Ari to her car, the same Toyota Corolla with frayed seat belts she had driven in law school. First-year prosecutors barely made enough money to cover the rent, groceries, and their law school loans. Some took the job as a stepping stone to a political career or a white-shoe defense firm down the road, some took it because it was available, and some took it because they wanted to put bad guys behind bars.

He knew Ari had taken all of those considerations into account, especially the last one. He also knew that prosecutors and defense attorneys swam in far murkier waters than simple wrong and right—but that was something she would have to experience for herself.

When he hugged her goodbye, she felt stiff. "Everything okay?" he asked.

"Just a lot of work."

He opened the car door for her. "Thanks again for coming. How's the new case?"

She slid inside and started the car. "Unsettling."

"What do you mean?"

"Have you ever heard of someone named Bentley Washington?"

"Don't think so."

"I'll fill you in later. I've really got to run."

As he shut the door and watched her reverse out of the parking space and pull away, he noticed that, for the first time he could remember, she never once looked back at him.

Part of him wanted to chase after her, and part of him, a very small part that he didn't want to admit to, wanted to go back inside the church and comfort Claire. With a sharp pang of guilt, he stood and watched Ari's car disappear in traffic, thinking of the good times they had enjoyed but also the way she had looked at him over the last few months, almost as a consolation prize to her work. He wondered if she was pulling away both literally and figuratively, and whether that had cracked a door with Claire he didn't want to open, and whether that entire line of reasoning was one giant, pathetic excuse.

A buzz in his pocket interrupted his thoughts. After reading the text on his cell phone, he strode quickly to his car, reversing and pulling away before the transmission had fully engaged.

<Phone records are here> the message from Chief Higgins read. *<There's something you need to see>*

13

As she drove away from the funeral home, Ari couldn't help thinking about how strikingly beautiful Claire Lourdes was.

Most of her friends thought Joe Everson's golden boy good looks had drawn her to him. In reality, it had almost kept them apart.

Ari had never wanted the popular guy, the confident Romeo, the flavor of the day. She didn't want someone who skated by on charm and good looks, and who didn't see, really see, the rest of the world. A month or so after she had started dating the detective, they had a light email exchange that had turned serious, ending with her asking what he believed in. Despite his past, she had not quite figured out where he stood with the question of religion.

What do I believe in? I believe in sunsets over still waters, Ari, and the way the breeze ruffles through the long grass in summer. I believe in little girls reaching for their daddies' hands in public parks, the mystery of the night sky, the irrational desire human beings have to create art, the taste of a cold beer after work, the callouses on my hands after the gym. I believe in the power of a good story, the sound of crickets when I fall asleep, standing shoeless in a mountain stream, and holding a mug of fresh coffee in the mornings. I believe in the way your hands wave too much when you talk, the smell of your skin after the beach, the way you gasp when we make love, the way you fight for your beliefs. I believe in your zealous devotion to your favorite authors, the way you dress like no one else and dance whenever you can and think too hard about everything. I believe in your inability to conform, the curve of your lips around mine, and the way you take a knee to talk to children. Does that answer your question?

Yeah. That.

She had printed out his response, folded it, and kept it tucked in a diary. He had won her heart that day, and everything since had only made her feelings stronger for the soulful detective with the troubled past and the deceptively pretty blond hair.

Yet if that was the true Joe Everson, why had she caught him staring at Claire at the funeral when he thought she wasn't looking?

Why had Claire hugged him so easily in the receiving line, as if his strong arms were hers to fall into?

Ari didn't want to be that kind of woman.

Claire's son had just been murdered.

But Ari couldn't stop thinking about how attractive she was.

Old insecurities she thought belonged to the past, products of her awkward teenage years, had returned tenfold.

Dammit, she thought. *Not him. Not Joe.*

She knew she hadn't been herself over the last few months. One of the hardest things about having a real job, especially a job like hers, was the inability to leave it behind. No matter what kind of day she was having, whether she was depressed or too full of life to possibly spend a whole day in the office, she had to put everything aside and focus. She couldn't phone in a prosecution or pretend to work while she surfed the Web. She had to give it her all.

Though maybe, she realized as she drove down busy Highway 15-501, easing into the brick skyline and narrow streets of downtown Durham, thinking again of Claire's impossibly long legs, throwing herself into her work was just what she needed.

Sitting at her desk in her interior office, more akin to a cubicle than a proper attorney's workplace, she rattled off a few discovery requests and then tapped her pen against a manila folder.

Despite her heavy caseload, Ari couldn't let go of Ronald Jackson.

The notorious drug dealer had hired Meredith Verela, one of the best defense attorneys in the city, to represent him. In a fair fight, Fenton could hold his own against her. But not with the facts they had.

All the neighbors around the reputed stash house interviewed by the cops had sworn they had seen nothing on the night of the murders.

They had no idea when Ronald had arrived, or if he was in the house at all. This was no surprise. Most residents of poor urban neighborhoods were terrified of narcing to the police. Without a murder weapon, and with no one to dispute Ronald's story, there just wasn't a case.

Except there *was* someone who disputed the story.

Ari didn't believe Bentley's testimony. She wanted to, but she didn't. But what if she was wrong? And why were they assuming facts not in evidence? Was she making a judgment call based on his appearance and reputation?

She decided to probe.

After an hour spent looking into New Hawk Holdings Inc., she was pleasantly surprised to learn that Bentley had told the truth about his business activities. Just as he had said, the company had a patent portfolio and a dozen apps under its belt, ranging from streamlining real estate searches to board games aimed at minority children. There were a number of stories online, mostly in local news columns, about how his company was known for investing in local tech start-ups in the African American community. He also co-owned a company that focused on affordable housing in low-income neighborhoods. She felt guiltier and guiltier about her assumptions.

Was it possible he was legit?

A few minutes on the Secretary of State website and a quick search in the business journals confirmed that Bentley Washington had indeed sold his software company in 2005 to a tech company in Austin. It was impossible to tell from an online search how successful his businesses were—did she have the budget to hire an accountant?—but judging from his investments, it appeared he had a substantial amount of money.

Okay, then. Maybe this could work. Even if his seedier reputation emerged—which they might be able to keep out—Durham jurors would appreciate his community service.

She found it extremely odd that New Hawk Holdings Inc. belonged to the same man reputed to be a sinister drug dealer. On second thought, maybe she didn't. Online reputations were easy to puff up or even invent. It could be that the software company had sold for ten thousand dollars, that the apps and the patents made no money, and that the entire portfolio was a front or a laundering scheme for the drug business.

Was Bentley Washington a self-taught polymath with a penchant for helping the community? Or a clever criminal who knew how to manipulate the Internet and public perception?

After making a few notes on her research, she walked down the hall for a coffee, mumbling greetings to coworkers along the way. By the time her mind started to perk, she had resolved to lay her own eyes on Bentley and Ronald's neighborhood, as well as the scene of the crime.

Ari left the office and drove east on Main. After a block of cute bars and boutiques on the tail end of the hip section of town, she passed a few blocks of staid government buildings and handsome brick churches, as well as her beloved Cuban sandwich shop.

Once she crossed Fayetteville Street, she entered gentrification territory, a mix of street-corner commerce and transitional housing the developers were snatching up like gold coins. Every now and then a condo tower or a refurbished warehouse would pop up, and the Golden Belt was nearby, a mixed-use artists' collective in a restored textile mill. It was not until she turned left on Alston that the scenery deteriorated into the grinding, semi-urban blight that had warranted Durham's rough reputation over the years.

She passed a slew of apartment buildings in such disrepair she couldn't tell if the people milling about were renters or squatters. Fried chicken shacks, discount marts, a boarded-up church, pawn shops with iron bars on the windows, no-name corner stores with parking lots busier than the inside of most bars on a Friday night.

Ari felt a dissonance as she drove, a visceral reaction to her environment that was more than just the poverty and the criminal presence. It struck her that the shortage of details was what made the scenery so jarring. The lack of paint on the buildings, not a tree or blade of grass in sight, the absence of those little touches of humanity that brought life to a place. Everything gray, bare, stripped to its essence.

Ari's left hand twitched on the steering wheel. She did not consider herself the type of person who locked her doors every time she entered a rough neighborhood. She had traveled to more than twenty countries, many of them on her own, and had traipsed through sketchy cities on three continents.

Still, as Bentley had mentioned, the inner-city ghettos of America were the closest thing she had ever seen to a true war zone. She decided to lock the door, surprised at how much thought she gave the decision. Did having a steady paycheck make her more cautious in life? A mile or so past Alston, she turned left again, into the residential heart of East Durham. This was a different type of poverty. A Southern one. Instead of contiguous row houses or sprawling ghettos, she saw block after block of bungalows and ranch homes, homes built for the working class gone to seed. Sagging front porches, broken windows, the roots of ragged oak trees cracking the sidewalks.

Most of the houses had good bones. Solid wood, wide front porches, craftsman trim on the eaves. Yet time and entropy, the dirty uncles of poverty, had taken their toll. An entire section of the city ground into the earth like the twist of a pepper shaker.

After checking her mirrors, she pulled to the curb in front of a green Cadillac, across the street from the address of the double murder. The shotgun-style house had a covered front porch, a weed-filled front yard, and a chain-link fence enclosing the rear of the property. Blackout curtains on the windows.

She could envision the night in her mind. The desperate ploy of a teenage girl kept as chattel. Convincing some gullible mark to help her hit the stash house so they could run away together. Or maybe it was true love—who was Ari to say?

Downing shots of cheap liquor for courage, hiding guns in their jackets, maybe pretending to have a message from Ronald as they knocked on the front door. No way that stash house had been empty except for the bodies before Ronald had arrived, as he had told the police. Someone must have been inside the whole time, guarding the product. Either someone had ratted out the would-be Bonnie and Clyde, or whoever was inside had overpowered them and held them hostage until Ronald arrived and left their brains dripping down the wall like spaghetti.

Ari's hands tightened on the wheel as she stared at the house. God, it was a violent world.

There was no one on the street. Plenty of vine-smothered oaks to support Bentley's claim he had hidden behind a tree. Unless someone had slipped into the backyard from another house, no one could have arrived unseen from the street, if Bentley had truly been watching.

Someone rapped on Ari's driver's-side window.

Startled, she looked over and saw a black teenager wearing an electric blue bomber jacket and a brown bandanna. He waved at her to lower the window. When she turned back to the street, ready to floor the accelerator, she saw an even younger kid in a faded army jacket standing right in front of her car. A similar brown bandanna hung from a pocket of his jeans.

Ari knew that roughly fifteen street gangs operated in Durham, pulling in youths as young as twelve. Sometimes even younger kids, emulating their family members, carried the culture to the elementary schools.

The kid beside her window smiled as he waved. The thinner boy in front of the car had lifeless, heavy-lidded eyes and a hand tucked under his jacket. Ari gripped the steering wheel and thought as fast as she could.

The knocking continued. She had to do something. Moving slowly, she reached for her purse with her right hand while she cracked her window to disguise the movement. If one of them pulled a gun, she would do what she had to: duck and floor the accelerator.

The smiling kid leaned down to speak into the cracked window. "Hey, pretty lady!"

"Can I help you?"

"Ah, we just wanted to say hi. Welcome you to the 'hood."

Ari had her hand on her purse. Her cell phone was inside. "Hi yourself," she said. "I have somewhere to be. Do you mind moving?"

The kid moved his face closer to the window. She guessed he was sixteen. "We need you to do something for us."

"What's that?"

"We're a little thirsty. Hey, how old you think I am?"

"Eighteen?"

He grinned wider, puffing out his chest. "You hear that, Devonte? She thinks I'm legal."

When she brought the purse to her lap, the kid in front of the car, Devonte, tensed and tucked his hand deeper inside his jacket. Ari stopped moving.

"You're not eighteen?" she said, trying to disguise her fear.

"I'm fourteen. Devonte, he sixteen. I look older though, don't I?"

"Fourteen and sixteen? Shouldn't you be in school?"

"Nah, we too smart for that. Tested out and shit. Listen pretty lady, we need you to buy us a bottle of something nice. Some Crown."

"I can't do that," she said.

He laughed. "Hey, I'm a nice guy, but Devonte, he don't like to hear *no*. Do you, Devonte?"

Devonte didn't twitch a muscle.

"Just unlock this door and let us in, okay?" He reached up with his left hand and put his fingers in the crack of the window. "We'll take you to the corner store, be done before you know it."

Ari had heard enough. She was scared, but these were kids, and she was a professional woman in a position of power.

"Do you know who I am?" she said, loud enough for Devonte to hear.

"Sure, pretty lady. You my boo, soon as we get some Crown."

That pissed her off. "What's your name?"

"Me? Jackson Brown. Action Jackson, like the movie."

"Jackson, Devonte, my name is Ari Hale, and I'm a prosecutor for the city of Durham."

That caused his fingers to slip away from the window. "A lawyer? Driving that thing?"

Keeping an eye on Devonte, who kept staring at her with those dull eyes, she reached into her purse and dug her government ID out of her purse. When she held it up, Jackson's smile cracked.

"I could have you arrested for truancy, solicitation to buy alcohol, assault, and attempted grand theft auto."

"Hey now, you don't need—"

"Add attempted armed robbery to that, if Devonte actually has a gun under that jacket."

"We were just playin—'" he said weakly.

"*Jackson*. Walk away, right now. Go back to school."

She took out her phone. He opened his mouth as if to retort, closed it, and slowly backed away. "C'mon, Devonte." The cocky smile returned, and he said, "Don't forget me, pretty lady. Run with me, I'll put you in a Beemer."

Devonte stepped away from the windshield and onto the curb. He was no longer looking at Ari or, as far as she could tell, anything at all.

As she drove out of East Durham, Ari noticed her hands had stopped shaking, and she didn't feel nearly as afraid as she thought she would. Instead she felt a heady rush of power that, instead of feeling good, made her feel conflicted.

The other thing she felt was a yawning sadness at the life of those two kids.

Soon after she returned to the office, an email popped up from Ronald's defense attorney, Meredith Verela, saying she wanted charges dropped against her client immediately for lack of evidence, before the grand jury convened. Meredith must have come to the same conclusion as the DA's office: They had nothing except Bentley's dubious testimony.

Just as Ari was about to leave for the night, her phone rang. An unlisted number that she let go to voicemail.

"Ms. Hale? Bentley Montgomery here. There's something I need to talk to you about—"

She snatched the phone. "This is Ari."

"I thought you might pick up, if you were in."

"What is it?"

"I'll just come out and say it. There was someone with me that night. A woman."

She sat up straighter in her chair. "The night of the murders?"

"That's right. I didn't say anything about it because, well, it's complicated. I've got a steady girlfriend, and this woman ain't she."

"I don't like being jerked around, Bentley."

"Who does?"

"She saw everything you did? And is willing to testify?"

"Just so."

"What's her name? I'll need to talk to her immediately. The defense is pressing us to drop the case."

He chuckled. "Y'all don't want me on the stand, do you?"

"When can we meet, Bentley?"

"Monday. I'll bring her in after her shift, at five o'clock. Make sure you're around."

"Why don't we . . ." Ari said, then trailed off because he had already hung up.

14

Preach strode into the station and went straight to Chief Higgins's office. As he entered, she opened a folder on her desk, revealing a small stack of spreadsheets broken into neat columns. Three months' worth of David's phone records, including the content of the text messages over the last ten days, thanks to the court order. "Take a look at October 1."

"This is the day before his murder," Preach said, as he scanned the printout. David had sent enough texts that Preach had to flip the page. The folder underneath likely contained a list of phone calls made and received.

"The string you want starts at 7:31 a.m.," she said.

"Right before school."

Using his finger to pinpoint the column, he sucked in a breath as he read the three lines of text that followed.

<*This is your last chance*> David had written.

<*Don't threaten me!*> came the reply at 7:32 a.m., from a phone number with the same area code.

And then the last one, sent by David almost immediately after the reply.

<*Tell her by Friday or I will*>

Preach stared down at the printout, his palms pressing into the top of the desk. "Are there any more exchanges between those two numbers?"

"Not after, no. There's a handful before, but nothing revealing. Short discussions about getting rides to practice and such. I assume you don't recognize the number?"

"Wait," he said grimly, thinking the number did look familiar as he dug his notebook out of his jacket pocket. He flipped back a few pages and read the phone number he had written down at Claire's house.

It matched.

Preach slowly looked up. "It's Brett's."

"Claire's boyfriend?"

He steepled his fingers against his lips and nodded, then read the texts again. "Last chance for what? Tell who by Friday? Claire?"

"You don't think they were . . . you know," she muttered.

"I hadn't thought of that. But I don't think so. By all accounts, Brett and David didn't like each other very much."

"Then what the hell is that about?"

"I don't know," he said, tucking the phone records under his arm. "But I'm gonna find out."

As eager as he was to confront Brett, Preach took the time to flip through the records himself. He went to his office and hunkered down, shutting out the ringing phones and the banter of the other officers.

On the night of his disappearance, the last time David had used his cell phone had been to call his mother at 6 p.m. Probably checking on dinner after practice, or asking if she needed something from the store. Preach found no other sign of Brett's number in the call log over the entire week. The only other number he knew at this point was Claire's, so until they compiled a list of phone numbers for the players involved, the call log wouldn't be much help.

Except for the exchange with Brett, the content of the text messages was unhelpful. He found plenty of innocuous exchanges with Claire, a slew of flirtatious texts with a slew of different numbers, and the usual coarse banter between teens.

Two hours later, satisfied he had learned all there was to learn at the moment, he clasped his hands atop the folders, leaning back in his chair as he thought. He found the lack of phone activity on the night of David's disappearance strange. What do kids do at that age when they're upset? They get on their devices and vent to their friends.

But wherever David had gone or whatever he had done after the argument with Claire, he had not texted or called anyone.

Which meant, most likely, that he had gone to vent in person—or something else had intervened.

Preach took Officer Terry Haskins with him to Brett Moreland's house. As soon as the businessman opened the door holding a coffee cup that read "I'm the Boss," his eyes slipped past Preach and focused on Terry's ferret-like face, no doubt wondering why a second officer had come along.

"Can we come in?" Preach asked.

Brett pushed up the sleeves of a ribbed sweater that was a touch too small on him. He was also wearing cotton drawstring pants, a class ring, and slip-on loafers. "Sure, sure," he said, his clipped tone failing to disguise his annoyance.

Once inside, Preach said, "Some new information has come to light."

He watched Brett closely for his reaction, noting how his thumb moved to the underside of his ring and began to rub it. The detective had already eyed his clothing and everything else within easy reach. Preach also kept an eye on the coffee cup in his hand. He'd once seen a guilty suspect throw a kettle of boiling water into the face of an arresting officer.

Brett remained standing a few feet inside the door. He was smart enough to stay quiet.

"Do you recall a text exchange between you and David the day before he was murdered?" Preach asked. "October 1?"

Brett's face reddened. "I said I wasn't okay with you looking at my phone records. Don't you need a warrant for that?"

"We didn't look at your records," Preach said calmly. He let that sink in, until the blotches started to drain from Brett's face. "Is there anything you want to tell us?"

Brett looked from one officer to the other, his stance firm and his eyes challenging, as if waiting for one of them to break.

"'This is your last chance,'" Preach said. It took a few seconds for Brett to realize the detective was not quoting a Spaghetti Western, but the text conversation with David. The businessman's face contorted into a snarl, and for a moment, Preach thought he might be foolish enough to rush them. The detective's hands opened at his sides, and he sank his weight into his heels.

"Your last chance for what?" Preach continued. "Why would David threaten you?"

"Get out of my house," Brett said.

"Tell who something by Friday—Claire?"

"Get *out*."

"I need you to answer me."

"I didn't kill David."

"I'm not sure you understand. I'm a homicide detective investigating a murder, and I'm asking you a question. What was the text exchange about?"

Brett locked eyes with him, balled a fist at his side, and then let it unclench. His jaw worked back and forth, and he said, "I want a lawyer. Right goddamn now."

"You're not going to discuss the texts with me?"

"That's right."

"Terry," Preach said, not taking his eyes off the other man, "read him his rights."

As Terry recited the Miranda warning, Preach unhooked the cuffs from his duty belt and took a step forward. Brett looked stunned. "What the hell are you doing?"

"Put the cup down and turn around, hands behind your back," Preach said.

"What? I—"

"*Do it.*"

Moving as if in a daze, Brett set the cup on a table beside the couch, turned around, and clasped his hands behind his back. "I said I wanted a lawyer."

Preach didn't hurt the other man when he tightened the cuffs, but he didn't make it pleasant. "That's your right. But saying those words doesn't keep you out of jail."

As Officer Haskins took Brett to the station for processing, Preach radioed for a forensics team, then performed a thorough search of Brett's house pursuant to a warrant he had obtained that morning. He had the team fingerprint every single one of the guns, swab the toothbrushes, collect the hairs on the counters, and commandeer the technology: Brett's laptop, phone, and even the Amazon Echo.

He preferred to have forensics deal with the electronics right from the start. Still, he couldn't help glancing at the recent texts on Brett's phone. The only thing he saw was a few normal exchanges with Claire that morning and the previous evening.

Everything else had been wiped.

After finding nothing of interest in the house, Preach left forensics to do their thing. When he returned to the station, he stopped by Terry's office and found the officer taking his navy peacoat off a hook inside his cubicle, preparing to leave for the night. With a wife and two kids in elementary school, he preferred the day shift.

Terry held his coat in his hand. "Did you find anything?"

"A wiped phone."

The junior officer frowned. "Don't much like the look of that guy."

"Me, either."

"You need me tonight? I'll stay if you do."

Preach debated asking Bill Wright to help him, then decided he'd rather wait on Terry. "The morning's fine. When you get in, check the history on those guns, then dig into Brett's life. Finances, school records, everything. You've got an accounting degree, right?"

"Never used it, but yeah."

Preach cocked his head. "You didn't feel like making some real money after school?"

"I tried. Couldn't get hired."

"Ah," Preach muttered, feeling bad about his comment. "Tough economy."

Terry was one of the more self-effacing men Preach had ever known, a small-town kid from one of those lost-in-time mountain valleys in western North Carolina. He didn't know him that well, as Terry preferred to come to work, do his job, and return home to his family.

"Anything else?" Terry asked. He had set his coat down and was taking notes on a sticky pad.

"His lawyer will try to stonewall, but I want a warrant ASAP on the phone records and laptop. I'll write that out tonight. Once we're sure we have access, I'll put you on those too."

Terry finished writing, then shrugged into his peacoat. His eyes possessed a hard glint that Preach wasn't used to seeing. "This job?" Terry said. "It was the only one I could get when we moved here. My wife files medical records for the county, and we need two incomes to survive. She made fun of me at first, and I laughed with her. Before my training, I'd never held a gun and couldn't win a wrestling match with my dog."

This was more words than Preach had ever heard Terry utter, in all of their other conversations combined.

"Anyway," Terry continued, "the first time I put the cuffs on someone, some drunk who gave his wife a black eye, I decided this gig wasn't so bad." He peeled the sticky note off the pad and stuck it next to his computer. "Catching someone that killed a kid?" He bent to pick up an insulated canvas bag with handles he brought to work every day, usually with a packed lunch inside. "Best job in the whole damn world."

After Terry left, Preach stopped by the chief's office to fill her in.

"So Brett's hiding something," she said.

"For sure."

"You think he's our guy?"

Preach had been thinking about that very question all day. Though Brett had looked genuinely surprised by the arrest, in the detective's experience, people with money never expected the shoe to drop. "I don't know yet. But I'm about to turn his life upside down."

"He'll get a good lawyer."

"He still has to tell us about those texts, unless he wants to take the Fifth and face the grand jury. My guess? Either he's guilty, or a night in jail will loosen his tongue."

Preach checked his watch as he left the station and then braced against the chill. A cold front had swept into town, threatening frost in the gardens and leaving the trees quaking in the wind, the streets clogged with fallen leaves. October in the Piedmont was as fickle as any lover. The temperature ranged from winter-coat nights to short-sleeve days and everything in between, depending on the range of sultry air pushing out of the Gulf, or the advancement of the cold fronts from up north. When the two collided, it spelled the sort of dark, heavy, too-still sky that threatened a tornado.

Seven-thirty at night. A good time to meet with the families of David's friends.

First he chose Victoria Summit, the study partner Claire had mentioned. From a records check, he knew her family lived on Hillsdale Street, the toniest section of Creekville. He pulled to the curb in front of a historic cottage with the name of the family carved onto a bronze placard in the front yard. The house had a fresh coat of ruby red paint with yellow trim.

A mousy teenage girl with saffron-colored hair opened the door. She was barefoot, thin as a spindle, and wearing a Creekville High marching band sweatshirt over a pair of blue scrubs. He noted she was about Claire's height.

She blinked at him with mischievous, intelligent green eyes. "Hi."

"Victoria Summit?"

"Yeah?"

Before he could ask if her parents were home, a tall and angular man with a handlebar moustache appeared in the hallway, followed by a woman draped in a fur shawl. Her arcing cheekbones and sour, lined mouth screamed to Preach that she had once been beautiful and would forever resent that fact.

As the man addressed Preach, he grabbed a sleek leather coat from the foyer, slipping it on over his high-collared blue dress shirt. "Can we help you?"

Preach flashed his badge and introduced himself. "I apologize for the inconvenience, but I was wondering if I could ask your daughter a few questions."

"About what?" his wife asked, in an acid tone.

"About David Stratton."

The man zipped up his coat. "Ah. What a terrible tragedy." He stuck out his hand. "Ted Summit."

Preach accepted the gesture, then glanced at Victoria, whose eyes had slipped to the floor.

The woman checked her watch and nudged her husband. He hesitated, then said, "Is Victoria in any kind of trouble?"

"Not at all," Preach said. "I'm just here to fill in a few gaps concerning David's school life."

"They weren't that close," the woman said. "They studied together a few times."

"I understand. I promise to keep it short."

"Vicky?" Mr. Summit said to his daughter. "Are you okay with this?"

The daughter sniffed and looked up. "Sure."

"Good. You won't mind if we step out, would you? We'll miss the show if we don't leave."

Victoria glanced at Preach, rolled her eyes, and said, "It's fine."

Ted clapped her on the shoulder. "We prefer to treat her as an adult. Unless you need us here?" he said to Preach.

"Not at the moment," he said evenly, wondering what kind of parents let their daughters talk to homicide detectives by themselves.

Ted tugged at his moustache and extended an arm to his wife. "We'll be home by midnight," he said to Victoria. "Make sure you lock up. Oh, and detective," his voice turned somber, "we're behind you on this."

"I hope so, Ted."

Victoria watched with an embarrassed look as her parents drove off. "What do you want to know?"

"How well did you know David?"

"Well enough, I guess. We met in study hall last year and became friends."

"You helped him with his homework?"

She laughed. "Is it the band sweatshirt? The football thing? He helped me with *my* homework. I'm lousy with essays."

"Sorry. I didn't mean to presume. Do you know anything about the night he was murdered? October 2? Where he went or what he did?"

"I don't."

"If you had to guess?"

Her jaw started to tremble, and she tried to speak but broke down. Preach gave her space, taking a moment to take his coat off and fold it over his arm. After finding a tissue and composing herself, she said, "He was very popular. To be honest, we didn't talk about our lives very much. I don't think either of us was that happy with them."

"Why wasn't he happy?"

"I dunno, he felt like everyone expected so much of him. His coach, his mom, his teachers, the fans. It's hard being the center of attention all the time, unless that's really your thing. It wasn't David's."

"If you didn't talk much about your lives, what did you talk about?"

She waved a hand. "*Things*. Books, movies, music, ideas. I don't think he had a lot of people to talk about that stuff with. We made out a few times too," she said, almost as an afterthought.

Preach wasn't quite sure how to respond to that, so he didn't. He sensed she was letting out some feelings.

"I know, it's surprising," she said. "I'm hardly in his league. And yeah, I was kinda in love with him. I think he did it out of a sense of duty or something. We never talked about it. It just happened sometimes, in our rooms."

"How was his relationship with his mom?"

"I don't really know."

"Do you know Brett Moreland?"

Her mouth curled at the edges. "Yeah. David couldn't stand him."

"Why not?"

"Because he's a rich douche?"

Preach smirked. "Did you ever hear about any fights or arguments they had?"

"It was always tense if he was there. We'd just go straight to David's room. I only saw him a few times a month or so. Even less during football season."

"Do you know if David had a girlfriend?"

"A steady one? No. Everyone would have known. He hooked up plenty, I'm sure, though he never told me details. He was good like that. A gentleman. Come on, I'll show you something."

She walked him down the hall and into her bedroom. It was filled with candles in colored sconces, a few plants, and vintage furniture with a beige-and-lavender theme. He hesitated, feeling strange entering her room without her parents in the house, then stepped inside and stayed close to the door.

Victoria hinged opened a cabinet set into her headboard and took out a leather-bound diary covered in occult symbols. She flipped it over and showed him the inscription on the back. "Magic Exists Within."

She started to tear up again. "He gave me this for my birthday. I'm Wiccan. It was a perfect gift."

He knew Wicca referred to some type of modern-day witchcraft. A harmless hobby, he thought, though he wasn't really sure. "Was David a . . . Wiccan?"

She gripped the journal in both hands. "He didn't know what he was. Just a searcher, a lost soul like the rest of us."

Victoria, Preach thought, was a little bit deeper than her parents. "Thanks for showing me. Can you think of anything else I might need to know? Anyone who might have wished him harm? Enemies at school?"

Her eyes slipped to the side, an evasive look Preach had seen a million times before. "Victoria?"

"I'm not sure I should say anything."

"Let me be the judge of that, okay?"

One of her feet turned outward, and she fiddled with a star-shaped earring. "Do you know who Ms. Waverly is?"

"I do."

"I'm not sure if this means anything, but . . ."

"Would you rather wait for your parents?" he asked gently.

She barked a laugh, dismissive. "I won't get in trouble at school for saying this?"

"Not as long as it's the truth."

After a slow nod, she said, "I've seen Ms. Waverly looking at David. A lot. I mean, who wouldn't? I didn't think too much about it, to be honest, because, well, let's just say that Ms. Waverly looks at anything with a pulse."

She broke off, and her face crumpled, as if realizing the heartbeat of the person they were discussing no longer pumped blood through a warm body. After a moment, she said, "Do you know about the Facebook post?"

"Yes."

"That same day, I drove home late. Band practice ran long, almost to six-thirty. We had a competition coming up." She stared at the journal again. "I went to dinner with a friend, then to someone else's house to study. By the time I headed home it was after nine. I drove right by Ms. Waverly's house. Everyone knows she lives on Blackburn Avenue because she runs through the park in a sports bra all the time. When I passed her house—I slowed down to be sure, because it was dark—I saw David's Jeep parked in the driveway."

15

"How did you know for sure?" Preach asked, keeping his face calm while he churned inside at the information. "That it was David's Jeep?"

"He has two stickers on the back. An OBX surfboard and a UNC heel."

Preach had seen both those stickers on the Jeep parked in Claire's driveway. OBX was local parlance for the Outer Banks.

"Was that the only time you saw his Jeep at Ms. Waverly's house?"

She sniffed again. "Yeah, but I don't usually go that way."

"Did you ask him about it?"

"I only saw him once after that. I just didn't . . . I didn't know how to start the conversation. Hey David, are you sleeping with the English teacher? Like I said, we'd never talked about those things before, so it would have been weird to bring up."

"Based on what you knew of him, do you think they were . . . together?"

Without seeming to be aware of what she was doing, she twirled the silk ribbon bookmark attached to the journal around one of her fingers. "I'd like to think they weren't. But I'm not sure I do."

Wild Oaks subdivision was less than a mile away. After returning to his car, Preach stopped by Wes Hood's house, the neighbor David had known since childhood.

Two signs, one protesting toxic coal ash dumping and the other objecting to fracking, bookended the front yard of the brick ranch.

Preach rang the doorbell. A trim black man wearing horn-rimmed glasses, slacks, and a white dress shirt with the sleeves rolled up answered. "Can I help you?"

After Preach introduced himself, his father looked down his nose at the detective. "Why do you need to speak to my son?"

"Just routine investigation. We don't know where David went the night he disappeared, and I'm gathering any information his friends might have."

"I see." The father took so long to decide that Preach feared he would deny his request, but finally he said, "I'll need to be in the room."

"Of course."

After introducing himself as Winston Hood, Wes's father led Preach down the hallway to the second door on the left. Bass-heavy electronica pulsed on the other side. "Wesley?"

The music ceased. "Yeah?"

"Can you open up?"

A sprawling computer cabinet filled with gaming equipment, hardware, keyboards, and speakers took up a large portion of the room. Under the stern gaze of his father, Wes Hood rose from his desk chair to shake Preach's hand. Almost as skinny as Victoria, the kid was saddled with the unholy triumvirate of male adolescence: glasses, braces, and zits.

"I hadn't seen him for over a week," Wes said, when asked about the night David disappeared. "Football season and all. I have no idea where he was that night."

"Wesley was here all evening," his father said to Preach, as if reading his thoughts. "With us."

"I assume David didn't stop by or try to call?" Both father and son denied that he had. Preach said to Wes, "David's mom mentioned you like to play video games together."

"Yeah," he said, with a glance to the side.

Preach read between the lines: the two kids had grown up in the same neighborhood, probably spent the night together a hundred times, but had grown apart over the years. David turned out to be good-looking and popular, and Wes hadn't.

Or was it that simple?

Wes's hand moved absently to the mouse, and he stared at the wall beside Preach.

"Someone I knew died in high school too," Preach said quietly. "My cousin." "Sorry."

"It's not fair."

Wes slowly shook his head.

"I know the wound is fresh," Preach said, "but if there's anything you can think of that might help, I'd appreciate if you told me."

"Son?" his father said. "Anything you have to say?"

"I think most nights he wanted to be here with me," Wes said after a moment, speaking so softly Preach had to lean in. He got the feeling the shy teenager was speaking to himself, or maybe even to David, rather than to the adults in the room. "He loved video games but almost never played them."

"Why do you think that was?"

Wes shrugged. "He liked other things more. He liked being popular. He liked girls." He caught himself, then glanced at his frowning father. "I mean, I like girls too. But David . . ."

He trailed off, embarrassed.

"I'm guessing you knew him pretty well," Preach said. "If David was upset, really upset, who do you think he would turn to?"

Wes pushed up his glasses. "I guess it depends on what it was about. Maybe me, maybe Vicky Summit. I think he liked talking to her. There was also this girl he used to work with. He liked her a *lot*. But it wasn't mutual."

"Mackenzie Rathbun?"

"Yeah." A grin slipped through Wes's façade. "I never thought there'd be a girl David couldn't get."

"They never went out?"

"Not that I knew of. And I think he would have told me."

"Can you think of anyone else?"

Wes lifted his hands. "You can try the football guys. I don't know them. I'm sure you know David hooked up all the time, with plenty of girls."

His father's frown deepened.

"Did he ever tell you about a fight he had with anyone?" Preach asked. "His mom, Brett Moreland?"

"He couldn't stand Brett. When they started dating, David came over whenever he was at the house. He felt like his mom and Brett ganged up on him."

That wasn't the impression Preach had gotten from Claire. Then again, kids probably saw those sorts of things differently.

"Ganging up in what way?"

"Never taking his side, just wanting to be alone all the time. It's tough when your mom's dating around."

"But no fights? Physical violence?"

Wes sank deeper into his chair, still fiddling with the mouse. "Not that I know of. Just that fight with Nate Wilkinson."

"So there was a fight? I've heard it mentioned but no one's confirmed it."

Wes looked up. "Oh, yeah. Nate has this good-looking chick who David used to see. I don't know how Nate got her, I guess because he deals—"

He cut off and glanced at his father, who had stiffened in his chair.

"Nate deals drugs?" Preach asked.

"Everyone knows," Wes muttered.

"Do you know what the fight was about?"

"Just that Nate didn't like him, I guess. They had it out after practice one night, in the school parking lot. David pounded him." He shook his head. "I don't know what Nate was thinking. Maybe that his friends would step in."

Preach compressed his lips. It was time to have a talk with Nate Wilkinson. "This happened when? Two weeks ago?"

"Something like that."

He decided not to upset Wes's father any further by pressing that topic. He could do his own investigation and come back as needed. After a few more routine questions, he left the house and returned to his car, driving slowly through the neighborhood. When he passed

Claire's house and saw the living room light on, he resisted the impulse to swing by and run the new information by her.

Realizing he had barely eaten all day, he ignored his hunger and swung through downtown, deciding not to wait another moment to visit Nate Wilkinson's trailer. As he drove, he digested the discussions with David's friends, feeling as if he were starting to develop a better picture of Claire's son.

But who, he thought, was she?

Weak light from a lone street lamp at the entrance to Carroll Street Homes glinted off the puddles of muddy water. A white van with flat tires and a for sale sign on the dash was parked near a line of mailboxes. A muddy ditch to Preach's left overflowed with litter. Though less than two miles from the center of town, just off the state highway that ran by the water tower, the mobile home park was as far removed from the progressive center of Creekville as it was from the Arctic Circle.

In the past, most of North Carolina's crowded mobile home parks were a ghetto for white people. These days, the residents came from all sorts of backgrounds. Rather than contributing to racial violence, Preach had observed that impoverished but multicultural communities thrown together in close confines tended to be more color-blind than homogenous wealthy neighborhoods. It was hard to hate the *other* when they were hunkered down in the same god-awful foxhole.

Tidy single- and double-wide trailers, parked along country roads or even tucked into city lots, were common fixtures in the South. Plenty of middle-class folk Preach knew had grown up in one. Trailer *parks*, on the other hand—not the ones near the entrances to state and national parks but the ones meant to provide bargain basement or transitional housing—were another story. Like their inner-city counterparts, living quarters were so tight and squalid it was tough to escape unscathed. Even then, some of the parks weren't as bad as the others, and they contained poor but hard-working residents who worked with the police to keep the bad elements out.

Carroll Street Homes was not one of those places.

Preach had gone there a dozen times in the last month alone, usually on domestic violence calls. Surrounded by woods and containing several hundred homes—huge by trailer park standards—it was a haven for drugs and gangs. Despite all this, fearing McMansions and bland office parks above all else, the residents of Creekville had lobbied hard over the years to keep the developers away. But crime in the park had gotten so bad in recent months that public opinion had started to shift.

Everyone had their limits, Preach knew, when it came to crime in one's own backyard.

Tolerance was all a matter of degree.

From the moment he pulled in with his window lowered to soak in the environment, he felt eyes on the unmarked cruiser, tracking his progress, wondering who he was and probably guessing correctly. A blond man in his late thirties, clean haircut, double-breasted overcoat, driving a nondescript sedan?

Either a property developer or a cop, and developers drove much nicer cars.

Carroll Street Homes resembled a trailer park graveyard more than a functioning community. The manufactured homes were strewn haphazardly over the lot, many of them mired in weeds and mud, as if they were abandoned relics from a former generation. Between some of the trailers, the junk was so dense it covered the entire yard. He saw stray dogs roaming the lots; windows covered in black tape; tarps in place of roofs; an open entrance with the door removed and leaning against a parked station wagon; screen doors banging in the wind; A/C units askew; rusting toys and bicycles in the yards; the remains of a demolished trailer on a concrete slab, as if struck by a localized tornado and left to rot.

Not many people were out. He rolled past an elderly white man returning inside with a basket of laundry, and a group of Latino teens gathered around an old Mustang, passing around a brown bottle and eying Preach like they were hunters and he was a wounded deer limping through the forest. Members of Los Viburos, he guessed.

Preach had pulled Nate's address from the system, though the kid's last arresting officer had moved out of state the year before. The cheap numbering had fallen off many of the trailers, but after figuring out the pattern and counting down a few homes, he guessed it was the peach-colored trailer streaked with rust on the back side of the park.

A bout of knocking produced no results, despite the lights in the living room and the television blaring through the thin walls. He took a step back and eyed the trailer end to end. None of the other lights were on.

He rapped harder.

Finally the door opened, revealing a short, obese woman with stringy auburn hair and brown spots on her teeth. She reeked of cigarette smoke. Just inside the door, a roach scuttled across a stack of empty pizza boxes.

"Mrs. Wilkinson?"

She looked him up and down, wary. "Yeah?"

When he produced his badge, her eyes narrowed even further. "I'm Detective Everson. Is Nathan Wilkinson your son?"

"Yep."

"Is he around tonight?"

"Nope."

"Do you know when he'll be home?"

She fished a cigarette and a lighter out of the pocket of her sweatpants. A pale green blouse with fishnet sleeves struggled to cover her voluminous bosom. "What's he done now?"

"I didn't say he did anything."

"You just stopped by to say hi?"

"Have you heard about the murder of David Stratton?"

She lit the cigarette in a corner of her mouth. "'Course I heard. What's that got to do with Nate?"

"Nothing, as far as I know. But I'm told the two of them had a fight at school. Did you hear about this?"

"Nope," she said, a little too forcefully. "A fight at school's hardly murder."

"I agree. I just want to talk with him."

"I don't see why."

Preach's eyes slipped beside her, noticing a cloth sofa and a flat-screen television sitting atop a coffee table. Cheap beige carpeting, unraveled at the edges, covered the floor.

"Like I said, he ain't here. He comes home late most nights, usually after midnight. Don't know if you heard, but he got suspended again. Two weeks this time. If he graduates, somebody better call the Pope, cuz it'll be a miracle the likes of Jesus coming back."

Preach handed her one of his cards. "I need to talk to your son. I'd like you to set up a meeting time and call me."

She blew a cloud of smoke that barely missed his face. "I'll see what I can do."

As Preach walked back to his car, he noticed the face of a teenage girl peering out of a window from a few trailers away, backlit by an eerie purple glow that reminded him of those gimmicky black lights that were popular when he had been a kid. When he turned, the face vanished as quickly as it appeared. The blinds were open but he couldn't make out anything inside the room.

If I wasn't someone who noticed things for a living, Preach thought, *I wouldn't have seen her.*

It was probably nothing, but the trailer park's vibe felt worse than usual, and he was frustrated about Nate. On a hunch, he walked over to the trailer where the girl's face had appeared, a grimy single-wide with a brown door and a homemade seesaw in the front yard, long since fallen into disrepair. Behind the trailer was a swampy tract of woods.

Just like at the Wilkinson's, it took repeated pounding to get anyone to answer. Finally, a willowy girl in her mid-teens, her face framed by long dark hair that needed a comb and trimming at the ends, opened up. She had a wild look about her, not just her hair and the skittishness in her eyes but the way she stood with her body angled away from the door, a deer ready to bolt into the forest. She was wearing a pair of old Doc Martens, jeans ripped in half a dozen places, a touch of black eye shadow, a studded leather band on her left wrist, and a black *Chinatown* T-shirt that depicted an image of Faye Dunaway's face floating inside the smoke wafting off of Jack Nicholson's cigarette.

She peered at the badge he was holding up, then at his face, her eyes unreadable.

"I'm Detective Everson," he said. "Is one of your parents home?"

She shook her head.

"Do you mind if I ask you a few questions?"

"Why?"

"You're not in trouble or anything," he said, trying to put her at ease. "Are you a high school student? At Creekville High?"

"Yeah."

"You've heard about the murder of David Stratton?"

"Sure."

"The night he was murdered—October 2—do you remember if you were home?"

"Probably." Her voice was tart, challenging.

"All night long?"

"I guess, yeah."

"Do you rememberirg seeing David that night?"

"Why would I? He doesn't live around here."

Preach's head bobbed as he thought. "That's a *no*?"

"Yup."

"What about Nathan Wilkinson? Was he around that night?" He pointed. "He lives in that double-wide over there."

"I know where Nate lives. And I have no idea if he was home that night. When I get home, I usually stay in my room."

"So you don't remember anything unusual about that night?"

She looked off to the side, her foot tapping. "Just another night in the big city."

He handed out another card. "What's your name?"

"Blue. Annie Blue."

"Thanks for talking to me, Blue. Let me know if you hear or remember anything about that night, okay?"

"Sure thing."

"Hey," he said, just before he walked away. "Good movie."

"What?" she said with a puzzled expression, before glancing down at her shirt. "Oh. Yeah."

On his way into town, Preach called the Courtyard to see if Mackenzie Rathbun was working. The Courtyard was a high-end steakhouse owned by her family, one of the local dynasties that had made its fortune in the early twentieth-century manufacturing boom. Textiles or tobacco or transportation, he couldn't remember which. Probably all three.

The restaurant was located just outside Chapel Hill. Mackenzie was a junior at UNC, and he thought it might be easier to catch her at work than at school. Unfortunately, the hostess informed him Mackenzie wasn't due in until Saturday. Depending on how the next day played out, he might try to track her down sooner. Though if David had been seeing the older girl, Preach had the gut feeling he would have confided in his friends.

Was it possible, he wondered, that David had taken a complete stranger home that night? Or at least someone no one else in his life knew about?

Another thought struck him—what if the mystery woman in the house was Nate Wilkinson's girlfriend? What if David had hooked up with her again, and Nate had found out, and he had taken revenge on the football hero who had beaten him up at school?

According to the principal, the kid's suspension ended on Monday.

Nate's mother sure wasn't going to help him before then, but Preach thought he knew a way to find him sooner.

His cell buzzed with a text. Claire.

<I need you. Can you swing by?>

After a quick reply, he turned right at the next intersection, cut across the north side of town on Spring, passed beneath a train trestle he and Wade Fee used to walk across as kids, and circled back to Wild Oaks.

After hearing him pull up, Claire met him in the doorway, wrapped in a lavender, knee-length, kimono-style wrap.

"You okay?" Preach asked, though he could tell by her red-rimmed eyes and the set of her mouth that she was not.

She curled a finger and turned inside. He closed the door behind him and followed her down a hallway to her bedroom. A black bra and a pair of matching panties tossed atop a pile of clothes drew his eye. The haphazard nature of the pile suggested a careless stripping of clothes each night. Pulling his gaze away from the intimate items, he noticed a pair of men's jeans draped across the white comforter.

"Brett's or David's?"

"Brett's," she said, her tone full of venom. She handed him a small, crinkly receipt. "I found this in the back pocket."

He took a closer look, stretching out the paper. The date immediately caught his eye. The night of David's murder. His eyes roamed lower and noted the amount, forty-seven dollars and thirty cents, and the place of business, a BP gas station.

"I looked up the address," she said. "It's the one on Simpson Road."

His eyes flew to meet hers. The BP on Simpson Road was about a mile out of town—and right on the way to Barker's Mill, the woods where David's body had been dumped. "Is that on Brett's way home?"

"From here? It's not far off. But he wasn't here. He told me he was home all night, working for a new client."

Preach checked the time on the receipt. Eleven forty-five at night.

The timing was right. He sucked in a breath and said, "I'll need to keep this. And the jeans."

After an absent nod, her face twisted into a snarl, and she pounded the wall with a small fist. "What does this mean, Joe?"

"It doesn't mean anything yet. Don't jump to conclusions. Listen, though—I took Brett into custody today."

"*What?*"

He told her what he had found on David's phone, and she sank onto the bed, her fist clamped over her mouth. "My God," she whispered.

He sat beside her. "It sounds suspicious, I'll admit," he said. "But maybe there's an explanation."

Her eyes flashed. "And maybe there's not."

As he looked away, tacitly conceding the point, she moaned and collapsed into him, burying her head in his chest. He started to pull away and then held her tightly, choking back his own emotions.

He didn't know how long they sat on the bed, but some time after the flow of tears had stopped, she pushed away and reached for a tissue on the nightstand. The chime of another text came in. He braced himself as he looked down.

It was Ari, letting him know she was working late and staying the night in Durham. As he slowly returned the phone to his pocket, Claire composed herself and said, "Are you hungry?"

"You know, I'm starving. But you don't have to—"

"It's okay. It will give me something to do. Grilled cheese and tomato soup?"

He spread his hands. "I won't say no to that."

"Good," she said, with a faint smile. "Because it's all I have."

The grilled cheese was just the way he liked it, white toast smothered in Velveeta with a touch of mayonnaise. She made him two. The soup was out of a box but had chunks of real tomato. After finishing it off with a few shakes of pepper, her chin trembled as she scooped it into a bowl and brought it to the table. "David loved this meal. I made it all the time."

"Thank you," he said quietly.

Her smile, soft and faraway, broke his heart.

She joined him in silence as he ate. When he finished, she poured herself a glass of red wine and offered him a beer.

"Sure," he said, after a moment.

After pouring him a Stella, she wandered over to the couch. He sat next to her, and Claire downed half her glass in one swallow. They drank in silence for a while, until she fixed him with a steady gaze. "What happens next?"

They were sitting a foot apart on the couch. He hadn't wanted to leave her in a distraught state, but he suddenly felt uncomfortable, as if he had crossed some unspoken line. "What do you mean?"

"With Brett."

"Oh." He felt foolish. Claire was hardly in a state of mind to think about anything other than finding her son's killer. "He'll have some explaining to do, if he doesn't want to stay in jail. And his explanation had better be good."

"You'll follow up on it?"

"Of course."

"Thank you," she whispered.

They drifted into silence again, until she crossed her legs underneath her, exposing a narrow sweep of thigh. "I don't love Brett. But you probably know that already."

He rolled the glass between his palms. "Why stay with him?"

"You probably know that too."

"The money?"

"I guess that's the crude answer, yes. To me, it's deeper than that. Security. Providing the right environment for my son. Brett paid the down payment on this house, enough that I could afford the note. I'm paying it back to him as a loan. With no interest."

"That was good of him."

"Was it?" she said. "He wanted something, just like I did. I just—" she put a hand to her forehead—"why is life so hard, Joe? Even without . . ." she buried her face in her glass and took a long swallow. "Not all of us got out, like you did."

"I didn't get out. I ran away."

She blinked at him.

"After my cousin Joey died, I just needed to . . . be somewhere else. Did you know I was a preacher for a while?"

She smiled. "I heard."

"That didn't last long. I tried being a prison chaplain after that, but that didn't last either. Being a cop felt right. I think most people who serve others, myself included, are really just trying to plug the hole inside ourselves. I don't even think it's selfless."

"The good ones usually don't," she murmured. "I've never tried helping anyone, except my son. I've never been in a position to."

"Being a parent is the most important job of all," he said, and then regretted it when her face crumpled. "Sorry," he mumbled, reaching out to touch her forearm. She leaned over and grasped his hand, clutching it tight, and the movement further loosened the belt of her kimono. He tried to ignore the crease of creamy skin revealed between her breasts but found it impossible.

She kept squeezing his hand, though her expression had an absent glaze to it, as if she were dreaming while awake. After a time she set her wine down, shifted again, and brought her knees tighter to her body, exposing more of her thighs as she tucked herself against him, resting her head on his shoulder. She slipped an arm through his, and the warmth of her hand and the curve of her breast beneath the kimono made him start to harden.

It felt like pushing through tar as he eased away and rose to his feet.

"I'm sorry," she said. "I didn't mean to—"

"It's just late. I should get going."

In response, she took her lip between her teeth and gave a small, disappointed nod. As he slipped on his coat and backed out the door, her eyes, a study in grief and silence, never left his own.

When Preach returned home, he started a fire in the potbelly stove on the screened porch, poured himself a bourbon, and shuddered as he eased into his hammock. He thought of Claire and wondered if the attraction was a new thing after all these years, or if those long-ago feelings had stayed buried within him like a virus, dormant until sparked to life.

He pushed those thoughts away and reflected on Ari and how much he wanted their relationship to continue. He debated quitting David's case, and then berated himself, because that wasn't fair to David or Claire. They deserved the best help they could get, and in Creekville, in maybe the entire Piedmont region, that was Preach. He needed to put his impulses in the rearview mirror where they belonged. With a deep sigh at the base nature of man, wondering at the purpose of it all, he finished his bourbon, poured himself another, and carried it to bed. He decided to take Ari out to dinner, and someplace special after that. A piece of his childhood that might lead him to Nate Wilkinson.

The day after tomorrow was Friday, and in every town from Maine to California, but especially in the South, that meant bright lights and football. Not only should most of the Creekville High students be there, but the games were a draw for drug activity in the shadows. Preach was betting he would find someone who knew where Nate was. That or Nate himself would make an appearance, even if suspended, lurking around the edges.

The next few days, he hoped, would yield some answers. Maybe Brett would talk, maybe Lisa Waverly would tell him why David had been at her house, maybe Nate Wilkinson would drift within the detective's orbit.

As he turned the light off, he felt relieved beyond measure that suspicion had shifted away from Claire. No one wanted a mother to be guilty of murdering her son, especially a mother he knew personally. Yet his last conscious thought left him with a feeling of unease: If Claire was guilty, then she was doing a very good job, from trying to seduce him in such an unassuming manner to her quiet displays of guilt to producing one of Brett's receipts from the night of David's disappearance, at deflecting suspicion.

16

The visit from the police reinforced the decision Blue had made to leave Creekville.

Things were too hot around the trailer park. Cobra was closing in, old Billy Flynn was about to make good on his promise, and the law was snooping around.

And what about the comment that blond detective with the shoulders like grapefruits had made, asking about her *Chinatown* shirt? Did he know something about the camera?

At this point, she no longer cared about the answers to the mounting questions. She just needed to get the hell out of Dodge, as her daddy used to say.

For a moment, just a moment, she considered turning herself in, either to the gang or the police. The gang idea she discarded as the height of stupidity. Going to the police wasn't much better. They wouldn't protect her, and if Los Viburos ever figured out she had narced, she was deader than Myspace.

What if the murderer was never caught, she wondered? What if the gang never stopped believing she was a witness?

She didn't have an answer.

For now, she had to run.

She started to hide her camera but realized there was no safe place to put it. Once she disappeared, her mom would turn her room upside down, and there was no basement or attic to stash it in. Blue lived in a trailer. A shoe box with a microwave.

Just thinking of leaving the camera caused her stomach to clench and her palms to sweat. She realized she couldn't do it. It was part of her now, a vital organ.

With *Night Lives* on hold, she decided to chronicle her sojourn into the underground instead. Maybe she could call it *Carolina Blue: A Forgotten Journey*. Yeah, she liked that. An artsy vignette of shorts documenting the underbelly of the Piedmont, from the trailer park to Southern urban decay. She could submit it around the circuit, Austin to Sundance, gathering acclaim while she worked on *Night Lives*.

She wondered how long it would take her mother to notice she was gone. She would probably appreciate the extra food stamps, especially after Blue made off with all her spare cash.

After packing her canvas satchel with clothes and toiletries, Blue dipped into her own secret stash. Every now and then, she stole a few dollars from an easy mark at school or one of her mom's boyfriends. Blue had over five hundred dollars hidden in her mattress, which she was saving for a trip to LA when the time came to promote the film. It pained her to disturb the fund, but staying alive took precedence.

Terrified someone from Los Viburos would catch her leaving, she crept out of the trailer at 4 a.m. and scanned the deserted grounds. Armies of cockroaches scuttled underfoot. Inspired by her new idea, she kept to the shadows and filmed her exit on the sly, capturing the litter and the silent trailers strewn like junked cars in the darkness.

The slam of a screen door in the distance caused her to flatten against the side of a van. When no one came her way, she shuddered out a breath. Enough. She had captured the essence. After hurrying to the tree line, she stuffed her camera in her bag and hurried through the woods, forcing away her fears of the unknown. Waiting in town for the bus was too risky, so her plan was to hitchhike to Greensboro and arrive around dawn. Hitchhiking posed its own risks, but she would take her chances over running into Cobra.

Leaving town would cement her guilt in the eyes of the gang, however. She knew there was no turning back. Not unless the police caught the murderer.

The woods closed in around her, deep and dark and chittering. To distract her mind from her surroundings, she pondered her decision to go to Greensboro. Charlotte and DC, the closest large cities, were too big and dangerous. Most of the others were too small to disappear. Richmond or Asheville might work, but she had been to Greensboro once before, on one of her few trips outside Creekville, when her father had taken her to see the circus. It might have been the best day of her life.

Once she arrived, she planned to find the cheapest motel possible, one with a weekly rate and a cash discount. After that, surely she could find work somewhere. Everyone needed a dishwasher, didn't they?

Relieved to leave the creeping darkness behind, she emerged from the woods and walked half a mile across town to the state highway. The lack of cars surprised her. After no one responded to her thumb, she ended up walking all the way to Highway 54, a busy road that led to Burlington, halfway to Greensboro. She could have walked the same distance in the other direction and tried the interstate, but that unnerved her. Visions of traveling serial killers and seedy truck drivers danced in her head.

Starving and exhausted, wondering if she would end up walking the entire fifty miles to Greensboro, someone finally pulled over as the pink light of dawn snuck through the pines. It was a red and white Ford Ranger, a low-slung relic with square headlights.

She eyed the driver as the vehicle came to rest: camo hat pulled low, gray sweatshirt with the logo torn off, worn jeans, grizzled beard covering a lined face and an unsmiling mouth.

That was okay. She trusted frowns more than smiles.

"Where you headed?" he asked.

"Greensboro."

"I'm only going to Burlington."

"I can take the bus from there." She shrugged off her canvas bag and opened the passenger door before he could change his mind.

After she buckled in, he pulled onto the road and said, "Little young to be hitching, aren't you? Don't you have school today?"

"I graduated in May," she said, with a rueful smile. "I came to Chapel Hill to party and ran out of money."

"Huh," he said, eying her clothes and the stuffed canvas bag. "Are you homeless, kid?"

"Um, *no*. You're not a creep, are you?" she said. "Because my daddy's a cop."

The driver flinched. "What? No. Hey, if your dad's a cop, maybe I shouldn't be doing this."

"It's okay," she said quickly, as the truck slowed. "I won't say anything, promise. He'd be super happy if he knew you were giving me a ride. I just don't want him to know I left. He's on a fishing trip and my mom's at her sister's. I don't do this a lot, you know. I was supposed to ride home with a friend but she left with some guy and, like I said, I ran out of money."

As he sped up again, Blue breathed a sigh of relief, amazed at how quickly the lies had flowed.

"What's your name?" she said, moving the conversation away from her.

"Greg Peters. I'm a contractor in Durham."

"You got work in Burlington today?"

"That's right. Say, where's your cell phone? I haven't seen a kid these days who wasn't buried in their phone."

"Out of battery," she said, with a sardonic grin.

The truth was that Blue was one of a handful of kids in the entire high school, maybe the only one, who didn't have a phone. Her mom couldn't afford the payments. It was very embarrassing.

She could tell he was growing increasingly suspicious, so she shut up and watched the road. Most of the scenery was woods or farmland, peppered by a few farmsteads and local businesses. Gas stations, a lumber yard, a garden shop or two.

Fifteen minutes later, they pulled into Burlington, a small town situated halfway between Durham and Greensboro.

"Where should I drop you?" he asked.

"A bus stop is fine. I have enough change to get home."

"All right, then. Which stop?"

"Anywhere downtown. They all go to Greensboro."

He didn't respond, and she could tell he was nervous and just wanted her gone.

After the highway crossed under the interstate and spilled into a tiny brick downtown, Greg let her off at a random bus station. "Watch yourself, okay kid?"

"Sure. Thanks for the lift."

She felt like also thanking him for not being a creep, but she let him pull away, unused to adults showing her kindness. The bus stop was deserted, the shops still shuttered. A grimy slick of oil mirrored the gray sky above.

Blue had never taken a bus before. It took her a few minutes to figure out the schedule, and she was relieved to find that a bus did in fact go to Greensboro. It arrived in ninety minutes and would take an hour to get there. Inspired by the bucolic emptiness of downtown, she filmed her environs for a while, then lay on her back with her head resting on her canvas bag as she waited for the bus.

17

As the moody, orchestral genius of Dmitri Shostakovich's Symphony No. 5 poured through the speakers, the black Lincoln Navigator rolled through the security gate and into the two-car garage attached to Bentley Montgomery's East Durham residence. A restored gem amid a sea of dilapidated properties, the house was a two-story American Craftsman with a broad front porch, three dormer windows, and a tall, spiked iron fence surrounding the property.

The plush Lincoln disgorged three other people along with Bentley and his hulking bodyguard. One was Javier Ramirez, the leader of the Los Viburos gang. Another was a dreadlocked white man in his thirties.

The third was Cobra.

Instead of entering through the side door, the bodyguard unlocked a steel door that fed into a stairwell. Before they had entered the Lincoln, he had confiscated the visitors' guns, patted them down, and checked their clothing with a metal detecting wand.

The white man, a drug dealer from North Durham named Van Mulkey, looked jittery as he followed Bentley down a flight of stairs to a large basement with a finished concrete floor, black leather furniture, and glass cabinets stocked with wine and expensive cognac. Video cameras overlooked the room from the corners. A range of African American art provided the decor, everything from whimsical folk sculptures to colorful chalk drawings, to framed and signed photographs of leading civil rights figures.

Van plucked at the sleeves of his Carolina Panthers windbreaker. "Nice digs, yo. I didn't know you cared about all this stuff."

"What stuff would that be?" Bentley asked.

"You know, politics and shit. I thought you's all about the money."

"Civil rights and the arts are vehicles of transformation. Politics is a social construct mankind has devised to impose order, since we cannot govern ourselves without descending into chaos."

"Whoa. That's deep, man." Van gave a wet hiccup of a laugh. "I guess that's why you're the boss."

Bentley opened one of the cabinets and poured himself a tumbler of Rémy Martin. "What do you think, Javi?"

Javier Ramirez, the thick-bodied leader of Los Viburos, shrugged out of his white anorak and flung it atop a sofa. "Politics depends on who's in the room. Two parties, huh? Which one's for me? The rich whites who want me back in Mexico, or the liberals who ain't got a clue how the world works? Shit, at least the right knows how to get paid."

Bentley arched his eyebrows and took a sip of cognac. "Cobra?"

The square-jawed face of the assassin seemed to sink deeper into the shadows of his black hoodie. "I don't have an opinion," he said quietly. His eyes had never left Van, who didn't seem to notice the attention.

"Stick with me and you will," Bentley said, with a chuckle. "I'll give you some books before you leave. Or maybe you think no one knows shit about shit, and that's why everyone has a worldview or a philosophy, or for less visionary men a political view, which they cling to like a life raft in order to feel grounded in the world. Is that perhaps what you meant to say, Cobra? Because I can respect that sort of apathy."

The assassin's eyes gleamed within the hood. "Sure," he said, his voice barely above a whisper.

Bentley turned to his bodyguard, a behemoth of a man with a wispy goatee and three lines of cornrows caught in a man bun. "Solomon? Would you care to opine on the topic? Grace us with your biblical wisdom?"

The bodyguard's arms bulged beneath his purple sweater like a line of baseballs. "I think niggers didn't have no say in any of it, so it don't concern me none."

"Now see," Van said, pinwheeling an arm, "how come y'all get to say nigger all the time, but if I say it, I'm racist as hell? I grew up in the same hood y'all did."

The room grew quiet.

"Are you telling me," Bentley said slowly, "that you've worked for me for over a year, and yet you somehow do not understand the basic difference between racism and prejudice?"

Expecting a laugh, Van looked as if he wished he had never spoken.

"Prejudice exists everywhere," Bentley continued, "against all things and among all people. I have a prejudice against dark roast coffee. I have a prejudice against goods made in China. I have a prejudice against the French and Italians and Vietnamese, in general. Racism is not prejudice, Van. Racism is *power*."

Van's hands fell to his side, and he looked down at the floor. "I'm just fooling around, man. I get it. I feel you."

"What is it that you get, Van?"

He looked confused. "Like you said, boss. Racism is everywhere."

"Racism is nowhere. Racism is an illusion."

"Huh?"

"Racism depends on a societal power structure. Look into the eyes of the most backward native in the Amazon and you still know he or she is a human being, capable of great feeling. Despite their petty prejudices, the vast majority of people would never even harm an animal. At least for no reason. So why did racism evolve? Choice, Van. Greed and choice. Human beings choosing to take advantage of one another for profit or sexual gratification or some other motive, then justifying it afterward with racism. It is not an innate behavior. It is learned. Purposeful. Taught by a few and embraced by many."

"Yeah, sure boss," Van mumbled.

"It is hard to swim against the tide, once the ocean is in place. Why disadvantage yourself and your children? But take away the power, and you take away the racism."

Bentley's eyes found Cobra's, and something quick and final passed between them. "Speaking of power and the abuses thereof," Bentley said, "my accountant seems to have found a discrepancy in your monthly report."

It took Van a moment to realize Bentley was talking not just to him, but *about* him. The dealer's eyes bugged, and his hands came up in a defensive posture. "Hey, boss, I would never—"

"Compounding theft with prevarication is never a wise idea," Bentley interrupted.

"Say what? Let me—" in the corner of his eye, he caught Cobra approaching, which caused the dealer to choke off his words and stumble away from the assassin.

A six-inch knife with a steel handle appeared in Cobra's hand as if by magic. Van shrieked and started circling the room like a cornered animal, moving among the men with pleading hands, trying to find an absolution he knew in his heart was not coming. "Please," he begged. "One more chance."

Cobra glided forward, but Bentley held up a finger. "Not you," he said, then pointed at Javier. "Him."

Bentley stepped back, all the way to the side wall, followed by Solomon. The bodyguard flicked a switch and the red lights on the overhead cameras started blinking. With a shrug, Cobra tossed the knife to Javier, then stepped back to join the other two men along the wall.

Startled, the leader of Los Viburos managed to catch the handle of the knife. He looked up at one of the video cameras in sudden acknowledgment, then looked at the bodyguard, gauging the situation. Solomon had one of his hands tucked under his sweater. Cobra had his arms folded, expressionless.

Javier, alone with Van in the center of the room, watched as the white man faced Bentley, got down on his knees, and begged for his life.

"I'll do anything, man. Anything. It'll never happen again, I swear. Never ever ever. I'm loyal, man. I just had to pay for my cousin's surgery. It was just one time. I'll pay it back three times over."

Javier glanced at Bentley, a silent inquiry as to whether this was a lesson or the real deal. Bentley gave a curt nod. Javier walked around and gripped Van by the back of his dreadlocks.

"Please," Van whispered, right before the leader of Los Viburos jerked his head back and slid the knife across his throat. No one in the room—except Van—flinched at the brutality of the act.

After the drug dealer bled to death in front of the other men, Bentley turned off the cameras. He asked Solomon to dispose of the body and clean the floor, then addressed Javier and Cobra. "Would you care to join me for a drink?"

"Hell, yeah," Javier muttered. "A double."

Cobra declined the offer. As Solomon slipped on a pair of latex gloves and stuffed Van's body into a thick plastic bag, Bentley handed cognacs to the other men and lit a cigar. He reclined on one of the couches and crossed his legs as he puffed. "Things are progressing at the park?" he asked Javier.

The leader of the street gang looked ready for a fight. Instead he pushed air between his teeth and gave a shake of his head. "Yeah, *ese*. You don't have to worry about that. In a few weeks, they'll be begging you to tear that shithole down."

Bentley sipped his Remy Martin. "Excellent. Keep at it. How is our drug diva holding up?"

Javier shrugged. "She seems fine."

"Keep an eye on her. She's more use to us alive, though if you think she's having regrets, bring her here. I'll provide a pep talk."

Javier clicked out of the side of his mouth and took a long swallow of cognac.

"And the girl?" Bentley said to Cobra. "What was her name again? A color, I believe?"

"Blue."

"Yes, thank you. Blue. You're sure she's the one?"

"I'm sure, but she skipped town."

"To where?"

"I don't know yet."

"How far can someone like that get?" Bentley took another puff and leveled his gaze at Cobra, who stared back without blinking.

The crime lord could read the motives of most men before they ever spoke. Cobra was different. The man's emotions disappeared into a black hole before they reached his face.

"Whatever piss-ant white trash town she ran to," Bentley continued, "go find her and take care of the situation."

Cobra acknowledged the command with a nod.

"Actually, don't go anywhere yet. Javier, why don't you put the word out with your gang? You have factions all over the Carolinas."

"I don't speak for the others. They might not like that I work for you."

Bentley gave a thin smile. "Tell them it's for you, then. Offer them a reward. Money speaks for everyone. Cobra, one more thing."

"Yes?"

"Someone else may have seen something. I need you to send another message."

18

On Thursday, after a coffee-fueled morning in the office filing paperwork and attending a monthly quality circle meeting, Preach called the Courtyard and learned that Mackenzie Rathbun was working the lunch shift. Surprised that something concerning a witness had gone his way, he hurried to his car to catch her before she left. Tracking down a college kid with a vibrant social life could be more challenging than finding criminals.

Accessed by a long gravel drive, surrounded by a tract of deep Carolina woods, the Courtyard was a swanky steakhouse built in the style of a traditional log cabin. A pair of roaring fireplaces bookended the dining room, but the real draw was the elegant flagstone patio that, for nine months or so a year, provided an unmatched natural ambiance. The place had been around for decades, but it was expensive, and Preach had only eaten there once.

The lunch rush had ended by the time he arrived. He introduced himself to the manager, asked to speak to Mackenzie when she freed up, and waited at a table in the corner. Soon, a young woman with all-American good looks walked over, untying her apron and shaking out her hair as she crossed the dining room. Preach noticed a mole on the left side of her neck, long blond hair as fine and shiny as galvanized wire, good posture that made him recall her upper-class roots, and star-shaped earrings with a blue stone in the center.

She sat across from him, looked him in the eye, and spoke in a self-assured voice. "You look familiar."

"I don't know that we've met."

"Do you work for my father?" The question was posed in a curious manner, rather than a rude one.

"I'm a Creekville police officer."

"Oh." She searched her memory for a moment, then said, "Were you at David's funeral?"

"Good memory."

Her eyes slipped away. "I'm surprised I remember anything about that. A bunch of us got really hammered afterward." She put a hand to her temple and took a deep breath. "God, how awful. He was such a sweet kid."

"I'm very sorry. How well did you know him?"

She started to answer but choked on her words. A tear fell from the corner of her eye, and he waited in silence as she composed herself.

"He worked here last summer," she said finally. "We talked a bit, mostly during the breaks and such."

"I've heard from a few people that he was . . . quite taken with you."

She flashed a soft, sad smile. "Yeah. I guess he kind of was."

"You didn't return the interest?"

"David? He was just a kid."

Preach arched his eyebrows. "Was he that much younger?"

"He was in high school." She laughed lightly and gave him a confident, knowing look that said, *I'm in college and know everything there is to know about the world.*

"I'm trying to piece together what happened the night he died. You didn't see him, did you? October 2, a Thursday?"

After she thought for a moment, her eyes widened. "That was *that* night? Yeah, he stopped by the restaurant. He seemed pretty upset."

Preach realized the actual date of David's death was not yet widely known. He leaned forward, intense. "Do you remember what time it was?"

"Around ten-thirty, I think. I was already rolling silverware. So yeah, had to be after ten, but probably not after eleven." She waved a hand. "I'm gone by then."

"How long did he stay?"

"Five minutes, maybe? He said he really needed to talk. I told him I was busy but he insisted."

"Had you seen him since the summer?" Preach asked.

"He stopped by now and then after a shift to say hi. To me and a few other people."

Preach wrote down the names of David's other friends at the restaurant, then said, "Please go on."

"We stepped outside so I could smoke—I usually have one after my shift—and he unloaded a bit on me. Told me he hated his mom and was moving out."

"Did he say why?"

"He despised her boyfriend, I forget his name, and thought they wanted him gone so they could be alone together. He said they couldn't wait until he graduated." Her eyes widened. "Wait—you don't think they . . ."

"Don't worry about that," he said.

Mackenzie put a hand to her cheek. "Christ."

"Did he say anything else?"

"Hey—do you mind if I smoke? I could use one right now."

"Sure."

After Mackenzie grabbed a beige, knee-length suede jacket from a closet, he followed her to the patio and wondered if her parents, one of the wealthiest families in North Carolina, insisted she help pay her way through college.

"What are you studying?" he asked, after she shook out a Benson & Hedges from the pack and used a black lighter with a stylish purple swirl to light up. Could he see her carrying a silver cigarette lighter? It didn't seem like her style. Mackenzie was less hipster and more international fashion model. Poised, intelligent, rich, the world waiting at her feet like an obedient lapdog. It was easy to understand why David had been smitten, and Preach couldn't help but think of the parallels between himself and David at that age, and Claire and Mackenzie.

"Global finance," she said.

"Big plans for the family company?"

"Something like that. I won't deny I have some advantages in life, but the expectations that go with it?" She rolled her eyes. "Those are a killer."

"I can imagine."

She took another puff, holding the cigarette delicately in her fingers. "To answer your question, I can't think of anything else we talked about. He did seem more distraught than normal. I didn't think much about it because I'd heard it all before—except the leaving part, which I assumed was just talk."

"You mean he'd talked about his mom and her boyfriend before, in the same vein?"

"A lot. It really brought him down."

"What happened next that night?"

She shrugged. "He tried to get me to take a ride with him, but I had to study."

"Where did he want you to go?"

"He didn't even say. I felt bad, because he seemed like he really needed someone. But I knew he had plenty of friends, and, well . . ." she trailed off and held a palm out.

He understood. She hadn't wanted to lead him on.

"What about someone else? Did he mention seeing another girl that night?"

"Not to me."

"Where did you end up studying?"

Her face clouded, and he regretted having to ask the question. "With a guy named Jared. Jared Wilson."

She took out her cell and gave him the guy's contact information. "Thank you," he said, then pursed his lips as he thought. "I want you to think very carefully. David's whereabouts that night are crucial to the case. You might have been one of the last people to see him alive."

That knowledge caused her to pale, a crack in her flawless poise. She fought back the tears again, and he remembered the feeling of being immortal when he was young. How far away and unreal death had seemed.

"I know this is hard," he said. "Did he mention where he was going next? Anything else that might be important?"

She pinched off her cigarette and dropped the butt in an ashtray she had carried out. "I asked him where he was going," she said, in a heavy voice, "and he said he didn't know. I told him to go home and talk things out with his mom, that I was sure she loved him."

"What did he say?"

She hesitated and wrapped her coat tighter, as if something besides the weather had given her a shiver. "He said she didn't love him anymore, and that maybe she never had. He said she was just like his dad."

Preach felt a great weight on his shoulders as he returned to the station. Mackenzie's words still haunted him. He could feel David's pain as he struggled through adolescence, struggled to find a place in the world, struggled to be loved.

Where had the hurting teen gone after yet another rejection, this time by the girl of his dreams? To whom had he turned?

Like most murders, Preach's gut told him someone David knew—and knew well—had stolen his young life.

The brainy deputy chief of forensics, Lela Jimenez, approached his cubicle. Short, athletic, and cherub-faced, her dark bangs brushed the top of her red-rimmed glasses as she tapped a manila folder in her hand.

Preach swiveled in his chair. "You found something?"

"It's what we didn't find. Hemp fibers in the woods. Not a trace outside a ten foot radius around the leaf pile."

"You checked in all directions?"

"All reasonable directions. Off the path, it's mostly just bramble."

Preach nodded, thoughtful. "Is that it?"

"For now. I thought you should know."

"You thought right. Thanks."

After she left, he considered the new evidence. No hemp fibers on the path meant someone had carried David a few hundred yards out of the woods.

Not dragged. Carried.

No way Claire could have done that.

He expelled a breath and tipped back in his chair. It didn't completely rule her out. She could have hired someone. But the evidence in this case was sounding more and more like the work of a man.

And, he thought grimly as he stroked his two-day stubble, there just so happened to be a male suspect sitting in a holding cell in the basement of the police station. Brett's lawyer had stopped by that morning, but until the businessman agreed to discuss the damning texts on David's cell phone, there was little his counsel could do.

Preach decided to eat lunch before he went downstairs. No need to go hungry while Brett sweated it out. After a Reuben sandwich from a deli near the station, he stuffed a pen and pad in the pocket of his overcoat and strode down the hallway of the holding chamber.

Brett was slumped on the cot with his back against the wall, shirt untucked, bleary-eyed, unshaven.

"How's the Internet business?" Preach asked.

"Fuck you, man."

"Kind of hard to run your empire from jail."

Brett gave him a defiant stare.

"You think this is hard?" Preach said. "You should try prison. Jail is for sissies."

"I'm not going to prison," he muttered. "I didn't do anything."

"No? Innocent people explain their actions. This won't get you anywhere, you know. I'm sure your lawyer told you that as soon as we haul you before the judge, he'll force you to comply. That or I guess you can stay down here forever, in contempt of court."

Brett's face reddened. "This is a civil rights violation!" he shouted. "You don't have the right to intrude on my private life!"

"I do when you're a suspect in a murder investigation. '*Tell her by Friday or I will*,'" Preach said, quoting David's text. "What did he want you to tell Claire?"

Brett hunched tighter on the cot.

"*Brett*."

With a snarl, the businessman jumped and started pacing. "You can't say anything."

"What?"

"To Claire. You can't tell Claire. If I come clean, you have to promise me she won't find out."

"I can't promise that, unless it doesn't involve the case."

Brett's arms flew up. "It doesn't. I swear."

"So it doesn't involve a receipt in the back of your jeans for a BP gas station on the night David was murdered? The BP on the road to Barker's Mill?"

Brett looked confused for a moment, then put his hands to his head. "Oh God—what—how did you find that?"

"I didn't. Claire did. She already knows, Brett. Whatever it is, she knows you were part of it."

Brett moaned. "I'm so stupid." He closed his eyes and roared in anger, then looked at Preach with stricken eyes. "I love her. I really do. I'm going to marry her."

Preach folded his arms. "What happened, Brett?"

"Lisa Waverly happened, the little slut. I slept with Lisa Waverly."

"Once?"

He swallowed. "A lot."

"And David knew?"

"Yeah. The little prick spied on me. Read my texts and followed me to Lisa's house one night."

"And he wanted you to tell Claire?"

Brett nodded, miserable. "He wanted me out of her life."

"You must have been pretty happy when he couldn't speak up for himself anymore."

"What? No." Brett's face screwed up. "I didn't want the kid *dead*."

"Then why were you pumping gas near Barker's Mill that night?"

"It was on the way to Lisa's house. That's it, I swear."

"The timing is awful convenient."

Brett raised his palms in a helpless gesture. "I didn't kill David. Don't be ridiculous."

After a few moments, Preach uncrossed his arms and let his hands fall to his sides. Though he would verify every inch of Brett's story, the man's emotional reaction felt real.

"You gotta let me out of here," Brett said. "Right now."

"I'll send someone down for a full statement. And let you call your lawyer."

"Let me out right now!" he shouted, then lowered his voice and tried to sound humble. "You can't tell Claire, okay? I'll talk it out with her. The thing with Lisa is over now."

Preach turned his back and walked away.

Back at his desk, Preach tapped his pen against his thigh and considered the new evidence. After the argument with his mother, David had gone to the restaurant, and then driven off again. Not long after that—had he gone somewhere in between?—he had returned home, where Sharon Tisdale had later seen him conversing with someone, most likely Claire.

That was a fact Preach couldn't reconcile.

Maybe Claire had been bombed out of her mind that night and had forgotten her last few moments with her son. Maybe she was sleepwalking, maybe David had locked himself out—maybe maybe maybe. Or what if Sharon Tisdale had her timeline confused, or had been drinking herself? The testimony was pretty weak.

Another thought hit him. What if David hadn't threatened to tell his mother and Brett about the affair in order to break them up? That line of reasoning would explain the Facebook post, but there was another option.

What if David, too, was having an affair with Lisa?

An affair that could ruin her career and land her in jail?

What if, for some reason—maybe to hurt Brett—David had threatened to go public?

Now that was a motive.

After a quick records search on his computer, Preach grabbed his coat and rushed out of the office.

Fifteen minutes later, Preach was knocking loudly on the door to Lisa Waverly's matchbox house wedged into a middle class neighborhood on the edge of downtown Creekville. The little cottage with blue siding and an uneven front yard was barely larger than a one-bedroom condo. The English teacher answered the door in a pair of Lycra workout tights and a white sports bra. Sweat dripped down her face and beaded on her bosom as she clutched a carton of coconut water.

"Hi, Detective." She wiped her forehead. "I just got back from my run."

"Didn't school just let out?"

"I carpooled in and ran home today. I do that three days a week."

"I see. Do you have a minute?"

She raised her arms over her head, arching her back as she stretched, drawing his eyes to her lean torso. "I'm all yours. Would you like to come in?"

"Sure."

She led him to a living room just to the left of the door, where a large bookshelf took up much of one wall. An array of potted plants accented the room and, while her house possessed a fresh floral scent, he mostly smelled the pungent aroma of Lisa's sweat-soaked body.

After toweling off, she slipped into a pair of sweats and joined him on the couch. She sat a few feet away, crossed her legs, and leaned toward him. *This woman has a strange sense of personal space,* he thought. He decided to get to the point and get a gut reaction.

"At best," he said, "you lied to me. At worst . . . well, we won't go there. Not yet."

She froze with the bottle of water halfway to her lips. "I don't understand."

"I think you do. I know David came here to see you. Trust me—it's better if you tell me the truth. All of it."

"Who told you that?"

"Doesn't matter."

Her eyes slid away. "Okay. Yes, he did. I'm sorry. I was scared."

"Of what?"

"It was selfish. But he was already . . ." her eyes teared up, and she replaced the cap on the water with a shaky hand.

"You didn't think you would get caught because he was already dead. Was it just the one time, or a longer affair?"

Her eyes flew up. "Wait—you don't think I would—that Facebook post wasn't about an affair with *David*. It was Brett Moreland. I thought that's why you . . . ah, I see. You were testing me. I would never sleep with a student. *Never*."

"So why didn't you tell me about Brett? Or David's visit?"

"For a long time, I didn't know Brett was Claire's boyfriend. I met him at a bar one night, and we started sleeping together. He never mentioned her. I have open relationships, so I never asked."

"When did you find out?"

"After David wrote *slut* on my Facebook page. That was the same night he came here to confront me. He hates Brett, but he also hated the idea of his mom's boyfriend cheating on her with one of his teachers. I swore to David I had no idea. To this day, I don't think he believed me. He took the post down and said all the right things to the principal, but he remained sullen with me."

Preach spread his hands. "Maybe because you were still sleeping with Brett?"

"David didn't know that. And it was none of his business."

"It was his *mom*."

"They weren't married. We're all consenting adults here, detective."

"Claire didn't consent to an affair behind her back."

"Maybe you should talk to Brett about that."

Preach sighed and rubbed his chin. "If you're so open to all this, then why not just tell me in the first place?"

"Quite frankly, it's none of your business. Or anyone else's. Creekville prides itself on being so progressive, but the attitudes toward sexual behavior, especially with women, are just as repressive and hypocritical as everywhere else. It's fine to be a lesbian or a militant feminist, but an openly sexual woman in her thirties, especially a teacher? God forbid. I kept it to myself because, whether I knew it at first or not, I had an affair with the boyfriend of a student's mother. That's all anyone would see, and I could get fired because of it."

"Was Brett here on October 2? The night of David's death?"

"He was."

"Do you remember when he arrived, and when he left?"

She unscrewed the water cap again. "He arrived around midnight and left in the morning."

"Isn't that pretty late for a date?"

"It was more of a rendezvous."

"He stayed the entire time?"

"As far as I know."

"And it was the just the two of you?"

She nodded, her eyes defeated. "You can check with my neighbors. I'm sure someone noticed his car."

"I will. How would you describe Brett's relationship with David?"

"He never talked about him or Claire."

"I get the impression he was terrified David would tell his mom about the affair."

"I'm sure he was, but he never told me. It was sex, Detective. Nothing more and nothing less."

After thinking through her testimony, Preach stood to leave. He would try to confirm her story, but at the moment he needed to stop by the station before he met Ari, hopefully followed by an audience with Nate Wilkinson. "Ms. Waverly?"

She looked up at him with a somber expression, her arms now crossed over her chest, protective.

"It would be best if you didn't leave town for a while," he said.

"How long?"

"I'll let you know. One final question: Who fell asleep first that night, you or Brett?"

At first she looked confused by the question, but when she realized what he was getting at, a drop of sweat trickled slowly down her jawline, plopping onto her bare arm. "I did," she said, almost in a whisper.

19

When Blue arrived in Greensboro, the first thing she did was go to the greasy spoon across from the bus station and order the eight-dollar breakfast platter. It was the biggest thing on the menu.

After stuffing herself with grits and bacon and pancakes and crispy hash browns, adding a country biscuit for good measure, she lingered over her coffee and thought about what to do next. The idea of running away to a big city had excited her, but now she felt alone and vulnerable. What if someone robbed her before she found a place to stay? Took her camera and all her money?

Blue paid her bill and left a quarter tip, then followed the waitress's directions to the Piedmont Inn, the nearest cheap digs. She was in a gritty, commercial section of town in the shadow of the skyscrapers. Greensboro was no Charlotte, but it had a few hundred thousand people, and to Blue it felt like New York City.

The Piedmont Inn was a typical roach motel. Flinching at the stare of the greasy-haired clerk with a harelip, Blue paid cash for the night and lugged her bag to her room. She had to find work quickly, or she would end up in the homeless shelter. Not a good place for a teenage girl.

After a long nap, sleeping atop the bedspread for fear of bedbugs, she put on her best jeans and a conservative denim shirt her mom had given her for Christmas. Blue asked the new front desk clerk, an older woman with a hard but honest face she trusted much more than the first guy, where the restaurants were. Following her directions, Blue hit the streets and passed a large statue of a soldier, an old general or something, then walked down West McGee to a gentrified part of downtown. At the corner of Elm, she looked in both directions and saw clean sidewalks lined with green streetlamps, brick buildings painted a variety of colors, and enticing shops at every turn: pubs, restaurants, wine bars, bookstores, coffee shops.

Peering inside the storefronts, Blue saw well-heeled people of all ages that made her feel poor and hopelessly awkward. Attractive couples sipping wine in window seats, fancy strollers with babies dressed in designer clothes, teenagers sporting the latest fashions. Blue's anxiety grew so pronounced that it paralyzed her, and she started to return to her motel.

No. That will get me nowhere.

As she always did when in distress, she thought of her father and the movies. She went even further and pretended she was in the eighties, and that she was Winona Ryder or Parker Posey, the coolest girl in town.

To her, the eighties were amazing. Not having lived through them, she could only judge the decade through the lens of its art. Apparently, everyone in the eighties ran around in bright spandex and had big coiffed hair, seemed to party all the time, and lived in new houses in the suburbs with sprawling green lawns. Even the cops were nice. What a time it must have been, she thought, wanting it to be true but knowing in her heart that it was all a farce, that there were people in the eighties and every other decade eking by in squalor just like her, that there had always been people on the margins and always would be. It was the way of the world, and unless one did something to change that fact, something radical . . .

Blue did not believe in fate or destiny. In fact, she despised those words. They implied a lack of choice. Such concepts might be good for a trust fund kid, or even someone born into the suburbs with a warm bed and loving parents. Someone who could afford to dream about an even better future that, if it came to pass, would be called *fate*. Or *destiny*.

Blue's destiny was a trailer park and food stamps.

So she believed in hard work and determination.

Maybe it wouldn't be enough, but it was better than rolling over and accepting the hand life had dealt her.

In the first restaurant she entered, a hibachi joint with shouting waiters and sizzling griddles of meat, she waited at the hostess stand with another teenage girl and her mother. Despite the chilly weather, the girl had on tights so taut Blue could see her butt crack. Both had long blond hair, and the mother had the bee sting kiss of collagen on her lips. After they flounced to a cocktail table, Blue gritted her teeth and asked the hostess for a job application.

20

When Preach returned home from work at 6 p.m. on Friday, he found Ari curled on the sofa in a long black skirt and a sweater, drinking a glass of wine and reading a book called *Dreamland* by Sam Quinones.

"Home by six?" he asked, as he took off his coat. "Was there a fire in the office?"

"You said dinner at seven. Don't you know a girl needs to wine down after work?"

He laughed at the pun. "New book?"

"I have an Amazon Prime addiction."

"I think the whole world does."

"Yeah, except for you. Is it time for a new coat yet? A pair of jeans?"

"It's hard to brood in nice clothes."

She curled a finger. "Come here, handsome."

He set down the case file and joined her on the couch. She threw a leg over his, pulled him close, and kissed him long and deep. As his hand slid up her thigh, she eased it away, eyes dancing. "Let's save it for later."

"Sure," he said, a little weakly.

She ran a nail down his cheek. "We have some catching up to do."

"I know."

"It might take all night."

He swallowed.

"So go take a shower," she said.

Her skirt had slid all the way up to the edge of her silk underwear. Pulling his eyes away from her creamy skin and pouting lips took a superhuman act of will, and he felt a little unsteady as he climbed the stairs to the loft bedroom. He grabbed some comfortable clothes for the evening, jeans and a dark sweater, and returned downstairs to shower.

Scrubbing down in the hot water felt like washing the grime of the case away, at least for a few moments. He felt good about the prospects of the night with Ari. For the first time in a while, she had seemed truly at ease. He knew all too well that everyone harbored deep wells of sadness inside them. Not just criminals and victims and detectives and prosecutors—everyone. His time as a preacher, as a listener, had taught him that. In the quiet of the soul, everyone wonders about the meaning of it all, and shivers at the darkness inside them, and reels at the disorienting nature of consciousness.

Who are we? What does it mean to be alive and aware? Why does the world exist, as David wanted to know?

How deeply one felt that transcendental sadness, Preach had often thought, and how one dealt with it, had a huge impact on personality. Poets and painters and musicians were people who had found a way to channel those inner demons into something tangible, something we could all relate to. Others flinched at the very thought of probing life's questions and appeared shallow, even though he saw it more as living in denial.

But the vast majority of people, like Ari, fell somewhere in the middle. They had bouts of depression and streaks of happiness and always the questions lingered, pinpricks of reflected starlight at the bottom of a dark well, crying out for answers, begging for purpose.

Love was the best tonic he knew. Our biological imperative told us to move from person to person, to propagate the earth. But that was a losing cycle. When we have found an equal, a friend or a partner to whom we can truly relate, someone to share the unanswerable questions with, then we can stop that hamster-wheel search for an escape or the next adventure.

Ari fulfilled him on a level he could only call spiritual. She was smart and poised and beautiful, but what drew him most of all was *her*. The edgy but still innocent persona. A woman hardened by a lonely childhood and life's truths, yet able to be moved by the simplest of things. That was a rare quality.

He didn't want to lose her.

After they cleaned up, he took her to a little Italian joint downtown with fresh flowers on the table and a waiter who shook their hands. Preach and Ari touched fingers as they sipped Chianti, decided to share an entrée and an appetizer, then rolled their eyes in pleasure at the house-made tiramisu. When the check came, he wiped a dollop of cream off her mouth, and they strolled arm in arm into the night.

"Are you really taking me to a high school football game?" she asked, as they headed to his car. The sky was clear and fresh, in the high fifties. Downtown was buzzing with a mix of college students, hipsters, older couples, tattooed drifters, and young professionals pushing strollers. The bars and restaurants were packed. Friday Art Walk was in full swing, and food trucks were parked on the corners. Preach still marveled at the transformation of his sleepy hometown.

"I am," he said.

"Do I look like that kind of girl to you?"

"What kind of girl is that?"

"The one who is almost thirty and still goes to high school football games."

"I've always thought you had an inner cheerleader."

"I have an inner cheerleader like you have an inner vegetarian." He laughed, and she said, "There won't be any there, will there?"

"Any who?"

"Former cheerleaders. You know, a posse of your ex-girlfriends? I'm not sure I'll last through the first inning if there are."

"They're called quarters, Ari. Baseball games have innings."

"Whatever."

"I expect the whole cheerleading squad from my class to be there. Why do you think I chose homecoming night?"

She gave him a playful smack on the cheek.

Preach scoured the parking lot as he and Ari pulled into the high school campus, keeping an eye out for Nate or packs of kids who looked suspicious. The game had begun, so there were no streams of people walking toward the stadium. No one at all, in fact, except for two teens kissing by the vocational building.

He parked in a spot reserved for security personnel. Earlier in the day, he had informed the principal and the security guards assigned to the game that he would be snooping around. As he and Ari left the car and walked toward the stadium, the roars from the crowd grew louder, the buzz of youthful energy vibrating the air. Once they stepped into the bright lights and smelled the popcorn and heard the trumpets from the band, a wave of memories rolled over him, causing him to grip Ari's hand.

"Did you see something?" she asked.

"Just a flashback. Kid stuff."

"Hopefully not about Claire," she said quietly.

He looked over and met her eyes. "Not about Claire."

"Good."

She squeezed his hand, and he felt as good about their relationship as he had in months. His physical attraction to Claire seemed trite and far away, as fleeting as the teenage years themselves.

"How's the case going?" she asked, when he paused at the bottom of the bleachers to watch the game. Creekville High had the ball and was ahead by a touchdown. The stands were as full and as raucous as he remembered, a sea of purple and white Creekville Tomcats.

"I'll update you later," he said. He had told her the purpose of the trip but little else.

"Do you have a gut feeling? You usually do."

She was right; after the initial round of witness and suspect interviews, he usually had a good idea where things were headed. With this case, however, he felt oddly at sea. Though he sensed the answers were within reach, he didn't quite trust anyone involved, and he felt as if there was an important piece of the puzzle missing, something unrelated to everything he knew so far.

It was a just a feeling, an instinct, but one he had learned to trust.

So what was it?

"I'll get back to you on that," he said. "How about you? Is your murder witness still bothering you?"

"Yeah," she said, in a distracted tone. "Let's not talk about that, okay? I'd like to enjoy the evening and not think about work."

"Good idea."

"I'm sorry I started it."

She looped an arm through his, and he led her through the home crowd all the way to the top row so he could have a view of the entire stadium and the grounds behind it. Plenty of people glanced his way as he entered: teachers, students, some people around his age he thought he recognized but wasn't sure. None of his closest friends from high school were in sight, Denny or Eric or Wade Fee. Nor did he see any ex-girlfriends, to his great relief. Though as much as everyone had changed, he supposed one could be sitting right next to him.

Just when he thought he was clear, someone called out, "Psycho Joe!"

On reflex, he turned at the mention of his old nickname. A few people down the row, he spotted a balding man with a beard and glasses, about his age, waving at him. Preach thought he recognized him: Craig Shinlever, a band member and golfer whose girlfriend, if memory served, had come on to Preach at a party. They ended up making out in a corner while Craig was in the other room, refilling her drink.

"Craig?" Preach asked, embarrassed by the memory. God, he wished he could go back and change some things. A *lot* of things.

The other man made his way over, squeezing between Preach and an older woman cheering wildly. "Been a while, huh?" Craig said. "Couldn't resist homecoming?"

"Something like that."

"My kid's on the bench," he said, as if apologizing for his own presence at the game. "I'm also a math teacher."

"You were always making the rest of us look bad in class."

Craig grinned and nudged him on the arm. "So were you, when it came to the ladies."

He made the comment without pretense or bitterness, and while Preach regretted his past, he also realized how trivial it was to the people they had matured into. Everyone made mistakes; everyone moved on and tried to become better people.

"Hey, I saw you on TV, with the case last year." Craig winced. "That must have been hard."

"Yeah. It was."

The math teacher lowered his voice. "You're working David's case now, aren't you? I heard about the teacher interviews."

Preach pursed his lips and nodded.

Craig's eyes roved to the sidelines, as if confirming the physical presence of his own son, safe and secure. "David was a really good kid." He stood and put a hand on Preach's shoulder. "Good to see you, buddy. The past doesn't feel so far away at these games, does it?"

"Not so much. Hey, Craig?"

"Yeah?"

"Do you know a student named Nathan Wilkinson?"

"Sure. Bit of a rough background. I think he's on suspension."

"You haven't seen him around tonight, have you?"

"He's not allowed on school grounds."

"Which means he'll want to be here even more," Preach said.

Craig chuckled. "You're right about that. You might want to check the parking lot by the baseball field. I've seen kids hanging out there during games. They're not supposed to, but it's a big campus."

"Thanks."

Craig pointed halfway down the stands and to his right. "See the Latino girl, puffy black jacket, sitting on the edge of the row?"

"With the cast on her leg?" he asked.

"Yeah."

Preach eyed a pretty, slender teen with short dark hair chatting with a group of girls. Her face was turned to the side, toward Preach, and her left foot was in a cast. A set of crutches was propped on the cement bleacher next to her.

"That's Alana Silver, Nate's girlfriend."

"Do you know how long she's been injured?" Preach asked.

"A few weeks, I think. Why?"

"Just wondering," Preach murmured. Crutches meant that Alana Silver was probably not the second person Sharon had seen walking through Claire's study.

After Craig wandered off, Ari said, "Psycho Joe?"

"Don't ask."

She gave him a soft poke in the ribs. "Really? It was that bad?"

"Trust me, you don't want to know."

As he debated approaching Alana, Ari squeezed his arm and said, "What's *he* doing here?"

"Who?"

"Opposite stairs, just coming in."

Preach turned to his left and saw, standing at the bottom of the stairs separating two of the bleacher sections, a young male with his hands in the pockets of his gray hoodie, standing in place as he scanned the crowd. Preach guessed he was in his mid-twenties, Latino American but darker-skinned than Alana, thick eyebrows, short but compact. His face was square and handsome, and his eyes moved among the fans like heat-seeking missiles, eerily calm and focused amidst the chaos.

"His name's Cristo Rivero," she said. "On the street he's known as Cobra. He's an enforcer for Los Viburos in Durham."

"I've heard of him."

"He's a real predator, Joe. A killer."

"Is there a warrant out?"

She shook her head. "Nothing's stuck, yet."

Cobra slipped his hood up, concealing his face, then climbed the stairs and took a seat at the top, just like Preach had. A vantage point to watch the crowd.

Preach rose and started scooting around Ari.

"Where are you going?" she asked.

"I'll be right back."

"Joe, maybe you shouldn't . . ."

She trailed off as he walked across the back of the stands, right next to the railing, and made his way toward Cobra. Though Preach had a different agenda that night, he couldn't stand the thought of a gang enforcer strolling into a high school stadium and looking for marks. *His* high school stadium.

Cobra saw him approach, studying him in silence. Preach sat right next to him. "Hey pal, are you an alum?"

"No."

"Do you know someone here?"

The gang member's eyes flicked to the field, as if deciding whether to claim he knew one of the players. "Is that any of your business?"

"You're a bit old for high school football, don't you think?"

"And you're not?"

"I went to school here."

"And I enjoy watching football."

"Do you also enjoy selling drugs to kids? Or recruiting them to gangs?"

Cobra's jaw tightened.

Preach slid his badge out and held it against his thigh. The people around them were chatting or focused on the game. "I'm a detective."

"Good for you. And what have I done wrong, officer?"

Cobra's voice was cold and measured, a professional for sure. "You joined a gang and came to the wrong place on the wrong night."

When Cobra turned back to the game, Preach gripped him by the forearm. It was a muscular arm, and Cobra tensed, but Preach was much larger and had an iron grip. "You should leave."

Cobra's other hand twitched. Preach prepared for action, sinking his weight into his heels and watching the gang member for signs of drawing a weapon. Instead of making a move, Cobra's voice lowered and took on a breathless quality, as if the thought of impending violence excited him. "Is there a law against watching a game?"

"Do you really want to do this?"

"It's a free country, isn't it?"

"Not around kids, it's not." Preach let his arm go. "Walk away, and don't ever let me see you around a school again. This one or any other."

Without changing his neutral expression, Cobra stood, eying Preach the entire time as he backed toward the stairs. As the detective continued to watch, the gang member turned and walked away, his focus straight ahead as he exited the stadium.

When Preach returned to his seat, Ari gave him a kiss on the cheek and squeezed his hand.

"What was that for?" he asked.

"For being you. Why do you think he was here?"

"I don't know," he said, recalling the members of Los Viburos infesting the trailer park where Nate Wilkinson lived. Was there a connection? Maybe he shouldn't have been so quick to run Cobra off. "Sending a message to someone, maybe."

When it was halftime, the band started playing, and people rose to make their way to the aisles. Alana was on the move too. She had picked up her crutches and was limping down the stairs, supported by one of her friends. Another girl trailed behind them.

"Sorry, got to run again," he said to Ari.

"I'm going with you this time." When he protested, she said, "If you trail those girls yourself, they'll think you're a perv."

He had to concede the point.

One of Alana's friends broke away at the concession stand. Alana checked her cell phone and nudged the third girl, a chubby redhead with a Mohawk and nose piercings. They started walking again, out of the stadium and down a paved walkway that ran behind the Driver's Ed trailer, spilling into the furthest parking lot from the main road. Off to the left was the baseball field, to the right was a patch of woods. Preach could see movement in the darkness of the infield.

Alana struggled along with her crutches, determined to get wherever she was going. Preach and Ari lagged behind, not wanting to spook anyone.

Cobra, too, could be there. Preach debated calling for backup and decided not to, but he also decided he couldn't take Ari any further. She protested again, but he insisted and told her to get the car and park by the baseball field.

After Ari left, he slipped closer to the dugout where Alana and her friend were headed. They didn't notice him and he stayed to the shadows, drawing close enough to see four boys sitting in a circle on the infield, smoking and drinking beer.

One of them was Nate Wilkinson.

As Alana and her friend managed the gate beside the dugout, Preach hopped the low fence, causing the boys in the circle to scramble to their feet. They gave him belligerent but guilty stares, trying to figure out who he was.

Nate looked just like he did in the yearbook picture Preach had seen. A skinny kid an inch or two shy of six feet, a face pockmarked by acne, oily dark hair, and ghoulishly pale skin. Not just white from lack of sun, but the unhealthy pallor of a poor diet and probably some drug use.

"Who the hell are you?" Nate said.

Two more kids stepped out of the dugout to back him up. They shared a similar dress code: ripped jeans, tattoos and piercings, vinyl jackets, and insouciant stares. Nate's gang, Preach presumed. At least Cobra was nowhere in sight. Preach thought he might have been here to distribute some product. If not, then why was he here?

The kids puffed their chests out and edged forward, emboldened by their leader. Preach held his badge out. "I'm Detective Everson with the Creekville Police."

That cowed them for a moment—everyone except Nate. After flicking his eyes at Alana, who was standing off to the side, he stepped forward and sneered. "Creekville Police? Don't you have some deer to round up? Old ladies to help across the street?"

Snickers rose from the group.

"How about a murder to investigate?" Preach asked.

Nate remained indignant. "What's that have to do with us?"

"I heard you and David Stratton had a fight a few weeks ago."

Nate's eyes slunk toward Alana.

"Busted you up pretty good, huh?" Preach said. "You get mad at him, decide to save some face?"

Nate shuffled his feet and ran a hand through his lank hair. "He jumped me the last time, from behind. I didn't have a chance."

Preach could tell by the shifting glances of Nate's friends that the truth lay elsewhere.

"Too bad he up and died on me," Nate said, which elicited a few snorts. One of the kids, the side of his cheek swollen with tobacco, spat and said, "Fucking pretty boy."

Preach leveled his gaze at them until each and every kid looked away. "One of your classmates is dead," he said quietly. "Show some respect." He turned to Nate. "Where were you on the night of October 2?"

"I didn't *kill* anyone, man."

"Answer the question."

He looked at Alana. "With my girl. At her place."

"Is that true?" Preach asked her. He could see her profile out of the corner of his eye.

"Yeah," Alana said. From her hesitation, he could tell she wasn't telling the truth, or at least not the whole truth. "He came in through the window and stayed the night."

"What time did he get there?" Preach asked. When Alana glanced at Nate, he cut her off with a palm. "I need you to tell me."

She shrugged. "Nine? Ten? Not that late."

Preach curled a finger at Nate. "You're coming with me."

"What? Why? I swear I didn't kill no one."

"We'll talk about that at the station."

"You can't just arrest me. I got rights. You got no evidence about that."

"You're trespassing on school grounds during a suspension," Preach said. "I have every right—"

Before he finished the sentence, Nate turned and sprinted through the infield. Preach gave chase, but a leg came out and tripped him, causing him to sprawl face-first on the ground. Spitting dirt and holding his knee, he cursed and lurched to his feet, unable to tell who had tripped him. He took off after Nate, watching him hop a fence on the other side and sprint into the outer edges of the blacktop. Grunting in pain as he ran, his knee on fire, Preach reached the fence and leaped to grab the top of the fence. He pulled himself over and dashed onto the pavement, just in time to see Nate disappear behind a shed. With another curse, Preach darted after him, realizing he had fled into the woods behind the school. Reaching for his cell phone as he ran, Preach flicked on the flashlight in time to illuminate a tiny footpath Nate had taken.

The detective pressed deeper into the patch of forest. With the chirp of crickets all around, he slipped on a fast food wrapper, then crunched on broken glass as he came upon a narrow stream with a makeshift campsite on the bank. Half-burnt piles of wood and cigarette butts littered the site, along with dozens of crushed beer cans. On the other side of the creek, a wider trail led alongside the water in both directions. There was no sign of Nate, and Preach wished he were a better tracker in the woods. He poised to listen, straining for the sound of footsteps above the insect chatter, but only the hooting of an owl interrupted the night chorus.

21

Preach lost Nate in the woods, and by the time the detective returned to the baseball field, there was no sign of any of the kids. Alana he could track down over the weekend, but he had the feeling Nate would go deeper underground than before.

Could he have murdered David?

It was possible, though Preach doubted it. What he did think was that Nate knew more than he was letting on.

After returning to the car, he filled Ari in on what had happened, and they headed home. Preach was annoyed at himself for letting Nate get the best of him, but he forced himself to shake it off and enjoy the rest of the evening.

In the morning, he planned to kick the investigation into high gear. Enlist some of the other officers to dig deeper into phone and email records, track down every lead, reinterview as many witnesses as possible.

There was an invisible thread running through this town that connected to David's murder; he could feel it.

When they arrived at his house, Ari poured the bourbon while Preach made a fire on the screened porch.

She curled into the hammock, and he slid in beside her, breathing in the familiar jasmine of her perfume. In this age of social media and information overload, things for which he had no intrinsic dislike but which in his opinion had far outstripped their purpose, he loved to lounge on the screen porch with Ari while the forest came alive around them, the pure deep black of the night sky replacing blue lights and tiny screens.

"It was nice to see that part of you," she said, the hammock gently rocking as the bourbon warmed their bellies. "The high school."

"It's a part better seen from afar," he said. "After a few decades have passed."

"At least you had a childhood. I was all over the globe."

Ari's parents, he knew, were teachers at international schools, and she had moved every two years her entire childhood. As she had once put it, her lifestyle was a "social death sentence for a kid."

He said, "I had cliques and keg parties; you had culture and travel."

"You had friends and dates; I dressed as a goth and had birthday parties with my parents. Who weren't very fun and didn't like my outfits."

"Maybe we should agree that we both survived our childhoods in one piece," he said. "Despite the circumstances."

She released his hand and reached up to stroke his cheek, though her gaze was in another place, another time. She had once told him, after drinking too much wine, that her parents had never wanted to have a child. He didn't know if there was any truth to that, but he knew she had begged them not to move schools, time and again, and they had always put their careers and travel lust first.

The troubles of the past fell away as they had another drink and began to kiss. When he tried to remove her jacket, they almost fell out of the hammock, and she put a finger on his lips.

"Not here," she said. "It's too cold."

He set his drink down and scooped her up. "That's better," she purred, as he carried her inside, locked the door behind them, and started toward the loft.

"The couch," she said, running her hands under his shirt and along the ridges in his stomach. "The bedroom's too far."

Thrumming with desire and feeling closer to Ari than any woman he had ever known, he set her down on the sofa, and she slipped out of her jacket and sweater. He slid a hand behind her back to undo her bra.

"Wait," she whispered.

"For what?"

"Music," she said, with a giggle. "I can't make love in silence. It makes me laugh."

"Makes you *laugh*?"

"Have you ever listened to yourself in bed?"

As he spluttered for a response, she grinned and slid off the couch, then padded to the iPhone dock in the kitchen. After a few moments passed and he didn't hear any music, he glanced over and found her studying his phone.

"Is the Internet down?" he asked. "I have a CD player."

No answer.

"Ari?"

Finally she looked up. "So did you swing by?"

"Sorry?"

She walked over to retrieve her shirt from the floor and slipped it back on. "When Claire texted that she needed you. Did you go?"

He stilled. "It wasn't like that."

"Twelve texts in the last three days?"

"It's my job, Ari. I'm working her case."

"No, you're not. You're working *David's* case. You don't even know that she's innocent. All of which is beside the point. *Did you go to her*?"

"I swung by her house to check on her, yes. That's all. She's emotionally . . ."

"Vulnerable? I bet she is. God, there are so many things wrong with this I don't know where to start. So I won't even try. I'll just finish it by leaving." She threw her jacket on and grabbed her shoes by the front door.

"There's nothing to explain," he said, though he winced at the half-truth. He decided, right then and there, not to be a fool and try to pretend nothing had happened. "She's beautiful, I admit. I had a crush on her once. I still find her attractive, as I'm sure you find many young and handsome lawyers in the courtroom attractive."

"Don't."

"But that's it," he said. "I don't want Claire. I want you."

"The texts on your phone, hidden from your girlfriend, say otherwise."

"I wasn't hiding them."

"You should have."

He sighed. "No, I shouldn't have let it happen in the first place. It's just that I've known her for years and her son was just murdered and I . . ."

"Jesus, Joe, it's not like I don't understand that. I'm not the jealous type. A text or an email twice a year is one thing, especially with someone who could never be a threat, but *I need you*? And then all those texts? From someone who looks like *her*?"

"Please don't go," he said softly, as she opened the door.

"Do you want someone like her? Older, taller, tanner? You never got over her, did you?"

"Ari—"

"I saw the way you looked at her at the funeral. I tried to tell myself I was overreacting, but it was the opposite. Is that why we went to the game tonight? In case she showed up?"

He shook his head. "Of course not. I'm sorry about the text."

"I'm sorry too."

He started toward her, but she walked out and slammed the door behind her.

22

Trust, Preach knew, is gained over time and lost in an instant.

And it can take years to claw back.

The content of his text exchanges with Claire was harmless. Yet sometimes it wasn't just the content that mattered.

The conversations had happened, he hadn't told Ari, and he knew he had hurt her. He felt as low as a slug crawling through the garden mud.

Too depressed to sleep and not feeling enlightened enough to read, he found himself flipping through TV stations in his loft, then watching a string of movie trailers, dozens of them, snippets of random adrenaline that unfocused his mind. Eventually he put on ESPN so he could lay on his back and stare at the ceiling and listen to mindless voices until he drifted off, jittery at the thought that he might have jeopardized his relationship.

Hoping for the peace of oblivion, he instead dreamed of an alternate reality where he had moved back to Creekville and started dating Claire instead of Ari. Everything felt so right, so natural. As the dream turned sexual, he woke with a start, the sheets damp with sweat as the memory of Claire's lean body coursed through him, convinced for a moment it was real.

With a snarl, he threw off the bedsheets and stomped to the bathroom, splashing cold water on his face until his desire faded. He checked the clock—5:30 a.m.

Unable to finish sleeping, he made a pot of coffee and sat with his laptop at the kitchen table. He ran through a batch of personal emails he hadn't checked in a week. In addition to an overdue electric bill, he found a notice that he had missed another porch drop for the homeless and would no longer be allowed to participate in the program. Every other Friday, he was supposed to leave canned goods on his front porch for delivery to local families in need.

Who gets kicked out of a charity program? He couldn't even get that right.

Browsing the daily news depressed him even further. Another school shooting. Another few kids found chained in the basement of some psychopathic family member. Another famous sexual predator, another genocide, another group of desperate immigrants dying on a raft while trying to flee their war-torn country.

As a detective, Preach spent his days wallowing in the muck of humanity. He struggled with how to balance the pain in the world versus his need to come home to a cold beer and unwind, to restore his mental equilibrium.

What kind of life was spent bobbing in the dark waters of Aleppo or Sandy Hook, or a neglected toddler who had frozen to death on the front porch while his parents mainlined heroin?

He knew from experience one had to come up for air. Yet what kind of life was spent warm and dry onshore?

He scanned the weekly departmental statistics. Another spike in the crime rate, with an abnormal amount of activity reported in and around the Carroll Street Homes trailer park. Was Nate's gang responsible, he wondered? Los Viburos? Both?

Were they competing for territory, or had one subsumed the other? If so, he doubted Nate had the upper hand. Had Cobra gone to the football game to check on him? Perhaps send a message?

If so, did it have anything to do with David's death?

Preach didn't see the angle. But it was worth investigating, starting with a long talk with Alana Silver.

After a breakfast of cheese grits and bacon, as well as another pot of coffee, a text came in from Lela Jimenez, the forensic investigator.

<Are you working today? If so, I have something>

Preach poured his coffee into a Durham Bulls travel mug.

When he arrived at the station, Lela met him inside and followed him to his cubicle. In her typical businesslike manner, she didn't mince words, extracting two photos from a manila folder and setting them on his desk. Each photo depicted a crusty yellow shoe print with parts of the tread missing. Sulfur casts made by forensics.

"Where'd they come from?" he asked.

"We found the first one in the woods, in the mud beneath the leaf pile."

He sucked in a breath and made a mental note to find out how deep the path led. Before he could ask another question, she continued, "Good news first?"

"Sure."

She pointed at the photo on the right. "That one matches the shoes found with David's body. It was found on the trail behind Claire's house."

"Which makes sense, if he was killed there and bagged."

"The bad news is that nothing is certain. The opinion on pattern evidence has eroded in recent years, ever since DNA became king."

Pattern evidence, Preach knew, referred to evidence identified by a repetition of common designs or markings, such as tire tracks, shoe prints, and fingerprints.

"Pattern evidence," she continued, "is difficult to cast perfectly, hard to interpret, and even harder to match to a particular individual. A solid fingerprint is one thing, because they're individual, but for a shoe print or a tire track to hold up in court, there has to be more than the identification of a particular tread. Do you know how many size ten Nikes there are in the world? We need a nail in the tire pattern, or wear and tear in a particular manner on the heel of a shoe. Even then, it's a subjective standard that has fallen out of favor in court."

Though talented, Lela sometimes got pedantic. He knew all of this already. "Speaking of tire tracks, have you found any?"

"Negative. No skid marks on the road, too much traffic for a latent print, and there are no impressions in the yard or near the woods."

He looked at the two shoe prints again. "These are different sizes."

"David was a size twelve. A large foot. The other one is two sizes smaller but still male."

"How do you know?"

"It's wider than a woman's shoe, and it matches a generic men's work boot from Walmart. Unfortunately, there were no other distinguishing marks."

"Not much help," he said, trying to remember what kind of footwear Cobra and Nate had worn. He thought he recalled a pair of brown hiking boots on Cobra, and scuffed tennis shoes on the kid.

"I'm afraid not."

She reached into the folder and set down three more photos. Each showcased another plaster cast, and they all looked similar: partial casts of a pieced-together rectangle with rounded edges. A few inches below each rectangle lay a circular impression less than a millimeter wide. "This is a tough one," she said. "They all came from the same shoe, we're pretty sure."

"A high heel of some sort?"

She nodded. "Good. Yes. An ankle boot, to be exact."

"Where'd you find these?"

"Under the leaf pile. In the mud next to the male prints."

He felt a little unsteady. "Can you tell the size?"

"It's hard to be certain, but my analysis is a female ankle boot, size six to eight, made at the same time as the print under the leaf pile."

"A woman," he said, almost in a daze. "A woman was there too."

"Claire wears a size seven," she said. "I checked when I was there. But half the women in Creekville, myself included, probably wear size six to eight."

"Any chance you could go through her shoes, or someone else's, and match the shoe with the print?"

"Almost nil. The print is a partial, and the impressions were shallow. That rounded point in the heel is as common as shoelaces.

Every woman I know has a pair of ankle boots with that general shape."

Preach knew she was right, but that was okay. There were other ways to catch a murderer. The fact that had rocked him was that two people had been in the woods with David that night.

And one of them was a woman.

Lela set another photo down. Though less defined, it looked similar to the tread on the work boot. "Final one. This has the same pattern as the size ten male boot. Is it the exact same one? Impossible to tell."

"Where'd this come from?"

"Sharon Tisdale's lawn."

"On the night of the murder?"

She blinked. "You don't know about last night?"

He stared at her. "Last night?"

"Someone tripped the alarm at her house around 4 a.m."

"What? Why the hell didn't anyone tell me? Who was on call?"

"Bill Wright. He thought it was a neighborhood kid, but he called me just in case. I didn't find anything except the print."

Preach couldn't believe what he was hearing. "Was the print fresh?"

"Very. I found it in a wet patch outside the sliding glass doors in the back garden."

Sliding glass doors. The same place Sharon had a view of Claire's study.

After thanking Lela for coming to him, he marched over to Bill's cubicle, didn't find him, and called him on his home phone.

Officer Wright sounded sleepy when he answered. "Yeah?"

"Bill, if you ever talk to a witness on your own during my murder investigation, you tell me immediately."

"I didn't—it was a false alarm. We didn't find anything."

"Except a print that matched another print found under the leaf pile with David's blood all over it."

There was silence on the phone. "Do we know whose it is?"

"Male, size ten, common work boot. Check the files and keep an eye out. What did Sharon say?"

"Someone pried the doors open and the alarm went off, but she never saw anyone. It's not all that unusual in that neighborhood. Bastard kids trying for an easy score."

Preach made a fist at his side. "Someone went there to send a message."

"But no one outside the office knows about Sharon's testimony," the older officer said, perplexed.

As far as Preach knew, that was true, though there was one person who might have put two and two together from watching the investigation.

Claire.

That, or the murderer had noticed a light on in Sharon's house that night.

"Next time," Preach said, "if you have something that involves an active homicide investigation—I don't care how peripheral you think it is—you let me know right away."

"I didn't have a chance to write it up," he muttered. "I was going to after lunch."

"*Right away*, Bill."

After hanging up with Bill and shaking his head at the lack of immediacy—major crimes just weren't in the man's skill set—Preach decided to drive to Sharon Tisdale's house.

Ignoring the magnetic pull of Claire's front door, trying not to think about the disastrous night with Ari, he greeted Sharon and had a conversation about the break-in. He learned nothing of import, though he could tell the retired professor was shaken.

"Will he come back?" she asked.

"I hope not," he said. "Keep your alarm on, even during the day. I'll make sure a patrol car swings by a few times each night."

"Thank you," she said, then plucked at the collar of her pink bathrobe. "Why do you . . . what do you think it was about?"

He decided to tell her the truth, even though it might upset her. "It's possible it was just a burglar, looking for an easy grab. An alarm system scares off most thieves. But given the similarity of the prints . . . I think someone wants you to forget about what you saw the night of David's murder."

She put a hand to her mouth. "You mean . . . am I in *danger*?"

"I don't think so. Not yet. But if we make an arrest . . . I'll keep you posted, okay? And please let us know if you notice anything strange."

"Should I leave town?"

"That's your decision, I'm afraid. If you have someone to stay with . . . maybe it's not a bad idea, for now. Just let me know what you decide."

She swallowed. "Okay."

"Can I ask you something else?"

"Of course."

"The two people you saw in Claire's house that night—is it possible one of them had crutches? Or walked with a pronounced limp?"

The whine of a boiling teakettle increased in the background. "I don't think so," she said, after a moment. "In fact, I'm sure of it. I've thought about that night a lot since we talked. I saw two people walk across the room, and neither of them had any sort of impediment."

"Thank you," he said. "Enjoy your tea."

A squat Latino woman with coiffed gray hair and a stern bearing answered the door to Alana Silver's working class cottage. As the older woman's eyes narrowed to regard Preach, she fingered a wooden rosary resting on top of a sleeveless blue blouse that had seen better days.

"Are you Alana's mother?"

"*Sí.*"

"Is she home?" He produced his badge and introduced himself. "I'd like to ask her a few questions about Nate Wilkinson."

At the mention of Nate's name, Alana's mother stiffened, her eyes opening so wide Preach worried he might have induced a heart attack. "One moment, please," she said, with a heavy accent.

A few moments later, a teenage girl came to the door who bore little resemblance to the confident wild child Preach had seen at the football game. Dressed in a conservative white shirt with puffy sleeves and a neck doily, Alana stood meekly at the front door, using her mother for support on one side.

"How can I help you, Detective?" Alana asked, pouring innocent charm into her words. "I'm afraid I don't know anything useful about Nathan Wilkinson. We only dated a few weeks and split up months ago."

Preach didn't have the option to play nice. He had a murder investigation to conduct. "I saw you at the game with him last night. On the baseball field."

Alana didn't miss a beat. "My friend Rebecca is dating one of his friends. I didn't know Nate would be there."

"Alana—" her mother began, but her daughter cut her off.

"That's all, mama. I swear we're not dating again."

Her mother spoke to her in rapid-fire Spanish, then turned back to Preach. "She will answer any question you need, for as long as it takes."

"Thank you," he said, though the support did him no good. During his questioning, Alana admitted that Nate still liked her, but she refused to concede she was seeing him. By the end of the conversation, Preach honestly couldn't tell where the truth lay. Alana professed to know nothing about Nate's criminal activities or his fight with David. She swore she was at home the night of the murder, alone, though her mother admitted she had not checked on Alana after midnight. When Preach confronted Alana about Nate's claim that he had visited her that night, she said she had only agreed to his remark because she was scared. Her mother put a protective arm around her and claimed that Nate was a dangerous influence.

Preach's one small victory was that, since Alana had changed her story, she could no longer confirm Nate's alibi. Whether she was telling the truth or feared her mother more than lying to a police officer, he couldn't tell.

"Do you know where Nate is now?"

She smiled sweetly. "Have you tried his home?"

"Of course," he said, working to control his temper. "Do you have any other ideas? His hobbies, who his friends are?"

"I'm sorry, I really don't know him that well. I tried to bring him to church but he would never go."

Her mother's grip on her arm relaxed a fraction.

"Alana," Preach said, "Do you realize that lying to me is an obstruction of justice? If I find out you're not telling the truth, I'll bring you to the station for formal questioning and possible charges."

"You better be telling this man the truth," her mother said.

Alana gave a solemn nod. "I would never dream of lying to an officer of the law."

As he left the Silver house, Preach felt like tearing his hair out. He needed to bring Nate downtown but didn't have time to look for him. He debated asking Terry to conduct a search, then decided he needed him on other things.

With a sigh, Preach stopped for lunch at the Buena Vista Café, an open-air coffee house and Cuban-themed sandwich shop. Nestled among a community of farms north of Creekville, the thatch-roofed, bohemian little joint was built atop a row of storage containers and had a covered, wraparound balcony that overlooked the rambling herb and flower garden surrounding the café.

The day was sunny and mild, and Preach relished the fresh air. He ordered the daily special, *picadillo* with fried plantains, and thought about how the people around him barely resembled the neighbors he had known growing up. There was so little permanence in the new republic of Creekville. Everyone was from somewhere else or was emulating another culture, opening Tibetan prayer centers and Honduran coffee collectives and African jewelry boutiques. Preach did not think these legions of new residents were vapid or disliked their country; he simply thought they no longer felt connected to their own heritage, to the piece of earth they called home. It explained the other half of the equation, the resurgence of rustic Americana, the tribes of local craftsmen and bluegrass bands and drinkers of craft rye whiskey. Yet even this was an adopted culture from the past and no longer an organic one.

Was it a backlash to technology? Disorientation in the face of globalization? The incessant migration of American workers and families to other states?

He didn't know. He just knew the people of this era, more than the one he had grown up in, seemed to be searching for an identity.

Or maybe we all grow up and think the same.

When the food arrived, he dug in with gusto, his thoughts refocusing on the case. A few raindrops turned into a downpour slashing against the corrugated iron balcony, blurring the view of the gardens.

All of us, he thought, were on the inside of our own little bubble looking out. True reality was filmy. Obscured.

The world of a murder case was even murkier. Who was telling the truth? Who had a hidden motive?

David and a woman had been in Claire's house that night.

Soon after: one shot to the gut, followed by a kill shot to the head.

A woman and a man were in the woods, disposing of the body.

The Brett and Lisa theory bore some weight. They had a reason to shut David up, and Brett had a temper. Yet Preach couldn't wrap his mind around this angle. Lisa did not strike him as a murderer, and Brett had a size eleven shoe.

Had Claire fed him the information on Brett? Planted that receipt to deflect suspicion?

Preach's sticking point with Claire was motive. Why would she help Brett, or anyone else, kill her own son? He didn't believe the fit-of-rage theory after the argument with David, or the run-away-with-Brett motif. She didn't even love the man.

He knew he had a bias, a visceral rejection of the thought of a mother killing her own child. It was a crime against nature itself, contrary to the natural order of things. Or maybe human beings were slowly going insane, devolving. That would explain the daily news cycle.

Could it have been an accident, he wondered? Followed by a cover-up? Maybe David had gotten his hands on a gun, argued with his mom about it, and then shot himself? Then Claire, or even Brett—worried Claire might be blamed—had delivered a post-mortem shot to the head to deflect suspicion?

He was reaching.

The rainstorm passed. Back at the station, he spent the afternoon rereading his notes, typing up new ones, and issuing orders.

To Terry: Dig into the lives of all the key players. Bring me a fresh angle.

To Bill: Track down Nate Wilkinson like your pension depends on it.

To Chief Higgins: Request info from the Durham PD on Cobra and Los Viburos.

To himself: Talk to David's other friends, have a frank conversation with Claire, figure out what to say to Ari, and talk to Wade Fee. His old friend had his finger on the pulse of the social scene in Creekville and might have some insight.

First, though, Preach had something else to do. A task he had put off for much too long. It might be nothing, but he needed to scratch a growing itch in his skull about the hidden thread he suspected tied this case together.

After wrapping up at the office, he drove over to the Wild Oaks subdivision for the second time that day. This time, he parked at the entrance to a public trailhead two streets over from Claire's house, striding into the woods from a different entrance point. The rain started up again, slow and dreamy this time. The smell of fecund earth, of mushrooms and soil and pine needles, stuffed his nostrils.

As he suspected, the footpath fed into the larger trail that led to the murder site. Preach kept walking. He had put off finding out where these woods led for long enough. A few hundred yards in, the trail intersected another, and then another. Both times, he plowed ahead on the main trail, staying more or less in a straight line.

When the trail split in two, forcing him to break left or right, he paused, wondering if he should wait until the government offices opened on Monday so he could find a plot map. Waffling, he peered through the trees, and was about to turn around when he thought he glimpsed something off to the right. A smudge of gray that might be a house or a building. He kept going, guessing he had walked a half-mile at most. Probably less.

The rain slacked off, exposing a patch of blue sky for the first time all day. As if a fog had cleared, he lifted his face and reveled in the blaze of fall sunshine. In the better light, the smear of manmade gray clarified, breaking the spell, and he realized with a start what he was seeing. Not a hundred yards away from where he stood, the trail spilled into the unruly sprawl of a trailer park Preach recognized by its decrepit condition and by the water tower squatting in the distance behind it.

Carroll Street Homes.

23

During her stay in Greensboro, Blue lost count of all the restaurants where she applied for a job, including the cheap diner where she ate breakfast every day. Eight of the places said they were looking for immediate help. Two said to come back the following Monday.

Emboldened by her success, Blue returned to the motel and changed clothes for the evening: ripped jeans, white T-shirt, and a green denim jacket. She would never have gone out by herself in Chapel Hill or Durham. This was a new start for her. As far as anyone in Greensboro knew, she *was* a budding filmmaker.

Camera tucked safely into her bag, Blue stuck twenty dollars in her pocket and left the motel. It was 8:30 p.m. Crisp. Dark. A street full of shadows.

Nervous at how many sketchy people were idling by her motel, pimps and pushers and addicts, she set her jaw and strode forward, clutching her bag tight, daring anyone to challenge her.

Blue returned to the popular district unmolested and relaxed, basking in the vibrant culture. She browsed the narrow shelves of the local bookstore for a few minutes, enjoying the comics and the pulpy smell of books. Feeling better about her money situation, she had a burger and fries at a diner, followed by a chocolate latte at a place advertising "coffee and libations." People glanced at her camera when she set it on the table, causing her to preen.

After browsing the bulletin board for a room to rent, fantasizing about sharing a refurbished loft with fellow artists, she left the café and began shooting the city, emulating the professional filmmakers she had seen in documentaries and on YouTube videos: kneeling for a better angle at a street corner, jumping to stand on benches, backpedaling from a crowd of pedestrians, capturing the graffiti scrawled on the side of a train as it passed in the moonlight.

Once all the businesses had closed and the people cleared out, she started toward her motel, as pleased with herself as she had ever been. When she was a block away, she noticed a young Latino wearing a black down jacket, standing on the corner near the Piedmont Inn. He watched her approach and looked down at his cell phone. Then he stared at her again, more intently than before.

As if matching a face to a photo.

Blue stopped walking and noticed the colors on the bandana tied around his left ankle. Gang colors.

Los Viburos colors.

Blue turned and fled.

Behind her, she heard the gang member cursing in Spanish as he gave chase, and Blue had a surge of adrenaline that scooped out a pit in her stomach and made her feel as light as a balloon, except this balloon had arms and legs pumping furiously as she ran. For the first few moments, she thought she could outrun Usain Bolt.

Whipping left at an intersection and sprinting twenty yards down another empty street, she risked a glance back and saw the Latino rounding the corner, stopping to peer in both directions. He noticed her and started running again.

Blue didn't recognize the guy chasing her, but Cobra must have known she was gone. She guessed the assassin had gone to the trailer park to look for her that morning and put the word out when he didn't find her. Her stupid mother had probably *told* him she had skipped town.

Was there a bounty on her head? Dead or alive? Delivered in the back of a trunk or the bottom of a canal?

She didn't want to find out.

A few quick glances over her shoulder revealed that her pursuer was medium height and stocky. She was faster, barely, but maybe he had more stamina. When he had surprised her at the corner, she had run back toward the nice part of town, since it was the only area she knew. Yet even if she managed to double back to her hotel, they would just break inside or wait for her to leave.

Blue scanned her surroundings as she ran, desperate for a place to hide. She reached the corner of Elm and West McGee, hoping to see a pedestrian or two, but everyone had gone home for the night.

A fire escape caught her attention, followed by a van she could hide under. Both were too obvious. To her left, after the shops, the street spilled into the high-rise district. Nothing but wide streets and empty sidewalks in that direction. To her right, she saw darkness and the stultified shuffle of the homeless, the unforgiving bowels of the city.

Directly ahead, a block away, the road led through an underpass. She couldn't see beyond it and didn't want to get stuck inside. For all she knew, a dozen gang members were waiting on the other side of that tunnel.

She had no time to decide. Her choices were poor. On impulse, she darted toward the underpass, then turned left just before she reached it, at the next block. She swallowed as the scenery took a turn for the worse. Addicts and homeless men prowled the street ahead, zombies of the night waiting for a warm body to wander into their midst. They would give her up in a heartbeat. After debating slipping over a low brick wall and hiding on the patio of a brewery, she eyed the embankment to her right. A grassy slope led up to a set of train tracks that crossed over the underpass.

The embankment intrigued her. Whatever was up there, if anything, was invisible from the road. It meant she would no longer have the chance to run into more people or even a cop, but she had lost hope in that. Greensboro had died on the vine after the shops had closed.

With a quick glance to make sure her pursuer couldn't see her, she bit her lip and raced up the embankment, slipping in the mud and wet grass, planting her palms on the slope as she scurried up on all fours, terrified someone on the street would yell at her and alert the gang member.

At the top of the slope, she pushed through a low thicket with a homeless camp hidden inside: a few pairs of old shoes, empty bottles, and a filthy blanket that smelled like urine. Thank God it was deserted. After emerging from the copse of undergrowth, she clambered over two sets of railroad tracks, one of which led to the underpass, before pausing to absorb her surroundings.

What she saw caused a shiver of unease to whisk through her.

Three more sets of tracks curved into the darkness opposite the underpass. Two of them dead-ended not far from where she stood, as if chopped up long ago. On the far side of the tracks, a flat plain filled with gravel extended for a few hundred yards, ending at the back of a line of buildings. It was hard to tell in the moonlight, but they looked like warehouses.

She had stumbled onto some sort of nether world forgotten by the city below, an abandoned terminus of roads and civilization. Isolated, deserted, eerie.

The kind of place people went to disappear.

A brisk wind cut through her coat. She felt the chalky taste of gravel on her tongue. She debated crossing over the underpass and slipping back down the embankment, but that would expose her to view. She looked to her left and saw nothing but tracks and gravel. Too open. Behind her, in the distance, a handful of skyscrapers rose like giant candles in the darkness.

Someone grunted at the bottom of the embankment. Without thinking, Blue dashed across the tracks and fled across the gravel plain, away from the overpass. She had to find a place to hide before her pursuer reached higher ground.

Puddles of water pockmarked the gravel. An abandoned railcar emerged in the darkness. She eyed an old propane tank, a mound of silt, and the outline of a station house in the distance. As the rustling on the embankment grew louder, she noticed a cement platform off to her right, about fifty feet away.

The railcar was too obvious, the old station house too far away. She veered toward the platform, searching desperately for a place to hide. She could make a dash for the buildings on the other side of the gravel plain, but she would definitely be seen, and then it was a footrace with no clear destination. Her pursuer would probably just shoot her in the back.

About three feet high and hemmed in by railroad ties, the cement platform extended for a hundred feet on either side of her, parallel to the tracks. What in the world was its purpose? She began to lose hope when she saw a square of blackness at the base of the platform, deeper than the night, almost hidden inside a thicket of weeds and low shrubs.

Thorny branches clawed her face and hands as she fought through the undergrowth to view the hole. A square had been cut out of the cement, two feet by two feet. Just enough to squeeze through. She peered inside and saw a pool of filthy water that had collected at the bottom of the opening.

Footsteps crunched on gravel behind her. A quick glance over her shoulder revealed nothing. She still had time to act. Left with little choice, Blue pushed deeper into the thicket, wondering if she could squat where she was and stay hidden.

No. She had to take this all the way. With a shudder, she squeezed into the hole, alarmed to find that the freezing water at the bottom was more than a foot deep. With a shudder, she squatted and wrapped her knees with her hands, recoiling as the plastic baggies and urban scum floating in the water brushed against her. She tried not to think about the gross things that might live at the bottom.

As the footsteps drew closer, Blue huddled alone in the hole, terrified of being discovered, her shoes and jeans already soaked through, so cold she had to bite down to keep her teeth from chattering. She tried to think of a movie to help her deal with the situation, but no fictional world she summoned gave her any comfort.

Even the movies, she supposed, had their limits.

24

Carroll Street Homes.

It seemed that everywhere Preach turned, the trailer park had a way of popping up during the investigation.

Maybe it was coincidence that David was killed on the trail to Wild Oaks. Maybe it was a coincidence that the crime rate in the trailer park had skyrocketed in recent months. Maybe it was a coincidence that Nate Wilkinson and a number of Los Viburos gang members lived there.

Or maybe there was something to it.

It was Sunday, and Preach decided to take the day off. Not because he wanted a break, but because his head was too cluttered. Sometimes a little time away aided the creative process. Allowed him to gain a fresh perspective and connect some dots on a tough case.

The day had started well. After a late breakfast, he took a slow jog over to his gym, a tiny sweatbox filled with rusting weights and rubber mats covered in chalk from the power lifters. No mirrors. No fancy locker rooms. Not even a front desk. The place was owned by Ray Logan, Preach's old wrestling coach, and Ray only gave the key out to people he trusted. Preach had the gym to himself that morning.

After his workout, he stopped at Jimmy's during the church hour. These days, a good cup of coffee and quiet contemplation brought him closer to the divine than sixty minutes of manufactured calm. It was a little hard to be a cop and wade through the muck of the world, then sing 500-year-old hymns and pretend everything was all right, even for an hour. That life, brief and visceral, was in his rearview.

He still cared deeply about life's questions. He still talked to God and wondered if He was listening.

He just couldn't do church.

Try as he might, he failed to spend the whole day away from the case.

As he munched on an afternoon panini, still at Jimmy's, his thoughts turned to how to attack the trailer park angle. Should he interview the residents and see if he learned anything new? Shake down the members of Los Viburos, bring them in for questioning? Do the same with any members of Nate's gang he could find?

Those were all possibilities. But first, he decided to follow the money.

Everyone knew a property development war was being waged in Creekville. It was all over the news. With the explosive growth of the Research Triangle and the cities it served, developers were chomping at the bit to exploit the quirky little gem within spitting distance of Chapel Hill. No matter that fashioning that uncut gem into a garish piece of jewelry would ruin the charm. The money would switch hands, enrich the fat cats, and everyone else be damned.

Except Creekville was different. Over the years, its residents had fought tooth and nail to keep the charm and local businesses in place, and Carroll Street Homes had become ground zero in the war. Developers wanted bland, mixed-use condominiums within walking distance of downtown. The progressives in charge of the city council trumpeted the impoverished trailer park as a bastion of low-income housing.

Preach knew better. Carroll Street Homes was not a historic neighborhood with deep community ties. It was a crime-ridden blight that no child should grow up in. While he hardly sympathized with the real estate developers, he had no illusions about the proletariat sanctity of the trailer park.

In the news, an attorney named Brink Dickenson kept showing up. An African American with a prominent Raleigh firm, Brink represented a variety of high-end commercial builders. He was the one lobbying the Creekville City Council for a zoning change for Carroll Street Homes. The current restrictions greatly limited the commercial value of the property.

Preach drove to the office, logged in, and did some more research. He learned the Rathbun family owned a ton of property in Creekville.

Half the town, it seemed. This was no surprise. They had been petitioning the council for a zoning change for years.

But the Rathbuns did not own Carroll Street Homes. After failing to reach Brink Dickenson, Preach made a few calls to local real estate agents who always worked on Sunday. He learned that Carroll Street Homes had been a coveted piece of real estate for some time. The previous owner, a crotchety old farmer named Homer Atkins, had owned the land for decades, always refusing to sell. Eight months ago, when he started to develop dementia, he finally entertained offers. A bidding war ensued. In the end, Homer sold the property for three million dollars to Edmund Pettis Properties.

On the one hand, three million dollars seemed like a huge sum of money for a dilapidated trailer park. On the other hand, the park comprised nearly five acres in the shadow of downtown.

But what did Preach know about such things? Almost nothing, so he asked the agents and learned the price was a premium. Speculation based on future profit in the case of a zoning reassignment. He also learned that Edmund Pettis Properties had outbid a "prominent local family" the detective assumed was the Rathbuns.

Preach assumed Edmund Pettis Properties was a rich local developer and was surprised to find that no one by that name lived in the area. In fact, a Google search revealed that Edmund Pettis was the name of the infamous bridge in Selma, Alabama, that Martin Luther King had marched across in 1965.

Odd.

Preach dug deeper.

Using a legal research tool to which the station had limited access, he learned that Edmund Pettis Properties was a subsidiary of New Hawk Holdings Inc. One of many subsidiaries, in fact. The name struck a chord. Preach thought he had heard it before. It took him a moment, but it came to him just as he finished typing the name in the search engine, and the results confirmed it: New Hawk Holdings Inc. was owned by Bentley Montgomery.

The witness in Ari's murder case.

The same man who gave her the shivers at night.

Preach let out a deep breath. *What in the world*?

The connection between his case and Ari's caused a wave of emotion to flood through him. He knew he had to reach out to her but wasn't sure how. What should he say? Did she even want to hear from him? Should he give her more time?

He debated calling her, then decided the next conversation should be in person. After running a hand through his hair, going back and forth as to what to do, he texted to ask if she would meet him for dinner the next day at a cozy little French bistro in downtown Creekville. Their favorite place for a nice evening out.

By the time he fell asleep that night, aimlessly flipping through channels as his stomach churned with worry, he had yet to receive a reply.

25

On Monday morning, as Ari waited in her office for Bentley to arrive with his mysterious witness, she had a hard time concentrating on the case.

I need you, Claire's text had said.

I need you.

I need you.

Ari couldn't stop saying it in her head.

It was such an intimate turn of phrase.

Had something physical happened between Preach and Claire? She honestly wasn't sure, and that scared her. She thought she had known him. She really did. But how could things have progressed to the point where Claire felt comfortable sending that text?

The one thing Ari *did* know for sure was that this woman had designs on her man.

Claire had just lost a son. Ari truly felt sorry for her.

But that didn't make the words disappear.

The door opened and Ari forced her feelings away, still not sure how to reply to Preach's text from the night before. She thought it would be hard to change gears, but once Bentley entered the room and Ari reminded herself that she was pursuing justice for a girl with no voice, her own problems fell away, and she let herself sink into the case.

A young African American woman dressed in high heels and a tight green sweater dress followed Bentley into the room. The woman had straight hair with obvious extensions, nervous eyes, and a svelte figure marred by a pouch of loose flesh around her stomach.

"Morning, counselor," Bentley said.

"Good morning."

He held out a palm toward the woman. "Ari Hale, Desiree Brown."

"Hi, Desiree," Ari said, with a warm smile. "Thank you for coming. Would you like some coffee? Water?"

"Nope. I mean, no thank you." Desiree took a seat next to Bentley, her hands fidgeting atop the table.

"Just relax," Ari said warmly. "We're on the same side here."

"I'm not so used to law firms."

"That's okay, because this is the prosecutor's office, not a private firm. We serve the people and make way less money."

"Go on," Bentley said. "Tell Ms. Hale what you saw."

Ari didn't like the way Bentley addressed Desiree as if she were beneath him. The dynamic felt less like a pair of lovers and more like an employer-employee relationship, or master and servant.

Following gentle prodding by Ari, Desiree proceeded to relate the same story that Bentley had told about the night of the murders. Throughout, she would glance at him for support or approval. A few times, when she hesitated, he put words in her mouth that she repeated verbatim.

"You have to let her talk," Ari said. "I've heard your story. I need to hear hers."

He put his hands up. "Just trying to help."

Once Desiree finished, Ari asked a few background questions. Normally she did this first, and she wished she had taken better control of the interview. "Where are you from, Desiree?"

"East Durham." She pronounced it *Durm*.

"You still live there?"

"My whole life."

"What do you do for a living?"

Desiree lowered her eyes and mumbled something.

"Sorry?"

"She said customer service," Bentley said. "She works in customer service."

"For who?" Ari said, looking straight at Desiree.

"For me," Bentley said.

Ari leveled her stare at Bentley. "I need Desiree to answer the questions. Ms. Brown, do you work for Mr. Montgomery?"

"Yeah."

"How long have you worked for him?"

Desiree's eyes slunk to her left. "A while."

"Two days, two months, two years?"

"About two years, I s'pose. That about right."

"What exactly do you do for Mr. Montgomery?"

When Desiree didn't respond, Bentley said, "She's a secretary."

"Desiree," Ari said, "would you mind stepping out of the room for a minute? There's a bench in the hallway."

Desiree looked relieved beyond measure to be excused. Once she left, Ari said, "Is she a prostitute or a drug mule?"

Bentley chuckled. "A fine young black woman walks in, doesn't speak so well, a little nervous, and y'all think she's hooking?"

"Is she?"

"Why don't you ask her?"

"I don't want to embarrass her."

"She has a legitimate role in my company. It's all on the books."

Ari sighed and put her palms on the table. "Bentley, do you understand that I'm on your side? I want your testimony to work, and I want Desiree to be a reliable witness. But these stunts you're pulling . . . opposing counsel will *eat you alive*."

Bentley was unfazed. "We'll see about that in court, won't we?"

"You're not hearing me. We won't *get* to court."

"Desiree's a secretary. That's all you need to know."

"Unfortunately, the legal system doesn't work that way. You've heard of cross-examination?"

"Even if Desiree is what you think she is, that doesn't mean she isn't a secretary too. You think she doesn't have two eyes and a mouth? That she can't see things like any other citizen? We have a word for that on the street, counselor."

"It's about her reliability as a witness. It's about her testimony that sounds like you fed it to her a few minutes before you walked in here."

Bentley's large head wove back and forth, chiding. "What's the line on plea bargains these days? Ninety-five percent? Ninety-seven?"

"Sorry?"

"You know why so many black people take the plea, counselor? Plenty of them could go free at trial, with a fair shake. No one in the hood goes to trial because black people don't beat juries."

Ari held her palms up. "What does this have to do with Desiree?"

He pointed a finger at her. "Because you're part of the problem, whether you admit it to yourself or not. You think you're all hip, with your tattoos and your social justice blurbs, but you're a prosecutor. The criminal justice system in this country, the whole prison-industrial complex, is a goddamn human rights violation. Prison is hell on earth, and your office sends black men to jail like they're going off to boarding school. They're treated worse than dogs, worse than lab rats, and sent back out to fail. And a branded felon? There's a name for that in this country. It's called Jim Crow. Can't vote. Can't get a job. What are they supposed to do, counselor? Go back and bring what they learned inside to the ghetto, that's what. You think Desiree is uncomfortable in this room and won't look good in front of a jury? You ever stop to wonder why? Desiree has never left *East Durham*. A trip to Chapel Hill would be like Disneyland for her. She vacations to Walmart and the 7-Eleven."

Ari leaned forward. "Why do you care so much about this case? About putting Ronald Jackson away?"

"Because he's part of the problem. He corrupts our youth. *He* needs to be in prison."

"And you don't?" she said, unable to help herself.

"This case isn't about me," he said quietly. "Desiree's telling the truth, she just doesn't say it very well."

He moved for the door, and Ari followed him out, wanting to speak with Desiree alone this time. But when she opened the door and peered down the hallway, there was no sign of her. Ari thought she might have gone to the restroom, but she never appeared, and when Bentley tried to reach her on her phone, she wouldn't pick up.

"I have to talk to her again," Ari said.

"I'll find her."

"We may not have time. Ronald's attorney wants him released yesterday."

"What do you mean? You have two witnesses."

Ari leveled her stare at him. "Neither you nor Desiree saw the actual crime. And I haven't decided whether I can use either of you."

"Ronald's a monster," Bentley said, unusually somber. "I'll get Desiree back here, I promise."

Bentley gave Desiree's phone number to Ari. She tried to reach her at lunchtime, and then during the afternoon, but Desiree never answered her calls. Just after five, while Ari was reading through police reports on a few other cases, a call came in from Meredith Verela, Ronald's defense attorney.

"Why hasn't your office dropped the case?" she asked Ari, after a curt greeting. Ari sensed Meredith viewed her as an untested adversary, not worthy of her time.

"There's another witness involved who just came to our attention."

"What? Who?"

"A friend of Bentley's who was with him that night. I'd prefer to keep her name private until we talk to her further."

"I thought Bentley was alone that night."

"So did we. It's a woman who, as he puts it, is not his girlfriend."

Whether true or not, talking about a betrayal caused the wound in her own life to open wider. Where was Preach today, she wondered? Was he with Claire?

"So you're supplementing your drug-dealing witness with a lover he's already lied about seeing? Your witness is a joke."

"We need to talk to her before we decide anything," Ari said, thinking Meredith was right, but that Ronald Jackson was guilty as hell. She just couldn't let the case go.

Also, she didn't want to let the older woman steamroll her. She had to talk all this through with Fenton, and he would ultimately make the decision, but Ari had to learn to stand her ground.

"I'll give you until Friday, and then I'm filing a motion to dismiss. With costs."

"What's your defense theory?" Ari asked, changing gears. She didn't want to pin herself down with a response. "About what happened that night?

Meredith hesitated, no doubt weighing what to tell her. Anything she said, Ari knew, would serve her own purposes. "It's very simple. Ronald said he arrived after the two victims were already dead. He has no idea who killed them. Off the record, he thinks Bentley is setting him up."

"I see. And you believe that?"

"Friday, Ari. Final deadline."

26

On Monday, Ari still hadn't responded to Preach's text. There was nothing he could do to force her, so he threw himself into the case to occupy his mind. He wanted to talk to Chief Higgins, but she was at a conference in Raleigh for the day.

Deciding to tie up some loose ends, Preach paid house visits to two of David's closest friends on the football team, Elliot Jacobson and Fisher Star. It was an in-service day for the public schools, and he found them both at home without their parents. He decided to go ahead and speak to them, though when they opened the door, he asked his questions from the porch. Both lived in the same neighborhood, a wooded enclave of renovated bungalows just south of downtown.

Elliot, a brawny redhead with a cleft chin and pointed ears, bawled as soon as Preach mentioned David. After calming the kid down, Preach learned no new information, except that David had not been involved with drugs. In fact, Elliott went out of his way to convince the detective of this.

Why bring it up? Preach wanted to know.

"You know," Elliott said, suddenly uncomfortable. "That's what everyone thinks at school. That drugs were involved."

"And you don't?"

"I *know* they weren't. Not Davey. He drank a bit, sure. Who doesn't? But he wouldn't touch drugs, not even when everyone else at the party—" he broke off, realizing he was talking to a police officer. "Anyway, he always said his mind was fucked up enough—excuse my language—and he didn't want to go there." He put his hand over his heart. "I swear, man. No one partied with him like I did. He was super clean."

Preach believed him. Or at least believed that David, if he was taking drugs, kept it from Elliott.

"What about selling them?" Preach asked. "Making a little money on the side? Even if he wasn't using?"

"No way, man. Why risk a future like his? He didn't really care about money, anyway. Not like that."

"What did he care about?"

Elliott thought for a minute. "Girls," he said, smiling as he wiped away another tear. "And football. That was pretty much it."

That was pretty much all he told *you* about, Preach thought.

Except for his African American heritage and orange tennis shoes, Fisher Star was a clone of Elliott Jacobson: muscular, preppy, polite, easygoing but one-dimensional. He, too, was crushed by David's murder. While he confirmed that Claire's son never touched drugs, he had nothing new to add.

By the time Preach returned to the office, just before 5 p.m., Ari still hadn't replied to his text. Her silence had opened a sinkhole inside him that crumbled wider and wider with each passing minute.

"Got a sec, Detective?"

Preach looked up from his desk and saw Terry Haskins standing at the entrance to the cubicle, carrying his vinyl messenger bag and offering a manila folder to the detective.

"What's this?" Preach asked.

Inside the folder, he found three pieces of paper. The first contained two photocopied images: a credit card slip and a sales receipt, both from Domino's. The second was a screenshot of Lisa Waverly dressed in a lacy nightgown on a website called Kixxxstarter.

The final image appeared to be a snapshot of a chat board for NC State grads.

"Check the dates," Terry said.

Preach found the time stamps and saw they were all from the same night. Or early morning, to be exact. "October 3," he murmured.

"Domino's delivered a pizza to Lisa Waverly's house at 12:30 a.m.," Terry said. "The delivery driver remembered seeing them both dressed in bathrobes. He said they looked like they had just gotten out of the shower."

"Need I ask what Kixxxstarter is?"

"It's the X-rated version of Tinder. Lisa posted a new photo—that one right there—at one fifteen in the morning."

"Her username is Hot for Teacher?" Preach said in disbelief, looking at the caption.

"I'm afraid so."

Preach shuffled to the third piece of paper. Halfway down the page, he saw the username BMoreland1 in a string of scattershot commentary that included the upcoming Wolfpack basketball season, gerrymandering, and the best route to Myrtle Beach. He looked up. "Brett commented at 1:45 a.m. None of this proves they weren't in the woods that night, but it's kind of hard to squeeze in a murder between pizza, sex, and chat boards."

"My thoughts as well," Terry said.

"Even if they had the time, it would take a couple of stone-cold sociopaths to murder a high school kid, take him across town and dump him, then go home and carry on like that. I've seen stranger things, but . . ." He set the papers down with a sigh. "Regardless of the affair, I think Brett's in love with Claire. And Lisa . . . I just don't see her as a killer."

"You want me to stay on them? Or move to something else?"

"Give them another shift, then check back in. Good work, Terry."

The junior officer tipped his wool cap and left for the night. After another hour of paperwork, Preach noticed the chief walk in. Before he could head her way, his cell buzzed, and he jerked his phone out of his pocket as fast as a gunslinger under fire. His stomach lurched when he saw Ari's name.

<I don't think dinner is a good idea. Café Driade at eight? One drink.>

At least she hadn't ignored him. He held the phone in his palm a few moments before he replied.

<Okay. See you then>

Before he could process the exchange, Chief Higgins stepped into the hallway, curled a finger at him, and retreated into her office. Preach followed her inside and slumped in the chair across from her desk.

"Do you mind?" he asked, picking up her yin-yang stress ball.

Her eyebrows rose. "That bad?"

"Just thought I'd give it a try."

"It beats alcoholism. I gave that a try once. Or twice."

Preach grunted. "I'm glad they were failed attempts."

"Oh, I was quite good at it. What's on your mind?"

As he caught her up on his research, she steepled her pointer fingers and tapped them against her mouth, making *mmm-hmm* sounds as she listened.

When he finished, she said, "This Bentley character owns the development company that bought Carroll Street Homes?"

"That's right."

She unfurled her fingers to pick up a pen. "I was at Durham PD today."

"I thought you had a conference in Raleigh?"

"I swung by Durham on the way home, said hi to a few people. I politic every now and then, you know."

He put a hand over his mouth in mock disbelief. "Say it ain't so."

"I know, I know. The price of fame."

"What'd they have to say?"

She rubbed her thumb against the pen, as if it were a replacement for the stress ball. "Los Viburos has been acting strange for a gang lately. Their activity is more methodical than usual. Durham thinks they might be taking orders from someone. As in, someone smarter than your typical gang leader."

"That's odd. Unless they're getting paid."

"Exactly. Gangs can hire out like any merc force. I'm not sure I'd ever turn my back on them if I hired them, but hey, that goes for the whole criminal world."

"Who does Durham think they're taking orders from?"

She leaned back in her seat. The setting sun in the window behind her mirrored the grease-fire hue of her hair. "They don't know."

"I'm not sure I'd call the increase in crime at Wild Oaks methodical, if that's what you're thinking."

"No," she agreed. "Unless maybe it is."

"How so?"

"I don't know. That's your job."

He nodded, contemplative. "I'll keep it in mind."

"So who do you have for this? If you had to say right now?"

"I don't really like anyone for it," he said slowly. "At least not anyone in play."

"You didn't like anyone for the last murder, either, if I recall." She gave him a thin smile. "Except for one person."

"Don't remind me."

"You think you'll ever live that down?"

"Not in this building," he said.

"Good answer. What about Claire? She seems the best fit so far." The chief folded her hands on the desk and leaned forward. "I've heard about your past with her. Are you sure you're seeing clearly, Joe? Do we need to bring in SBI?"

"I'm fine," he said, more roughly than he intended. "There's no motive. Why would a mother kill her son?"

"Do you think mothers need different motives from other criminals?"

"Yes. I do."

The chief sat back. "It happens, you know," she said after a moment. "Murder-suicides, mothers drowning their babies after they're born, leaving them in dumpsters or hot cars."

"Those are usually mental health issues."

"Not always."

"Claire raised David by herself for *seventeen years*. I just don't . . ." He cupped the back of his neck and let out a sigh, knowing his emotions were clouding his judgment.

Instead of responding, the chief put a palm out, and he handed over the stress ball. On his way out he saw her kneading it angrily in her palm, over and over, as she stared out the window.

A short while later, after showering and changing into jeans and a gray sweater, Preach arrived at Café Driade fifteen minutes before eight o'clock. On spring and summer nights, the patio of the little café on the outskirts of Chapel Hill was lit with strings of golden lights, the forest warm and thick all around. During law school, Ari used to virtually camp out here, and the two of them had spent many a weekend morning sipping coffee on the birdsong-filled patio or in the cozy stucco interior, ensconced in a book or a magazine, surrounded by local art and the smell of roasting coffee.

Jimmy's was his place, and Café Driade was hers. While they had enjoyed them both together, he knew her choice of venue was a statement.

The night was chilly, so the interior was packed, and he couldn't find an open table. He ordered a beer and hunkered down in his overcoat on the back patio, hoping a seat would open up. Ten minutes after eight, Ari walked through the back door holding a glass of red wine.

"Hi," he said, as she approached.

"Hi."

"I've been waiting for a table. We can stand inside if you prefer."

"I'll last for one drink." She set her wine down and buttoned her knee-length, plum wool coat before she sat. Beneath the coat, she wore a cream-colored shirt, dark slacks, and black boots with high heels. She looked stunning, though he wondered if her extra makeup—she usually wore very little—was a statement of some sort.

"How are you?" he said quietly.

"Busy."

"I hear that." He took a long swallow of beer. "Listen, Ari, I really wanted to see you. But I also wanted to run something by you. About work."

Her eyebrows rose. "Yours or mine?"

"A possible connection between cases."

She swirled her wine, crossed her legs, and leaned back. "Work first."

Her guarded body language spoke volumes. He wanted to reach out and take her hands in his, but instead he told her what he had discovered about Bentley's purchase of Carroll Street Homes. "Do you know anything about this?"

"I'd have told you if I did," she said. "I do know he has multiple business interests."

"Are they legit?"

"As far as I can tell. I'm sure if we dug deep enough we'd find irregularities, but his business empire isn't our focus. What are you thinking?"

"I'm thinking there's a lot of noise around this trailer park," he said. "I'm thinking David was a few hundred yards from it when he was killed."

"He was also close to his home. It could easily be a coincidence."

He took a sip of beer, the bare trees watching in silence from the forest edge. "Do you remember my favorite quote on coincidences?"

"Remind me."

"G. K. Chesterton said they're spiritual puns."

The hint of a smile lifted her lips, quickly withdrawn.

"Your opinion on Bentley stands?" he asked. "That he's bad news?"

She shivered into her coat. "He's one of the most manipulative people I've ever talked to. Are you going to interview him?"

"Probably. First I want to probe this angle a bit more. I have a feeling cornering him with what I've got right now would be pointless."

"You're probably right."

"Durham PD mentioned someone might be pulling the strings of Los Viburos. You think it might be Bentley?"

"I wouldn't put it past him. Even if he is . . . what does this have to do with David?"

"I don't know," he admitted.

"Do you think he might have been working for him?"

"Based on the people I've talked to, I'd have to say no. But you never know. And that second gunshot, the one to the head . . . it smacks of a gang."

Her eyes sparked. "What if he stumbled onto something in the woods that night?"

"Something unrelated that got him killed?"

She nodded, and he felt the familiar tingling spread through him whenever they brainstormed a case together. He wanted so much to reach out to her, take her hands in his, but he knew she would pull away.

"Maybe David went into the woods for some reason," she continued, "or even to the trailer park. Is there a girl there he knows?"

"Good question. If he did go there, maybe he ran into Nate on his home turf, or even stumbled into a drug deal." He was starting to like this line of reasoning. "Maybe he *was* with Claire in the study that night, and maybe she *was* too drugged up to remember. Maybe none of that was sinister at all, and I've been making all the wrong assumptions."

When he mentioned Claire, Ari drew back in her seat, and he instantly regretted it. They drank in silence for a few minutes, until the silence grew uncomfortable.

"We could have had this conversation over the phone," she said finally. "About work."

"You're right. I wanted to see you."

"Why?"

"To tell you I'm sorry."

She pursed her lips and said, "You're investigating her, Joe. Have you considered the fact that you might have a duty to recuse yourself?"

"I'm not compromised."

"I would argue otherwise."

"Her son was murdered. She needs me."

As soon as he said it, Ari's face crumbled, and he wanted to flog himself for his choice of words. While he fumbled for something to say, her expression hardened, and she drained the last of her wine.

"That's not what I meant," he said. "I'm the most experienced homicide officer we have. The *case* needs me. That's all."

She stood. "I think it's exactly what you meant."

"Don't go."

"Why shouldn't I? You've already admitted you're attracted to her."

"We can't help who we respond to in that way. There are millions of people in the world who physically draw us. You're so much more to me than a simple attraction, Ari. A universe more."

A teardrop formed in the corner of her eye. Her voice never quavered as she wiped it away. "I can accept that. And I don't think you were cheating. But I do think you were flirting, and the main thing . . . I'm just not convinced you weren't seeking something I haven't been giving you. And that maybe I never can."

He said quietly, "What can I do to convince you?"

"I don't know."

As she started to walk away, he rose. "Ari."

She turned.

"Stay with me tonight."

"I can't, Joe."

As she moved out of the soft glow of the patio, swallowed by the night, he felt something break apart inside him, as if a foreign substance had just dislodged.

And he knew in his heart that no matter what happened between them in the future, things would never be the same.

27

The next morning, as Preach arrived at the station with his cup of coffee from Jimmy's, he saw Officer Wright stepping out of his car in the parking lot.

"Detective," Bill said, hustling to catch up with Preach on the stairs. The burst of exertion made the older officer red-faced and a little breathless.

Preach held the door for him, hoping Bill never had to chase down a criminal. "Did you find Nate?"

"Not yet, but I talked to someone at the trailer park."

Preach perked up. "Who?"

"I put the squeeze on a high school kid I busted for meth last year. Piece of shit named Adam Krusky. Kid couldn't go clean for a week if his life depended on it. Could barely keep still when we talked."

"He's still a kid, Bill."

"Oh yeah? You know what kids are into these days? I swear, if I see one more goddamn punk covered in tattoos, standing on a corner and—"

"*Bill.* What'd he say?"

The older officer looked flustered and eager to please, as if trying to compensate for his earlier screwup. "He hasn't seen Nate in a few days, doesn't know why."

"I heard Nate has a gang of some sort. Do you know if that's true?"

"He's got a posse of white kids in the trailer park called the Rat Fuckers. Real classy, huh?"

"And?"

"According to Adam, after I threatened to haul his ass to juvie again, he told me Nate's been pulling off petty crimes for years. Small stuff like hitting unlocked cars at night. But lately he's been stepping up his game."

"Such as?"

"The only thing Adam knew for sure—and he didn't want to tell me—is that Nate's running drugs for Los Viburos."

Preach whistled. "How sure are you about that?"

"Kid's about as trustworthy as a pawn broker with the rent due. I believe him on this, though. He wants to stay out of juvie."

"Does he have any idea where to find Nate?"

"Nope. I get the impression Adam's fallen out of favor. He did say Nate's still seeing Alana."

"No surprise there. Good find, Bill. Stay on it."

The noose was growing tighter, Preach could feel it.

Nate ran drugs for Los Viburos. Both Nate and the gang were connected to the trailer park. David and Nate had bad blood between them.

Had Claire's son, angry after their clash at home, gone to pick a fight with Nate at Carroll Street Homes? Had someone intercepted him on the way or met him at the park and taken him back to the woods? Had someone from the gang fired the head shot? Who had been the woman in the woods? Alana?

Preach felt sure he was still missing something that tied it all together. On a hunch he decided to pay a visit to his old pal Wade Fee. The two of them had grown up together and were inseparable until Preach's senior year, when he had cut ties with his old crew, Wade Fee included, and joined a church. That led to his brief stint as a preacher, a few tough years as a prison chaplain, and then a period of soul searching that eventually led to the Atlanta PD.

Preach regretted none of those choices. They all added up to the man he was today. If the day came when he thought he was no longer fit to be a detective, then he would move on from that too. Maybe he would retire to the forest one day, surround himself with grandchildren and logs to split and a pile of good books.

But that day was a long way off, and he had a murderer to catch.

In the parking lot of the Rabbit Hole Café, he found Wade's car: a restored, maroon and white '57 Chrysler New Yorker. After Ricky's death, Wade had taken Preach's abrupt switch the hardest. Unable to express what he was feeling and sure his friend would not understand, Preach had never discussed his decision. It was simply no more parties, no more hell-raising together.

Even today, he felt as if the air was not fully cleared between them. They had crafted an uneasy peace, one of mutual respect and a shared past, but he knew their childhood bond was severed forever.

As far as Preach knew, Wade still worked at the Rabbit Hole, an eclectic little café popular with hipsters and college students. He used to supplement his income by running minor drugs on the side. Preach hoped he had stayed straight.

On his way inside, he spotted Wade on the back patio by himself, smoking a cigarette and staring into the pines. As Preach made his way over, crunching on the wood chips covering the ground, Wade turned and raised the tip of his cigarette in greeting.

"Afternoon, Joe." Wade's voice was a soft growl. "Been a while."

"How you been?"

"Peachy, man. Just peachy."

"You on break?"

"Yep."

Wade's thinning black hair and handlebar moustache, twisted at the ends, had not changed since the last time Preach had seen him. He was also wearing rimless glasses, Carhartt work pants, and his hipster T-shirt du jour: an image of Sheryl Lee with the caption, "Who Killed Laura Palmer?"

"Can you talk for a sec?"

"Anything for you, buddy," Wade said, checking his watch. "I can take five more."

"Thanks." Preach sat across from him on the picnic bench. "How connected are you to the scene these days?"

"And here I thought you were gonna ask me to join a bowling

league." Wade turned his head to blow smoke away from the detective. "The scene? What scene you talking about?"

"The drug scene."

"Ah." He looked away and said, with a touch of bitterness, "I'm not in the game anymore."

"I'm glad to hear it. Truly."

"Yeah. Well."

"I understand you're out, but word still gets around."

Wade took another puff. "Not sure I follow. And not sure I want to. Shoot me straight, why don't you."

Preach spread his hands. "Fair enough. You've heard about David Stratton's murder?"

"The football kid? Sure. Murder's still big news in this town. You're working it?"

"I am. I assume you haven't heard anything relevant?"

"Nope."

"What about David Stratton? Any idea if he was selling? Using?"

"No idea. Even if I was back in, I'd never sell to kids."

"Ever heard the name Nate Wilkinson?"

"Nope."

"Okay. Okay." Preach weighed how much he should disclose versus his need for information. "You've heard of Los Viburos?"

"Sure."

"What else do you know about them?"

Wade shrugged. "Not much. Like I said, it's past my time."

"Ever heard of a guy named Bentley Montgomery?"

"Out of Durham?"

"That's right."

Wade's eyes narrowed. "Him I've heard of. He's supposed to be real bad news."

"What do you know about him?"

"I don't *know* anything. Just that a few guys from the old life mention his name now and again. I try not to listen too hard these days."

"What do they say?"

"That he wants to be king and will do anything for the throne." Wade put his hands up. "I don't know specifics, so don't ask."

"Does he give orders to Los Viburos?"

"No idea. Listen, man—" he checked his watch, "I should get back. I'd help you if I could, but you're barking up the wrong tree here."

"Can you point me to someone who might know something else?"

Wade smirked, and Preach knew he had crossed a line, asking him to rat out his contacts who were still in the business. That said, he didn't have time to dance around his old friend's loyalties to his criminal connections. "Wade?"

"No, Joe. I can't." He stood, picked up the pack of Marlboro Lights, and rolled it into the sleeve of his T-shirt.

Preach rose as well. "Thanks anyway," he said, a little coldly.

Wade hesitated, fiddling with the end of his moustache. "There is one thing."

"I'm all ears."

"Rumor has it there's a new player in town, in control of the local product. Has been for six months or so."

Preach had heard of no such thing. Then again, someone that new might not have hit the Creekville police radar. Or they might be good at staying hidden. "How firm is this rumor?"

Wade looked him in the eye. "Firm."

"Who is he?"

"I don't know. But you're a sexist pig, Joe, because it's not a *he*. It's a *she*."

Preach felt a little wobbly. "A she," he repeated. "What's her name?"

"I just told you I don't know. The guys I mentioned, they don't know either, or I'd have heard. My guess? She's a level or two above their pay grade and reports in to Durham. Maybe to this Bentley guy."

Preach stood still atop the wood chips, trying to process what he had just heard.

"Joe? I gotta get back."

"Ask around, okay? If you get a name, or anything, let me know. I swear it won't come from you."

"Sure. Hey, it's been real. We should do this more often."

Preach didn't respond. He didn't even notice when Wade stepped aside, leaving the detective alone on the patio as a breeze stirred, causing a patch of colored leaves to swirl like faerie dust in the parking lot. All Preach could think about was that a woman might be running the drug show in Creekville. A woman who might be the missing connection between Nate and Los Viburos and Carroll Street Homes, a woman who could have made the footprint under the leaf pile in the woods the night David was killed, a woman who Sharon Tisdale might have seen with David in his house that night.

A woman who might have killed David for a very different reason than Preach had suspected so far. A reputable citizen with a secret identity, a drug queen David might have threatened to reveal to the world.

Whether Claire was the guilty party or not, the logic behind her primary defense had just crumbled.

Now she had a motive.

28

A few hours after Blue had heard the last of the footsteps crunching on gravel near her hiding place, cramped and numb from the cold, she had wriggled out of that god-awful hole inside the concrete platform and spent the rest of the night concealed inside the muddy thicket. She had kept her camera dry and had fifty dollars in her pocket, but she knew she dared not return to her hotel.

When the sun rose on Greensboro, she finally descended the embankment and emerged into the city, miserable and starving and exhausted to the bone. She had to get out of town and decided to risk a bus. No one would pick her up on the side of the road looking like she did.

During her overnight ordeal, she had had plenty of time to think through her options. No way could she go home yet, and she was almost out of money. Hungry. Desperate.

The way she saw it, she had three choices. The first two were hide out on the streets or find a homeless shelter to hole up in. She quickly discarded living on the streets. It was just too dangerous, and she would probably starve or freeze to death. No, that was the absolute last resort. A homeless shelter was a much better idea, except for the other creeps who would be living there, and a higher risk that Los Viburos would find her. Shelters were full of drug people, any of who would give up her location for a single hit.

Her third option was very different and, in some ways, frightened her even more than the other two.

After her father had left, once her mother had realized he wasn't coming back and hurled his belongings into a dumpster, Blue had pawed through the trash and found a photo album from her father's childhood. She even found a letter from a cousin addressed to her father at his old house.

She still knew the address. Her father had grown up in Old Fort,

North Carolina, a speck on the map in the shadow of the Blue Ridge Mountains, not far from Asheville. Her father's childhood home was a mythical town to which she had never been, her last place of refuge.

Blue had enough money to get there. She could take a bus to her father's hometown and beg one of her relatives to take her in.

Yet what if they rejected her?

That was something Blue wasn't sure she would survive.

After scurrying to the Greensboro central bus station, she checked the timetables and learned her father's hometown was so small there wasn't even a bus stop. The closest town was Black Mountain, a touristy spot about ten miles from Old Fort on the way to Asheville. The lack of bus service made her decision easier. She could go to Black Mountain to get away from Greensboro, then decide whether or not to visit her father's family.

She bought a one-way ticket to Black Mountain and a cup of coffee, then hunkered down in the most secluded corner of the station she could find. During the wait, she didn't spot any gang members. With any luck, they would bank on her returning to her hotel or running back to Creekville.

Though the wait had her biting her nails to the flesh, by the time she boarded her bus, just after noon, she was sure no one suspicious was watching her.

A few hours later, when Blue arrived in Black Mountain, she stood on the sidewalk and took a few minutes to inhale the fresh mountain air, eying the sweep of shaggy peaks that cradled the town. It was beautiful, an entirely different world from the Piedmont. As if the rise in elevation had also raised her station in life, or at least lifted her spirits. Yes, that was it. The change was internal. The mountains inspired her, transformed her into a more soulful being. She already felt closer to her father.

After spending a couple of bucks at Goodwill on a clean pair of jeans and a Montreat sweatshirt, she bought two hot dogs for a dollar at a gas station. There wasn't much to the town that she could see, a few blocks of quaint shops and restaurants, but there was lots of activity. Tourists and hikers and parents walking their kids to school. It was a bucolic place, a place out of time, and she loved it at first sight.

After freshening up as best she could in a public restroom, she sat cross-legged in a public park full of gnarled old trees and debated what to do. She supposed she could walk the ten miles to Old Fort. How long would that take her? Half a day? It didn't sound very enticing. She could also try to thumb a ride, or maybe she had enough money left for a taxi. No—she wasn't spending the last of her funds on that. She would need those dollars. And hitchhiking was dangerous. She had pushed her luck once already.

Blue sat in the park for a very long time, knowing she was stalling, enjoying the crisp mountain air and the ancient wisdom of the trees. At the end of the day, she trudged toward a homeless shelter she had noticed on the ride in, nervous about spending the night in such a despondent place, but terrified even more by the thought of knocking on the door of the house where her father used to live.

29

"Christo, pass the salt please."

"Yes, Mama. For the beans?"

His mother reached over to pat his hand. "They just need a little help. Thank you for cooking."

Christo Emilio Rivero, known on the street as Cobra, reached across the kitchen table to pass the salt to his mother. His father had died on the family's harrowing flight from Honduras when Christo was ten years old. Like the buried remnants of a terrible nightmare, he retained only flashes of the journey: leaving his childhood village in tears; an exhausting march through a mosquito-infested jungle with armed men prodding them along; eating insects and roots and hoping not to get sick from the water; the screams of women and young girls at night; his father never leaving Christo or his mother alone during the day and tying them all together with a belt while sleeping; Christo understanding nothing except the village had no work and they were going to a paradise called *Los Estados Unidos*; the hiss of rattlesnakes and bitterly cold nights in the Mexican desert; feeling as if he would die of suffocation when stuffed with thirty people in the back of a stifling hot truck for eighteen hours during the border crossing.

Most of all, he remembered the shootout with the group of armed Latino men in a small town in Texas, soon after he and his family had crawled out of the truck. Later, he had learned that a local gang had not liked the fact that the handlers for Christo's village had tried to cut out the middlemen. Back then, he knew only that one of the bullets had caught his beloved father in the throat, and he had bled to death on a cracked piece of asphalt in their brand-new country. Forced into another truck, Christo had no idea what had happened to his father's body.

He could never get the beans right. Though he worked odd hours and sometimes gave his mother a break by cooking lunch, the main reason he tried to make it home as often as possible was the curly-headed boy sitting to his right.

His name was Hugo, after the grandfather he had never known.

Every now and then, Cobra liked to read books for laymen on theoretical physics. Books like *The Elegant Universe* and *A Brief History of Time*. He didn't understand all the concepts, and certainly not the math, but he was fascinated by the universe and all its inconceivably bizarre wonders. One thing he did know was that the scientists were all searching for something called the theory of everything: a way to marry macro and micro behavior models, Einstein's theory of relativity with the bizarre world of quantum physics.

It was easy, he thought. The theory of everything is sitting right beside me. Why did anyone need to search anywhere else?

Cobra and his mother had struggled mightily in Texas, managing to eke out an existence picking fruit in the daylight hours and cleaning toilets at night. Yet it still wasn't enough. In addition to paying for room and board in the cement block they shared with two other families—how was this better than the fresh air and fertile soil of his childhood village, Christo wanted to know?—they had to pay back the men who had smuggled them across the border, who charged an exorbitant interest rate.

They would never pay them back, he had finally realized. These men hadn't brought them across the border out of the kindness of their hearts, or even for the initial fifteen hundred dollars they had charged.

They had brought them over to work as slaves.

Maybe it would have been different if his father had lived, and maybe not. But once Christo turned twelve and realized this was their fate, this half-life of menial labor and filthy living conditions, he took the only avenue of escape he saw for him and his mother.

He joined a gang.

It turned out he was more suited to crime than tossing watermelons into the back of a dusty pickup. A natural athlete, smart and desperate, Christo rose steadily through the ranks, graduating from petty crime to slinging rock to armed robbery. After surviving an ambush by a rival gang and slaying two of their members with a folding knife, he was promoted to the coveted position of *asesino*. Christo had never wanted to hurt anyone, but he found that once he started, he developed a taste for it. Not only that, but he knew too much about the activities of the gang to ever leave, and he owed them ten grand for a loan to move himself and his mother to an apartment complex near Chapel Hill. The gang wanted to expand in the Triangle region, and Cobra wanted his son to grow up in a safer place. It was a good fit for everyone.

"Papa, stay and play this afternoon."

"I wish I could."

"Please please please?"

Christo waffled. "Maybe for a bit. Just for a few minutes, though. Papa's very busy."

"Can we play trucks?"

"Sure."

"Hey Papa, watch this!"

Hugo giggled and folded the two middle fingers of his right hand into his palm. As he held his hand proudly in the air, sticking out his thumb and pinky and index finger, Cobra turned white and yanked his son's hand across the table. He unfolded the fingers and covered Hugo's hand with his own. "Where did you learn that?" he said, though he already knew. His was not the only gang family living in the cheap apartment complex.

Though Cobra was a feared enforcer, he was paid very little. It was another form of slavery, he knew, but at least one that came with respect and a far better standard of living. Though Cobra would do almost anything the gang asked, one thing was not for sale: his son's future.

Cobra had traded his soul for security for his family, but if anyone tried to recruit his son, they would find out exactly how Cobra had earned his nickname.

And so would everyone they held dear.

"Someone showed me," Hugo said, his soft brown eyes lowering, aware something was wrong.

"Never do that, okay?" Cobra said. "It isn't a nice thing."

"Okay, Papa. I'm sorry."

Cobra pulled his son into a hug and pressed his lips to the top of his head. "It's okay, niño. Papa loves you very much."

"Can we play trucks now?"

"Sure."

The buzz of a text vibrated Cobra's pocket. He pulled his phone out and checked the message. It was Javier. Someone in Greensboro had spotted the girl, Blue, but she had slipped away again. The gang leader wanted Cobra to step in. Ensure the job was done right.

He replied to Javier and replaced the phone. After indulging his son by playing trucks for fifteen minutes, Cobra went to his room to pack. "I have to go away," he told his mother when he returned downstairs carrying a small duffel bag. "I'm sorry."

"We'll miss you," she said, as she finished up the dishes. She never asked questions. She knew hard choices had been made.

"I hope it's just for a day or two."

After turning the water off, she dried her hands and hugged him. "Take care of yourself. Don't worry about Hugo."

"Don't let him play with the older boys, okay? They grow up too fast these days."

She patted his arm. "You're a good father."

"I love you, Mama."

"I love you, too."

Before he left, to Hugo's great delight, Cobra swept him into a bear hug and carried him through the front door, all the way to his black-and-red Yamaha R3 in the parking lot. His mother followed them out. After letting Hugo sit in the seat and rev the motorbike a few times, Cobra released the boy into her arms and drove off.

30

A cold, fierce wind whistled through the streets of downtown Creekville, ruffling the leaves of the oaks, bending the limbs of smaller trees, cutting through the worn fibers of Preach's forest-green overcoat. After lunch, he had taken a walk to think through the case.

Was it enough, he wondered?

If Claire had a drug business, would she have killed her own son to protect it?

There were two parts to that question. The first was whether *someone* would do such a thing. The answer to that, unfortunately, was an emphatic *yes*. Just last year, in North Carolina, a doctor was arrested for having his wife killed in order to protect an illegal prescription opioid drug ring.

The second part to the question—could *Claire Lourdis* commit such a terrible deed—was a different story. Was this single mom and fashion boutique clerk, former high school knockout from Preach's own past, living a double life as a drug queen?

Maybe the chief and Ari were right. Maybe he was too close to the case and should recuse himself.

But what if they were wrong? What if Claire was innocent and needed him more than ever? Could he put everything aside and treat this case as he would any other? Could he look at the evidence fairly and arrest Claire if he had to?

His answer mattered. Not just to the case but to him. He didn't want to be the kind of person who answered any of those questions in the negative. He didn't want Ari to see him as a man who could not overcome his juvenile crush on another woman.

But he had to be honest with himself as well. He had to do the right thing for David, even if it meant admitting his own weakness.

The station was just around the corner, less than two blocks away. The chief needed to hear what Wade had told him. A decision loomed.

At the next intersection he stopped at the light, running a hand through his hair and clutching the back of his neck. Traffic flowed like quicksilver in both directions. Pedestrians eyed him as they passed, and it felt as if the whole town was spinning on an axis around the spot in which he was standing. Stuffing his hands in his pockets, buffeted by the wind, he knew he could not step away from the case and still live with himself. This was his job. His calling. His town.

In a strange way he did not fully understand, he knew failing David would be like failing Preach's younger self as well.

A lost and fallen ideal he had already failed before, in so many ways.

The light turned yellow and then red. The traffic ground to a halt. His face numb from the biting wind, Preach hunched his shoulders and took a step that felt like pushing through tar, joining the flow of people crossing the street.

Chief Higgins's stare bored right through Preach when he told her about the new drug czar in Creekville. *One chance*, the chief had said. *One chance to get this right, or I pull you from the case.*

When Preach returned to his desk, he leaned back in his chair and debated the best course of action. His thoughts returned to his earlier questions about Claire's lifestyle. Even if Brett had paid the down payment on the house, what about everything else? How had Claire lived before Brett? Was there a long string of extravagant expenses?

One did not step into the middle of a drug operation without experience, he knew. Creekville was small beans, and it might not take long to rise to the top, but it was not exactly applying to the local grocery store. There would be a history there.

He had to admit Claire had the perfect cover: a soccer mom raising the town golden boy. Who would suspect her? She could even have met her drug mules in the woods between Wild Oaks and Carroll Street Homes.

After spending the afternoon looking into her finances, he didn't like what he saw. Claire's vehicle history showed a string of fancy new cars. Leases on a Land Rover, a Lexus, and an Infiniti coupe. How much did she make at the boutique, he wondered? Fifty thousand at most?

Before her current house, she had rented a two-grand-a-month townhome. How did she afford that rent, those cars, the country club she had belonged to for years, and also raise a child?

It didn't add up.

Preach called Terry over and asked him to give Claire's financial history the third degree. *Trace it all,* he said. *Every single loan, credit card, and tax return. Figure out her job history. Tally up her expenses.*

After that, Preach checked in with Bill, who hadn't made any progress on finding Nate. Frustrated, he told the older officer to keep looking. Preach left the station and had a lonely lunch at a Mexican joint that shared space with a Buddhist center, thinking of all the times he and Ari had eaten there, dreading what he planned to do next. After lingering over a second basket of chips and dabbing the last bit of habanero sauce off his mouth, he stepped into the parking lot and prepared to meet Claire.

Sometimes the best way to get an answer to a question, he knew, was to look into someone's eyes and ask them.

The freak windstorm earlier in the day had left debris and broken branches strewn throughout Wild Oaks, as if an angry god had gone on a rampage. Preach wound through the neighborhood as the soft cloak of dusk settled onto the placid lawns, the residents working to clear their yards before the light failed completely.

Claire answered the door in a beige, fringe suede jacket she had thrown over a white slip. Preach's eyes fell, unbidden, to her bare feet and the tanned striations of her calves.

A frail smile fluttered on her lips. "How was your weekend?"

"Eventful."

"Do you . . . have any news?"

"I thought I might find Brett here," he said, switching subjects.

She stiffened. "We decided to take a break for a while. Probably forever."

"I'm guessing he didn't take that very well."

Her eyes flashed. "He should have thought of that before he put his—" with a struggle, she composed herself and stepped to the side. "Come in. It's cold."

"Thanks."

After she shut the door, Claire retreated to the couch, sitting by the gas fire with a glass of red wine in hand. He left his coat on a hook and joined her, though he sat further away than last time.

"Is he still a suspect?" she asked.

"I've haven't ruled anyone out, but he has a pretty solid alibi."

Her lips curled in derision. "Lisa Waverly?" When he didn't answer, she took a long drink of wine. "Why'd you leave the ministry?"

Surprised by the personal question, he chuckled and said, "Everyone wants to know that. Do people ask that question of electricians and bankers?"

"People are fascinated by ministers, whether they admit it or not. Probably because they wish they had that kind of faith."

"Ministers are fascinated by people who don't have a compulsive need to think about those things all the time. Still, it just never felt right to me. I need my feet on solid ground, wearing out my shoes."

She stared down at her glass, into the blood-red depths of the wine. "Does any of this . . . your job, the things you've seen . . . cause you to wonder where God is?"

There was a defeated look in her eyes. Was she grieving, he wondered? Acting?

Questioning her decisions? Asking him to tell her something she wanted to hear?

"The families of the victims ask that a lot," he said quietly, pushing up the sleeves of his sweater to relieve the heat from the fireplace.

"And what do you say?"

"That if we're looking for Him, then we must want Him to be there."

"That doesn't mean He is."

"It means something."

She set down her wine, removed her jacket, and threw it atop a chair, leaving her slim arms exposed. "I hope you don't mind," she said. "It's hot, and grief does not lend itself to modesty."

His gaze caught the contours of her breasts beneath the creamy fabric of the slip. She was not wearing a bra, and Preach felt heat from a different source rise within him.

"So if Brett's not a suspect," she said, "who is?"

He looked her in the eye. "You are, Claire."

His hope for a reaction, a gut response to the accusation, was unfulfilled. Her expression didn't change, though she sipped her wine in silence for a long moment before she answered.

"In high school, I thought I was going to be famous," she said. "A model or an actress or the wife of someone glamorous. Anything to rise above this town. That's okay. Dreams die. That's why they're called dreams, right? Because they're not real. Do you want to know what my new dream was, before my son died? I wanted to see him off to college and start a pop-up clothing boutique. Maybe I'd run it like a food truck, drive around in a sexy vehicle of some sort, maybe even a Silver Stream, and sell my fashion designs around the Triangle. That's not too much to ask, is it?" When he didn't answer, she repeated the question. "Is it?"

"Claire."

"Do you know I haven't said his name since he died? I don't dream anymore, Joe. At least not when I'm awake. I think about the future, sometimes. That's about as close as I get. Do you know what I think about?"

"Claire—"

"I think about my funeral. When I'm going to join my son. When I'm fucking going to die, because that's all I have left."

She set her wine glass on the coffee table with a shaky hand. Some of it sloshed onto the rug. She brought her knees to her chest and hugged them, her face pale as she stared through him. "There's only one reason I care whether or not you arrest me," she said. "Because that would mean you're not chasing the bastard who killed my son."

"I need your phone, Claire."

"It's on the kitchen table," she said, in a monotone. "Take it."

"I'm not saying I think you're guilty yet. I'm saying I have to look at the facts and investigate them as best I see fit."

"I'd ask for nothing else. Can I ask what led you to this absurd conclusion?"

"Your story about the night David died doesn't match up with what a witness saw."

"I already told you about that. I don't remember seeing him again."

"We also found footprints in the leaf pile with David's blood on it. Prints from a man and a woman. You argued with him before he died. More than one witness has told me David resented you . . ." he trailed off when he saw the hurt his words had caused, as if he had just taken a knife, slipped it between her ribs, and twisted it. She stared past him, face white and hands trembling.

"To be honest, none of that was enough for me," he continued. "Not for this. I heard something else today, though. I heard there's a woman drug dealer in Creekville with ties to the Carroll Street Homes trailer park."

Her eyes slowly lifted. "You think I'm a drug dealer? And what? David found out and threatened to turn me in? So I *killed* him?"

"It's something I need to get to the bottom of."

Her gaze went distant again. After a long moment, she said, "It's something more than love, you know. What you feel for your child."

"I'm sure that it is."

"It's deeper than anything else. So deep it . . ." her voice had thickened, and she hugged her knees tighter. "I can't take it, Joe," she whispered. "I can't accept that he's gone."

He couldn't bear to watch her suffering. Whether or not she was guilty, the pain was tearing her apart. Of that he was certain. He moved closer and put a hand on her arm. "I'm so sorry, Claire. Can I suggest a grief counselor?"

"I don't want a grief counselor. I want my son back. I want his murderer to burn in hell."

As he started to pull away, she reached up to grab his hand. "Stay with me."

"Sure," he said. "I have a few minutes."

Her hand slid up his forearm, her nails tracing lightly against his skin. "I mean stay with me tonight. Make me feel better. Make me feel anything. You can arrest me tomorrow."

"You know I can't do that, Claire."

"Of course you can." She unfurled from her position and put one leg on the floor, leaving the other bent and resting against the side of the couch. The shift exposed a silky patch of underwear and the shadow of her sex underneath. Her nails moved to the underside of his forearm and stroked it, giving him chills, and her other hand moved to the spaghetti strap of her slip. "I know you want to stay," she whispered. "I can see it in your eyes."

Time seemed to compress and bear weight as she continued to stroke his arm. It wasn't enough, he knew, to leave in that moment. Without knowing who he truly was.

"Desire is a tiny part of the equation," he said. "We desire many things in life. It's how we act on those urges that matters."

"Let's finish what we started all those years ago. One night. No strings attached." She pushed the strap off her shoulder, and it fell away, exposing the pink tip of a nipple. As she reached over to remove the other strap, he caught her wrist. "Get some sleep, Claire."

"Look at me, Joe," she said softly, arching her back and causing the slip to fall even lower, exposing her breast in full. "This was always meant to be."

As if taking the last sip of water in a desert, his eyes drank her in, all of her, the parted lips and smooth skin, the firm swell of her chest, the stabbing memory of his youthful desire, all the weak and lonely urgings of the flesh.

"I need you," she said, leaning in so close he could feel her breath on his lips, her hand sliding up his arm. Her scent enveloped him, musk and butterscotch, and he felt light-headed, his thought processes muddled.

When she tried to kiss him, he pulled away at the last moment, pushing off the couch on wobbly legs. "Don't leave town for a few days," he said, aware of how husky his voice sounded. "Try to get some rest." On his way out, he grabbed her cell phone off the kitchen table, and her stare of disbelief followed him out the door.

Outside in the cold air and bright stars, the passion started to ebb, and he knew it for the shallow thing it was. After releasing a deep breath, he drove through the streets of Creekville with a purpose, the past exorcised, thinking about the case and what to do next.

His cell rang, and he checked the caller. It was the station.

"Detective Everson."

"It's Bill. I've got a tip on Nate tonight."

Preached eyed the dash—9:17 p.m.

Bill had taken his edict seriously.

"Where are you?" Preach asked.

"At my desk."

"I'll be right there."

31

As Preach drove through downtown Durham at night, he marveled at how much the city had changed over the years. Bright city lights, bars and restaurants in every direction, plenty of pedestrians on the street. Unlike in the days of his youth, these pedestrians were strolling languorously, talking and laughing instead of hurrying as fast as possible to their destination, terrified of being mugged.

In the rare times when Preach and his friends had ventured to Durham during his teen years, always without their parents' knowledge, he vividly remembered the aura of danger that permeated the streets after dark. A wasteland of abandoned buildings, criminals, and addicts that the rest of the Triangle treated like a quarantine zone. Taxi drivers had refused to go there at night.

Was it really that bad? he wondered. Yes, to some extent. The crime rate had been astronomical compared to the rest of the state. The drugs and loss of jobs and urban blight were real. But during the recent boom times, Durham had not magically imported a few hundred thousand people. Like waking from a bad dream, the city's long-suffering residents had embraced the change and poured their energy into making Durham one of the most vibrant downtowns in the state.

That didn't mean all of the problems had disappeared. Many of them were swept under the rug, pushed further out from the city center. Even now, his practiced gaze caught the menace lurking on the edges of society. The pair of men eying passersby like prey near the entrance to a parking garage. A group of teens with gang colors disappearing down an alley. A still-abandoned building with broken windows.

He parked across the street from the Pinhook, a grungy music venue on the eastern edge of downtown. A few blocks down, past Mangum, the city got eerie real quick at night.

One of the kids Officer Wright had rousted in the trailer park claimed Nate went to the Pinhook on Tuesday nights for the all-ages shows. Unsure what to expect, Preach opened the door, greeted by a blast of electric guitar and synthesizers. He paid the eight-dollar cover and got his hand stamped for the first time in years.

Red-painted walls and a black ceiling. Dim lights. Scuffed wooden floor. The sticky-sweet stench of stale beer.

Inside, to his right, a group of people around his own age occupied a pair of booths along the wall. This was not the wine bar crowd, however. The patrons resembled aging band members more than young professionals.

At the bar, he spied a long-haired bruiser in a tank top, a woman with Goth makeup and a full-length leather coat, and a guy wearing a felt cape over a repurposed bath robe dyed in psychedelic colors.

No sign of Nate.

Preach checked inside the photo booth just past the booths along the wall, earning a few annoyed stares, then squeezed between the bar and a chalkboard wall covered with band flyers. A bartender of uncertain gender, with pierced lips and a green Mohawk, gave him the eye. Preach guessed this was due to the group of stringy-haired teens at the far end of the bar who looked barely old enough to vote, let alone drink.

Preach knew he stuck out like, well, a detective in a musty green overcoat at an alternative music venue. If Nate was here, he needed to find him fast, before someone tipped him off.

Past the bar, the club opened up a bit. The stage was just ahead, on the other side of a small dance floor. To his left was a pair of low-slung chairs and an old leather loveseat. He thought Ari might like the band. They reminded him of a modern Duran Duran, a moody vocalist merging synthpop and rock.

Stay alert, Preach.

A white man in his sixties was doing a weird line dance by the loveseat. He looked like a retired professor. Definitely tripping. After a glance into the bathroom, Preach edged into the crowd near the stage and noticed a seating area wedged along the wall, invisible from the front of the club. Nate was drinking a beer on a chartreuse couch with a group of friends, nodding along to the music. He saw Preach at the same time Preach saw him. For an instant, both of them froze, and as Preach started forward Nate jumped up and darted down a hallway beside the stage.

Preach cursed and pushed through the crowd, causing a stir. The hallway was short, ending at a door to the outside that was just closing. Preach burst onto a tiny patio in time to see Nate struggling with Bill Wright, who Preach had planted by the back door. After pushing the flustered older officer into the low wall surrounding the patio, Nate fled to his left, down a concrete walkway. Preach followed, yelling at him to stop. Nate didn't listen, and Preach had little choice. He wasn't about to shoot a kid in the back.

Nate slipped around a patio table in the middle of the walkway and overturned a pair of chairs. Preach jumped over them. The path continued along the back side of a line of tall brick buildings. To the right, across a parking lot and then a wide avenue, Durham's modern performing arts center gleamed in the glow of streetlights.

At the end of the path, Nate squeezed through a weird jigsaw section of wall that partially concealed a generator. Once Preach got through, he saw Nate dashing through a private parking lot, aiming for a waist-high iron fence that separated the lot from the street. Preach sprinted at full speed for the gate. No doubt Nate knew the nooks and crannies of the city, and he probably had a car or a bike stashed around the corner.

Just before Nate made it over the fence, Preach lunged and caught the back of his sleeveless gray vest, trapping him atop the iron bars. Nate struggled to no avail and, as easy as lifting a bag of groceries, Preach picked the kid up and hoisted him to the ground. While Nate sulked, Preach patted him down, then led him by the arm to a corner off to their left, where the gate met the brick building.

By that time, Bill had caught up to them, glaring at Nate with his hand on his gun. Preach put a palm out to calm Bill. "Long way from home, aren't you, Nate?"

"Fuck you."

"Is that really how you want to start this off?"

Nate brushed a limp bang out of his face and looked away. His eyes were as sunken as ever, his skin as sallow as candle wax in the weak ambient light.

"Believe it or not," Preach continued, "I'm not here to arrest you. I just want to talk."

"I already told you, I don't know anything about David."

"Then why do you keep running away from me?"

Nate snorted. "Because you're the cops, man."

"So? None of the rest of the people in the club ran away."

"That's because they don't know you."

"Maybe. So why are *you* running?"

Nate swore again and lit a cigarette. Preach didn't object.

"I don't like cops," Nate said. "You're always nosing around. Arresting people for doing nothing."

Bill took a step forward. "Listen, you punk—"

Preach cut him off with a raised hand. "I hope that's not the case," Preach said gravely. "To my knowledge, I've never arrested someone for doing nothing."

Nate guffawed.

"I believe you about David," Preach said. "At least for now. That's not why I'm here, though. I need your help with something."

Nate blew smoke and didn't respond.

"I know you deal drugs around town."

"Don't know what you're talking about."

"Nate."

"You ain't got nothing on me."

"I've got you twice for avoiding arrest, and more importantly—" Preach held up an evidence baggie of heroin he had found hidden in Nate's bedroom on the way over, less than an hour ago—"we found this in your dresser. That's a Class I felony."

"You searched my *home*? My damn mom—"

"Your mother tried her best to keep me out." Preach reached into his coat and produced the warrant he had obtained from a quick call to a judge, also that evening. Though unhappy about being disturbed at night, the judge had agreed the warrant was important. "I'm working a murder, Nate. You ran away from me, you had a fight with David, and multiple people have told me you deal."

"That stuff's not mine," Nate said, with a snarl. "One of my friends must have left it there."

Preach gave him a sad look. "What happens next depends on you."

"What do you mean?"

"Who's your supplier? Who do you take orders from?"

Nate waved a hand, dismissive.

"Bill?" Preach said.

Officer Wright stepped forward with a pair of handcuffs. Nate shrank against the building. "Hey now. Listen."

"That's what we're here for," Preach said.

Nate sucked down his cigarette and lit another. "God*damn*, man. She'll kill me if I rat."

Preach exchanged a glance with Bill. "So it's a she?"

Nate swallowed and puffed even harder.

"Is it Alana?" Preach said.

Nate laughed.

"Your mother?"

"You don't know anything, do you?"

"Lisa Waverly?"

"What? Get off, man."

"Is it David's mom?"

Nate kept dragging on the cigarette, though his eyes widened ever so slightly.

"Nate, is it Claire?" Preach said quietly.

"Felony I, kid," Bill chimed in. "You know what that means?"

Preach held up a hand again. "If you're telling the truth, she's going to jail. She can't hurt you from there."

The kid's eyes roved from one officer to the other. "And what happens to me, if I say something? I go free?"

"That's the DA's call. But if you can give us details on the record, I'll strongly suggest your sentence be reduced to a misdemeanor. And in my experience, the DA usually takes my advice."

Nate finished his cigarette, sniffed, and stubbed out the butt.

"Is it Claire, Nate?"

The kid flicked the butt away and flexed his fingers, again and again, as he stared at the ground.

Preach stepped closer. "I need to know. Right now. You have my word I'll go to bat for you. Does Claire Lourdis give you drugs to sell?"

Nate shoved his hands in his pockets and looked up, and Preach felt his chest tighten when he saw the acknowledgement in the kid's eyes. "Yeah," Nate said. "It's Claire."

A few hours later, with blue lights flashing on the street behind him, Preach knocked on Claire's front door for the second time that night. After they had taken Nate to the juvenile detention center and processed him, he had refused to say more without an attorney. But he had said enough to arrest Claire.

As Preach waited for her to appear, he couldn't get a quote from Kierkegaard out of his mind.

"The truth is a trap," the philosopher had once written. "You cannot get the truth by capturing it, only by its capturing you."

The detective's pace slowed as he approached the door. A light was on in Claire's living room, even though it was 1 a.m. He could see her silhouette through the gauze curtain.

When the door opened, she was still wearing her white slip. "Change your mind?" she asked.

"You need to get dressed and come with me."

"You need to get undressed and come with me." She seemed to ignore the flashing lights, and he could smell the alcohol on her breath. She reached up to stroke his cheek, and he grabbed her wrist. "Don't."

"Not in front of the men, you mean?"

"Get dressed."

"Do you want to know what David and I argued about that night?"

His eyes scanned the house behind her and saw no sign of a weapon. Just a pile of dirty dishes in the kitchen, the living room as he had left it, and a collection of empty wine bottles in a paper bag by the door.

"We argued about Brett. David told me about the affair that night."

"That's not what you led me to believe."

She shrugged. "I was embarrassed. You know what I told David? I told him that I didn't care. I said it out of anger. I meant it, of course, but I should never have said that to my son. To think that was our last conversation."

"What did he say?" Preach said quietly.

A soft, ironic smile creased her mouth. "He said that makes me a whore. I said that makes me a good mother." She slumped to the ground, her back against the door, arms folded across her chest.

"Claire."

Her eyes slipped upward.

"We have to go."

"I'll get dressed and leave with you," she said, after a moment. "But listen to me, Joe. Whatever it is you think you know—it's wrong."

Preach took her downtown and saw to her processing himself. After that, he returned to her house to get an update from forensics. As soon as he arrived, Lela Jimenez led him to the guest bedroom, where the bedspread and sheets were gathered in a pile on the floor. After pointing out a slit in the queen-size mattress, Lela handed him a notebook they had found tucked into the barely noticeable hiding space. The notebook was filled with Excel spreadsheets divided into four sections: date, carrier, amount, and a final column labeled *product* that contained shorthand notations consisting of two letters, most likely a code. Likewise, two initials made up each line of the carrier column. One set of initials that appeared with frequency was N. W.

Preach felt confident that N. W. stood for Nate Wilkinson. He felt even more confident, because he had seen similar notebooks often enough during his career, that he was looking at a drug ledger.

32

After work on Wednesday, Ari met Fenton Underwood at the bar of 21C, a luxury hotel and art gallery in downtown Durham. The cocktails were so fancy she didn't recognize most of them. Elaborate sculptures of jungle animals in a variety of artistic styles hung on the walls, and in combination with the beige leather stools and the brown marble bar that resembled a piece of sleek wood, the room evoked a pan-African vibe.

How very Durham, she thought, and she had to admit she liked it.

Fenton picked up his drink, grinned, and waved at her to follow. Curious, she took her vodka martini and stepped into a leather-padded elevator that took them to the basement, where a cocktail lounge had been fashioned out of an old bank vault. A pair of doors with rusting iron bars separated the rooms, and the original copper-plated safety deposit boxes still lined the walls from floor to ceiling. Inside the vault, Durham's business set sipped cocktails on velvet sofas while flapper-era jazz cast a spell on the room.

"One of Durham's little gems," Fenton said, as they squeezed into a corner of the lounge.

"Nice digs," she said, though she felt a little claustrophobic. "I never knew this was here."

"You could almost imagine a gangster with a tommy gun bursting in and holding the place up."

She agreed, though it brought an unwanted image of Preach to mind and how safe she always felt with him. Ari had lived and traveled on her own for years and did not need a man to protect her. But Preach had an undeniable strength of presence about him, years of experience with keeping the bad guys at bay.

She supposed Claire felt the same way.

Fenton removed his jacket and draped it across his lap as he sat. After loosening his tie, he removed the lemon rind from the lip of his

Sazerac. “How’s life?” he asked, taking an exploratory sip and nodding in approval.

Pretty shitty, she wanted to say, but she didn’t know Fenton well enough to vent her personal issues.

“Busy.”

“Take some advice from an old man. Set boundaries with work. The law is a harsh mistress, as I’m sure they told you in law school. Some cases, you could grind twenty-hours a day for months, and it wouldn’t change a thing.”

“What’s the trick?” she asked.

“Knowing when to call it a day, and when to put in those twenty-four hours.”

“I don’t think I’m quite there yet.”

He chuckled. “You’ve been on the job what, five minutes? You’ll learn to step back and see the big picture. Misdemeanors, white collar, a murder one: Stakes aside, they’re all the same in the end. What’s the balance of the evidence? What will a jury think? Where can you make an impact?”

“The Ronald Jackson case . . . I don’t think it’s going too well.”

“Talk to me.”

During her update, Fenton sat quietly and held his Sazerac, sometimes taking a sip. He was a good listener. Just like Preach.

Too bad Joe listens to other women as well.

Since the night at the café, he had tried to call her at least three times. She had ignored his efforts, not to be mean, but because she didn’t know what came next. While part of her yearned to give him another chance, part of her couldn’t shake the sense of betrayal.

The whole ordeal had left her feeling numb on the inside, and she wasn’t sure what that meant. Was she protecting herself? Had her feelings changed?

Did work have anything to do with it, she wondered? Had the two of them been growing apart even before the text from Claire? If so, then why? His job hadn’t changed—was it her?

She didn’t like that thought very much.

Who was she becoming?

Fenton leaned back in his seat. "What's your next move, counselor?"

"Sorry?" she said, startled by the question.

"How do you recommend the office proceeds with Ronald Jackson?"

"Oh." *I was kind of hoping you would tell me,* she thought. But she knew what he was doing, and she appreciated it. He was doing his job as a mentor. Pushing her to learn.

"Ronald is guilty. I'm convinced of that."

Fenton cocked a grin, as if to say, *so what*? "Do you think we can convince a jury of that?"

"What if we don't have to? What if we get a plea instead?"

Was Bentley putting words in her mouth, she wondered? Had that been the point of their last conversation, a hidden directive disguised as a civil rights lecture?

"Do you think we have enough?" he asked.

"What if we make a show of moving forward? I think Ronald is terrified of what a jury will do."

Fenton's eyebrows lifted. "You figured that out quick. It usually takes at least a year or two to become a cynic."

She buried her face in her martini.

"Playing that game is risky," he said. "Meredith is a pit bull. We might get smacked hard by credibility questions for these witnesses."

"Don't we owe it to the victims to try?"

"We answer to the law, Ari. We want justice but not rogue justice."

"Is it justice if the system can't convict a murderer?"

"The alternative is worse. You don't want a system that can be manipulated to convict whoever you want."

Isn't that what we have already, she wondered?

God, I *am* a cynic.

Her phone rang, and she dug it out of her pocket. "It's Meredith Verela," she said to Fenton. "Do you want to take this?"

"She called you."

"She probably wants to tell me she's sick of waiting for Desiree."

Fenton waved his glass. "Give her hell, counselor."

Ari stepped into the hallway.

"Have you heard?" Meredith said abruptly, as soon as Ari answered.

"Heard what?"

"About Ronald. He's dead."

Ari stilled. "What? How?"

"He was stabbed in the throat this afternoon, in his cell."

"Oh my God."

"You've been played, Ari."

"Excuse me?"

"The man who stabbed Ronald is also a murder suspect. His name is LeDarius Milton. He's been in jail for a year awaiting trial."

"A year?"

"Three different lawyers have been appointed, there's no bond, and your boss keeps stalling. LeDarius is accused of killing a twelve-year-old girl in a drive-by, and maybe he's guilty, but everyone deserves their day in court."

"But why did he kill Ronald?"

"LeDarius is from East Durham. A known enforcer. He was transferred to Ronald's cell block just this morning, a request put in through LeDarius's attorney. Do you want to know when the transfer request was submitted?"

In the ensuing pause, a prickle of gooseflesh crept down Ari's arms.

"The same day Ronald was sent to prison," Meredith said. "Do you know who this attorney also represents, Ari? I did a little digging, on a hunch."

Ari couldn't bring herself to say the name.

"Bentley Montgomery. What did he promise you, Ari? That he'd return with this new witness soon? Maybe by next week?"

By Friday, Ari thought.

"There's more," Meredith said. "The male victim killed in Ronald's stash house, Lionel Braston? The police tell me he was on Bentley's payroll. One informant went so far as to call him Bentley's protégé. Do you understand what happened, Ari? Your client set my client up."

Bentley sent Lionel and the girl to rob the stash house that night, then informed on them behind their back. Bentley wanted Ronald to kill them so he could call the cops and have him arrested, even though he knew it probably wouldn't stick.

"It's easier to kill a rival drug dealer in prison than on the street," Meredith said. "Your client is a chess player, Ari. He sacrificed a knight to kill a king."

Later, when she replayed the conversation in her mind, Ari thought she had said something in response. But she could never remember what.

"Congratulations," Meredith continued. "You're now a pawn in Bentley's private drug war."

33

When Preach entered the station Thursday morning, he found Chief Higgins beckoning him into her office. As he settled into the chair across from her desk, she slapped down the morning's edition of the local paper and jabbed a finger at the front page. He looked down to find a photo of himself standing on Claire's doorstep on the night he had arrested her.

The camera had caught Claire in her white slip, reaching up to stroke his cheek in an intimate manner.

"Not a good look," the chief said.

"No."

"Want to tell me about it?"

Thinking back, he remembered seeing a news van, though he had no idea how they had arrived so fast. David's case was the biggest news in Creekville, so they had probably trailed the police cars when they had pulled out of the station.

"She had just opened the door," he said. "I grabbed her wrist and pulled it away. Obviously, this doesn't show all of that."

"That's unfortunate."

"What can I say?" At this point, he was far more concerned about the damage the photo might do to his relationship with Ari. "Put me in front of a camera. I'll set the record straight."

"It's not the public I'm worried about. You think she's innocent, don't you?" the chief said.

"I arrested her."

"That wasn't the question."

Preach fiddled with the yin-yang stress ball on her desk again, weighing his words. "I spent half the day yesterday looking through her phone and email."

"And?"

"Nothing."

The chief folded her hands. "If she's dealing, she has a burner. Maybe an email account we don't know about yet."

"All true."

"What else did Nate give you?"

"He clammed up and asked for an attorney."

"Which means he's going for a deal." When Preach tipped his head in affirmation, the chief continued, "And Claire's extravagant expenses?"

"Still unaccounted for. I'm planning to ask her about them today."

"She hasn't lawyered up?" the chief said, surprised.

"She told Terry she doesn't need a lawyer."

"Why Terry? You haven't seen her?"

"Not yet."

"Why not?"

Preach kept kneading the stress ball. "I don't feel comfortable judging whether she's lying. I'd rather trust the evidence."

"So you believe her."

"I don't *dis*believe her. There's a big difference. And the consequences . . ." he sucked in a breath. "I don't want to get this one wrong."

"I should hope that's always the case." With her hands still clasped, the chief started tapping her forefingers against the backs of her palms. "Do you have another credible angle?"

"Not right now," he said slowly.

"We found her *ledger*, Joe. I would hate to think you're not thinking clearly. She's a striking woman, I'll admit."

"Don't," he said. "I'm just doing my job."

"Make sure you are. I hate to do this, because I see us as partners and I don't like to give orders to my partner. But I have to forbid you from digging deeper into this case for any suspect other than Claire. If you have leads to follow to cement her guilt, then fine. Otherwise, we have more cases to work."

"Why don't you give me a week—"

Her eyes flashed, and she jabbed her finger at the newspaper again.

"Have you taken a good look at this? It sure doesn't look to me like you're about to arrest her. It looks like you're about to—"

He rose, his face flushing. "Are we good here?"

"I don't know, are we?"

He stood rigid in front of her, choking back what he wanted to say.

"Joe? If I find out you're chasing this case, I'll send you home."

After his conversation with the chief, Preach headed down to the basement of the building housing the police station. He hadn't planned to confront Claire so quickly, but he needed to know a few things.

Maybe she would answer, maybe she wouldn't. Maybe she was telling the truth, and maybe not.

But he needed to hear for himself.

Since the arrest, she had refused to answer any questions, sitting stone-faced through all attempts at interrogation by the other officers. What game was she playing? Was she trying to manipulate him by not cooperating? Waiting to see him alone?

In a low-ceilinged cell with white cement walls, he found her huddled on her side, her long hair splayed across the front of her cot. Even without makeup or a shower, her regal beauty transcended the cell.

This time, though, it failed to move him as it had before. In fact, it brought a sharp pang of longing for Ari, her earnest laugh and lack of guile, lying beside him in the hammock by the warmth of the fire.

He put a hand on the diamond-patterned cage that separated them. "Why haven't you asked for an attorney?"

"I don't need an attorney." She pushed to a sitting position and leaned her back against the wall, her legs folded underneath her.

"Why not?"

"I just need you."

"Don't."

She smiled softly. "I'm not talking about that. That was the other night, drunk and reckless. This is now, thinking of my son. I need you, Joe Everson, detective. The best cop in town. I need you to help my son."

"What was the ledger for?"

"It wasn't mine."

"Whose was it?"

"How should I know?"

"Maybe because it was in your house? Where did all the money come from, over the years? The cars and vacations and country clubs?"

"Seriously? You haven't figured that out yet? Good god, you are smitten." As he glared at her, she waved a hand, careless, and said, "Men, Joe. Boyfriends. Lots of them. It's how I gave my son the life I did."

He blew out a breath. "I have to tell you, Claire. It doesn't look good. You should get an attorney."

"You still don't get it. I. Don't. Care. Anymore. Not about myself."

"You should," he said quietly. "He would want you to."

Her jaw trembled, and she took a moment to compose herself. "There's a poison that infects you when your child dies. Especially in a way like this. I don't know if the poison's going to drive me insane or kill me, but I do know I'm not getting any better."

"You will, with time. I know it doesn't seem that way. But you will."

"I don't *want* to. We can't get better if we don't want to, can we?"

"Ask for an attorney, Claire."

She stared in silence at the wall, refusing to talk further.

After lunch, Preach got the call he had been both dreading and yearning for.

Ari.

"Hi," he said.

"I assume you're off the case?"

No icebreaker. No head games. Just an honest rebuke, delivered with an utter lack of emotion.

She had seen the photo.

"The chief wants me to see it through," he said.

A long silence. "At least tell me you know she's guilty."

"Ari, it wasn't what it looked like. I opened the door to arrest her, and she reached up."

"Wearing a slip, of course. To meet a detective."

"She lost a son. She doesn't care anymore. The camera caught us in the wrong moment."

"What an incredible coincidence."

He felt defeated. "Listen, I know how it looks. I pulled her hand away as soon as she touched me."

"I bet you did, since half the force was watching."

"There's nothing between us. I want to see you, Ari. Make it up in some way."

"Do you think she's innocent?"

"I . . ."

"Do you? Answer me."

"Of killing her son? I honestly don't know."

"You don't *know*? What do your instincts say?"

He swallowed, unable to lie to her. "My gut says she is."

"Is what?"

"Innocent."

"Oh my God. You found the *ledger*, Joe. And that's just what's in the news."

"This isn't about us. I still have to do my job."

"I don't think we should see each other anymore."

"Ari, let's—"

"I can't talk right now," she said, with a quaver in her voice.

About to respond, he ended up lowering the phone instead, since the other end of the line had gone dead.

34

Twenty-four hours.

Nineteen phone calls.

Fifteen in-person interviews.

Nine cups of coffee with a dash of cream.

One tuna and egg sandwich choked down.

No new evidence.

As frazzled as he had ever been, devastated by the breakup with Ari but unable to dwell on it, running on two hours of sleep and fumes, Preach put his head in his hands and knew he had to give it up. He had to let the case go.

Even before their conversation in jail, Preach had realized Claire's charm was all manufactured, and that Ari's was all real. Claire was a user and would throw anyone under the bus—including him. But did she murder her own child?

He agreed with Ari that he should recuse himself. He agreed, based on logic, with the chief. Even his own gut instinct, which screamed that Claire was innocent, could no longer be trusted. He was too close to the case. He was in danger of suspension if the chief found out.

So what was he doing?

Was it a perverse sense of duty to a past that no longer existed?

Or was it something else?

Maybe a way to prove to Ari, and to himself, that he hadn't fallen under a siren's spell?

He stood and paced his cubicle, scratching at the stubble on his cheeks. Nate had turned on his supplier awfully quickly. He had never asked for police protection. Was he not worried about blowback?

He was just a kid, though, behind the tough exterior. A scared and lonely kid.

And the ledger—why leave it in the house with that much heat around? Why hadn't they found it during the first search? The assumption was that Claire had removed it after David's death, knowing the police would search the house, and then replaced it. Yet she must have known they could search her house during her own arrest.

Or had she been so secure in her story—or in her hold over him—that she thought the arrest would never come?

The case against Claire fit. Preach had to admit that. It all fell nicely into place.

So why couldn't he accept it?

An email ping from his computer interrupted his thoughts. He leaned over and saw Ari's name as the sender, causing his pulse to spike.

The message had nothing to do with their relationship. It was an update on her case, written in a very businesslike tone. She wanted him to know what had happened with Bentley and Ronald Jackson.

Ronald was dead? he thought. *Killed in prison by an associate of Bentley? And Ari thinks Bentley might have orchestrated the whole maneuver, starting way back with the stash house murders?*

He had never heard of anything like that. But he thought of someone else who was currently sitting in jail and who might have a connection to Bentley.

Someone the ruthless businessman and criminal might also want to silence.

Claire.

In need of a change of scenery, Preach migrated to Jimmy's to fuel up again. The caffeine shakes had his fingers twitching and his mind racing. He debated telling the chief that Claire might have a ticking clock, then discarded the idea. One, the chief would probably send him home. Two, she would never buy such a theory without more proof. He wasn't even sure *he* did.

Even if they decided to protect her, what else could they do? She had her own cell for the time being and was due to appear before the judge on Monday. Assuming she stayed in custody, she would probably languish in jail until trial.

Yet if Bentley truly had it in for Claire, if he thought she might cave, then nowhere was safe. The best thing Preach could do was find a link between David's murder and the drug ring—if any existed—and go after Bentley himself.

Preach hunched in his seat in the corner and listened to the hum of a refrigerator stocked with cream sodas and local dairy products. The café was quieter than normal. Forcing his attention inward, he ran through the events of David's last day for the thousandth time.

On the morning of October 1, the day before the murder, David and Brett had exchanged a series of hostile texts. Preach no longer believed Brett or Lisa Waverly had played a part in the murder. But the texts might have set the stage for David's blowup with Claire.

David had gone to school. Nate Wilkinson had been suspended at this point. From the interviews Preach had conducted over the last twenty-four hours, talking to everyone who might have had contact with David, he did not think that David and Alana, Nate's girlfriend, had interacted for some time.

After football practice, David had come home for dinner. He did some homework and then argued with Claire outside the house. Sharon Tisdale had heard the fight, which devolved into shouting.

David had been hurt and angry with his mother. Assuming Claire was orchestrating a drug ring, had her son known about it? If so, had he threatened to tell the police? Had this led to the murder? If so, Preach guessed David had threatened to expose her *before* he left the house, giving Claire time to call for help. Said help had arrived before David had returned home, which afforded Claire time to ambush her son.

Preach sucked in a breath. If Claire had called for help, then that was premeditation.

In North Carolina, that could mean the death penalty.

Not that it mattered to him if she had really killed her son.

He ran a hand through his hair, stood with his coffee, and stepped outside to stretch his legs. The crisp air felt nice on his cheeks. An aroma of mulch and pine.

What else did he know?

According to Mackenzie Rathbun, David had gone to the restaurant in a distraught state. He tried and failed to convince her to leave with him. Preach had verified her story with the rest of the staff. It all checked out.

The next time anyone saw David was around midnight, when Sharon Tisdale claimed to have seen him—or someone with a similar profile—through a window. She had also seen a woman in the house, though Claire claimed she had taken an Ambien and didn't remember seeing David again.

Could someone besides Claire have been in the house? Either male or female? If so, who?

He couldn't think of another theory that made sense.

As the chief said, Claire was the most likely suspect.

According to the timeline, David had arrived at the Courtyard to see Mackenzie around 11 p.m. He had stayed fifteen minutes at most. That left an hour or so of time unaccounted for. None of David's friends knew anything about this time period. The most obvious conclusions were that he had driven around town by himself, distraught, or went home.

Preach paced back and forth on the wooden patio. Two kids licking Locopops had run outside to play, cavorting around a set of giant Legos.

Think, Joe.

He felt the case slipping away. He needed a new angle. Something outside the known evidence. If Claire was guilty, then no such angle existed. But if she wasn't . . . then he was missing something.

Something big.

A thought hit him. About five years ago, on a case in Atlanta, one of his colleagues had uncovered a key piece of evidence in a rape case by looking through the other cases that had come in during the year preceding the rape. It turned out the rapist had been arrested for an armed burglary but had gotten off on a technicality. The burglar's mug shot had been similar to the rape victim's sketch and, while that evidence had not been admissible in court, a new investigation had led to an arrest.

It was a long shot, he knew. But Creekville was a small jurisdiction. He could knock out the case files in a few hours.

It was worth a try, at least.

Back to the station he went.

Compared to the mean streets of Atlanta, the crime log in Creekville was a joke. To start, he went back a month, searching all arrests. A few dozen DUIs, open container violations, domestic violence calls, trespassing, possession of marijuana. An A&B here and there. A few harder drug arrests in Carroll Street Homes. In fact, the majority of the rough stuff was associated with the trailer park.

But he already knew that.

Three months back, then six. Nothing struck a nerve. He tapped his pen on his desk and widened the search to complaints filed by private citizens. This was a real stretch and included everything from deer incursions to broken lawn ornaments to a report that Jimi Hendrix had stolen someone's guitar for a show in an underground government bunker that housed aliens.

Moving right along.

After going back two months on the complaints, something caught his eye. A local documentary filmmaker named Alyssa Carson had reported a missing camera, a Canon EOS C100, worth over three thousand dollars. He read the whole complaint and then gripped the page. He couldn't believe what he was reading.

Alyssa had also reported missing a silver cigarette lighter. One with a floral pattern on the sides. The value was listed as sentimental.

Just to be sure, Preach hurried to pull up his own evidence report from the day he had found the bloody leaf pile in the woods. His notes confirmed it. "Silver cigarette lighter. Floral pattern etched in gray lines along both sides."

He turned back to the report. Someone had stolen the silver lighter from Alyssa Carson on August 21, when she had attended a meeting of local documentarians at the Creekville Arts Center. During a restroom break, she had left her purse and camera on the sink, thinking no one else was around.

But someone must have entered quietly behind her.

Someone who had stolen the lighter and left it in the woods behind Claire's house, possibly on the same night as David's murder.

35

It took Blue two full days to work up the nerve to go to Old Fort, her father's hometown. Telling herself she was afraid of hitchhiking was a copout, and she knew it. She wasn't scared of hitching. At least not very much. Staying too long in the Black Mountain homeless shelter was a much greater risk, though the place wasn't as bad as she had thought. She had enough food and her own cot in a great big room that smelled like ammonia. The shelter was for women only, which was comforting. But she knew Cobra was looking for her, and there were too many desperate people around who might rat her out. She lived in fear of hearing the gang assassin's motorcycle rumbling outside the shelter door.

She had to move on.

After half an hour of thumbing on the main state road out of town, Blue managed to hitch a ride down the mountain, ten miles east to Old Fort. A white-haired farmer in a Ford Bronco as old as Father Time gave her the lift.

Before she knew it, before she had time to second-guess or even process her decision, she was standing on the desolate Main Street of Old Fort, breathing in the sharp air, surrounded by mist and the bluish-black humps of the mountains. The town had a far different feel from the energizing vitality of Black Mountain. This place felt old and worn out, used up, discarded. There was no sign of tourism and very little life on the street. Where was everyone?

She thought of her father and what it must have been like to grow up in this place. She imagined it had been much different back then. A vibrant soda shop where all the kids gathered, a few diners where everyone knew each other, a baseball field with emerald-green grass and plump bases as white as doves. Not this shell of a town she saw around her: crumbling brick storefronts with no sign of gentrification, broken windows, abandoned buildings, missing signs, unpainted shutters.

Or maybe, like everything else she associated with her father, she had distorted the image. Maybe the town was better off than ever, and he had grown up in abject poverty with bad teeth and white trash neighbors and bare feet covered in coal dust. It pained her that she didn't even know.

Blue couldn't seem to make herself walk down the sidewalk. Now that the reality of the moment loomed, she was absolutely paralyzed by the thought of knocking on her relatives' door.

What if they turned her away?

What if *he* was there, and *he* turned her away?

As much as she worshipped his memory, she had never forgotten the rejection. It had stayed with her like a permanent stain, a full-body tattoo that only she could see.

You think he loved you, Blue?

So why did he leave you behind?

Why had he never written?

Never visited?

He left you there to rot.

No. He didn't have a choice. There was a reason, a good one. There has to be.

On the bus out of Greensboro, the passenger beside her had let Blue look up her father's old address on her phone. The house was a few blocks off Main. A quarter mile from where she was standing.

Yet she couldn't bring herself to do it.

The memories of her father, the one thing good and true in her life, were too precious too risk. They were too special. They were *everything.*

Shaking, she stood in the center of the tiny town she idolized and feared above all places on Earth, willing her feet to move, eventually taking her camera out and chronicling this stage of her journey. That helped her to breathe. Removed her from the situation.

After walking up and down the main drag for the tenth time, she popped into McDonald's for another cup of coffee, trying to summon her nerve. She sat in the back and picked up a dog-eared copy of a Buck Rogers novel that looked older than Mick Jagger, and which someone had left on a table. Science fiction was cool, she thought. Our world was so on the edge of being a sci-fi novel. The next twenty years could make the last century of progress seem like the Bronze Age.

What sci-fi movies did she love? The original *Blade Runner*, oh yeah. *Alien, Dune, Inception, The Matrix*. The Eighties were a glut of riches. *Robocop, ET, Terminator, Return of the Jedi, Tron*, the list went on and on.

Speaking of movies, there was one kind in particular she hated. The pretentious, postmodern ones where rich and famous people flitted in and out of fancy hotels and European cliffside resorts, going from one disillusioned conversation to another, complaining about the meaningless of their lives. Some clever critic in an online article had referred to these movies as reflecting "a culture of numbness."

Really?

These people might want to live for a few weeks in a housing project, or the trailer park where Blue grew up.

Maybe they would make a different movie.

Redefine their definition of *numb*.

Blue realized her foot was tapping incessantly under the table. She knew she was avoiding reality by thinking of the movies again. She was out of money now. It was her father's family or the homeless shelter. A middle-aged man in a faded army jacket opened the door, and Blue caught her breath. Could it be her father? He was the same age and trim build, and her father had a jacket just like that. He had served in the Gulf War before Blue was born.

The man faced her way, and she scoffed. This man had the face of a ferret. Her father looked like a young Daniel Day Lewis with short hair. The one from *The Boxer*.

An hour later, she started getting stares from the employees. Blue slid out of her chair and stepped outside, hugging her camera against her chest, and started walking toward the house. *One foot after another*, she told herself. That was all we could do in life.

And then she was there: standing on a sharply sloped street off Main, in front of a house with beige siding and maroon shutters. The house had its own yard with its own mailbox, and a flagpole that proudly displayed the stars and stripes. There was a groomed flowerbed, a gravel driveway, and a layer of rocks on the slope near the street to ward against erosion. It was small and simple, yet perfect. An embodiment of the American Dream.

Even if her father wasn't inside, someone in that house, a relative, would know where he was.

Why in the world had she waited so long? He would be thrilled to see her! The new chapter of her life was about to begin, the last decade a bad memory!

With her legs feeling like twigs unable to bear her weight, she approached the front door and rang the bell. Moments later, a gray-haired woman in her sixties answered. A kind smile softened a pinched face that had a lifetime of hard work etched into its craggy lines. Blue tried to picture her father in this woman. She thought she could see it. The crinkle at the corner of her eyes, the firm jaw.

"Yes?" the woman said, with a hint of suspicion.

"I, um . . . do you know if Donnie Blue lives here?" she blurted out.

"Who?"

"Donnie Blue," she repeated, sure the old woman had misheard her. "He's my father," she added shyly.

"There's no Donnie Blue here, honey. You sure you got the right address?"

Maybe a distant cousin had moved in, Blue thought. She described him and asked again. The woman still looked confused.

"Who's there, Meryl?" a male voice called out.

The old woman turned her head. "Someone for Donnie Blue. You know the name?"

"'Course I do. That's the family we bought the house from."

"How long ago was that?" Blue managed to croak.

"'Bout ten years now, I reckon," the man called out, as he walked into view. He was burly, with tanned arms and a dome of thinning white hair.

Blue had to swallow a few times before she could speak. "Do you know where they live now?"

"Moved to Ohio, I believe. Job transfer. Father's name was Jesse. Donnie rings a bell, and I know they had a son. That must've been him." He shook his head. "He didn't live here when we bought the house, though. I've never met him myself."

Blue trudged up the steps to another homeless shelter on the edge of Old Fort. It was called the Promise House, and it housed runaway teens and single mothers. She had no choice. Unless she called her mother or sold her camera, neither of which she was willing to do, she had to find enough work to eat and leave town again. That or resort to stealing.

At the moment, she didn't really care. Learning that her father's family no longer lived in Old Fort had floored her. A far larger part of her than she cared to admit had held out hope that he would open the door and sweep her off her feet.

She knew in her heart, of course, why she had never tried to come to Old Fort before.

Because if he had wanted to see her, he knew where to find *her*.

It might be better if he was dead. Then she could tell herself he had wanted to come back for her.

After the staff checked her in and led her to the tiny cubicle where she would spend the night, Blue fell onto her cot and heaved silent sobs, feeling as if a part of her was gone forever.

When Blue woke the next morning, she felt a tiny bit better. She was a resilient person. She knew this about herself. Depression did not become her. She would let herself wallow in her misery a while longer, lock away her father's memory once again, and carry on. Find a way out of that gloomy little town and start over in a better place. Maybe Asheville, this time. The city had a reputation for welcoming artists and drifters.

She stepped out of her cubby and looked around. Built into the repurposed basement of a Methodist Church, the shelter was little more than a dining hall and a large room full of cubicles separated by five-foot-tall plyboard partitions. The dingy, cramped interior made her think of runaway teens and serial killers again.

Which made her scoff. She had read once, after watching *The Silence of the Lambs*, that at any given time there were a few dozen serial killers operating in the United States. Though disturbing, this was not a large number, compared to the population. Funny how terrified we are of imaginary things when our reality is far more desperate.

Toughen up, Blue. You'll get a job today. Work for a month and move to Asheville. Rent a pad with some other kids, find another job, and start filming again.

Not wanting to lug her camera around all day, wary of being robbed, she wrapped the Canon in her jacket and asked the director of the shelter to keep it in the office. Thankfully, he agreed.

After a long day hitting up every place in town she could think of for a job and having no success, she debated hitchhiking to Asheville the next day. On her way home, a few blocks from the shelter, she heard the whine of a motorcycle. Almost afraid to look, she glanced back and saw her worst fear manifest behind her, less than a hundred yards away.

There were a few people on the street, but Blue knew it wouldn't matter. This was not some punk kid on the lookout. This was the most feared enforcer she knew.

As Cobra whipped his motorcycle into a parking space and jumped off, Blue turned and fled, cutting down a side street marked by a flashing red light across from a bait and tackle shop. A hundred yards down, she could tell the street dead-ended at a school of some sort. That did not look promising. Well before she reached the school, she saw a paved byway on her right, more an alley than a road. She dashed down it, deciding to take her chances with the unknown.

There was no one around. No one to hear her cries for help. Footsteps pounded the pavement behind her. The alley was dotted with the backs of a few houses, lonely and shuttered. A barking dog strained at its leash to get at her as she sprinted toward a Hardees sign in the distance. She was in a town, not in the woods. Someone there could help her.

The footsteps drew closer and closer. Blue kept running, arms and legs churning as fast as they could. As she passed a trailer hitch parked in the weeds off to the right, a hand grabbed her by the shoulder and spun her around. Before she could scream, Cobra covered her mouth and pulled her to the ground. Like oil on water, he slid effortlessly atop her, pinning her arms and holding a knife to her throat.

"What do you want?" she said. "I don't know anything."

He wasn't even breathing hard. "I know you were there. Who have you talked to?"

Blue was about to spout that she had talked to no one, then thought better of it. Once she admitted there was no more evidence, he would kill her. Through the fog of her fear, she made a snap decision. "Yeah, I saw it. I *filmed* it."

Cobra grew very still. "You did what?"

"On a digital camera I stole."

"Where is it?"

"I don't have it."

He pressed the knife tighter.

"In Creekville," she said, feeling a trickle of blood on her neck. "It's in Creekville."

"No," he said, after a moment. "I don't think so. You wouldn't have left it behind."

"Well, I did. I buried it in the woods." Blue tried to slip her hips to the side, but she couldn't budge. "Let me go!"

Cobra's voice was low and calm. "Take me to it, if you're telling the truth. I know you have it with you."

"You'll just kill me, no matter what I do."

"If you give it to me," he said, "I promise there will be no pain."

"No pain?" she said, in a panic. "So you're going to kill me!"

He put a hand over her mouth and pinched her on the shoulder, in a soft spot that sent arrows of pain shooting through her. His palm muffled her scream, and he pressed the tip of the knife against her eyelid. "You'll give it to me either way," he said, in that emotionless voice she found so terrifying. "That I promise you."

Blue believed him with all her heart. Unable to think of a good way out of the situation, she told him where to find it, praying he might send her inside the shelter alone and give her a chance to run or call for help.

The knife disappeared into his jacket as swift as any illusionist's trick. He rose and jerked her to her feet. "We'll see together if you're lying," he said, crushing her hopes. "And if you think of trying to escape, I'll kill you before the cops arrive."

She had a few blocks to think of something, though she knew it was hopeless. His grip on her shoulder was like a bear trap. Cobra would never let her get away, not when he thought she had witnessed a murder.

"And then?" she said. "If I get it for you?"

"We will see who else you've told."

"I didn't tell anyone or see anything. Take the camera and you'll know what I mean."

"You were in the woods that night."

"I'll take that to my grave. I swear."

"I know you will," he said quietly, and pushed her forward.

36

On Friday afternoon, as a bank of storm clouds gathered in the distance, Preach pulled into the gravel drive entrance to Carroll Street Homes. The nucleus of it all. The gravitational center around which the case swirled.

He realized someone unknown could have stolen the camera and the lighter and pawned them. The items could have ended up in anyone's hands, including Claire's. In fact, it looked like just the sort of fancy silver lighter she would carry.

Yet calls to the handful of pawnshops in Creekville and Chapel Hill had gotten him nowhere. He had even widened the search to the entire Triangle area, enlisting Bill and Terry. If that didn't pan out, Preach had a few other ideas, but first he was going to shake down the trailer park. A camera like the Canon would have stood out.

As he rolled through the park, he recalled the girl with the *Chinatown* shirt from his last visit. She seemed clever and aware. Maybe she had seen something. A long shot, he knew. But sometimes the tiniest detail could break a case. She had also lived close to Nate. What if Alana had entered the women's restroom and stolen the lighter and the camera?

If the *Chinatown* girl didn't know anything—he thought her name was Blue—he would go door to door if he had to. That lighter had a connection to the murderer, he could feel it. Maybe Claire herself had dropped it, and maybe not.

But he was going to trace it back.

While he was pondering why the lighter had turned up a hundred yards from the leaf pile—had the pair of murderers split up in the woods?—another thought came to him.

What if one of the two murderers hadn't dropped the silver lighter? What if someone *else* had? Someone totally unconnected?

He stopped where he was, struck by an idea.

What if someone else had witnessed the murder?

A witness in hiding, running for his life? The lighter, the stolen camera . . . could someone have *filmed* it with the stolen camera?

Good God. If that was the case, or if someone connected to David's murder even suspected it was, then another life could be in grave danger.

He let out a breath. Things were spiraling. He needed answers.

Earlier, he had talked to Alyssa Carson on the phone. She was on location filming a documentary in Charleston, South Carolina. Unfortunately, she had nothing to add, aside from reiterating the value of the camera and shouting at him that priceless footage from a recent film session was stored inside. What were the Creekville police doing, she wanted to know? Why couldn't they find her camera?

Good question.

The trailer park was busier than usual, hourly workers starting the weekend early and kids playing in the muddy streets after school. The same thugs as before lurked on the edges, eying Preach as he rolled through. He tried Nate's mother first, just in case, but she screeched at him to go away, demanding that he send Nate home. Preach asked her about the camera, which elicited a blank stare and another round of shouting.

Gritting his teeth, he knocked on Blue's door. No answer. All the lights were off inside. After that, he went door to door and talked to a few more neighbors, including a wiry retiree who lived across from Blue. Dressed in overalls with no undershirt, his teeth and nails stained yellow from tobacco, the old man's rheumy eyes wandered to his left, focusing on a trio of children at play, as he answered Preach's questions. When asked about the camera, the old man got a clever glint in his eye, right before he said he had no idea what Preach was talking about.

"A hot piece like that wouldn't last five seconds around here," the old man, whose name was Billy Flynn, said. "Someone would pawn it off quicker than a raccoon fart."

"I never said it was stolen," Preach said quietly.

He stuttered for a moment. "Well then how else in the Sam Hell would it end up here? Look around you."

Preach stepped closer, invading his space. The old man's breath reeked like spoiled meat. "Why don't you think a bit harder?"

Billy shuffled back a step. "You can't just come on in here."

"Is there a reason I would want to?"

"I don't know. You're the one came round."

"I think you've seen that camera before. I want to know when."

He leered at Preach, defiant. "I'm telling you I haven't."

Preach stared right back at him, until the old man lowered his eyes and retreated another step inside his trailer. On the kitchen table behind him, Preach spied an open laptop that looked twenty years old.

"How about I take that computer back to the station with me? I wonder if there'd be anything on there that shouldn't be?"

Billy started, his eyes slipping again to the kids playing in the street. "You can't do that. You ain't got no warrant."

"Mr. Flynn, I'm investigating a homicide. You have no idea what kind of authority I have. Don't believe what they tell you on TV. Now do you want to tell me something, or do I take your computer with me and see where you've been going on the Internet?"

"Aw listen, now," he said, waving a hand. "It's just that girl Blue." He pointed. "Lives right over there. I seen her with a camera once. Ain't got no idea if it's the same one, but it had to be stolen. She was prancing her little tush around at night filming stuff, pretending she was a fancy director." He cackled. "Kids got to dream when they grow up round here, don't they?"

"When was this?"

He shrugged. "Dunno. Couple weeks ago?"

"What else?"

"What you mean?"

"What else do you know about the camera? Does she still have it?"

He drew back as if Preach had insulted him, suddenly self-righteous. "Why would I know shit about that girl? I only seen her once at night with the camera, that's all."

"How often do you watch her at night?"

"What?" he said, sullen now. "Never."

"Except that one time."

"I was looking for my cat. It ran away."

Preach gave him a long, hard stare. He knew his type. Besides a probable pedophile, Billy was a man who would sell out his own mother to save his skin, living on the margins of society like a rat, gnawing at whatever came near. Preach sensed the old man was holding something back, too, though maybe it had nothing to do with David's death. Preach could come back and lean on him if needed. Right now, he had to find Blue.

"When was the last time you saw her?" Preach asked.

"The girl? Dunno. I ain't her pops. I s'pose it's been a few days, but like I said, I don't look out for her or nothing."

Before Preach could press him, Billy pointed a crooked finger over the detective's shoulder. "Why don't you ask *her*, now. That's her mother coming in from work."

Preach turned to see a tall, lean woman with dirty blond hair tied in a ponytail approaching Blue's trailer. The woman had Blue's narrow shoulders and graceful neck, but none of her poise. He could tell she once had been a stunner, but now she looked exhausted and defeated, a dirty dishrag that her forty-odd years had wrung the life out of.

"Excuse me," Preach called out as he hurried over, catching her just before she shut the trailer door.

"Oh," she said, holding it open. "Do I know you?"

He pulled out his badge. "I'm Detective Everson with the Creekville Police."

She waved a tired hand. "Annie isn't here. I haven't seen her in a few days. I just came home for a bite to eat."

"Annie is Blue?"

"That's right. I'm Gigi Stephens, her mother."

"How many days?"

She looked genuinely perplexed. "I . . . I'm not sure."

"And you're not worried?"

"About my daughter? I only said I hadn't seen her. I assumed she'd been in her room all week. She only comes out for school or money."

Preach had a hard time believing what he was hearing. "Are you telling me you don't know for sure if you're daughter's been home this week?

Blue's mother looked uncomfortable now. "I'm not neglecting her. I work long hours, and she's just at that age, you know? Teenage angst and all that. Convinced the world is against her."

It kind of looks like it is.

"What'd she do this time?" Gigi said, with a sigh.

"She might have come into possession of a stolen camera. Have you seen one around?"

"No," she said, "though I wouldn't be surprised. She's obsessed with movies."

Preach sucked in a breath. "Is that right?"

"She's always talking about going to Hollywood one day—as if anyone over there would have her. Not just Annie," she said hurriedly, sensing Preach was judging her. "I mean someone from," she waved a hand, "you know, from around here."

"Has your daughter ever owned a camera?"

"You mean a real camera? A movie camera?" Her laugh was self-deprecating, ashamed. "I can't even buy her a cell phone."

"Ma'am, I need you to listen carefully. I think your daughter may be in danger."

"What? Why?"

"I'm not positive—not even close to it—but there's a chance someone believes Blue witnessed a crime. A murder."

Gigi slowly lowered her hand from the door. "Who?" she said, almost in a whisper, then clapped a hand to her mouth. "Oh my God."

"What?"

"Someone else was here looking for her. Just yesterday. He said he was a friend from school, though he looked a little old for that. I thought maybe he'd been held back a year or two."

"What did he look like?"

The description she gave him, a young Latino male with an athletic build and intense eyes, caused a lump of dread to settle in Preach's stomach. "What did you tell him?"

"Just that I hadn't seen her. Who was he?"

"Let's just find Blue as quick as possible and see if we can clear this up."

"Okay. Okay." She took a deep breath. "Do you want to come in?"

"Sure."

After searching Blue's room and coming up empty, Preach accepted a glass of water and sat across the kitchen table from Gigi. The cheap plywood surface was covered in coupons and scratch-off lottery tickets.

Blue's mother looked shaken. "She took my spare cash," she said. "I haven't checked the drawer in a while. She wouldn't have done that unless she was leaving."

"Do you have any idea where your daughter might have gone?"

"She's never run away before. Not for real."

"Does she have a hideout? A special place she goes when she's upset?"

Her mother thought for a while, then held out her palms, helpless.

"What about a relative?"

"My family lives in Utah. We never talk."

"And her father?"

Gigi looked at an old photo attached to the refrigerator, of herself holding a baby in a city park. "He left a long time ago. When Annie was nine."

"Were they close?"

She started chewing on the tip of her thumb. "She worshipped him," she said distantly, still staring at the photo. "And he never came back. Not even a card on her birthday. Not once."

"Where did he go?"

"He ran off to California with a girl he met at a bar. And that, Detective, is the whole of the story. We fought from the beginning, and I can forgive him for leaving me. But Annie . . . he hurt my little girl so bad."

As he decided what to ask next, Gigi reached for a pack of Camel Lights sitting in a wooden bowl in the center of the table. After fishing out a cigarette, she lit up, crossed her long legs, and leaned back in her chair. "I stayed in this shithole trailer because I'm too poor to leave. My family in Utah is even worse off. God gave me blond hair, a healthy daughter, and little else in life. She's everything I have." Her chin quivered, and she swallowed. "Please find her for me."

"I'll do everything I can. Is there anywhere else she's familiar with? Has she ever been out of town before?"

Gigi thought for a moment. "She's been to the beach a few times. Day trips to Wrightsville. Her father took her to the circus once, Raleigh a few times . . ." she shrugged. "That's about it."

"Where's her father from?"

"Old Fort. A little hick town outside of Asheville."

"I know it. Has she ever been there?"

"Nope. Her father wasn't close with his family either. Had a falling out about an inheritance." She rolled her eyes. "A piece of swampland worth about five thousand dollars, mind you. Hardly the Biltmore fortune."

"Did Blue know about this?"

"We always kept that from her. After her father left, she never asked about his family."

"She knows where he's from, though? The town?"

"Yes."

"What about the address?"

"I'm not sure she knows it."

"But you have it?"

She told it to him. Preach gave a grim nod and dropped a card on the table. "If you hear anything, call me immediately."

"You're leaving? Where are you going? She could be anywhere."

No, he thought. *Not anywhere*. People don't go just anywhere. They go to someplace they know, and which they think others don't. If Blue knew someone like Cobra was after her, she wouldn't stay in Creekville. It was too dangerous. She would go away but not too far, and she would go someplace where she had a connection. By all accounts, this girl with big dreams had no one to turn to. No friends, no family, no sympathetic teachers at school.

Nothing except the memory of a beloved father, preserved in the amber of her own mind.

37

After pulling out of Carroll Street Homes, Preach grabbed a coffee to go and made the drive to Old Fort in under two and a half hours. A towering granite arrowhead, the only distinguishing feature as far as he could tell, marked the intersection of the two principal streets.

He went straightaway to the childhood home of Blue's father and was told the family had moved away years ago. He was also told a young woman had visited earlier that day, looking for Donnie Blue. The new residents had no idea where the girl had gone. He was glad to have his theory validated, but this was a problem. If Blue left Old Fort, then she could have gone anywhere, depending on her funds. Though if he moved quickly enough, he might be able to find her before she disappeared. He drove back to the center of town, parked his car beside the arrowhead monument, and tried to think it through from her perspective.

If I were a girl of sixteen, on the run with no help, where would I go?

Would I return home? Not under the circumstances.

Would I keep running? Maybe, if I had enough money.

And if this was the end of the line, at least for now? Where would I go? What would I do?

Though Preach had only met Blue once, he sensed both resilience and desperation in her eyes, strength and vulnerability, someone unsatisfied with her lot in life and who knew she had to make a change or risk drowning forever.

He didn't think she would crumble. That girl he had spoken to briefly was tough. Yet the news about her father's family might have hit her hard. He imagined that, in her mind, she had nurtured a secret hope that her father would one day return for her, and that he might help her now.

She wouldn't be ready to leave town. Not yet. She would stay a few days to process this final betrayal, this severing of a lifeline.

But where would she go in Old Fort? Again, it depended on her funds. She might check into a cheap motel, or even find a room for rent. Somewhere she could pay cash. How many hotels were in town? He had not seen a single one. Somehow, he doubted Airbnb was thriving here either.

First, he would check the obvious. Blue was young and poor. She had stolen petty cash from her mother. Unless she had sold the camera, which he doubted, she was probably desperate for money. Before she took a job or thought about whether to resort to stealing again, she would need a place to sleep. The streets were exceedingly dangerous for a young woman. Winter was coming on. It was cold at night. Yet there were options, shelters for the poor.

He imagined Asheville, only half an hour away, had plenty of choices. But a quick Google search told him there was a shelter right here in Old Fort, just a few blocks from where he was standing.

The Promise House. A home for runaway teens and single mothers.

Disappearing in and out of the mist, the mountains seemed to breathe around him, living monuments to an ancient age. The tallest peaks had a crown of early snow. He blew on his hands and got back in his car. There wasn't much to the town. An abandoned industrial plant sat like a scab near the exit off the interstate. Barely any pedestrians. A few elderly people doddering toward a funeral home. The directions to the shelter led him to an old church with a granite base and a newer second story with plank siding. A pair of teens loitered on the front steps. The cold climate had already stripped the leaves from the chestnut trees in the scraggly front yard, bare limbs clawing at the sky. An abandoned shopping cart rested against the brick sign at the head of the sidewalk.

Inside, he saw a familiar despairing sight. A short hallway that opened up into a common room divided into cubicles. Linoleum floors and the smell of disinfectant. A line of shabbily dressed mothers sitting in folding chairs at the front of the room, keeping an eye on a group of children watching cartoons on TV.

The head-high partitions were a nice touch, he thought. They gave the quarters a little dignity. Preach had visited plenty of shelters over the years, both as a pastor and as a police officer. They all made him sad, but it was the kids that got him the most. Not so much because of the physical circumstances, because kids were resilient. Give them stable love and food, and they didn't care about much else.

But take away one of those two, and you had problems.

Not that any normal parent didn't love their child. But life on the edges was rarely normal.

Times were always tough. Fortunes rose and fell. A few of these young mothers, maybe more than a few, would manage to pull out and reenter society. Yet most of them, due to addiction or abusive relationships or a cycle of poverty that had started when they were young, would fail.

And they would drag their kids down with them.

He didn't have the answers, but his thoughts about mothers and children drew him back to Claire, and Blue. Two people whose lives he had a chance to affect. As his eyes roamed the shelter for someone in charge, a spindly white-haired woman approached and asked if she could help. "Betty-Anne Clark," the nametag read.

According to Betty-Anne, Blue had checked in the night before and left around nine that morning, dressed in the same clothes as the day before.

"Do you remember if she had a camera with her?" Preach asked.

Betty-Anne tapped a finger against her sapphire ring as she thought. "I can tell you she wasn't carrying anything when she left this morning."

That was good, he thought. She had just left for the day and was planning on coming back.

"I'm sorry I can't help you more," she said, after Preach displayed his badge and explained the situation. "Our regulations prohibit random property searches."

He could get a warrant if needed, but that was okay. If the camera was in the shelter, it wasn't going anywhere. And Blue wasn't going back inside without him noticing. He knew both of these things as facts, because he planned to plant himself outside the shelter and wait as long as it took for her to return.

On second thought, Preach decided to park on Main Street, a block away from the Promise House. He still had a view of the entrance, and he didn't want to scare Blue off if she noticed a suspicious sedan parked right out front. She was skittish the first time he met her, even before she went on the run. If she saw him first, she might bolt and disappear.

As daylight faded, he drew stares from the handful of pedestrians who passed by on the sidewalk, unused to strange men camping out in parked cars in their town. A local officer stopped to question him, then brought Preach a cup of coffee and said to holler if he needed help. The coffee was weak and stale, but it worked its dark magic.

Just as he began to wonder if Betty-Anne had seen the wrong girl and Blue was on a bus to Charlotte or Atlanta, he heard a rumble in the background. Nothing too unusual, just a street bike, though on second thought he hadn't seen too many crotch rockets in Old Fort. He had seen zero, in fact. A pair of bearded old men on Harleys had cruised past him on the way in, and that was about it.

In the rearview, Preach saw a rider bearing down on a young woman walking his way on the sidewalk. He thought he recognized Blue's gangly form and swagger, as well as Cobra's lean build. Preach spilled his coffee in his haste to leave the car. By the time he had opened the door and jumped out to shout at her, Blue had turned and noticed Cobra, yelled, and dashed down a side street. The gang member quickly parked the bike and gave chase.

Preach didn't think either of them had heard his shout. He debated getting into his car and then took off on foot, reasoning they would be veering off the street. By the time he drove down the street and parked, they might already be gone.

Without taking the time to call the local police for help, worried he would lose them, Preach pulled his gun and sprinted after them, startling a hardware store owner who had stepped onto the street to lock his door.

Preach turned left at a flashing red light, down the same street Blue had fled. Neither of them were in sight. With a curse, he kept running, scanning to the sides for a hedge or another place where Cobra might have taken her. Preach dreaded hearing a scream or the crack of a gunshot, and he prayed the gang member wanted her alive.

Why wasn't she calling out? Was she saving her breath? The street dead-ended at a large building up ahead, set back from the road. Too exposed; he doubted she would have chosen that direction. Where, then? Had she headed to the creek bed on his left, partially hidden from view? What if he went that way and lost her?

As he raced through his options, pulling out his phone to call for backup, he passed a paved alley and thought he heard voices. He slowed, breathing hard, but saw nothing except for an unhitched equipment trailer squatting in the weeds, halfway down the alley. Maybe those voices had belonged to the neighbors. After whispering his location to the Old Fort police, Preach pulled his gun and crept forward. He had to balance his desire for surprise versus waiting too long and risking Blue's life.

Moving in a swift crouch, gun gripped in both hands and aimed at chest height, he drew to within twenty feet of the equipment trailer. Just as he got close enough to hear shuffling, Cobra emerged holding Blue by the arm with one hand, a knife pressed against her throat with the other.

"Police!" Preach shouted. "Step away from the girl!"

"Put the gun down," Cobra rasped.

"Not gonna happen."

"Do it!" Cobra said, pressing the knife tighter. Blue arched to relieve the pressure, her eyes wild with fear.

Cobra was shielding his own body with Blue's, making an impossible target. Preach was a good shot, but not good enough to hit a sliver of Cobra's head or arm while ensuring the bullet missed Blue. As far as

Preach could tell, the gang member wasn't carrying a gun, though he could have one stuck in the back of his black jeans. "Let the girl go."

"I can't do that."

"Why not?"

In response, Cobra began dragging her toward the other end of the alley. "If you follow, I'll kill her."

"There's nowhere to go. The local police have the roads out of town sealed."

Cobra gave a thin smile, and Preach knew that, to a man with a weapon and no compunction about hurting people, there was always an option.

Still, the odds were not in Cobra's favor. Preach didn't care if he escaped dead or alive at this point. He just couldn't let him escape with Blue. That would sign her death warrant.

Yet how to intervene without Cobra slitting her throat?

"It's the camera, isn't it?" Preach said, trying to buy time.

The gang member didn't react, but the comment caused Blue to wriggle harder in his grasp. Cobra had one of her arms pinned at her side, and she wasn't strong enough to get loose.

"I know who killed David," Preach lied. "You don't need her anymore."

Still no response. Cobra, his dispassionate eyes locked onto Preach, kept walking backward. Twenty feet to go before he reached the end of the alley and the greater freedom of the street. Preach advanced at a steady pace, gun still raised.

"Let her go, and we can strike a deal," Preach said. "I promise I'll talk to the judge—"

"One more step, and I'll slit her throat." Though Cobra hadn't raised his voice, the emotionless tone of his delivery convinced Preach he would do just what he said.

Preach stopped moving. They were ten feet from the end of the alley. *Think, Joe.*

"If I see you or any other cop on my way out," Cobra said, "I'll kill her on the spot."

"I can't let you take her," Preach said.

"You don't have a choice."

"There's always a choice. Do you have friends, family, kids? You'll never see them again." In Preach's experience, there was always at least one person that even the hardest criminal had a soft spot for. A friend, a grandmother, a son or daughter. "There are three roads out of town, Cobra, and they're all covered. Backup will be here in moments. You're only at kidnapping right now. Don't be a murder one."

They were five feet from the end of the alley. Cobra continued dragging Blue backward, eyes locked onto the detective. Preach had no choice but to follow. Cobra could hole up with his hostage in a house, but he couldn't get her in a car or on his bike without exposing himself to a shot.

Blue had gone limp in his arms, resigned to her fate. Preach would have to wait it out and pray he could reason with the assassin, or somehow pressure him into giving her up.

As they reached the end of the alley, and Cobra turned the corner with his hostage, Blue gave a sudden violent twist and threw her free hand into the assassin's face, clawing at his eyes. Before he could react, her fingers found purchase, and the gang member screamed in pain. When his free hand reached for his injured eye, Blue spun out of his grip, though the knife etched a red line into the side of her throat. Before Cobra could grab her again, Preach fired twice into his chest, dropping him.

Preach dashed forward, gun raised, wary of a concealed firearm. As he drew nearer, Cobra lunged at him with the knife, forcing Preach to shoot him again, this time in the shoulder. The knife clanged to the pavement as Cobra slumped on his back.

"Stay!" Preach yelled at Blue, as she fled down the alley holding her neck. When she hit the corner, she turned left and disappeared.

Preach patted down the gang member. No other weapons. Preach kicked the knife away and took in his condition. The two chest wounds, both near the heart, were pouring blood. Cobra's face had paled and his eyes looked dim and unfocused.

"Did you kill David?" he asked.

No response.

Preach snarled and knelt next to him. "It was you, wasn't it? Who else was with you?"

"*Lo siento*," Cobra whispered, as he stared at the sky.

"You're sorry? For what?"

The gang member started murmuring in Spanish as the whirr of sirens cut through the air.

"Who else was it?" Preach shouted, over and over, but Cobra wouldn't say another word. The moment local police appeared at the end of the alley, Preach took off after Blue.

38

Preach cut back to Main Street, racing toward the shelter on foot, guessing he would arrive faster than backtracking for his car. Maybe Blue had gone in a different direction, but he was betting she wouldn't leave the camera behind. He could sense it had come to represent something far greater than material value to her.

Though grateful he had saved her from Cobra, if the gang member died from his wounds, then his knowledge of the night of David's murder would die with him. And if Blue slipped through the cracks again . . .

Preach ran faster.

The smell of burning leaves drifted to his nostrils. Cold mountain air crackled in his lungs. The adrenaline from the confrontation in the alley started to fade, leaving him ragged and nervous, jittery with desperation to find Blue.

As he stepped onto the cement path at the entrance to Promise House, she burst out of the front door carrying a canvas satchel slung over her shoulder. Blue's fingers and the side of her neck were stained crimson from her wound. She saw him at once. After leaping down the front stoop with a single bound, she took off across the lawn as Betty-Anne tottered out of the door behind her, bearing a look of horrified confusion.

Summoning another burst of energy, Preach ran after Blue, shouting that he only wanted to talk. Nothing slowed her, and her long legs churned with the swift and easy stride of a deer. She might have evaded him, except clearly she had not walked the grounds yet, because the path she chose dead-ended at a six-foot wooden fence beside the house. With Preach steps behind her, she tried to cut through a hedge of holly that led to a neighboring yard, crying out as the edges of the nasty shrub bit into her flesh. Preach pulled her out, holding her at arm's length as he spoke as soothingly as he could.

"It's okay," he said, releasing her and raising his badge at a distance to show he meant her no harm. She was backed against the hedge and had nowhere to go. "We got him. He'll never come after you again."

At first, Blue looked as if she might try to slip past him or put up a fight, but then she collapsed on the ground and hugged her knees. Her jaw quivered, and she composed herself with an angry shake of her head.

"Let me see the wound," he said.

"It's just a scratch."

He peered closer and saw that she was right. Though messy, the knife swipe across her neck had already stopped bleeding. "Let me take you home," he said, offering to help her up.

She stared at the outstretched hand. "Is he dead?"

"I don't know."

"I hope he is."

"Either way, he's in custody. He'll go away for a long time."

She fiddled with the sleeve of her jacket. "I can't go home. They know who I am."

"And who are you? What do you know?"

"I don't know *anything*. They just think I do. And nothing I say will convince them I don't. You don't know them."

"I do, Blue. I know exactly who they are."

"You're just a Creekville cop."

"Blue," he said, taking a knee to look her in the eye. "You overestimate them. Most of them are scared kids, just like you. And I spent more than a decade working homicide in Atlanta. I've dealt with gangs far, far scarier than this one."

She looked away again. "Doesn't change anything."

"I'll tell you what *will* change things."

"What?" she said, turning sullen.

"Catching the other person in the woods that night. You know what I'm talking about, don't you? I believe two people murdered David Stratton, and one of them was Cobra. Do you think the same?"

Slowly, untrusting, she raised her eyes to meet his gaze. After a moment, she nodded, once.

"Do you know who the other person is?" he asked.

"No. I swear."

"I'll protect you either way," he said. "But if we can catch the other one, then there won't be any need for protection, will there?"

She thought about it for a moment. "What if they think I talked?"

"These guys aren't the mafia. They're small-town thugs. However this turns out, I'll have a talk with them and let them know you didn't say a word, and that if they ever lay a finger on you, I'll spend every second of every day making sure they regret it."

"You will?" she said, almost in a whisper.

He stuck out a hand. "You have my word."

After another hesitation, she accepted his gesture, and he pulled her to her feet.

"How will you protect me right now?" she asked.

"Didn't you steal a camera?"

"Yeah," she said, wary again. "Why?"

He gave her a tight smile. "No one told you that sort of thing can land you in jail?"

On the ride home, Blue told him everything she knew about the night of David's death: how she was filming in the woods and heard voices she could not identify, the muted gunshots, dropping her bag and stepping through the rotten log, the terrified flight through the forest.

Poor thing, he thought. She had lived in fear for weeks.

Unfortunately, her story didn't do him much good beyond confirming what he already knew, and they were no closer to discovering the identity of the second person in the woods. He hoped to change that back at the station. While Blue said there was nothing helpful on the camera, the video techs might say otherwise.

On the drive home, he insisted Blue call her mother and tell her she was okay. After a phone call that turned tearful, Preach took the phone back and told her mother about his plan to keep Blue in a holding cell for a few days, where he could keep an eye on her. Gigi gratefully consented.

When they arrived at the station, he had never seen anyone so content to sit behind bars. Blue looked relieved, exhausted, and grateful beyond words for a hot meal. He ordered Bill to find some books she liked from the library and bring them over in the morning. Claire, who was three cells further down the hallway, never saw them come in. When he had questioned Blue earlier, she had claimed she knew who David's mother was but had never met her.

Preach kept Blue's incarceration off the books, both to ensure her record stayed clean and to keep her off the radar of anyone who might be snooping. The only people he told at the station were Chief Higgins and Terry Haskins. They had video surveillance, and Preach would sleep at the station if he needed to.

When the chief asked why he was off in Western North Carolina running down a camera, he said he wanted more evidence to pin on Claire. The chief had glared at him but let it pass.

Early the next morning, Lela Jimenez hovered over a large monitor in the Chapel Hill crime lab, booting up the department's latest video enhancement software. Both she and Preach had viewed several times the footage Blue had shot on the Canon the night of David's death. Starting with Blue's video of the trailer park, the entire film was less than two hours long. The relevant portion was much shorter, the few minutes in the woods when Blue had tried to catch a rendezvous on film. Date notations on the video feed made it easy to pinpoint the exact start time: 12:43 a.m.

"She didn't know what she was doing," the forensics expert said, as the enhancement program loaded. So far, almost nothing could be seen. The footage was too dark and grainy, the subjects too far away. "The low resolution, poor lighting, background noise, shaky picture? That's not the camera. It's the operator. This camera is a Cadillac. And that EF-L lens? If she'd known how to use it, she could have shot a snail's slime on a tree from a hundred feet away."

"Can you restore anything?"

"It's not restoring," Lela chided. "It's enhancing. Used to be," she said, as the home screen for the software popped up and she inserted a USB drive with the footage into the computer, "this would take hours, at least. We had to convert, stabilize, register, de-warp, sharpen. Trust me, it was a huge pain. All manual and error-prone." She snapped her fingers and grinned. "Watch this."

Her fingers went to work, running through the choices onscreen faster than Preach could follow. Eventually the beginning of Blue's footage appeared. Lela clicked the mouse, a percentage bar zoomed from zero to one hundred, and the image began to clarify. "Super-resolution-based reconstruction algorithm," she said, her normally taciturn personality bubbling over with excitement. "De-interlacing, dynamic lighting correction, stabilization. Hours of hard work in minutes. And better results."

"Just find me something," he murmured.

"I can't believe the department splurged on this software. Used to be this was fed territory. DOD and FBI."

"What's that?" he said, pointing at the screen. "That's new."

At the edge of the picture, two shapes had appeared, clarifying into distinct human forms. The camera lost them again, and Preach cursed.

Moments later, the shapes returned. They were still quite a distance away, shadowy and anonymous, but one of them was clearly shorter than the other, with longer hair. They kept walking toward the camera, and Preach gripped the back of the chair he was leaning over. He had seen this before, though not as clear.

"That isn't Claire," he said.

"What? How can you tell? There's no face yet."

"Her walk. It's different." He leaned back on his heels, feeling as if a great weight had just lifted.

"Different how?"

"This woman and Claire both have good posture, but Claire's gait is less . . . bouncy."

"Really? You can tell that?"

"I'm a detective. I'm paid to notice things."

That, and the way Claire sways as she walks has been burned into my memory for twenty years.

He knew something like that would never hold up in court, and he was embarrassed for recognizing it. But that was okay. He was sure it wasn't Claire. *She didn't kill her own son.*

But who had?

The people stopped moving and began talking. Even with the enhanced resolution, their faces remained unclear, and they were too far away to make out the words. As Preach knew from repeated viewings, after the short conversation, the two people moved offscreen, the gunshots sounded, and they never reentered the footage.

Except this time, in the long pause before the second gunshot, a flicker had appeared at the edge of the screen. A barely visible man stepping out of the foliage to the left of the clearing, then walking forward with a gun in his hand. The man took a moment to scan the clearing, and for a brief instant, his face was visible.

Cobra.

"Got you," Preach said, staring intently at the screen. One down.

"That's your guy?"

"Yep. Can we boost the volume?" he asked. "Try to hear what they were saying at the beginning?"

"It's already at the maximum."

"Damn." He ran a hand through his hair. They let the portion in the woods run to the end again but never saw a second face. "Back it up."

"Where to?"

"Right before they go offscreen, before the first gunshot. I thought I caught a flash of something."

"Me too. Probably just a trick of the light."

"Try it anyway. We need something."

She rewound the video and caught the last instant the pair was visible before walking offscreen. The shorter person with long hair, the woman, had her back to the camera.

"A little bit more," he said. "Right as she's turning. Keep going . . . keep going . . . there! Did you see it?"

"Absolutely," Lela said, leaning closer to the screen. "Can you enhance it any more?"

"Yes. But we'll lose clarity."

"Do it."

Lela complied. Despite the gradual blurring of the image, before they reached the brief glint of light he had seen, Preach was astonished to find they could now see the victim's face enough to make out who it was.

David.

"That's two," he said, letting out a deep breath. "Who are you, mystery woman?"

David's enhanced face now filled the screen. The blurry resolution made Preach feel uncomfortable, as if the boy's ghost, haunting and inchoate, had been summoned from the ether. Though his features were warped by the enhancement, the expression Preach saw, the searching eyes and parted lips, surprised him.

David didn't look angry or afraid or in trouble. In fact, he looked the opposite.

He looked as if he was about to kiss the person in front of him.

"Pan out," Preach said. "Get the flash we saw."

It took Lela a dozen attempts to catch it, but she finally isolated the almost instantaneous sparkle they had both caught onscreen. It came right as the woman, who they could now tell had blond hair, entered the image. For an instant, they caught the side of her head just before it turned completely away from the screen. And in that moment, caught like a piece of glitter from the heavens, a twinkle in the lambent moonlight, was a silver earring in the shape of a star, inset with a deep blue stone.

Lela gave an approving whistle. “Is that a blue diamond in the center? And white diamonds lining that silver star? That’s a serious piece of jewelry. Very rare at the least, maybe even one of a kind.” She looked up. “You might be able to track this!”

“No need,” he said, reaching for his coat. “I already know who it belongs to.”

39

Before he bet it all on one horse, Preach wanted to be one hundred percent sure. As night settled in and the deep Carolina sky faded to black, he drove fifteen minutes away to the Orange County Juvenile Detention Center, a smattering of depressing brick buildings surrounded by barbed wire. Preach pulled up to the gate and told the guard why he was there. Once inside, he parked beside the last bus and hurried inside the main building. It took him half an hour of conversation and paperwork to secure an audience with Nate Wilkinson, and the detective's thoughts spun in a thousand directions as he waited in a white-walled holding area.

He thought he knew all the players now, but what had happened that night in the woods?

What was David's role in all of this?

What had gone so terribly wrong?

His sneer in place, Nate slumped into a metal folding chair on the other side of the table from Preach. After waving off the guard, the detective leaned forward, clasping his hands atop the table. "I don't have much to say tonight, because I don't think you know much of anything."

"I've been telling you that, man."

"But I do think you're lying about something."

Nate rolled his eyes and scratched the side of his nose.

"Who gave you the idea?" Preach said quietly.

"Huh?"

"Who told you to lie about Claire?"

"I told you what I know, and my attorney made a deal. I'm out of here in a month."

As he leveled his gaze at Nate, Preach's voice hardened. "I'm going to make this real simple. You're here on a drug charge. Minor time. Even less with the deal. But son, if you lie about a murder, and someone goes to jail for that, and it comes out later what you did . . ." he shook his head. "Not only does that invalidate the deal, but you don't even want to know the kind of trouble you'll be in."

Nate stared off to the side, unresponsive.

"Did Bentley Montgomery tell you to lie?"

Preach saw the kid's hand twitch ever so slightly atop the table.

"I think Bentley told you what to say," Preach said, "and planted that ledger at Claire's house. I believe you about the new drug queen in town. All that info you gave the DA has the ring of truth. I just don't think it was Claire."

Though Nate still hadn't spoken, his posture was deflating, all the fight seeping out of him.

"You're scared, aren't you?" Preach asked. "Of Bentley?"

Now sitting rigid as a flagpole, Nate slowly mashed his lips, churning inside and out.

"We'll talk about that later," Preach said, "but I'll make this easy on you. You don't have to say anything. I'm going to give you a name—the name of your supplier—and I just want you to nod. Okay?"

"I can't go against him," Nate mumbled, so low Preach could barely hear him.

"Like I said, we'll deal with that later. But unless you want to risk being tried as an adult and doing serious time, I need to clear Claire's name—the name you gave us—and put David's real killer away."

Nate swallowed, and Preach felt a rush of sympathy for him. The kid was out of his depth.

"I was never here today, okay?" Preach said.

"Okay," Nate whispered.

Preach gave him the name, and after a long moment, one in which Preach second-guessed his intuition and his legwork, a moment in which it felt as if the whole balance of the case teetered, Nate sniffed and tipped his head.

And Preach knew.

More of a modern day castle than a private residence, it was the kind of house that existed only in fairy tales, or in documentaries about the titans of industry of centuries past. It was the kind of house that was as unobtainable to a police officer on a government salary as was reaching past the Milky Way to visit another galaxy, thousands of light years away.

That was okay. Preach had never cared much about the finer things in life, and he didn't resent those who did.

What he cared about was those who broke the law to get them.

This time, though, he wasn't certain it was the owner of the house who had taken a few shortcuts. There were still pieces of David's case he hadn't put together, but he was certain he knew the salient parts. The *who* and *where* and *when*.

He just didn't know the *why*.

Patches of clouds obscured the majority of the stars. The glow of a pregnant moon softened the night, and the manicured lawn emitted a wonderful aroma of late fall blooms. On his way to the front door—or at least he assumed it was the front door, since there appeared to be five separate entrances on the rambling limestone facade—his shoes padded softly across the cobblestone walkway, and he spied a clay tennis court through the trees to the left. The house was silent and imposing, all spires and steeply pitched roofs, designed to evoke a French chateau.

A butler in a white tuxedo answered Preach's knock, which took him aback. He did not realize such things still existed in America.

"Mr. Everson. Good evening. The gate attendant mentioned you would like to speak with Mr. Rathbun, but I'm afraid he and the missus are away for the week."

"It's *Detective* Everson, and I'm here to see Mackenzie. Not her parents."

"Ah. I see."

"I was told at the restaurant she was having a little party."

"I'm unaware of this."

"Is that why I see a dozen cars parked on the street outside?"

As the butler spluttered, Preach held up a finger, silencing him. In the distance, coming from somewhere behind the house, he heard the rising thump of bass, followed by a shriek of laughter.

"Take me to her," Preach said. "Right now."

Looking as if he might be ill, the poor man had no choice but to comply. The interior of the great house passed by in a blur of fine art, luxurious carpet, and furniture that looked like it belonged in the court of Louis XIV. They passed through half a dozen rooms before the butler threw wide a set of French doors that opened onto a rectangular pool stretching a few hundred feet away from the house, flanked on both sides by a lawn as pristine as a putting green. At least a dozen college kids were swimming in the heated pool illuminated with track lights on the bottom. A few more people were in the hot tub, and another group was wrapped in towels and clustered around a trio of outdoor heating lamps that sprouted from the lawn like giant exothermic mushrooms. A pair of outdoor speakers on the deck area blasted out a rap tune. Bottles and cups were everywhere.

Except for a pair of kids snorting coke off a silver plate on a wrought-iron table, who scurried to hide the evidence, no one paid much attention as Preach stood at the edge of the pool and swept the crowd. When he found Mackenzie lounging in the hot tub in a white bikini, she was staring right at him. She looked away as soon as his eyes found hers.

As he approached, she put her elbows on the flagstone and leaned back, arching her breasts as her lips curled into a coy smile. "I remember you," she said.

"Mackenzie, you need to come with me."

"A cop, right?"

"Detective."

"Maybe you should grab a beer and join us. The water's nice."

"Don't make me ask again."

As the other people in the hot tub stared at them, she laughed and made little circles in the water with one of her feet. "Can't we just talk right here? Getting out would be a real buzzkill."

He walked over to her, leaning down so no one else could hear. "I'm arresting you for the murder of David Stratton. We already have Cobra." When he said that, her feet stopped moving in the water. "I'll cuff you right here if I have to, but I thought you might want to avoid a scene."

After seeing how serious he was, Mackenzie pulled herself out of the hot tub, wringing water out of her long blond hair. A friend tossed her a towel. She dried off and wrapped her athletic body in the thick cotton. "I'll be right back, y'all. Keep the party going."

As the butler watched in dismay, Preach took her inside and recited her Miranda rights. He had Bill Wright, who was waiting in a separate car, drive her to the station and process her.

Forensics was already en route. After ordering the butler to send the other kids home, Preach went ahead and started searching. Within minutes, he had found the star-shaped earrings in Mackenzie's bedroom, and he dropped them in an evidence bag.

Hours later, weary in body and mind, aching in his soul, Preach returned to the station and updated Chief Higgins on the new developments. He had called her on her cell phone at home, and she had decided to come in. Though after midnight, the Creekville police station was buzzing like it was midday.

"So you found three more drug ledgers in her apartment," Chief Higgins said, warming her hands around a cup of herbal tea behind her desk. Dark circles floated under her eyes, and her flame-red hair was greasy and unkempt. Preach sat across from her, sipping a cup of coffee, knowing his appearance was just as haggard.

"Going back over a year," he said. "She's been running meth, coke, heroin, mommy pills. Half her business is college students."

"Jesus. Have you talked to her?"

"I'm about to."

"She didn't lawyer up?"

"Not yet. Her phone call was to her mother."

"So Claire isn't involved with this after all?" There was no trace of pettiness in the chief's voice. Only grudging respect.

"Once they saw the noose tightening around the circumstantial evidence, I believe they thought Claire would make a good patsy and planted the ledger at her house. The way Claire sleeps," he cleared his throat, "I mean with the drugs she takes before bed, it wouldn't be too hard."

"Who's they?"

"Los Viburos. I don't know for sure, but I'm guessing Bentley is the mastermind."

The chief threw her hands up. "The mastermind of what?"

"Turning Carroll Street Homes into such a crime-ridden swamp that the Creekville City Council will vote to change the zoning and let Bentley's company develop it. That property is worth millions. Maybe tens of millions."

"Okay," she said, nodding, "I can buy that. But how does David fit in?"

"That," he said, pushing to his feet and tucking the case file under his arm, "is what I hope I'm about to find out."

"Was he dealing for you?" Preach asked, as he slid into the chair across from Mackenzie in the station's lone interview room. Wrapped in a cashmere shawl and jeans, her hair loose around her shoulders, she looked tired, scared, and completely and utterly lost.

Yet there was another emotion Preach saw in her eyes. One which he planned to exploit.

Mackenzie Rathbun, he thought, looked relieved.

The truth will do that to you.

"Dealing? David? No," she scoffed. "As far as I know, he didn't touch the stuff."

"Then what happened that night?"

She covered her face in her hands, lowered her head, and began to quietly sob. When she had composed herself, she looked up through tear-streaked eyes and said, "I didn't kill him. I didn't."

"I believe you. Did Cobra pull the trigger? Shoot him in the head?"

She nodded.

"You fired the first shot, though, didn't you?"

She moaned and covered her face again. "It wouldn't have killed him. It was just a stomach wound. They made me do it. I tried to back out after that, I swear. He made me. Oh, God—he made me!"

"Who did?"

She opened her mouth to speak, then slowly closed it again.

"Was it Cobra? Bentley Montgomery?"

"I can't say," she said, in a near-whisper.

"Even though he put you here?"

"I . . . I can't."

"Okay," he said, sensing empathy would get him much further than a show of force. "We'll talk about that later. But I need to understand why you did it, Mackenzie. What happened between you and David?"

Her lips parted, as if ready to speak, but then she started to cry again. He could tell she was genuinely distressed, burning up with guilt.

"Talk to me," he said. "I'll help you if I can."

As she struggled to gain control of her emotions, someone knocked on the door to the interview room. The detective turned to see Chief Higgins pushing the door open, followed by a sixtyish man in a pin-striped suit, as well as a paunchy man with squinty eyes and a head full of regal silver hair. Preach recognized the silver-haired man from the news.

Jerry Rathbun II. Mackenzie's father.

"We need to talk," Chief Higgins said to Preach. "Mackenzie's father is here with their attorney, Paul Sanderson."

Instead of the lawyer, Jerry Rathbun stepped forward. As his jowls quivered in anger, laced with the red veins of a heavy drinker, he said, "This ends here."

"Excuse me?" Preach said, as he scooted his chair back and stood.

"You came into my house and arrested my *daughter*. I can assure you my lawyer—"

"Okay," interrupted Chief Higgins. "You've asserted your rights. Now let's—"

"What are you talking about?" Mackenzie said, turning to face her father. "They're my rights, and I haven't asserted anything."

"Shut up, Mackenzie," her father said. "Don't say another goddamn word."

As her lawyer started talking about due process, Mackenzie rose and pointed a shaky finger at her father. "You don't get to do this," she said. "Not anymore."

"I said *not another word*."

"Shut up, Daddy!" she screamed. Preach could see in her eyes that something had snapped, some pent-up demon with an origin far older than the events of the last few months. "You're the reason all this happened! *You!*"

After a moment of shocked silence, Jerry put a palm out, bobbing it up and down. "Now just calm down. We can talk about this later, with Paul. Your mother and I just flew in from Florida because of this. We're leaving this station together, right now, while Paul clears things up."

"Leaving?" A hysterical laugh escaped her. "Didn't they tell you what I did?"

"Shut *up*, Mackenzie!"

The lawyer stepped forward, and Jerry put a hand on the man's chest.

"I just wanted to help Bentley show you up, you know," Mackenzie said. "That's all. Develop that property and put you in your place for once. I never meant to . . ."

"Paul," Jerry said, his voice as taut as a suspension cable, moving his hand off his attorney's chest, "sort this out."

The lawyer started to speak, but the chief held up a hand and turned to face Mackenzie. "As you said, it's your decision. Are you asserting your right to a lawyer?"

"I am," she said, "but not yet, and not him." With a twisted, melancholy smile, she looked right at Preach and said, "First I'm going to tell you—and only you—exactly what happened. I'm going to tell the truth for once. David deserves it. And Bentley can go to hell."

Looking unbalanced and grief-stricken, ignoring the strenuous objections of her father and his attorney, both of whom the chief led unceremoniously to the hallway before she shut the door, Mackenzie Rathbun sat with Preach and proceeded to do exactly what she had promised.

40

Mackenzie's father never hit her, but he might as well have. Always the looming presence, a thundercloud ready to burst, watching every move, criticizing, controlling, disparaging. The verbal abuse against Mackenzie and her mother. What to wear, what to say, how to act, when to do it.

They might as well have been slaves in that house.

It was all about the money. Of course it was. What else did that fat, drunken patriarch, other than providing sperm to her mother, have to offer her?

Mackenzie cared about money as only the super wealthy can: She both took it for granted and understood how rare and precious it was. A ruthless sort of cynicism. Yet as much as she wanted to break free, her trust fund would never be hers while *he* was still alive. To get paid, she had to walk the path he had charted. A path she hated.

Go to school for global finance. Help run the family empire. Report to him every day. Marry whom he says. Buy the house he picks. Every last detail of her life planned out.

Why couldn't she just walk away?

She asked herself that question every single day.

But she didn't have the courage, either for running away or confrontation, so she had chosen a different, timeless route of protest: rebellion.

The drug money came easy. It felt good to earn something for herself, real money, and thumb her nose at her father (silently) in the process. Imagine if he knew! It was almost as good as telling him off to his face!

Bentley had set her up with the supply. She had a nose for business and plenty of friends to get started, and her reputation spread from there.

That was supposed to be it. The extent of her foray into crime. But then she sat in on a family meeting and heard her father talking about some old farmer who was ready to sell Carroll Street Homes, a property she knew her father had coveted for some time. Purely to antagonize him, she passed the opportunity on to Bentley, and he conceived the idea to buy it at any cost, knowing he could flood the trailer park with crime until the Creekville City Council changed the zoning.

The family had a vast investment portfolio, but with the factories long shuttered, Mackenzie's father made most of his new money from property development. She would hit him where it hurt. Steal an investment in his own backyard. She would tell him about it one day, too. Right before she walked out with all her drug money and started a new life someplace else. She would beg her mother to come, but that would never happen. Her mother's tea bag had steeped for far too long, the golden handcuffs twisted so tight she couldn't twitch a muscle.

Rebellion became sedition, and nothing Mackenzie had ever done had felt quite so good. Now, sitting in that white-walled interview room with the detective, in one of those moments of true reflection that sprang from hitting rock bottom, she was self-aware enough to know she had done these things to get her father's attention as much as hurt him. She both loved and hated him, just as she did herself.

And she despised him all the more because of it. He didn't deserve an ounce of her love.

It was all going well until that fateful night at the restaurant. Bentley came in now and again, when he wanted to impress a girl. Take her away from the mean streets of East Durham and ply her with steaks and ambiance. It was how he and Mackenzie had met. She had waited on him a few times, heard about his reputation on the street, and approached him one night on the patio, when he had come in alone and stayed until closing. Had he known at the time? Sensed her vulnerability and wanted her to approach him? She wouldn't put it past him.

They hashed out their new arrangement on a cocktail napkin, which he burned in the candle flame flickering inside a mason jar in the center of the table. He rarely came in after that, but she met him in other places from time to time, always at his request. He avoided public recognition, didn't need flash and attention like other gangsters. He had never made a pass at her or asked her to do anything she didn't want to do.

Not until David.

A handsome kid, sure, but just a high school student. A busboy over the summer. Mackenzie knew he had a major crush on her, and he was a good listener, but he was not in her orbit. Not when it came to dating.

Still, they talked much more than anyone knew. Whenever she needed a friendly ear, or a dinner companion, he would meet her at the drop of a dime. One night in late September, unbeknownst to her, he had parked in the employee lot behind the restaurant, waiting for her shift to end. Feeling restless, he had left his Jeep and used a young crepe myrtle to climb atop the roof. He lay on his back and contemplated the starry sky as well-heeled diners bit into filet mignons and consulted the sommelier. He told her all this later, before his death.

This happened to be a night that Bentley himself had driven to meet Mackenzie and talk business. As David lurked overhead, unseen in the darkness and wondering what the fancy black Navigator was doing behind the restaurant, Mackenzie popped out during her shift, responding to Bentley's text. Before David had a chance to react, Bentley lowered his window, puffed on a cigar, and talked in a low voice—but not too low for David to hear—in the otherwise empty back lot.

David didn't hear much. Mackenzie would argue that point later, with Bentley, after he gave his terrible order. Only then would she understand just how merciless and vicious the crime lord was, so domineering he made her father seem like a timid, weak-willed minion.

She was never quite sure how Bentley knew David was there. David claimed he never made a sound, but Bentley said he heard a scuff on the roof after the conversation, ran the plates in the parking lot, and figured it out. However it happened, David himself confirmed it, when he confronted Mackenzie about her life of crime.

That was the worst thing of all. Despite how besotted the kid was, he didn't ignore what he had heard or tell her it was cool.

He tried to convince her to stop working for Bentley.

He tried to make her a better person.

Even now, the knowledge made her shudder.

The next night, Bentley invited Mackenzie to his house for the first time. Down in his basement, after plying her with expensive cognac, he told her that David had overheard their conversation and said she had to kill him.

Had she heard correctly?

Kill him? *Me*?

Hell, no, she said.

Oh yes, he replied, in that chill-inducing voice, as hard as it was well mannered. *You will indeed. You will do it in this way, and with this gun, on the very next night he comes to see you.*

It was all so dreamy, she thought. Unreal. She wasn't going to kill anyone. She wasn't going to kill *David.*

But if she didn't, Bentley said he would kill David himself, and frame her, and make sure she went to prison for the rest of her life.

How can you threaten me like that? she had said. *I'll just tell them you set me up.*

His answer to that was a long, booming laugh.

Eventually she agreed. What choice did she have? He wouldn't let her go, and she would say whatever it took to get out of that basement. Except before she left, the last thing he did was make her watch the video he had just recorded.

The one where Mackenzie had vowed to kill David.

So you see, Bentley had said, *it is all ready for you. The boy is already dead. Your only choice is whether you will choose to live the rest of your life in freedom or rot in jail.*

Except her freedom, she knew as soon as she left that evil house, was already gone. Bentley owned her now.

Please, Mackenzie had begged David in her mind. *Leave town or quit school or run away to Siberia. Don't ever come to see me again.*

What happened next was a blur. Everything moved so quickly. David came to see her a few nights later, the night of October 2. He usually respected the barrier between them, the one where she called him if she wanted to see him, but that night he came into the restaurant distraught about his mother. They had just had a huge fight. He loved Claire very much but hated her relationship with Brett. David knew why she was dating him and despised the situation. They didn't need the money, he kept telling his mother. Just each other. Just their love. They could live in a trailer in Carroll Street Homes for all he cared. Just don't be a whore because of me.

David said he had told his mother exactly that, and she had slapped him. Hurt and angry, he jumped in his Jeep and fled to the restaurant, where he begged Mackenzie to go somewhere with him, anywhere. When she walked him to his Jeep, thinking only of what she had to do, he said he wanted to be more than friends. They had to go somewhere and talk it out, he said. Tonight. After her shift.

Her cell had buzzed, and she turned away to read it.

<Do it now>

She swallowed. *Oh God. He's watching.*

Moving as if in a dream, she told David to meet her in half an hour behind his house, so they could take a moonlit walk in the woods. He had taken her to his house once before, when his mother was away, and showed her the path in the backyard. This was Bentley's idea. He wanted someplace David would feel secure, but isolated enough for Cobra to clean up the mess.

Mackenzie hated the crime lord's devious mind. She kept telling herself she wouldn't do it. There had to be another way out of this nightmare. Yet half an hour later, one of Bentley's associates dropped her off at the edge of Carroll Street Homes, and she found herself slipping through the woods to David's house.

How'd you get here? he asked in surprise, when he left the house to meet her.

Uber. Didn't you see?

Nope, but I was showering. Why didn't you knock?

I wasn't sure about your mother.

He waved a hand. *She's out cold. What's in the backpack?*

Just a few clothes. Her lips curled. *In case I need a change in the morning. Didn't you say your mother never goes in your room?*

He slipped an arm behind her back, pulling her in for a kiss, but she pulled away and traced a finger across his lips. *Let's see about that midnight stroll. The woods are sexy at night.* She patted the backpack. *I might have a blanket in here too.*

David grinned. *In that case, we're gonna need some refreshments.* He took her by the hand and, before she could protest, led her through the back door into the house. *Mom takes a handful of pills every night. She wouldn't know if an elephant came through.*

As he grabbed a bottle of Four Roses bourbon from the study, Mackenzie was both terrified someone would see her and elated by the delay. She wanted a way out, she really did. She wanted his mom to wake up or the cops to come or a tree to fall on the house.

But she knew deep down, without a doubt, that Bentley would kill David no matter what happened. David had heard him discussing business and seen the crime lord's car, maybe even his face. He could put him away. A chink in Bentley's armor who couldn't be allowed to live.

On the way out of the house, David locked up and took Mackenzie by the hand, leading her into the woods, never noticing the nine millimeter she had tucked into her jeans underneath her baggy sweater. When they reached the appointed spot in the clearing, she stopped and took him by the face, kissing him long and hard. At the end of the kiss, unable to help herself, she started sobbing.

Why are you crying?

I just . . . you're just so good to me. So kind.

I like you too.

No, you don't understand.

Understand what?

David . . .

Talk to me. We've always been able to talk. This doesn't change anything.

I'm sorry, she whispered. So very sorry.

Sorry? Why? He lifted her chin and smiled. *For not doing this sooner?*

Tears poured down her cheeks. *Yes, that. Very much that.*

He gently wiped her eyes. *Is it the drugs? I forgive you, you know. And I know why you're doing it. But you have to stop. Your dad isn't worth it.*

Oh, David.

You're only hurting yourself.

When he leaned in to kiss her again, she shot him in the stomach. It felt like an out of body experience, as if someone else had taken control of her hand and pulled the trigger.

In disbelief, he moaned and staggered back from the force of the bullet, right before the pain hit him like a wrecking ball. As she dropped the gun and went to him, unable to follow through, her entire body shaking as she helped him to the ground, Cobra glided out of the trees as smooth and silent as a shadow.

Move, he said.

We don't have to do this, she begged. *He won't tell anyone.*

I said move.

No. I won't.

He nodded at her backpack. *You were supposed to put the tarp down. There's blood everywhere.*

I forgot. Don't do this. Don't kill him.

Unable to cope, she buried her head in David's back, still holding him from behind. In disgust, Cobra jerked her away by the hair and tossed her aside.

Then he stood over David and shot him in the head.

41

As Preach stood in front of Claire's cell and unlocked the door, all he could see was an image of the last night he had spent with Ari, making love as rain slashed the windows, the rise and fall of her chest as she slept, thunder rattling the panes, his gaze lingering on the sharp angles and delicate curves of her face, the fine-boned features radiating strength and mystery and integrity, a woman he loved inside and out.

How could he have been so stupid?

"You're free to go," he said to Claire.

She sat up on her cot, blinking the sleep away. It was 6 a.m. Sunday morning. Preach had spent the night at the station, dealing with Mackenzie and the aftermath, unable to sleep as the adrenaline ebbed.

"What happened?"

"Mackenzie confessed."

"Mackenzie? *David's* Mackenzie?"

As Preach gave her an abbreviated version of the story, Claire's face turned whiter and whiter, until she clenched the bedsheet and jumped to her feet. "That *bitch*. I can't believe . . . oh God, Joe. Oh my *God*."

He held the cell door open while she sobbed, understanding the power of closure. He didn't try to comfort her, and she didn't ask him to.

When she calmed, she dried her eyes and shrugged into a gray sweater. "You kept investigating, didn't you? After I was arrested?"

"I did."

"Why did you believe me?"

"Just a gut instinct."

"Well," she said, tossing her hair and lacing her pink designer tennis shoes before she stepped into the hallway, "thanks." She said it in a flippant manner, almost coldly.

"It's my job."

"I still can't believe you arrested me," she said, with a shake of her head.

He shut the cell door behind her. "Is that right?"

"I just, you know."

"I'm afraid I don't."

"I didn't think you would do it."

"You mean because I was in love with you?"

"I wouldn't go that far . . . maybe lust is a better term?"

He pressed his lips together, nodding. "You think you're pretty special, don't you?"

"I just did what a mother had to do. To get justice for my son."

"You think I worked the case because I was attracted to you?"

"No, I think you worked it *harder* because of that." She took a step closer and laid a hand on his arm. "Didn't you?"

He pulled his arm away. "I'd say we'll see each other around, but we probably won't."

"It was nothing personal, Joe."

He smiled at her, soft and knowing. "I finally figured it out, you know."

"Figured out what?"

"You still want to know why I believed you?"

"Sure," she said, her voice cold and distant once again.

"Something about your involvement in the case—about you in general—always struck me as off. I never could put my finger on what it was until last night. I'm a detective, see. I'm trained to look for incongruities. Contradictions. You're a very good actress, Claire, but what kills any great lie is a kernel of truth that shines through. In my world, it's usually guilt. But in your case, I realized the only thing about you that was genuine was your grief."

After seeing Claire out, Preach went back to the holding cells to check on Blue. She was still sleeping soundly, curled on her side like a child.

It struck him how young and brave she was. He wished he could do something to improve her circumstances, to bring back her father, but maybe this experience would be a wake-up call to her mother.

He decided to let Blue sleep, but he made a vow to do something for her that very day.

Just as soon as *he* got some rest.

Because he had a feeling he would need it.

Later that evening, as the fading sunlight backlit the horizon, whorls of pink dancing through wispy banks of clouds, Preach parked outside Bentley Montgomery's two-story house in East Durham. He was out of his jurisdiction, but he didn't care. It was not meant to be a visit made in his official capacity.

This one was personal.

One of Bentley's black-suited goons opened the door. Preach flashed his badge right away to ward off trouble. "I'm here to see Bentley."

"Yeah? Why?"

"Just tell him it's Detective Everson."

The bodyguard closed the door. When it opened a few minutes later, Bentley himself stepped outside, dressed in dark slacks, a purple dress shirt, and an ankle-length wool overcoat. "Walk with me, Detective."

"Where to?"

Bentley had already left the front stoop. "To see the neighborhood. Unless you're too afraid of East Durham to take a little stroll?"

Preach stuffed his hands in the pockets of his double-breasted overcoat. "Lead on."

A few inches taller than Preach, thicker even than the bodyguard, Bentley patted his ample belly and said, "I have to work in my evening constitutional, and I thought it might be good for you to visit your own backyard."

"I know East Durham."

"Do you now?" he chuckled, as they started down a sidewalk warped by tree roots. "Or do you just know the pimps and pushers you arrest?"

"Speaking of arrests, Cobra has stabilized."

"Who?" Bentley said.

Preach didn't give him the benefit of a reaction. "I'll be interviewing him in the morning. Durham PD gets him next."

When Preach glanced over at Bentley, he was chilled by the utter lack of concern in his eyes.

"That house right there," Bentley said, pointing at a tiny bungalow with windows covered with shredded plastic, "belongs to the widow of a war veteran. The government says they overpaid on her husband's disability. They're claiming a hundred grand in back benefits. She's eighty-five and works two jobs, because neither employer gives her any health benefits. Slave labor, is what it is."

"I'm sorry to hear that," Preach said quietly.

"That brick ranch over there, with all the junk in the yard? Momma's a crack whore, raising three boys by herself. I give them about a year before they end up in juvie or dead."

"Or working for you on the corner."

Bentley's lips parted in a faint smile. "Durham's so progressive these days. I love that we got all these initiatives for clean energy, net neutrality, save the trees, save the planet, save the universe. Those are worthy things, detective. Lofty goals. Well, how about this—I got people living around me with no heat or air conditioning, moldy roofs, using food stamps for potato chips and soda because they can't afford anything else. I got kids getting sick from filthy water. Kids sleeping in the gutter. Kids with every male relative they know either in prison or unable to get a job because they just got out."

"Don't forget kids getting hooked on the crack you sell."

"The dire situation in Yemen? Honduras? The Sudan? Americans have no clue how people live in their own backyard, not to mention some continent they've never been to. How about all of these civic-minded people around here look around and fix the damn ghetto? The place right in front of their noses where kids are actually living in terrible conditions and actually getting sick and dying? What's the difference between Durham and the Germans who watched the Holocaust and did nothing, except a matter of degree? Slow or fast, it's murder all the same."

"I know what you're doing to the trailer park, Bentley. I know about David too."

"Then why don't you put the cuffs on? Or is this my last walk of freedom?"

Again, the lack of concern in his voice unnerved the detective, as if the man already knew what Preach was going to say and didn't care one bit.

"I've been reading up on stress and the stoics," Bentley said. "Did you know there's a human propensity to sort everything into good or bad news? It's evolutionary. Combine that with a twenty-four news cycle that preys on fear, and you got an entire country worried *about all the wrong things*. Clear eyes and mind, detective. Clear eyes and mind. Cancel the noise. See what's in front of you, the truth, and act on it."

"That sounds a lot like my job," Preach said. "Do you know what I think the truth is? That an extremely small percentage of ruthless, ambitious, sociopathic criminals always make life miserable for the rest of us."

"You're talking about the President, now?"

"I'm talking about you."

"Tsk tsk. I thought we were having a pleasant walk. Why make it personal? Trust me, you don't want to make it personal."

Preach stopped walking, and Bentley did too. Preach stepped closer and said, "Are you threatening me?"

Bentley didn't flinch. "You should walk away, Detective."

"From what?"

"From East Durham. From this. From me."

"I'm afraid I don't have that choice."

Bentley laughed. "Choice? We have a wasteland of choice.

That's the defining nature of humanity, especially in your America. You don't have to go to war on a daily basis, farm for food any more, cut your shelter out of the jungle. Your people don't have to do anything but slave away to get shit you want, play video games, watch other people's lives on TV. So just choose, detective. Choose to *walk away*."

"What should I do, leave a manila envelope for you in my mailbox?"

"You heard me."

"One thing I learned as a prison chaplain. The true criminals of the world actually feel at home in prison, because they know they're in the right place. They may not like it, but they know they're home. I look forward to stamping your passport."

"I believe our walk is over."

"I didn't come out here to warn you that I'm about to arrest you. You're right, this isn't my jurisdiction."

"I trust you can find your way back? It gets dark out here rather fast. There's not much artificial illumination to light the way."

They had stopped walking at an intersection marked by a cheap, two-story housing complex that looked in danger of falling over. A host of rundown sedans and pickups were crammed into the parking lot, and a group of shifty-eyed men were drinking on the concrete balcony, eying the two men.

Preach leveled his gaze at Bentley. "The girl, Blue, you sent Cobra after."

"I don't know—"

"Shut up." Bentley went rigid, as if no one had ever spoken to him like that before. Preach continued, "She was in the woods that night but didn't see or hear a thing. You have my word on that. There was something on the camera, but it was too dark to make out. We used video enhancement software to build our case, and she knew absolutely nothing about it. Still doesn't."

"You telling me this to hear yourself talk?"

"I'm telling you this because no matter what happens to you and Cobra, if you or any of your people touch a single hair on her head, I swear to God I'll spend the rest of my career making sure you'll regret it. Trust me when I say it will be the worst decision you've ever made."

"That's a noble sentiment, detective."

"She's innocent. Let her live her life."

"What happens if you're not around to protect her anymore?"

Preach backed away, very slowly, boring into him with his eyes. "Not one single hair."

42

ONE MONTH LATER

Neutral ground.

That was what Preach thought of Ari's request to meet him after work at Café Driade again. As before, she was making a statement. Someplace along Highway 15-501 in Chapel Hill, neither in Creekville nor in Durham. A place that belonged to her past but maybe not to her future.

He sensed the Ari he had once known, the carefree law student with dreams of changing the world, the cool girl with the ripped jeans and flashing eyes and chip on her shoulder, the iconoclastic traveler who had overcome an awkward and lonely childhood with strength of will and good literature, was in the midst of a transformation. A chrysalis set to emerge.

Would Ari settle happily into her new role as an attorney? Or would she fight it tooth and nail, longing for the freedom of her past life? He knew she was still caught in between, figuring out who she really wanted to be, what she really wanted from life.

That was okay. It was all okay.

He just wished he could be a part of it.

The past was never fully truthful, he thought. Nor was it complex. Just like witnesses in a murder trial recalling the scene of the crime, cherry-picking details, the human brain selects what details from past relationships it wants to remember. Not only that, it takes a *position*. Bombarded by information, weeding out extraneous info, our former lovers are viewed either through a rose-colored prism or through a shattered lens.

He knew how Ari thought of him now, and it made him sad. Even if they couldn't be together, he didn't want her to remember him in that way.

It was cold and gusty outside. Luckily, he found a table in the corner across from the counter, tucked beside a pair of wood-paneled French doors.

When Ari arrived a few minutes after eight, strolling into the café with her dark hair askew, observing him with a gaze both earnest and defiant, a woman who wanted to trust the world but didn't, Preach felt a thorn of shame and regret stabbing him in the side. A surge of attraction coursed through him as well, one so strong it harkened back to the early days of their relationship. He realized that, along with all the other mistakes, he had even taken Ari's unique beauty for granted.

Dressed in high-heeled black boots, gray slacks, and a chartreuse wool jacket he had never seen before, he thought her transformation to *new woman* was complete until she turned the chair across from him around, facing backward, and sat with her arms crossed on the table, leaning forward as her mouth curled into a sly smirk.

"Howdy, stranger," she said.

"I see you're picking up the local lingo."

"If you can't beat 'em, join 'em."

"Now *that* isn't the Ariana Hale I know."

Her smirk broadened. "Don't believe everything you hear."

"From an attorney? I wouldn't dream of it."

She rolled her eyes. "Exactly what I would expect a seasoned police officer to say."

"How did we ever get along?"

She shook her head sadly. "I have no idea."

He was surprised by her playfulness. He had expected her to tell him when she was coming over to collect her things.

"Do you want a drink?" he asked, rolling his beer between his palms.

"Maybe in a minute," she said, looking him in the eye. "If I decide to stay."

He let the bottle come to rest between his palms. "And what does that depend on?"

Instead of answering, she held his gaze so long he knew she was testing him in some way. Finally she said, "One thing I love about the Triangle? I can wear jeans and a sweatshirt to a coffee shop and still be one of the best-dressed people."

"I think you've far surpassed that."

She plucked at the lapel of her coat. "Work clothes don't count. I'm talking about Saturday morning, roll out of bed and get a latte clothes."

"Then yeah, you've got that covered. Though I never thought you cared about that sort of thing."

He wondered if that would offend her, but she said, "You know, when I first got to know you, all blond and handsome and wounded, I thought you'd be one of those guys who knew everything there was to know about women."

"And?"

"How wrong I was."

"Guilty as charged," he said.

"Oh, it's not just you. You're probably better off than most. Guys don't know much of anything about women, period. No matter how dressed down a woman is in public, never let her tell you she isn't aware of what the other women are wearing. It's not that I care about being the best dressed. I just don't like to feel pressured."

He waited for the hammer to drop, the one where she told him exactly how stupid and callous he had been.

"It's a good place," she continued, still riffing on the local scene. "Both urban and rural. Progressive but tied to history. You get all the seasons. Durham, especially, has a good mix of people. This area . . . it feels real. I respect it for that."

Where was she going with this, he wondered? Was she about to tell him she was settling down with a corporate attorney in the suburbs?

Her expression darkened. "Have you ever come across someone like him before?"

It took him a moment. "You mean Bentley?

She pressed her lips together, nodding, as she twisted one of her silver thumb rings. Her nervous tic.

"No," he said slowly. "Not quite."

"He played me—played on my emotions—in a way no one ever has. I feel like he's this Pied Piper of crime or something. I think he believes in what he's doing on some level, in that help-his-people bullshit he spews . . . but he's as ruthless as anyone I've ever met."

"Is there any progress on his case?"

"We had to drop it. After Mackenzie recanted, we didn't have anything."

Though bitterly disappointed, he was not surprised. A week after her confession, though she stayed true to the rest of her story, Mackenzie had refused to testify against Bentley before the grand jury. She said that Cobra, not Bentley, had recruited her and supplied her with drugs. Citing her fear of reprisal from Los Viburos, she said she had made up her initial testimony about Bentley, and that it had always been Cobra.

The gang assassin, who had survived the gunshot wounds, did not contradict her story. In fact, he confirmed every single bit of it, with no deviation.

Someone had gotten to them both, Preach knew.

And it didn't take Sherlock Holmes to figure out who that was.

"Her initial confession holds no weight?" he said.

"Not if we go to trial and she stands in front of a jury and says the opposite. She's terrified, despite the fact she's staring a murder charge in the face."

"He must have threatened her family," he said.

She looked up at him. "I'm not giving up. We'll get him another way."

Preach lowered his eyes, torn. He wanted very much for Ari to never go near Bentley again, not even with an ironclad case. He wanted her to quit her job and leave town and not be within five hundred miles of that sociopathic bastard. But instead, knowing that was her choice to make, he said, "Be careful, Ari. I mean it. You don't want to stay on the radar of someone like that."

"He made me feel abused, Joe. As if I was an object he could order around. A piece on his chessboard. How many other people has he manipulated? Murdered? I want him to go *down*," she said, with a glint in her eyes that took him aback.

"Just don't provoke him, okay? Let us take him off the board for something big. That's our job."

Her palms were pressed into the table. Finally she relaxed, stepped away from her chair, and went to the counter for a drink. She returned holding a glass of red wine, turned her chair the right way around, and sat with her legs crossed. Modern jazz notes floated softly in the background, interrupted at regular intervals by the grind of the coffee roaster.

Instead of questioning the significance of the glass of wine, he said, "What about Cobra? How's his case going?"

"Oh, he's going down hard."

"I wonder why he took the hit for Bentley? He doesn't seem like the type to scare."

"My guess? He has a five-year-old son."

Preach reflected on the day he had chased down Cobra and shot him, then gave a slow nod.

"I haven't been paying attention to the Creekville news," she continued. "How did the council vote on Carroll Street?"

"Not to tear it down. Over the last month, we've kept a police presence there 24-7. The crime rate fell off a cliff." Preach took a swallow of beer. "Though I get the sense Bentley can absorb the financial hit."

"You think it's a good thing? For the people who live there?"

"I think it's there or somewhere else."

She swirled her wine with a troubled expression. "What about Blue? Is she doing okay?"

"Can you believe the filmmaker she stole the camera from pressed charges? After all Blue went through?

"What!?"

"The judge counted Blue's jail time—when I kept her locked up at the end—as time served. He also persuaded the principal to let her back in school with no repercussions. She'll graduate, I hope, and after that . . . I don't know."

"I can tell you care about her."

"She's had it rough. And her father . . ." he sighed. "Life just isn't fair. There's some good news, though."

"Oh yeah?"

"Another local filmmaker heard about the case. She's making a documentary about the trailer park, with Blue playing a part. *And* she's taking her under her wing and teaching her how to direct."

Ari clapped a hand to her mouth. "That's amazing."

"Yeah," he said softly. "She's a tough girl. I think she'll be okay."

They sat without speaking for some time, sipping their drinks as they stared in different directions.

"Ari," he said.

"Mmm?"

"What's next?"

"What do you mean?"

"Why'd you ask to meet me tonight?"

She tensed, one hand gripping her wine glass, the other fidgeting on the table. "You hurt me, Joe."

"I know. I can't tell you how sorry I am."

After a moment, she said, "I'm not sure what I want yet. And I don't know, maybe you're over me already."

"I'm not."

Her eyes flicked upward, finding his. "I wanted you to be that guy, you know? The one. The perfect one. But you're not. You're just a . . . a *guy*."

He stared back at her, knowing she was right, wishing he had something to say.

"But none of us are perfect. We can never know for sure what another person is thinking or feeling, not even our partner. Nor would we want to. Doubt is part of human nature. I think it takes getting hurt to realize that and to be able to live with it. Maybe some people never doubt, I don't know. Maybe some relationships are perfect."

"They're not," he said simply.

"I don't think so either." She took a moment to swirl her wine. "A few days ago, I stopped by the Trader Joe's down the street. I go there sometimes, if I'm out this way."

"I know."

"I saw Claire."

His eyebrows rose.

"I walked by her, not expecting to talk, but she stopped me and told me something."

"That she was sorry?"

"Um, no. I don't think that crossed her mind."

"Then it was definitely Claire you saw."

"Yeah. She was pretty arrogant. But she told me you stayed true, despite everything she threw at you." Ari's smile was distant. "She said no man could resist that kind of temptation—not unless he was in love with someone else."

"She thinks a lot of herself."

"Claire really is beautiful."

"She's skin deep, Ari."

She smirked. "So are most men. Anyway, there are plenty of people who choose to do the right thing, even if they're not in love with someone else. Or even for all the wrong reasons."

"That's true."

"You know what I think? After giving it some thought?"

He shielded his anticipation with a sip of beer. "What's that?"

"I think a relationship untested is one waiting for a test."

"And?" he said, guardedly hopeful.

"I think you failed."

He sat back in his chair.

"It wasn't a zero, though. Just a sixty-five or so."

"A sixty-five," he repeated, absorbing her words. "Is there any hope of extra credit?"

After one of the longest moments of his life, one in which he truly did not know what outcome to expect, she reached a hand across the table, palm up. "Maybe. But it's not a second chance. It's a trial period."

He took her hand. "I'm not sure I understand the difference. Though I think I probably should."

"Have you heard of the Socratic Method? It's how classes in law school are taught. The professors answer questions by asking another question in response."

"Forcing the students to come up with their own reasoning."

She tipped her head in agreement. "So you tell me. Is there hope of extra credit?"

"I've never had classes as difficult as law school," he said. "But I'll do my very best, and let my prof decide."

"Good answer."

"How long does the term last?" he asked. "A quarter? A semester?"

"Think of it as a PhD program. It's over when the dissertation is complete."

"I can accept that."

"Did you have a choice?" she said, as she drained the last of her wine and stood. After setting the empty glass on the table, she gave him a long, unreadable look and then left the café without a backward glance.

His first test, he supposed, was whether or not he should follow.

ACKNOWLEDGMENTS

Thanks to my indefatigable agent, Ayesha Pande, and the team at Seventh Street Books for all of their hard work and wonderful support for the series. I'd also like to recognize John Perdue for graciously lending this novel a lifetime of criminal justice and law enforcement expertise, as well as Luke Bumm for providing legal acumen and insight into the Durham District Attorney's Office. Finally, a special thanks to my wife, whose beauty, wit, and devotion inspired the novel, and whose literary ear helped shaped it.

ABOUT THE AUTHOR

Layton is the author of the Detective Preach Everson novels, the popular Dominic Grey series, and other works of fiction. His novels have been optioned for film, nominated for multiple awards, including a two-time finalist for an International Thriller Writers award, and have reached #1 on numerous genre lists in the United States, the United Kingdom, and Germany. Layton is also the co-editor of International Thrills, an online magazine for International Thriller Writers (ITW) that interviews crime authors from around the world.

In addition to writing, Layton attended law school in New Orleans and was a practicing attorney for the better part of a decade. He has also been an intern for the United Nations, an ESL teacher in Central America, a bartender in London, a seller of cheap knives on the streets of Brixton, a door to door phone book deliverer in Florida, and the list goes downhill from there.

Layton lives with his family in North Carolina. You can also visit him on Facebook, Goodreads, or on his website (www.laytongreen.com).